D0505979

THE
INTERLOPER

By the same author

THE HUNTING SEASON
WOLF'S HEAD
CRY HAVOC
A SHRED OF HONOUR
THE MASTERLESS MEN

THE
INTERLOPER

J. K. Mayo

MACMILLAN

First published 1996 by Macmillan

an imprint of Macmillan Publishers Ltd
25 Eccleston Place London SW1W 9NF
and Basingstoke

Associated companies throughout the world

ISBN 0-333-65237-1

A CIP catalogue record for this book is available from
the British Library

Typeset by CentraCet Limited, Cambridge
Printed by Mackays of Chatham PLC, Chatham, Kent

Chapter One

A man squatted on his heels outside the circle of firelight, and watched and listened to the three men who had settled there to wait for sunrise. It had become clear to him that they were not going to sleep, but were going to sit out the few hours the night had left to it.

They had a pot of coffee keeping warm on the edge of the fire, and a bottle of whisky to lace it with, while the man with the guitar and a stetson on his head kept the other two entertained and gave them music to sing to.

Jason Wildgrave found it one of the most incongruous scenes he had ever witnessed – three Americans on the edge of an African forest imitating the actions of their pioneer forefathers. Even the song with which they were, at this moment, astonishing the creatures of the night came from the Old West.

> *'Goodbye, old paint,*
> *I'm a-leavin' Cheyenne,*
> *I'm a-leavin' Cheyenne.*
> *I'm goin' to Montana,*
> *I'm a-leavin' Cheyenne.'*

Behind them, illuminated by the flames of their fire, stood the truck which had brought them here, these three men bent on murder. Some yards away the weapons they had brought in the truck to effect the destruction they planned rested patiently, pointing up to the glittering canopy of the stars and with the generator humming

1

quietly behind the music. The men sang the verse again but changed their destination on the fourth line to sing:

> 'I'm goin' to Mombasa.
> I'm a-leavin' Cheyenne.'

'I don't think so, boys,' Wildgrave said to himself, and a rotten smile crossed his face.

He rose silently to his feet, made himself comfortable, made himself one with the rifle, and put off the safety catch. They were in mid-song when he took them with three shots: first the one on the left, then the one on the right, and lastly the man in the middle who sat there, for the single second of time before he died, with the guitar gone silent on his lap.

Wildgrave brought down the rifle and put the safety on again, and with that in one hand and a pistol in the other, he crossed into the firelight to make sure they were dead.

He set off to where he had left the Land Rover, a mile away. He walked warily, with his eyes and ears alert, through the African night, for even the hunter can be hunted. As he went he heard behind him the demented yell of the hyena. The three who had sung so carelessly round their campfire were not men now, not even dead men. They were carrion.

By the time he reached the Mombasa road the sun was up. After half an hour he turned off the road and bumped over the red dust until he drove into a clump of trees which hid the vehicle from both ground and air.

He climbed on to the truck bed where four wheels, fitted with tyres, were stored, and dropped them to the ground. He put the jack in place and went to work, and in an hour the Land Rover was standing on the wheels that it had carried through the night, and the wheels that had carried it were ready to be disposed of.

For Wildgrave was a careful man, and knew the Americans would be out to revenge themselves against whoever had killed their singing campfire trio. By his standards they were not all that competent, but they would know enough and be motivated enough to make moulds of the tyretracks that had followed their men into the middle of nowhere. Most of the journey had been over the same kind of arid terrain that surrounded him here, but there had been places last night where the truck he was following had passed over softer ground, which would have registered the treads of his tyres.

Now it remained only to dispose of the telltale treads: if a thing was worth doing it was worth doing well, and he would sleep easier if the tyres had ceased to exist. He dug a shallow trench, and when it was done he hacked the tyres off their wheels with his hunting knife and tossed them into the hole. He took a can of petrol out of the back and poured it over them, and set it alight.

After the fire was out and the last whiff of black smoke had vanished into the air, he shovelled the dirt he had dug out back on to the stinking mess, and then put the empty petrol can, the shovel, and the four wheels that he had shorn of their tyres, on to the truck bed and secured the tailgate.

He rested then, sitting with his back against a tree, and drank a pint of water. While he rested he scanned the ground to be sure he had left nothing, let nothing fall from his pockets, to satisfy himself that when he was gone there would be no sign of his having been here.

He rose at last, and stood gazing up into the sky with an enigmatic smile, as if the sky and he shared a secret; then he took a final look round and climbed into the Land Rover.

He had one more thing to do out here before he returned to the road, and he drove on till he came to the Galana River.

There were crocodiles basking in the sun on the river's edge, and Wildgrave, tired after an active and sleepless night, had no intention of going to war with them. He ran the truck slowly along beside the river and came to a place where a swift reconnaissance showed that the coast was clear, both of crocodiles and of humans.

The river was deep enough here for his purpose. He hurled the rifle far out into the water, and the four metal wheels he threw out a few feet and watched them vanish, one by one. He got into the driver's seat, lit a cigarette, and decided that yes, that was the last of it. He had left no spoor to lead from the campfire killings to himself.

He stubbed out the cigarette and headed for the road, and when he reached it, he set off at what speed the old Land Rover would make for Mombasa. He thought that, if it could be done, it would be rather neat to get there before Provensal.

Not far from where the three men lay dead beside the ashes of their fire, the elephants came out of the trees and confronted the barren ground before them. It ran for about a mile, a stretch of cracked and pebbly scrub, before the trees started again.

The old bull elephant was in a bad mood. It had been a disturbed night. An outburst of the banging sounds made by man when he is out killing had sent the she-elephants into a panic. With their calves at heel they had run crazy, crashing through the forest with no other aim than to put space between them and the noise that meant danger.

After that it had taken hours to get back on course – for the small herd was not a bunch of aimless wanderers, it was on a journey. They had been obliged to work round full circle almost to where they had been when the scare came, and now right in their path was this strange humming. The bull could not see what was causing it. Between him and the trees ahead there was a dip in the land, and it was from down in the dip that the humming came.

Man again, undoubtedly, for this was an alien noise: at the presence of this thing, whatever it was, right in his path, the bull's irritation expanded. He showed no caution, but threw his trunk up and trumpeted and made straight for the place where the ground fell away. Two young bulls followed him but the females with their calves and the three other bulls hung back, following slowly at a circumspect distance.

When he came to the ridge the bull saw no living creature, and what he did see he had no names for.

Down in the hollow, untended by man, and here in the middle of Africa incongruous to the last degree, was a stand of ground-to-air missiles. Connected to this by black cabling was a generator,

4

busily using up the last of its fuel, and issuing the humming that had so irritated the bull.

He looked and listened and smelled, and liked nothing at all about this object sitting there buzzing at him. He went down the slope and approached it and without pause kicked it over and stamped on it. As it died the generator coughed and spluttered, then fell silent under the clouds of dust that flew up from the massive feet, for still the old elephant trampled on it until its organs and intestines fell out, and these too he crushed into the arid ground.

The young bulls with him caught his fever and attacked the gleaming stand of missiles which quickly gave up their innards, and here too everything that came out was trampled and crushed, until whatever threat the generator and the missiles might have presented to the elephants was reduced to nothing more than a scatter of small stones and pebbles.

As the frenzy of destruction was ending, a strange bellowing came from the sky close above them, and the elephants burst out of the hollow. As they moved on they gathered again as a herd, making for the trees that were the next stage in their journey.

The plane came over the trees at five hundred feet, flying into a sky aflame with the wild colours of the breaking day.

'Look there, Mr Provensal,' said the man with the shaven head. 'There it is. Spot on Wildgrave's map reference.'

The man called Provensal looked down and saw a small group of elephants gathered round some object. 'Binoculars, Daniel,' he said. 'Tell Saidu to fly round again.'

The aircraft came round in a wide circle and he gazed through the binoculars. He passed them to Daniel. 'Is that it?' he said. 'I can't tell for sure.'

'Yes, sir, it is,' the first man said. 'It's all a bit of a mess, but that's a missile, absolutely, out there on the edge.' He handed the binoculars back. 'Look quickly, one of the elephants is going for it now.'

'Yeah, I got it.' Provensal laughed. 'They're all steamed up, these creatures. I wonder why.'

'Smell of man, I imagine, and maybe it was just in their way. Yes, they're finished with it, they're moving on. Shall I tell Saidu to resume course and height?'

Provensal nodded.

The aircraft straightened and began to gain altitude.

Provensal, lounging there in the comfortable armchair, was a long slim-built man. The face was lean and stern of look, with a large nose, full lips, and a strong jaw that came to a point. He was bald on top, and short tight-curled hair, partly black and partly grey, clothed the sides and back of his head. He was in repose now, and this showed a mouth that in its rest wore a faint but neutral smile. To people who did not know him well, this smile was deceptive, since it was an expression of himself, and told nothing of his attitude to those with whom he might be dealing. The eyes were brown and lively, but behind the life in them something brooded, as if the inner man inhabited a state of perpetual and hidden thought.

Provensal's roots were in West Africa, his progenitors from the Asante. Daniel and the other bodyguard in the cabin – his brother Lucas – were of the Ndebele people, from here in East Africa. They were of the size and musculature of heavyweight boxers, each with fists that could have felled an ox.

Provensal went on looking down from the window, and as if he was dropping a message to the ground below, said softly: 'Well done, Wildgrave, and thank-you.'

The plane was a Hawker 195 with eight seats in the cabin, furnished with leather and walnut. It was a luxury private jet, with seven on board: the crew of pilot, co-pilot and steward and four passengers, Provensal, Daniel, Lucas, and in the rear of the cabin, which was curtained off, a woman.

When the Hawker touched down at Moi International Airport outside Mombasa, the sun was a white glare in the sky. The pilot taxied to a spot three hundred yards from the terminal and parked there. A limousine appeared as if by magic and the passengers, the one woman and the three men, got into it.

The car left the airport and took the road through Port Reitz to the city. It crossed the causeway and drove down the middle of Mombasa Island to the Old Town, a warren of Arab houses built along narrow lanes which barely admitted the car.

At the mildest touch of the horn a pair of tall wooden gates opened and the limousine eased its way into the courtyard of an establishment which had been created out of half a dozen of the old houses, the entrance and courtyard having been contrived at the expense of removing one of the houses altogether.

The men who had opened the gates closed them again at once, and the party descended from the car. Provensal raised a hand in greeting to a man sitting on the first-floor balcony.

He turned to the woman, who was as tall as he, her eyes level with his. Unlike her companions, she was not African, but a woman from the mountains of the Caucasus. 'Shouana,' he said, 'I must talk with Wildgrave, and you will want to freshen up after the journey. I shall come to you soon, and we can discuss what you would like to do with your day.'

Those eyes of hers that looked into his were golden. Her skin was copper, and her features and the shape of her head were incomparable. But it was a distortion of the mouth which, paradoxically, made her beauty unique. The ends of the lips turned down to such an excessive degree that they appeared to signify a burden of ancient and unassuaged grief. The effect of this accident of nature, of this, her mouth's given, sculpted shape, was to suggest that one who was able to sustain a grief so profound, and who conducted herself with such arrogance, must have known afflictions so appalling that they had made her a being apart, separated from the rest of the human race.

Shouana's golden eyes regarded Provensal with a gravity, almost a coldness, that spoke of a kinship of the spirit, and not of the heart. 'Yes,' was all she said to him.

She took his arm and they went into the house and up the stairs. He opened a door for her, she passed through the doorway, and he closed it behind her and continued to the balcony.

Wildgrave sat on one of two rattan chairs with coffee on the table between them. Provensal sat down. 'Well, Wildgrave. You have had another success.'

Wildgrave was a long, narrow figure. For a man working in Africa he had an oddly unconvincing tan, with a matt texture to it as if it had been acquired on a sunbed. It was closely matched by his hair, of a dull sandy colour. His nose was long, and he wore a thin line of moustache above long thin lips. The face was expressionless: it made the usual movements that faces make, but gave away nothing beyond the reaction of the moment.

All in all, then, here was a dull, khaki-looking man: dull, that is, until you became conscious of the eyes. They were a bright blue, and their gaze was startlingly alert and focused. Here too, however, there was a complete absence of meaning. The bright stare shone out at you in an oddly dissociated way, as if all the life in them was in the shining, and had nothing to do with the being to whom they belonged.

He shrugged. 'We have good people,' he said, 'and I had a bit of luck.'

'What kind of luck?'

'I saw the truck arrive at that house they keep outside Nairobi. High wall like that,' and Wildgrave waved at the wall across the courtyard. 'I thought it might be worth investigating. Never seen a truck that size there before. I went over the wall and took a look and saw what she was carrying. Ground-to-air? Well, you were going to be flying in, and we knew you were on their shit-list. I had an intuition, and when that happens to me I trust it. In this business, it's better to be safe than sorry. So I kept a watch and when the truck came out two days before you were expected, I just followed on. You know the rest.'

Provensal surveyed Wildgrave, this dummy of a man with seemingly electrified eyes, dressed in bush jacket and shorts, who referred so carelessly – 'we knew you were on their shit-list' – to his gift for gathering intelligence and spoke so matter-of-factly of his instinct about the truck and the actions he had taken as a result of it.

'You're worth your weight in gold, Wildgrave,' Provensal said.

'Maybe more, with the money I've had from you,' Wildgrave said. 'I don't carry a lot of flesh on my bones.'

Provensal laughed. 'You take modesty too far.'

'It's not modesty,' Wildgrave said. 'As to my weight, I'm a skinny article, always have been. As to the rest, so long as I'm paid what I'm worth I don't need congratulations.'

'Well, damn, doesn't a word of enthusiasm for what you've done mean anything to you? Make you feel good?'

'No.'

'I don't believe you, Wildgrave. Anyone who achieves what he sets out to do and gets recognition for it has good feelings come up in him.'

'I don't.'

Provensal did not take to being rebuffed like this, and he sought to put the other man on the defensive. He produced a mocking laugh, and said: 'Are you trying to tell me you are a man without feelings?'

An imitation of a smile briefly animated Wildgrave's face. 'Feelings?' he said. 'I don't feel anything, Mr Provensal. I'm as feelingless as that woman you brought with you.'

Provensal, who had been leaning forward to project the force of his personality upon Wildgrave, recoiled, like a duellist from the thrust of his opponent.

'What do you know about Shouanete? You've never met her.'

'I saw her down there.' Wildgrave pointed his long nose at the courtyard. 'I took a good look at her, as who wouldn't? Like recognizes like.'

'You're being insolent to me, damn you.'

'No, I'm not. To be insolent you have to recognize authority, and I don't do that. You were being intrusive so I came back at you, that's all.'

The hardness that entered Provensal's eyes would have done credit to Shaka the Destroyer, but the anger in them bounced off Wildgrave's impervious stare like a butterfly being thrown by the wind.

'I'm your employer, Wildgrave. You owe me some respect.'

'People owe respect to each other.'

'All my employees show me respect.'

'Mr Provensal – observe, at least I adhere to your wish to be called Mister – this kind of talk really bores me. If I don't suit you, say so, and I'll take myself elsewhere.'

Provensal kept on looking at him, but the hardness had gone from his face. 'I guess I'll just never be able to make you out, will I?'

'I don't see why you shouldn't,' Wildgrave said. 'I'm quite a simply constructed fellow. Do I take it that you don't want me to quit just yet?'

'No, I don't want you to quit.'

'Then I'll stick around.'

'The boat's ready for tomorrow?'

'She's ready,' Wildgrave said. 'Fuelled, armed, crew and captain on board.'

Provensal's face lifted and at the same moment Wildgrave came out of his chair and turned, for, even sitting at his ease, he had the alertness of an animal in the wild, and had sensed that someone was approaching him from behind. It was the woman Shouanete.

Provensal presented them to each other. Wildgrave inclined his head to her, and instead of shaking his hand, she touched him on the upper arm. She said, 'Wildgrave. A name that means something.'

Her cold golden eyes met his bright perpetual stare, and stayed, taking the feel of him.

She was simply dressed, in a white skirt to the knee, a white silk shirt, and a white jacket, with a panama hat on her head. Standing so close to her, Wildgrave felt a strangeness. There was a power in her that he could not name, except to think that this woman was a consort for a god, not a man.

'I have kept you waiting,' Provensal said to her.

'No,' she said. 'I find that tonight I want to be with a woman. I am going to Maria.'

'Very well.' Provensal showed no sign of being disconcerted by this news. 'Do you want one of the boys to drive you there?'

'No, I will walk. I can look after myself.'

She turned and went along the balcony and into the house, and

10

the two men sat down again. Soon she crossed the courtyard below them, a small door was opened for her, and she left.

The two men on the balcony watched her departure in silence, and Provensal said: 'Shouana is bisexual.'

'That's lucky for her,' Wildgrave said.

'Why do you say that?'

Wildgrave glanced again at the now closed door across the courtyard. 'It gives her a richer life than most of us.'

Provensal rubbed his hand over his face and sighed.

'Yes,' he said. 'You're certainly an unusual man.'

Then he rose to his feet. 'All right,' he said. 'I'll order the car for eleven o'clock tomorrow, and then we'll visit my island.'

'Very well,' Wildgrave said.

Provensal pressed his shoulder as he went by.

Wildgrave hardly felt it. As the woman went out of the door she had turned to look at them, and he had felt her gaze touch him with that cool indifference of hers, and with that waft of utterly emotionless sexuality.

Chapter Two

Harry Seddall was taking his ease over his second cup of seriously good espresso in a restaurant in Duke of York Street, while he read a book called *The Ruin of Kasch*. Italo Calvino was quoted on the dust jacket as saying: '*The Ruin of Kasch* takes up two subjects: the first is Talleyrand, and the second is everything else.'

For Seddall a new book on Talleyrand was an event, and he had bought it that morning with a great sense of acquisition. He had read thirty-odd pages, and discovered that all he had achieved in the reading of them was to make a reconnaissance, in, so to speak, the dark. The author, Roberto Calasso, had an intellect capable of holding in its grasp such a chaos of thought, history, antithesis, quotation, anecdote and God knew what else, that Seddall had barely glimpsed what Calasso was showing him. He was going to have to go back to the beginning and start again, and read slowly, maturing each passage in his mind before he went on to the next.

This was a discovery that filled him with pleasure. He was embarking on a month's leave, part of which he meant to spend in refreshing the use of his intelligence. Signor Calasso had provided him with the perfect medium.

Seddall was a man over middle height, but not quite tall, with strong shoulders and a bullish set to his round head which was emphasized by a pugnacious chin. The eyes were of an unusual brown, almost yellow; and full of life, as if he was alert for any surprise he might encounter on the wayside.

He closed the book, laid his fingers on it affectionately and possessively, sat back and took out a cigarette. He was about to call for more coffee when a man approached, said, 'May I?' and sat down across from him, hooking his umbrella on to the edge of the table.

'To tell you the truth,' Seddall replied, 'I was rejoicing rather in my own company, and there seem to be plenty of other tables available.'

'Colonel Seddall, I am here because I want to talk to you.' There were enough words in this speech for Seddall to hear that the accent was American.

Seddall lit the cigarette and looked at the creature, at black pin-stripe, white shirt, white handkerchief, some unknown club tie, and fair slicked hair over a face which – regular, featureless and commonplace – at thirty-something had not yet begun to live: all the appearance, in short, of a rectitudinous little shit. Seddall had a prejudice against Americans who aped the English style.

'Where'd you get the brolly?' he asked him.

'Swayne Adeney,' the creature said, with the self-satisfied air of one who perceives that he has come well prepared for an interview.

'I might have known. I very seriously do not want to talk to you, so go away,' and he raised a lazy arm at a passing waiter, and asked for another coffee.

'They warned me that you might be difficult.' The creature was holding his ground.

The older man gave a sudden and exceedingly disagreeable smile, like a fox lifting its nose to the scent of chickens in the night. At sight of this repulsive leer the creature's head gave an involuntary jerk and the control on his face collapsed, much as if he had been lying in the bath and spied a cobra in the rafters.

Seddall was not at all like the senior men with whom John Brady (for that was his name) was accustomed to deal back at the office. What Brady was looking at was a fiftyish man in a crumpled linen jacket and a blue cotton shirt, both of them overdue for a visit to the dry-cleaner; a man with a round head that had a bald patch on top and brown hair with grey in it, well enough cut, probably, but right now in a complete mess, as if he'd been running his fingers through it and hadn't bothered to put it straight.

The picture was that of a raffish remittance man. It was really quite extraordinary to find him wearing such an utterly uncouth appearance in a restaurant just off St James's.

'I'm on leave,' Seddall said, and the creature saw that the yellowish eyes had read him like a book. 'All right, sunshine. Who are "they"? Who sent you?'

'I'm not at liberty to tell you that.'

'An anonymous message, then. Spit it out.'

The coffee came. The waiter replaced the ashtray in which Seddall had just extinguished his cigarette. When he had gone the creature leaned forward and spoke in a low voice.

'It is not just a message. It is a warning. We know you are on leave. If someone makes a proposal to you that concerns something near the Equator, you will be wise not to accept it.'

Seddall stared upon him with a face like teak and eyes like stone. He said nothing. It was utterly unnerving. At last, he too leaned forward, in a confiding manner, and Brady responded to this first indication of unhostile behaviour by moving a little closer himself, and waited, poised and expectant, for Seddall's response.

When it came, he was thunderstruck. A hand darted out and snatched the wallet from his inside pocket, and Seddall riffled through it till he found what he wanted: a card showing that Brady was with the commercial attaché's department at the American Embassy in Grosvenor Square. Seddall scrutinized this, and then the card and the wallet were tossed on to the table.

'Bloody amateurs,' Seddall muttered as if he were quite alone. 'I wonder what they're on about.'

'You had absolutely no right to do that,' Brady said.

The hand that had so deftly picked his pocket waved about in the air as if to brush away an irritating insect. Seddall's eyes were narrowed and reflective, with no focus in them. Brady felt as if his own existence had simply been forgotten.

Brady stowed away the ID and the wallet.

'What answer am I to convey?'

The face tilted up at him regarded him as if he were no more than a shape discerned vaguely in the mist. 'None,' it said.

'Well, I really do have to give some indication of your response, you know.'

The face became alive and almost benevolent. 'Brady,' it said, 'whatever they're up to, your masters are playing out of their league. And as regards your own interest, I doubt if you'll learn much about life from them. If I were you, I should take up some other occupation.'

In spite of himself, Brady responded to this. 'Such as?'

'Leave government service altogether. Forget the state. Forget the business of state. The state has no real existence. Go footloose about the world.'

Brady was pleased to find reserves of scorn within him. 'Go to Nepal, you mean, like a sixties backpacker? No, thank you.'

And as if to demonstrate the distance between himself and the hippie culture, he took a mobile phone from his pocket and punched in a number.

'I've spoken to Seddall,' he said. 'No go. His response is positively hostile.' He stowed away the phone and unhooked his umbrella from the edge of the table.

'Mr Brady,' Seddall said, and quoted in French, by way of tribute to Talleyrand. 'What I am saying to you is, "*Point de zèle.*"'

The zealous and aspiring Brady hefted his umbrella and strode out of the restaurant.

'He leaves, I'm afraid, no vacuum,' Seddall said to the man who brought his bill; and who smiled politely, as at a jest not understood.

Seddall went out into the sunshine, and strolled towards his luncheon appointment with Jane Kneller.

Chapter Three

Elsewhere on that summer's day in London, in that part of it known as Whitehall where the art of government was once practised and is now imitated; where lies flourish and are admired as if they were prize blooms at the Chelsea Flower Show; and where infirmity of purpose is expressed with a belligerence that might almost make you think great men had come again: in that part of London, soon after noon on this smiling, sunny day, a man left his office and went out for luncheon.

He was Sir David Harington and he was the Foreign Secretary. He was tall and thin and his grey hair was coiffed with the care of a woman's, so that it lay across the front of his head in a long curl, and at the sides was swept back like the wings of a bird at rest.

As he sank into the back seat of the Jaguar his mind ran over the encounter from which he had just come. He gave a sigh, and said to himself, 'The things I do for my country.'

'I don't think I understand,' had been the first words of the Secretary of State for Energy, a rubicund man whose face habitually expressed an impeccably intelligent cheerfulness: this was a mask which rarely deserted it, even when he was at the dentist. His name was Edward, known to his family and friends as Eddie, Loring. His job title signified not that he was expected to run up mountains every morning and play furious games of squash in the afternoons, but that he had a mandate to occupy himself with the affairs of Britain's fuel industry, of fuels both fossil and nuclear.

'Really? I shouldn't have thought it was that intricate,' was Sir David Harington's reply.

Loring leaned forward over the table, big-shouldered and ebullient, with his hands planted on his thighs. He looked like a sumo wrestler at the start of a fight.

'David,' he said. 'Intricate be damned. You're lying to me. You're keeping something back.'

'Oh, come now,' said Harington, and deprecated what he felt to be the unseemly violence of Loring's speech with an ineffable movement of the hand, which a choreographer at the Royal Ballet would have noted down on the spot. 'I am, after all, no more than the messenger. It would not become me to run ahead of my brief.'

Harington was the sort of man Loring could never like. A long drink of water was one description that came to him, and dissimulative bastard was another.

Loring could play it tricky himself when he had to, but this display of fastidious alarm on the part of Harington, at the mere suggestion that he held a supply of deceit in his armoury, filled him with contempt.

'Kyanite mining,' Loring said, 'and in particular kyanite mining overseas, by a British-American corporation I've never heard of before, and on an island in the Indian Ocean that I've also never heard of, has bugger all to do with my department.'

'It has relatively little to do with the Foreign Office,' Harington pointed out. 'It is simply that there has to be some government oversight of such a development. All your department will have to do is deal with the licensing arrangement. Mines, you know, whether kyanite, bauxite or coal, are still mines. I daresay it will be pro forma to your people. Kyanite is vital to our defence interest.'

Loring got up, patted his pockets as if to make sure nothing had been filched from them while he sat here, and said curtly, 'I'm off. No decision. I'm going to think.'

'What do you mean, no decision? It is not your decision to make, it is the Prime Minister's decision.'

Loring stood there on the other side of the desk, glowering down at the Foreign Secretary. 'I don't like the smell of what you're trying to sell me, Harington. And as for the Prime Minister and his decisions, you can put them where the sun don't shine.'

Harington's head flicked to the side as if he had been struck, and Loring, looking thuggish and pleased with himself, took his departure.

Harington, alone in his over-sized office, allowed himself to look tired and disenchanted. He didn't like this Matetendoro project one little bit. He sat frowning and twiddling his thumbs. He hoped that Simon Ainley would have better luck, this evening, with that reputedly maverick Intelligence colonel – what was his name? He opened the file in front of him and turned over the pages. Yes, here it was: Seddall, Colonel Harry Seddall – than he had just had with Loring.

He looked at the clock, thanked his lucky stars that he was lunching alone, and called for his car.

Harry Seddall did not care for this kind of party, where all there was to do was stand around with a drink in your hand and engage in pointless chatter with people you hoped never to meet again.

Still, only about half an hour to go. He'd made a deal with Jane Kneller that they should not stay for the banquet but take their leave at half past seven, and he had made a point of booking a table for dinner at eight. The man and woman with whom he was, God knew why, presently engaged were rapidly forming a mutual admiration society over their common view that the Balkans would never change.

Between their heads he sighted Jane further down the room. She was not the most beautiful woman there – in a gathering of the Great and the Good such as this there were inevitably a score or so of what used to be called society beauties – but to him she was far and away the best-looking.

With her usual indifference to what was appropriate for a forty-something senior Home Office official at a formal gathering like this, she was not wearing, like all the other women, a skirt of respectable length, but a silk shift dress of dark green that stopped several inches above the knee, glossy black tights, and green ankle boots.

She caught his eye and smiled, and he smiled back and raised the hand with the cigarette in it and tapped the watch on his wrist, and she laughed and nodded.

'Seddall,' a voice said in his ear, and, 'Do excuse me, but I must have speech with him.'

The two Balkan experts barely interrupted their discussion to acknowledge the intrusion, and Seddall turned to find out who had rescued him from this ennui. Lieutenant-General Simon Ainley gave him a pleasant look and took him by the arm.

'Let us see if we can find a private space,' Ainley said.

He was a tall strong-built man with a red and rough-looking farmer's face.

'Hello, Ainley,' Seddall said. 'A private space with somewhere to sit would suit me down to the ground.'

They left the room, Seddall hijacking an ashtray as they went just to be on the safe side, and in the wide corridor found a table with a couple of chairs against the wall.

'How goes it?' Ainley said. 'You're just off on a month's leave, I gather.'

'Indeed I am, God be thanked. Weekend in the country, with a friend of Jane's called Peter Hillyard, then next week we're off to Martinique to visit a friend of mine.'

'If I may say so,' Ainley said. 'I do think you're a fortunate man. Jane Kneller is a most excellent woman.'

'You may say so,' Seddall said. 'What is it you want to talk to me about?'

'Yes, well,' Ainley said, and looked along the corridor in both directions as if to be sure the coast was clear. 'It's about your weekend in the country, actually.'

'Why, do you need me for something this weekend?'

'No, no. Nothing like that.' Ainley's face creased into many lines as if the combine harvester had broken down and the fine weather was due to break. 'I hope you won't take this amiss. I have been commissioned to say to you that Peter Hillyard has gone what they used to call in the civil service, rather viewy.'

'Viewy?'

19

'What's meant by that term in his case is that he's become an enthusiastic Green. Interested in the environment, ecology, all that side of things.'

'Bully for him, surely? For a man in his seventies that seems a healthy way to go.'

'I can't disagree with you there. However, what's exercising the powers that be is that Hillyard appears to have got an inkling of something they don't want broadcast.'

'And?'

'And they have a sense that he may ask you to take some action in connection with this particular matter.'

'This matter that they don't want broadcast?'

'Yes. And what is wanted of you is that, whatever he tells you, you will not only utterly abstain from having anything to do with it, but also, you will forget everything he has to say and convey nothing of it to anyone else.'

Seddall leaned back in his chair and looked at the ceiling, and sat up again and stared down at the carpet, and then came slowly to his feet and wandered slowly off along the corridor until he reached the far end, where he gazed out of the window for a while. Then, just as slowly, he came back.

'Ainley, Peter Hillyard is an old friend of Jane Kneller, and it is on the strength of this that he has invited us to Dovestone. From what I hear of him, he is a man to respect, and further than that, his loyalty to his country and his sense of duty have never been questioned. So what on earth am I to make of this stuff you're passing on to me from our political masters? For I presume you are simply the messenger of the politicos.'

The general's face tightened. 'What you are to make of it, Seddall, is that the Prime Minister himself has asked me to speak to you about this. And he has done so because I am your superior officer, and I am therefore able to express his will as a direct order, and I now do so.'

There was a very tough expression on Ainley's face now, but Seddall's face was like granite and his eyes as hard as Ainley had ever seen them. Then Seddall rubbed the back of his neck and he sat down and took out a cigarette and lit it, and something like humour replaced the inflexible look on him.

'Sir,' he said, and watched not without pleasure the vexation which awoke in the general at the military formality of this mode of address, 'a command from a superior officer, the disobeying of which does not render the recalcitrant junior subject to court-martial, is not a proper military command.'

Ainley appeared to be not in the least fazed by this display of barrack-room lawyering. He stood up and leaned over Seddall. 'In the sort of field we have been discussing, Colonel Seddall, there are other sanctions than courts-martial. You know what the Prime Minister wants of you, and you know what I have told you to do. I trust that your common sense will supply you with the appropriate response.'

He straightened up and took out a cigarette case, not a thing you saw often these days, and lit one for himself.

'Damn it, Seddall, you always take these things so personally that sometimes there's no dealing with you at all. I've done my best to do this pleasantly, and you know it's not the kind of chore I like. You don't help, do you? Are you going to give me an answer I can take back to the All-Highest?'

Seddall accepted this with a rueful and self-mocking turn on his mouth. 'Ainley,' he said, 'what's it all about? Can you tell me that?'

'I don't know, damn it,' Ainley said. 'I'm simply told it's a matter of the gravest importance to the State.'

'And you believe that? I'd be more inclined to believe it's a matter of the gravest importance to HM Government.'

'Enough of this,' Ainley said, and Seddall knew that the general was half of the same mind as himself. 'Do I have a response?'

'I think you could say that Seddall was taking it very seriously indeed. Let them make what they want of that.'

Ainley put out the half-smoked cigarette in the ashtray Seddall had brought from the room where the reception was taking place.

'I've done all I can, I think. I'm off. You watch your back, Harry, but better than that, for God's sake try to be sensible about this.'

'Thanks,' Seddall said. 'Appreciate it.'

General Simon Ainley went off down the corridor towards the great staircase, without returning to the reception: from which it was not difficult to deduce that he had come here for the express purpose of conveying to Seddall what the Prime Minister wanted of him.

Harry took another turn up and down the corridor and looked at his watch, and went back into the hubbub of well-bred voices to find Jane.

She was halfway up the room, making a vivacious presence in a group of people there but glancing about in search of him, and when she saw him she left the others without a word and came towards him with her long springing stride.

'Well, Harry Seddall,' she said, 'you're jolly nearly late.'

'But not quite,' he said. 'A minute in hand.'

'Shall we go? Where are we having dinner?'

'Nowhere very posh,' he said, 'but you'll like it. And I think it's possible that they'll like you.'

'And why should they like me?' Her sea-green eyes were bright with merriment as she fished for the compliment he plainly intended to make.

'Oh, mostly because you're not too unintelligent.'

'Is that so? Then stand by to repel boarders, because I'm going to embarrass you to death until you say the kind of thing a woman likes to hear.'

And she put one arm round his neck and the other round his waist to pull him into her, and began to force a real kiss on him. Seddall, partly despite himself and partly not, began to return this embrace with enthusiasm, and after a little he was aware that the buzz of chatter round about them had diminished.

'There,' she said, standing away but still holding him, 'will that do it?'

'Where were we?' he said, with one of those wicked and sarcastic grins of his.

'God, you make a girl work for it,' she said. 'You are now going to give me the real reason why they'll like me in this restaurant we're going to.'

He put his hands on her shoulders and said, 'You know bloody well why, because you look terrific and because you're showing off very nearly all of the best legs in the seven continents.'

'Prettily said,' and she stepped away and brushed down her skirt so that she could look at them. 'I take it from that we're eating Italian again.'

'We are eating Italian.'

'Career woman and sex object,' she said. 'Who could ask for more? Let's go.'

'Snogging in public, Kneller, won't help your career.'

'Then to hell, Seddall, with my career. I'm old-fashioned. I'd much rather have a reputation than a career.' She put her arm in his and headed for the stairs. 'And now that I have established myself as a woman of reputation, I think I'll do my best to build on it. Lead me to these Italians.'

'The Italians? What's the connection?'

'My dear Harry, if a woman wants to develop the art of seduction, the Italian man is the fellow to practise with.'

'Why?'

They were out on the pavement now, and as he raised his arm for a taxi, she struck the pose and looked at him under half-lowered eyelids and spoke in her best imitation of an American accent. 'Because Italians respond, babe. Italians respond.'

'Dear God,' he said, opening the door of the cab, 'this is going to be a steamy evening.'

'Evening,' she said with excessive breathiness into his ear as he sat beside her, 'and night.'

'Well, goody,' he said, 'and I don't want to put a damper on what you have in mind, but while you're practising the arts of seduction on our Italian friends, I have some solemn things to tell you about my encounter with a certain General Ainley, which concern your friend Peter Hillyard.'

The car streaked down the outside lane at ninety-five, a Renault Savannah with only eleven thousand miles on the clock, Jane

Kneller's car, but Harry Seddall was driving. He went like the wind for a number of reasons: driving off with Jane for a weekend in the country on an afternoon of glorious sunshine had raised him to an exhilarated state, the prospect of contention with his political masters had set the adrenaline running, and, in particular, they had started hellish late.

Jane had put her seat back, and had gone to sleep soon after they set off, but it was time to wake her, and as he let the car's speed drop he put a hand on her thigh.

'We're leaving the motorway,' he said to her. 'Get ready to navigate.'

'So soon.' Jane yawned and stretched and then brought her seat and herself upright. 'OK. We follow this road for about fifteen miles and then I'll pilot you along the complicated bit.' She looked at the dashboard clock. 'You've made good time. We'll hardly be late at all.'

They came to Dovestone up an avenue of lime trees. It was a sixteenth-century manor house, a simple stone building hardly more than a large farmhouse, with a porch set off-centre and a gravel path running up to it between lawns. The curve of the drive took the car up to the side of the house, and they dismounted.

A man with white hair and moustache came to the door and Jane ran to him through the boisterous greetings of a golden labrador while Seddall got the luggage out of the back, using a degree of graceful delaying tactics to let the two of them have full measure of their greeting; for he knew how strong was the bond between them.

Before dinner they had sherry in a long low drawing-room, with two windows looking over the grass at the front and two on either side of the fireplace at the east end of the house. Jane had sent Harry down before her, so that he and Peter Hillyard could meet for a little on their own.

Both men were wearing shirts open at the neck, since Hillyard had said he didn't go in for dressing for dinner. Harry, seeing that there were ashtrays in the room, pulled out his cigarettes and offered one to his host.

'Gauloises,' Hillyard said. 'I should just think so.'

He was an upright figure, thin and weakening slightly with age, but still energetic and with a lively human warmth coming from him. The face was authoritative and handsome, even debonair, with that wide white moustache flourishing on it.

'Jane thinks a lot of you,' he said to Seddall. 'She says she's never met a man she trusts so much, apart from me.'

'That's generous of her,' Seddall said. 'I shall study to live up to it.'

'I believe you will,' Hillyard said, and the bright blue eyes examined him. 'I know you will. I intend to trust you myself, if you'll let me, with something very important to me, but we'll keep that till tomorrow. Tonight we'll simply enjoy ourselves. I don't see Jane often enough, and though she gives me a high report of you, I'd like to get to know you before I confide in you.'

Seddall had a liking for the easy candour that came to some people as they grew old, and because of it, he felt obliged to reciprocate in kind.

'I have to tell you something,' he said. 'I had of course no idea you planned to confide something to me, then last evening out of the blue I was given an official warning, by a General Ainley who said he was speaking to me on behalf of the government, to pay no attention to whatever you might tell me, to take no action on it, and thereafter to put it out of my mind.'

'The devil you say,' Peter Hillyard said. 'Still, I am no more than mildly surprised.'

'You do perceive the implication? I don't know if they're opening your mail or listening to your telephone calls, or if they have gone so far as to break into this house and plant bugs in it, and doubtless at the same time look at your private papers, all that kind of thing; but for them to know that you intended to lay a matter of importance before me does suggest that they've got their information by some underhand means. The only alternative is that you have seen no need for discretion and have been proclaiming to all and sundry that I was coming here, and what it was you were going to say to me.'

During this speech Hillyard sat with his head leaning on his hand and gazed at Seddall unwinking, and seemingly unperturbed.

'Yes,' Hillyard said, 'I see the implication. It would be hard to miss it. The only allusion I've made to your visit here has been to Jane on the telephone, and all I said was that I was glad you are who you are – she'd told me you were Military Intelligence and what sort of fellow you are – because I'm carrying a burden on my back and I need to share it with a reliable man. Jane has no idea what it's about, any more than you do at the moment. Apart from that I have kept silent. I've not been broadcasting it to all and sundry.'

'Has it occurred to you,' Seddall asked him, 'that they might be listening to us right now?'

'Oh, yes, certainly.' The old man had a curious gift for looking serious and humorous at the same time, as if his own spirit and his understanding of the world reposed in a perfect balance.

Seddall stood up and went to the alcove where the drinks lived and brought back the sherry decanter and, at Hillyard's nod, refilled both their glasses.

'It doesn't sound to me,' Seddall said to him, 'as if you are at all offended by the idea of being eavesdropped on.'

'To be offended by people like that? That would do them too much honour.' Hillyard took a swallow of sherry. 'What we'll do tomorrow is devise a meeting-place that will prevent them from overhearing us, and a way of getting there that will ensure we're not followed. We'll go out for luncheon, I think that would be the best thing. After what you've told me it would be unfair to embroil Jane, in view of her Home Office job, so she can stay here and sunbathe or amuse herself as she pleases.'

'Talking about me?' Jane said, entering the room all legs and leggings, with a white shirt belted at the waist.

'We were discussing your imperfections, my dear,' Hillyard said, 'but we seem to have run through them quite quickly.'

'Men are like little boys when they get together,' she said. 'How many imperfections do I have?'

'Only three, I think,' Seddall said, 'personal vanity, intellectual arrogance, and I've forgotten the other one.'

'So have I,' Hillyard said. 'Give yourself a drink, Jane.'

In the course of the evening Harry's first impression was confirmed. Peter Hillyard was one of the best men he had ever met. Straight as a die, humane, intelligent and large-hearted. He had been born in Kenya, served in the war, went into international investment banking and retired when he inherited this house from his uncle. He had farmed its five hundred acres till he was sixty, and then he let most of the land out to neighbours whose land marched with his.

The house and garden were looked after by a married couple, the Taylors, who lived in a cottage hard by. Sitting outside among the roses after dinner as dusk fell, Seddall found it hard to conceive of this contented man living so comfortably in the peace of his years, deep in the Warwickshire countryside, as being a thorn in the flesh of the government.

Seddall had been intrigued by what Hillyard had said earlier about contriving to hold their vital meeting tomorrow free of surveillance, and said so.

'I think it's secure enough out here to talk,' he said, 'if we keep our voices low and make it brief. We're going on the assumption, I think, that the house is probably bugged, so they'll know what we've planned for tomorrow. How do you propose to escape their attentions?'

'Oh, that's easy enough,' Hillyard said. 'We can assume that they've put a tracer in my car, and that they're quite likely to put one on Jane's Renault overnight if they didn't do it before you left London. I'll take a gun out first thing tomorrow and see if I can bag a few rabbits and pigeons, and I'll call in on John Baldock who's harvesting these fields over there – ' he waved an easterly hand – 'and ask him to watch out for us about noon, and block the road after we've passed with a tractor and trailer.'

'Yes, but if there's a tracer?' Jane said.

'Thought of that,' Hillyard said, his eyes gleaming like a schoolboy's up to mischief. 'We'll drive like the wind for Rugby, hire a car there, and vanish like smoke into thin air. You'll drive, Harry, I'm not up to this kind of high-speed work these days.'

'Golly,' Jane said. 'You talk as if you do this sort of thing all the time.'

'It's no more than tactics,' Hillyard said. 'I hope you won't think

I'm a bad host if I go off to bed now. I want to be up betimes – you won't mind breakfasting without me – and it's going to be a busy day tomorrow.'

'We shan't be long behind you,' Jane said.

Hillyard crossed the lawn, turned at the door and held up a hand, and went inside.

They sat there for half an hour in the scent of roses as the dusk grew, looking out over the rolling fields and listening to wood-pigeons calling in the trees. Then they went to bed.

They never saw Peter Hillyard again.

Chapter Four

The temperature had fallen dramatically overnight. After breakfast they walked the mile-and-a-half to the village – the Seddall cigarette supply was dangerously low – under a sky of white clouds driven by a brisk north-east wind, and on their return they saw, as they approached Dovestone, a police car parked on the gravel.

'Police,' Harry said. 'I wonder what's up.'

They went into the house and through to the drawing-room to find a police sergeant and a constable standing there, and Mrs Taylor in a chair with tears on her face.

Jane went to her and knelt on the floor beside her. 'What's wrong, Ida? What is it?'

'He's . . . he's . . . Mr Hillyard's dead,' the weeping woman said.

'Oh, God. No, no,' Jane said, and seized the other woman's hands and bowed her head, and began to cry herself.

The sergeant said to the constable, 'Stay here,' and came up to Seddall. 'Let's go outside a moment,' he said, and led the way to the porch.

They stood just outside the door and the sergeant said: 'My name is Welford, and you are?'

'Seddall is my name. We're here for the weekend. Mr Hillyard is, was, an old friend of Jane's.' He nodded back at the house to indicate who Jane was.

'Not an old friend of yours?'

'Met him yesterday for the first time.'

'Do you have identification of some kind?'

Seddall gave him the piece of Defence Ministry paper with his name on it. 'What's this about? How did he die? Heart attack, stroke, what?'

'It looks like a shooting accident. Usual thing, going through a fence and the gun went off. Head-shot.'

Seddall turned to face the sergeant for the first time, and saw a large, country-looking man in his thirties with a big square face.

'Shooting accident? As I told you I hardly knew Mr Hillyard, but I'm pretty sure he wouldn't be fool enough to let himself get caught up in a fence with his gun loaded and not broken.'

'Yes. I would have thought the same, but, you know, he was an old man, and when people get old they tend to forget things like that.'

Beside them in the bed along the front of the house the roses, red ones, yellow ones and white, were tossing in the wind, and in the distance, framed in the avenue of lime trees, a line of bullocks passed one by one as they trekked across a field. These were Hillyard's roses, that was the view from his front door.

'This is a hellish thing,' Seddall said. 'He seemed to me one of the best men you could want to meet.'

'I know, sir. I know.' The sergeant sighed. 'I must just deal with the formalities, sir, and that's really why I want to speak to you rather than the ladies. There will be an inquest, of course, because of the way he died. And because it is a violent death the body has been removed for post-mortem examination. The ladies ought not to see it in any case; the face is just shot away. Can I ask you to explain these things to them – about the inquest and the post-mortem, I mean? This is not the time to tell them, and I must be off, sir.'

Seddall was abstracted now, thinking. 'Tell me, where did it happen?'

'If we go across the orchard I think I'll be able to point out the place from there.'

They passed through apple and plum and pear trees, showing promise of a good crop to come, and came to the far wall of the orchard. In front of them was a shallow valley with a small river meandering through it.

30

The sergeant pointed. 'Do you see that strip of wood coming down over the hill? About twenty feet – in fact we measured it, twenty-two feet from the corner post along the base of the wood, that's the spot.'

'Right. Thanks.'

They started back to the house. 'I know it's an old wives' tale,' the sergeant said as they left the orchard and crossed the grass, 'but strong sweet tea, lots of sugar, wouldn't do the ladies any harm. And it's not just the tea, it's having someone do something for them.'

'You're a kind man, sergeant.'

'No, sir. It's my job. Mr Hillyard now, he was known for a kindly man.'

The police were gone. The two women had taken their strong sweet tea. Frank Taylor had heard the news and come up from the pub where he had been having his Saturday pint and game of darts, and taken his wife home.

Jane had said she wanted to go to bed and be alone for a while, and Seddall said he would go for a walk, not far, back in an hour.

'I shan't disturb you,' he said. 'I'll wait for you to come down when you're ready. Is that best?'

That was best, and he left her and set off for the wood.

He crossed the river by a footbridge and climbed the gentle slope to the fence that bordered the wood. It was old but well maintained. There was rabbit wire halfway up it, above that two strands of plain wire and a top strand of barbed wire.

The police had cleared the ground punctiliously of the human wreckage left by the shotgun blast, to the extent that in front of the fence there was a large patch of bare earth. It was not a job Seddall would have liked to do; he knew what a shotgun blast could do to the human head.

He sat on the grass and looked about him. He had no idea what he was looking for. He did not even know why he had come here.

The selfish thought rose in him that he was glad he had not known Peter Hillyard well, for in the little time he had spent with him, he knew how much there was to mourn in his dying. Seddall's feelings, therefore, were with Jane. She had met Hillyard ten years ago on one of those group walking holidays in Spain, and since then it was as if he had become, in her own words, an unofficial godfather to her.

He looked down at that small and simple house below where she lay grieving for the man who had lived there. He came to his feet and looked again at the fence.

He thought of the kind of man that Hillyard was, trained to firearms in his Kenya childhood, who in his youth had fought as a soldier in the war, and a man who had been as used to going out with a gun as others were to going on to the golf course.

He thought of all this, and he thought of the meeting with General Ainley, and the fear the government had of Hillyard, and of his own certainty that Hillyard was under surveillance and his phone tapped and the house itself, very probably, bugged.

He said aloud, 'No, I don't believe it. This was murder.'

A man came through the trees, dappled in leaf-shadow and sunlight, a young man with wild dark hair and a brown gipsy face, wearing a black sleeveless tee-shirt and worn khaki shorts and old tennis shoes on his feet. His arms and legs were brown and thick with muscle. He came to the fence and stood there across from Seddall and stared at him with intense black eyes.

'If it was murder,' this apparition said, 'what are you going to do about it?'

'Who the devil are you?' Seddall said.

'My name's Steve Tschiffely. And who the devil are you?'

'And what are you?'

All this won him was a thin smile. 'I'm a man standing in a wood, looking at a stranger. Fair's fair. I gave you my name. So tell me yours.'

'Seddall. Harry Seddall.'

'Are you police?'

'No.'

'Uh-huh,' Tschiffely said. 'We'll see. It seemed to me that you came from that house down there.'

'Dovestone? Yes, I did. I'm staying there.'

The black eyebrows went up. 'You're a friend of Peter Hillyard?'

'I think perhaps yes, I was, but I only met him yesterday.'

'Then how come you're staying there?'

'I wonder why you expect me to answer all these questions,' Seddall said. 'This one, and no more: I'm a friend of a woman called Kneller, who was a friend of Hillyard's.'

'Ah,' Tschiffely said, 'the tremendous Jane Kneller,' and he put a hand on a fence-post and vaulted over as light as a deer.

'You know her?'

'I should bloody think so.' Tschiffely's eyes were full of laughter. 'Jane's visits here have been highspots in my social calendar. Wait a moment. You're not the fellow – yes, by heaven, you are – you're the man she fell in love with. I never got the name, just that it had happened. Is it you?'

'Well,' Seddall said, overwhelmed by this sudden outburst of enthusiasm, 'we've taken up with each other, yes.'

'Don't be so tight-arsed about it.' Tschiffely seized his hand and shook it vigorously, and then executed a kind of dance, shaking his head and clapping his hands, and dropped on to the grass. 'You got a cigarette about you? Good. Then for God's sake let us sit upon the ground and tell sad stories of the deaths of kings.'

So they sat on the grass and smoked their Marlboros (no Gauloises in the village shop) and gazed out over Dovestone, and Tschiffely grew quiet again. A few times he looked at Seddall sideways, as if there was something on his mind.

At last, hissing the words out in a kind of spasm as if he could not contain himself, he said, 'I saw it done.'

'What? What d'you mean?'

'No. I shouldn't have said that.' Tschiffely threw his cigarette on the grass and kicked down on it with the heel of his shoe as if he was extinguishing more life than the fire in a piece of ash. 'I'll wait till I've seen you with Jane. I can't be a hundred per cent sure yet that you're who you say you are. Let's go down to the house.'

'You realize that Jane is terribly upset.'

Tschiffely was up on his feet. 'For Christ's sake, of course I know that. What do you take me for? I know how much she loved him.'

Seddall stood up too and gave him a long look.

'When I left the house she was resting,' he said. 'So I want you to take it easy, that's all. I don't want any of this impassionated stuff you seem to be full of coming down on her. What do you do here? Do you have a weekend cottage, or do you live here, or what?'

'I live here.' As they started down the hill, Tschiffely waved a hand vaguely over the landscape. 'I'm a poet.' He gave a sardonic laugh. 'I have been a poet. Haven't written a bloody poem for nearly two years.'

'So what have you been doing?'

Tschiffely gave him a contemptuous eye. 'You don't know what life's about, do you? I've been not writing poetry, that's what I've been doing.'

'It's not my field,' Seddall said. 'Why am I supposed to know what it's like, being a poet?'

'Quite right. Why should you?'

When they went into the house Jane, in a white towelling bathrobe, was coming down the stairs, her face pale and her eyes red.

'Ah, Steve,' she said, and gave him a quick hug. 'It's so good to see you. Isn't it awful about Peter? It's so damned awful.'

She went to Seddall and put an arm round him and laid her head on his shoulder.

'I'm cried out,' she said. 'I came down to get myself a drink. How was your walk?'

'Good,' Seddall said. 'Enriched by meeting this man. Why don't you two go and sit in the garden and I'll bring your drink out. It's not so warm as it was, but it's better talking out there than in here.'

Jane got the message at once. 'Yes, I think I'd like to be outside. I'd like a stiff brandy.'

'Beer,' Steve Tschiffely said.

Harry took out a glass of brandy, and the bottle too, which he put beside his chair, and two beers.

'Is this man treating you right? If not, I'll horsewhip him on the steps of his club. I believe that's the thing to do.'

'I'd like to be there when you try it,' she said. 'But, oh yes, he's treating me all right.'

'He's a tough hombre, is he?' Tschiffely looked at Seddall. 'Of course, you're one of these cloak-and-dagger guys. Well, I'm a lot younger than you and very fit, and I've taken up kick-boxing this past year. What would you do about that?'

'Oh, I think I'd manage,' Seddall said vaguely.

The laughter with which she was trying to raise her spirits soon left her, but except for the pain in her eyes Jane's face did not return to the grief-stricken lines it had shown before Harry went out. She became composed and thoughtful.

'Harry, I've been out shooting with Peter, and he was a safe man with a gun. In fact it was Peter who taught me to shoot – I'm a city-bred girl, after all – and he was meticulous about safety. I don't understand how he could have let this happen.'

'No. That's been on my mind too.' He reached out and took her hand. 'Are you feeling stronger? I know you're a strong woman, but it's been a dreadful blow to you.'

She pressed his hand and let it go. 'Yes, I think I am. I was full of grief and I will be again, and I'll just let it come, but I feel quite calm just now. Why do you ask, though? You know you can say anything to me. We may be thinking the same thing.'

'That it wasn't an accident?'

She nodded, slowly as if her neck was stiff, and bit her lip. 'Yes, that it wasn't an accident. And if it wasn't an accident,' she put her face to the sky and came out with it, 'if it wasn't an accident, then someone else did it, because Peter would never kill himself.'

'Are you sure this is the time to talk about it?' he said. 'Would you rather wait a few days?'

'No,' she said violently. 'Now. This is the time. I don't want to hide from anything. It's terrible enough as it is and we should deal with everything, we should deal with the truth.'

'All right,' he said. 'Then we might as well use the words and not bother with euphemisms, is that right?'

'Yes.'

'I believe he was murdered.'

Jane turned her head to look at the house, to look at Peter Hillyard's house, and when she spoke her voice was a whisper. 'Yes, I believe so too.'

Harry said, 'I think Steve here knows something. Are you strong enough to hear it?'

'Oh, God,' she said. 'Yes. Yes I am. Tell me, Steve.'

'This will be hard to hear,' Tschiffely said, and Seddall was surprised to hear the gentleness in his voice, since it did not at all fit the image he had of the man.

'Whatever it is,' Jane said, 'just bloody tell it, damn you.'

'Okay,' Tschiffely said quietly. 'I saw it done. I saw them kill Peter.'

Jane began to weep and pulled a handful of tissues from the pocket of her dressing-gown. She dried her eyes and blew her nose and sat up straight and leaned forward.

'I see,' she said, and a transformation came over her. She looked, suddenly, more like Kneller of the Home Office than the Jane who had lost a loved friend. 'Go on. Details.'

Tschiffely held a cupped hand out to Seddall and made a demanding motion with his fingers, and Seddall gave him a cigarette and lit it. The poet drew deep and blew out smoke and put his hands on his knees and gazed at the ground.

'Tell it, Steve,' Jane said. 'And make it quick, don't beat about the bush.'

'It was early morning,' Tschiffely said. 'I don't know when exactly, six or seven. I'd been in the wood since dawn. I go there sometimes, often, and just sit there and feel the trees about me. I watch the sun come up. No one's about then.

'Jesus,' he said, and gave a huge sigh as if reliving the scene was too much for him. 'I saw a man coming up to the edge of the wood. I was deep in the trees and couldn't see who it was. And then there were men running round the corner of the wood, I couldn't tell how many, all I could see was the movement.'

Jane lifted a hand and said, 'Fill my glass, Harry.'

Seddall filled it and handed it to her and she took half of it at a gulp.

'Right, Steve, go on.'

'The men gathered round the other man and there was a shout and I had a feeling of a struggle, so I began to move closer, and then there was a shot.' He wiped his brow with his hand. 'I got nearer, moving quiet and careful. There were three of them. Two of them were holding a man, a dead man, his head all bloody, a bloody mess. They were folding him halfway through the fence, under the barbed wire, holding up the barbed wire and pushing down the wire underneath him. I knew the dead man was Peter by the white hair and the clothes, the tweed jacket and the blue cords, the trousers, I mean. I knew it was him.'

He stopped and Jane held out her glass to him. He drained it and shuddered and went on.

'One of the men had a shotgun. They'd shot Peter with their gun, not his own. I suppose somehow they'd known what kind of shot he went out with in the mornings. When they'd finished arranging his body they loaded his gun – Peter's gun – with cartridges from his own pocket and the third man took the gun and ran away round the corner of the wood and fired it once. He must have fired into the air over the trees, I heard the shot fall through the leaves behind me, a good way behind.'

Tschiffely wiped the back of his hand across his mouth. The hand was shaking. Jane was intent upon him, as still as if she were made of stone.

'So,' Tschiffely said, and he spoke as if he was at the end of his tether, as if to tell the story to the end was as great an effort as rolling a giant boulder up a mountain, as if it was taxing him beyond endurance.

'So. The man with Peter's gun stood beside the body and jerked the gun so that it fell about six feet away, which of course would be natural if it had gone off and killed him, and his hand had let go as he died.

'Then that man, who was obviously the boss, said, "First rate, let's get out of here before the world wakes up," and they went off round the corner of the wood, and vanished the way they had come.'

He dropped his face into his hands and after a while looked up, first at Harry then at Jane.

'I went through the trees to Peter and touched him goodbye on the shoulder, and then I went up through the wood, and I went home. I sat there hating myself because I hadn't known it was going to happen, because I hadn't been able to save him. And hating myself, to tell you the truth, because the savagery of it, the absolute callous cold-blooded savagery of it had terrified me. I'd never met anything like it before. I never have in my whole life seen anything like it.'

He said, 'Give me a minute,' and walked a few paces away and stood looking out over the garden and the fields. He turned round but stayed where he was, his face like a soul in torment, and fixed his eyes on them.

'A couple of hours later I went back, through the wood again, you understand. The police were there, so someone had found the body, and they'd got a Land Rover up and put Peter in it on a stretcher and taken him away. I stayed well back among the trees while they did whatever it is they do, and then at last they went away.'

He directed his gaze at Seddall. 'I just sat on in the wood after that, thinking about Peter, what a great man he was, what a great human being he was. And then you came.'

The silence ran on. It was Jane who ended it. She spoke briskly and in a tone of great resolution. 'I'm going to get some clothes on,' she said. 'And listen, you two. Mourning is one thing, but we're going to do something about this. We're going to nail these bastards.'

They watched her as she strode off into the house.

'She's some woman, our Jane,' Harry said.

'Yes, indeed. Hey, what's this?'

This was a car coming up the drive, which turned out to be a dark blue Ford Mondeo with three men in it. They emerged with vigorous slamming of the car doors and came over the grass, three men in what Harry classed as rectitudinous suits, and walking with a strong sense of purpose.

They hove to three paces away. 'Good afternoon,' the one in the middle said. 'Metropolitan Police,' he said. 'New Scotland Yard. We have to inspect these premises.'

'Goodness,' Seddall said, in a slow, insulting drawl. 'Does that mean the Midlands don't have their own Special Branch?'

'This is a special case. I am Superintendent Wardle. This is my identification.'

Seddall took it, glanced at it, and retained it. 'What do you mean, a special case?'

'That is not for you to know, but I can tell you that Mr Peter Hillyard was doing secret work for the government. We are here to collect his papers.'

'Here's your ID,' Seddall said. 'It does appear convincing, but I'm afraid I'm not convinced. And as to Peter Hillyard doing secret work for the government, that's simply a lie.'

Colour rose in Wardle's face, which was characterlessly handsome, with boyish rust-coloured curls turning a dirty grey on top of it.

'We are going into that house,' he said angrily. 'And just what makes you think you have any rights here at all?'

'I am the invited guest of Mr Hillyard.'

'Mr Hillyard is dead, so you no longer have any locus here.'

At this, Tschiffely came in. 'Actually, Harry, Peter told me that his will left everything to Jane, so you are the invited guest of the living and present owner.'

'Follow that,' Harry said to the angry man.

'And who are you?' Wardle said to Tschiffely.

Tschiffely sat and smiled and said nothing.

'Well, who are you, damn it?' Wardle said to Harry.

'Don't you know? You must have been badly briefed. But that's only what I'd expect of you people.'

'What do you mean, "you people"?'

'You know perfectly well what I mean by it. I think you've run out of steam, Wardle. And if you don't think so, I'll tell you what

I'll do. I'll toddle into the house and phone a man called Commander Gerald Kenna of Special Branch in London and ask him if he knows of a team sent here today.'

All of a sudden Tschiffely leapt up and said, 'Wait, I have an idea. I'll just go and consult Miss Kneller, the beneficiary of the estate, you know.'

His tone to the intruders had been quite friendly, and Harry was left wondering what this abrupt move was about. While they waited, the three men became a bit more relaxed, as if they could now see some hope of fulfilling their mission.

Tschiffely came bounding out of the house again and ran over the lawn, and when he was about five yards away whipped a camera up to his eye and began clicking it, over and over, as he advanced.

'Masters,' Wardle said. 'Get that camera.'

The man on Wardle's right, with a confident sneer on his mouth, took something that looked remarkably like a cosh from his jacket pocket and went for the oncoming photographer. At this Seddall began to get up but he was still halfway out of his chair when Tschiffely threw the camera far behind him and as Masters came within reach brought his right leg up and kicked him on the side of the head. The man fell to the ground and lay there clutching his face and making unhappy sounds.

Wardle went to him and whatever it was he did in the way of ministering to his subordinate led to a loud yell. He rose and bore down on the warrior-poet.

'You've broken his jaw, damn you,' he said.

'Yes,' Tschiffely said, 'I'm getting good at this.' He gave ground, his eyes gleaming with excitement and a mad grin on his face, jumping up and down in the kind of dance Seddall had seen already that day, but always keeping himself between Wardle and the camera. 'Stand off or you'll be next, and I don't like you, shitface, so I shan't be so gentle this time.'

Wardle's other sidekick took his chief by the arm. 'Come on,' he said. 'Don't you see he's an expert? We're not armed and that creep will half-kill you. We might as well go, we're not winning anything here. And we've got to get Masters to a hospital.'

Wardle left the field to Tschiffely and turned round. 'All right, all right,' he said. 'I thought Masters was supposed to be a hard case.'

'No,' the other man said. 'He's just a bully, same as you. Not the same thing. Let's get him in the car.'

'You watch your bloody language, Bailey, or you'll be out on your neck.'

'Fat lot I care.' He bent over the casualty. 'Come on, matey, up you get, nice and easy. We'll have you patched up in no time.'

With no help from his superior, he managed to get himself seated in the back of the car with the head of the injured Masters resting on his lap.

'What's that in aid of?' Wardle said. 'He's a grown man, do you think he needs a bloody nursemaid?'

'You try sitting upright with a broken jaw in a moving car,' Bailey said. 'You drive, and be careful, remember this man's in pain.'

'Who do you imagine is running this show?' Wardle said.

'I think running would be too strong a word, don't you? So stop trying to rescue your ego. Just get in and drive.'

To Seddall's surprise, the car went off smoothly and slow. Tschiffely, who had retrieved the camera, ran after it and stooped to take a picture of the number plate. Then he came back to join Seddall and dropped into his chair.

'Phew!' he said.

'I'm lost in admiration,' Seddall said. 'What came over you, that business with the camera? I've known people twenty years in this kind of business who'd never have thought of such a thing.'

'No call for praise,' Tschiffely said. 'Get tied into a trade, whatever it is, and you get into a rut. Keep the mind and spirit free, that's the way to go, and whatever turns up, you're ready for it.'

'Your kick-boxing certainly paid off, you can't deny that.'

'Oh, shoot. Princess Diana could have done that.'

'Yes, but she wasn't here, and you were.'

When the car had disappeared down the drive, Jane came out of the house clad in jeans and sweatshirt. She carried a tray with a loaf, cheese, pickles, plates and attendant knives.

'We seem to have missed lunch,' she said. 'So this'll hold us for now. Steve Tschiffely, I saw that kick. I didn't know you were an athlete.'

'I'm no athlete, Jane, just supple and sadistic, that's all. That Stilton looks good. Aha, yes.'

The two men began to eat as if they were starving, but Jane sat quietly with a plate settled on her thigh, apparently lost in thought.

She looked at Harry and said, 'What did those men want, and do you have any idea who they were?'

Harry was wrestling with an over-ambitious mouthful of bread and cheese, so Tschiffely got his word in first. 'Not the same three I saw this morning, I can tell you that much.'

Harry gulped down bread and cheese. 'Said they wanted to go through Peter's papers, on the pretext that he'd been doing some secret work for the government. And no, I don't know who they were. I pretended to know, though I didn't specify. Of course they might be MI5, but they might be anybody. Thing is we don't know what it's all about, so we don't know who might be involved. Ainley said it was about the environment, and that Peter had gone excessively Green in his old age. That may or may not have been a specious fiction; no way to know.'

'Well then,' Jane said, 'we'd better go through his papers ourselves. Right away.'

Hillyard's study was at the back of the house. They found nothing in his correspondence or on the bits of paper in his drawers, but on his desk were half a dozen books on East Africa and two on the western littoral of India. In one of them was a slip of paper and the page it marked referred to an island in the Indian Ocean, four hundred miles or so off the coast of Africa, called Matetendoro.

On the floor, propped against the desk, was an atlas. It was Jane who picked it up to have a look at the Indian Ocean. Round the island of Matetendoro, Hillyard's pen had drawn a circle, and beside it, an exclamation mark.

She showed the map to the others. Tschiffely started to speak but Seddall clapped a hand over his mouth to shut him up.

'This is all a waste of bloody time,' Seddall said. 'There's nothing here at all. Let's go out and get some dinner.'

They found a pub beside a river where they ordered food and sat under the trees with mugs of refreshing warm beer. Above them was an astonishing sky of irradiated clouds.

'Look at that,' Tschiffely said. 'Straight out of William Blake.'

'Yes, yes,' Harry said. 'To business. Someone has to go to this mysterious island of Matetendoro. I mean it may be an utter waste of time to go there, but it's the single, solitary, slightest chance of a clue we have to whatever it was that had caught Peter Hillyard's interest in a way that worried the government.'

'Agreed,' Jane said. 'It's not much to go on but it's all we've got. But who's to go? What you're talking about is a bit of private secret intelligence work, and you and I are booked for Martinique next week, and everyone knows that, which means "they" know that, whoever they are.'

She flipped a wasp away from her beer glass and took a couple of swallows and continued.

'And they also know Peter wanted to bring you in on this thing, whatever it is, so that ties us in with him. And now that he's gone, and what with us being here when he died, we shall both, to put it mildly, be under observation. If we cancel Martinique now and fly south instead of west they'll guess we're heading for Matetendoro; which means our secret intelligence work won't be all that secret.'

'Waiter coming,' said Tschiffely, who was facing the pub. The man unloaded cold meat and salad and all the fixings and departed.

'Listen,' Harry said. 'First of all it was just me who was being regarded with suspicion, now it's you as well. Where does that leave you, as a senior Home Office person?'

'Don't care,' Jane said. 'I'm beginning to find I don't want to spend the rest of my life in the higher reaches of the Civil Service. I won't pack it in now, it would be too much of a signal. But come Christmas, I intend to be a free woman.'

'Hey,' Tschiffely said, 'hot stuff. But what will you do?'

Jane bent a strong regard upon him. 'I shall do what I feel like doing, and what I find rewarding. I might run a hotel, or a delicatessen, or the Tate Gallery, or devote my energies to the cause of feminism or become a *poule de luxe*. To an active and intelligent woman the whole world is open.'

Tschiffely gave her a huge smile. 'Just asking.'

'Meanwhile,' Seddall brought them back to the matter in hand, 'that leaves us with the question: who to send to this Matetendoro place. You're right. We have to go to Martinique as planned. And we can't send any of the chums, like Sedgwick or Carver, because they're identified with us.'

'I'd go like a shot,' Tschiffely said, 'if you thought I'd be any use. Trouble is I can't afford it.'

'Come on, Steve.' Jane was amused and sceptical. 'What do you know about this line of work? He couldn't possibly be any use, Harry.'

But Seddall had other ideas. 'You know, I think he might. He thinks fast. Bringing on the camera was a good idea in itself; and the way he did it – when he went into the house he had these people believing they might be going to have their way after all. So he's good at being deceitful. And he can handle himself, that kick-boxing is a useful weapon.'

'Well, thanks for that encomium, Harry,' the poet said, 'but like I said, the snag is that I can't afford it.'

'I'll foot the bill, don't worry about that. And Jane, the other thing is that Steve is the last kind of guy anyone would think of as being an intelligence agent, a spy, if you like. To the outside eye he's just a poet, a bloke who doesn't live in the real world at all – at least not what our enemies, whoever they may be, think of as the real world.'

'Gosh, Harry, you're learning,' Tschiffely said.

'Yes,' Jane said, 'but if he buys an air ticket to Nairobi or Mombasa or Dar es Salaam, they'll be on to him like a shot. He's been with us all day and they'll know about that. They may not watch him like they'll watch us, but they'll keep an eye on him for a bit all the same.'

Seddall gave Tschiffely a witty and affectionate look. 'Oh, yes,' he said. 'But he won't buy an air ticket. He'll take a pup tent and a motorbike and he'll travel down to Marseille or somewhere really subtle like Sète. All right so far?'

'Fantastic,' said Tschiffely, who was sitting forward and watching him raptly.

'Good. He'll get himself on a ship across the Med, and take that ship or another one through the canal down to somewhere in East Africa. Then get himself passage on a dhow or charter one, or whatever he can get to take him out to the island. How does that sit with you, Mr Tschiffely?'

'Oh, God,' and Tschiffely's volatile face was wild with delight. 'Who would have thought that a hard-boiled character like you would come up with a gift like this. What a great journey, man. How could you invent a journey like that? Just for me.'

'Steve,' Jane said, 'you can be such a child at times. It's not just for you. It's an espionage mission, that's what it comes down to, and if Matetendoro turns out to be the key to this mystery we've inherited from Peter it could be dangerous, and I mean really dangerous. There's nothing in your life that says you're cut out for this kind of work.'

Tschiffely's eyes went dark and the smile left him.

'You can blow that out of your shorts, my dear Jane,' he said coldly. 'And don't patronize me. Do you think that because you've spent twenty years carving a career among the suits in the Home Office you know what tough looks like? Do you know that he whom you would doubtless regard as the effete poet Rimbaud ended up running guns in Egypt?'

'You could get killed,' Jane said, her cheeks colouring at the sarcastic vigour of this response.

'Killed?' Tschiffely laughed. 'So what? Then in case I do, get yourself a copy of Tennyson and read this:

> 'Sunset and evening star,
> And one clear call for me!
> And may there be no moaning of the bar
> When I put out to sea.'

45

'I didn't know modern poets had anything to say to Tennyson,' Seddall said.

'Plenty of them don't,' Tschiffely replied, 'but I'm not one of the modern poetic herd. I just ain't street enough.'

'Let's finish our food,' Seddall said, 'and think about it while we eat.'

So they ate their good plain meal while above them swifts and swallows darted and jinked about the evening sky, and far off a hawk screeched, knowing that night was coming and it was time to surrender the hunting ground to the owls.

When they'd finished Seddall went into the pub to get some more beer.

'Was I patronizing?' Jane said.

'Yes, you were.'

'I didn't mean to be. It's only that I like you so much as the man I know, the wild boy, the intelligent undisciplined fool, the poet: I don't see you as action man.'

'Holy hell, Jane,' Tschiffely said roundly. 'Just because I am, yes, pretty much who you say I am, and not sixteen stone of macho mindlessness, that doesn't mean I'm not ready and able to fight for my own hand if I have to.'

'You're telling me I've been stereotyping.'

'Certainly. Because it suits you to have that view of me.'

'Ouch.'

'Yes. Ouch.'

Seddall came back with the beer.

'OK,' he said. 'If you're still keen on making this expedition, Steve Tschiffely, I have to tell you I have decided that you're just the man for it.'

'Then you're on.' Tschiffely's eyes were alight again. He lay back and stretched luxuriously. 'I've always wanted to go to Matetendoro.'

Seddall threw him a cigarette. 'Always wanted to go? You didn't know it existed till today. None of us did.'

'Well, you're getting there, I think,' Tschiffely said, 'but you just haven't got yourself round the poetic psyche yet, have you, Harry?'

'I'm a slow learner.'

Tschiffely raised his pint mug. 'Here's to the pearl of the Indian Ocean, and may all her sharks be little ones.'

'They won't be,' Seddall said, 'but you can always kick them in the face.' To himself he thought, there are sharks in London too. I'll go back there tomorrow and see if anything strange swims my way.

The three of them clinked glass, and drank.

Chapter Five

Seddall dreamed, and, still fantasizing about expeditions into the great unknown, was conversing with a crocodile in a tropical swamp (it spoke with the voice of Talleyrand) when something nudged his head. It was the black cat Sacha, who was normally content to spend the night either foraging in the wilds of Kensington or in her basket in the kitchen.

'Hello,' he said sleepily, and then saw that in the space where she had pushed her way past the door, there was the faintest suggestion of light. He came wide awake. The light went, and then a little later, there it was again.

He listened, and thought he heard the slightest sound below. He got out of bed, tightened the cord of his pyjamas and secured it with a double knot, and moved, softly as the cat herself, to the chest of drawers. The service revolver was locked away downstairs, but in his sock drawer was a Colt Woodsman .22 target pistol.

Sure and silent in the dark of his own home, he went as far as the corner where the stairs began. Yes, a torch was in use down there. He stopped halfway down. The torchlight came from the drawing-room. He went down a few more steps until he could see that there were two men rummaging at his desk. The sound he had faintly heard was the shuffle of papers: not simple thieves then, no mere burglars these.

He went slowly and quietly backwards up the stairs, keeping the drawing-room doorway in view. He went back into his bedroom and silently closed the door, took the mobile phone from his bedside table, went into the bathroom and closed that door and called the police.

He gave his name and address and said, 'Two men – at least two men – have broken into my house. They do not know that I am aware of them. At the moment they are going through my desk in the drawing-room on the ground floor. You will send a car? Good. How long? Very well.'

He stayed only to put on a dressing-gown and went out again and noiselessly down the stairs once more and into the hall, where he stood, back to the wall three feet from the drawing-room door with his pistol in his hand, and waited.

He did not have to wait long.

He saw a flashing blue light through the glass of the front door and the torch in his drawing-room go out.

'Christ!' a voice said. 'It's the police. Come on, Charlie, out of this.'

He moved into the doorway and turned down the light switch. Two men were coming at him, who stopped when they saw the gun aimed at them.

One had a bundle of correspondence in his hand and other papers were lying about the floor in disarray. He turned as if to escape through the arch that led to the dining-room, and slipped on the polished floor and fell. The other man, holding the torch, was startled and blinking in the bright light from the chandelier, but he was quick to react. He simply dropped the torch and his hand flew to his shoulder.

Seddall shouted, 'Stop that!'

The hand stopped, and then fell.

Seddall took one pace forward. 'Now listen to me,' he said. 'Take your jacket off your shoulders. Not off, but off your shoulders, so that it restricts your arms.'

The man was raring to go. He was twenty years younger than Seddall and built like a rugby forward, but he did what he was told. The gun in its shoulder-holster came into view.

'Jesus Christ, Charlie,' the man on the floor said. 'For God's sake do something. I've broken my bloody knee.'

'Shut up,' Charlie said.

'Quite right,' Seddall told Charlie. 'I'm going to relieve you of that weapon, and I'll tell you this for free, I'm a marksman and I would dearly love an excuse to kill you, so if you try anything I'll shoot you in the eye.'

He saw some of the rage desert Charlie, and uncertainty and a trace of alarm come into his face. Seddall went up to arm's length and lifted the automatic from its holster, and stepped back again. Without taking his eyes or his aim off the man he tossed the automatic across his body on to a chair.

'Now, Charlie, the next thing you will do is this. You will kneel down beside your friend, you will take out his weapon with thumb and forefinger, and you will hold it up in the air. This time, if you make a false move I'll shoot you through the brain, always supposing you have one. Is that clear?'

'Yes.'

'Yes, sir,' Seddall said, intent on demoralizing the man further.

Charlie lowered his head and stared, but what he saw in Seddall's face quelled the incipient mutiny.

'Yes, sir.'

'Very well. Now do it.'

Charlie knelt beside his colleague, who had gone silent but was still clutching his leg and grimacing with pain. He lifted the gun and Seddall took it from his hand and threw it after its fellow.

'We got to do something for Mick,' Charlie said.

'Let him be. It won't be broken, only twisted.'

'God, you're a right bastard,' Charlie said.

'Yes, I am,' Seddall said. 'Now, you lie on your front beside young Mick and lock your hands behind your head, while I let the police in.'

Charlie stared at him like an indignant bullock.

'Do it.'

Charlie did it.

Sacha appeared and after assessing the two strangers on the floor with sight and smell, jumped up on to the grand piano, a coign of vantage she favoured when she was in the drawing-room.

The police came in the shape of an armed response team, an inspector, a sergeant and two constables, all of them armed and wearing flak jackets. There was also a paramedic on a motorcycle.

When they were in the drawing-room, the inspector flourished a card and gave his name as Radley, and said, 'That's a nice pistol, sir, but you can put it away now if you please. I take it you have a licence.'

'Yes. It's Ministry of Defence issue.'

'Is it so? You don't say Army issue, you say Ministry of Defence.'

'Yes. I'm in Intelligence.'

'Curiouser and curiouser. What do you know about these men?'

'Hardly anything. That's Charlie, and that's Mick, who's hurt his leg, poor chap. Their weapons are there on the couch. They were standing at the desk, going through the drawers – you can see the papers they've scattered about. I was in bed and the cat woke me.'

'I gather Charlie is unhurt?'

'Not a scratch on him.'

'Handcuffs, Simpson,' the inspector said.

The sergeant, with his head a bit to one side as if he was asking himself a question, was studying Charlie.

'Yes,' he said as if to himself, and then to the room at large, 'I've seen that one before. He was in court, giving evidence. He's with one of those security consultancy firms.'

'Flowery language for what we used to call a private eye,' Inspector Radley said.

'I've a nasty feeling about this one,' the sergeant said.

The inspector looked at him hard. 'And what's that?'

'I forget what the case was, though I'll look it up, but we investigated these lads a bit, and it's in my mind that they have been used by the Security Service.'

'MI5?' Inspector Radley said. 'Well, well, and dearie, dearie me, and so forth. This one's going to be fun. And you, sir,' he said to Seddall, 'would it surprise you if these fellows turned out to be connected with MI5?'

'Not a bit,' Seddall said breezily.

The inspector took him into the hall. 'Now that we're alone, sir, can you please tell me why you wouldn't be surprised if MI5 were involved in this?'

'Let me think for a minute.' He thought, and could see no disadvantage to himself in telling the tale, but in a discreet version. He did not mention the Foreign Secretary or the general, but told Radley that before his visit to Dovestone, he had been given an official warning, on the Prime Minister's behalf, to ignore anything Peter Hillyard might have to say to him; and that Hillyard had been murdered before he had a chance to open himself to Seddall.

'Do you mean to say,' Radley asked him, 'that you see it as quite possible that this armed break-in is connected with this official warning to you, and with Mr Hillyard's murder?'

'I don't think you need my speculations, Inspector.' Seddall examined his fingernails. 'I think your investigations will bring the truth of this affair into the light of day.'

The inspector gave a wry laugh. 'As to the light of day,' he said, 'we may well find the truth of it, but it's all of Lincolnshire to a five-pound note that someone will intervene to stop it seeing the light of day. These men will go down all right, but I'd be surprised if any connection with officialdom is mentioned in court.'

'Quite,' Seddall said.

There was a silence, which was eventually broken by the policeman with a question which, Seddall could see, he had been uncertain whether to ask. 'What do you think they were after?'

'Anything they might find that could be used to put pressure on me.'

'Pressure to do what?'

'To conform to the Prime Minister's wish in regard to Peter Hillyard.'

'Have they reason to suppose you might not?'

Seddall smiled. 'You could say so. I believe I conveyed the impression that until I had heard what Peter Hillyard wanted to say to me, I must decline to commit myself to oblige the Prime Minister in this regard.'

'Deep waters, these. And what,' Radley went on, 'would their chances be of finding something among your papers that they could use to put pressure on you?'

Seddall's smile was both deprecating and amused. 'Nil. Absolutely nil. I can't claim to live a blameless life, but I am guilty of no crime, and as for any other kind of thing, I don't give a damn for my reputation.'

'Then,' the inspector said, 'may I, unofficially and off the record, offer a word to the wise?'

'Please do.'

'Make sure nothing has been planted in your house – I don't know what, papers of some sort, drugs. And make sure nothing has been paid into your bank account. It's not so easy as it once was to put money into a man's account without his knowing of it, but the, ah, level of people you are talking about have more power than the rest of us.'

'That's extraordinarily amiable of you,' Seddall said.

'What do you mean?'

'What you have just said. The advice you give me.'

'I have said nothing.' The policeman's expression was as bland as buttermilk. 'And I recall giving you no advice.'

'I must have been day-dreaming,' Seddall said.

'In case it's of any use to you,' Radley said, 'here's my card. It's the one with my home number on it as well. After all, we must stand together against the ungodly, whoever they may be. I'll take Charlie and Mick away now. You'll hear from me about whether you'll have to testify, but I think it most likely you won't. I think these lads are likely to find it worth their while, if you take my meaning, to plead guilty.'

Seddall took the card and studied first it, and afterwards Radley, with a lot of perceptible thinking going on in him. He jerked his head towards the back of the hall and led the way to the kitchen. When they were there he closed the door.

'Mr Radley,' he said. 'Am I mistaken in the impression that you are, in a manner of speaking, on my side?'

Radley gave a great sigh, and looked about him as if at vast horizons. He sat himself on the edge of the table, took out a pack of cigarettes, absent-mindedly put one in his mouth and then offered the pack to Seddall.

'I put a foot wrong once,' he said. 'I'd have been superintendent, perhaps chief super, by now, if I'd followed orders. I, ah, I pursued an investigation into an incident involving a man whom I shall describe as a government official. I'd been warned off, but I'm a policeman, and my job is to uphold the law. From the career point of view it was reckless to the point of folly, but I don't regret it.'

'Well done you,' was Seddall's comment. 'But I want to say this: I seem to be up to my neck in a business that so far I know nothing about, and I don't want you to get into any more trouble on my account.'

'That will be my choice, my decision. If you're up against who I think you're up against—'

Seddall interrupted. 'Why are we pussyfooting about like this? Who was that so-called government official of yours?'

Radley extinguished his cigarette, apparently to give himself time to reflect before he answered this one. 'It was a bloke from MI5. Quite high up.'

'And you think these fellows tonight were hired by MI5. I don't know about that. Maybe, and maybe not.' Seddall put his own cigarette out. 'I should tell you, Radley, I've been a bit maverick myself in my time, and it might do you no good at all to be associated with me. I'll take you at your word, though, and if anything comes up that I think you might be able to help me with, you'll hear from me.'

'That's the ticket,' Radley said. 'What I shall do, Seddall – ' they were acquaintances now, the formalities gone – 'is read up on you, and see if you're safe to know. Right, I'll be off. Let's go and clear that ullage out of your drawing-room.'

Left to himself, Seddall sat in the drawing-room, purifying it of the late intrusions with a recording of Mozart's Second Violin Concerto, and considered what to do next.

The question that exercised him was whether to go down to the office in the morning to brief Mick Fawcett, the man who was standing in for him while he was on leave, on the recent events. In the end he decided to do so. Although it would, on the one hand, be unfair to rope Fawcett in to what was going to be not a part of their official duties but a private war (a war, very likely, against their own political masters), on the other hand Mick was man enough to stand the racket. And he would want to be in on it, and would be furious if he was left out.

The concerto came to an end, and he went upstairs to return to his sleep and his dreams, secure in the knowledge that the vigilant Sacha was roaming the house and would awaken him, as surely as the geese on the Capitol of ancient Rome awoke the sentinels there, if any more intruders broke in.

In the morning he showered and shaved and dressed decently for his visit to the office, walked to the hotel down the road for breakfast, went out and found a cab, and told the driver to take him to Whitehall.

'The boss!' said Major Mick Fawcett, rising from behind the desk to his great height as Seddall walked into the office. 'I thought you were away by now, pig-sticking in Uttar Pradesh, or playing polo against Hodson's Horse.'

'I'm not that old, you insolent, jumped-up, third-rate apology for a soldier, and you know damn well we're going to the Caribbean. Well, with luck.'

'With luck? Something up, Harry?'

Seddall threw himself into a chair and told him what was up.

'My word,' Fawcett said at the end of the recital. 'That is quite a tale. General Simon Ainley, no less, warns you off Jane's friend Peter Hillyard, and within forty-eight hours Hillyard is murdered. And before any of that this twerp from the US Embassy also warns you to steer clear of any – what was it? – oh yes, any proposal to do with corporate business. I can't make head or tail of this, Harry, but I have a nugget to throw in myself.'

'What's that?'

'Tell you in a minute.' He looked askance at Seddall. 'Did I pick you up correctly, that Ainley said he spoke on behalf of the Prime Minister, not for the government? So it would sound like Intelligence business. MI6.'

Seddall lit a cigarette. 'Might be. What I'd like, Mick, is for you simply to write down what I've just told you and file it; the written record sometimes comes in handy.'

'Will do.' Fawcett slid the ashtray across the desk. 'It's noticeable that this man from the US Embassy Commercial Attaché's office is markedly low-level. I suppose so that he can be disowned if it comes to the bit.'

'I should think that's right. What's this nugget you've got to throw into the pot?'

'I've been warned off something too, and at ministerial level.'

'Give.'

Fawcett got up and walked around. 'There's no connection, I can't see a connection, it's just that it was odd. The very first day of your leave I was summoned to Prynne's office, the Minister of State. He told me this, that if we heard of any happenings on the East African coast that seemed to us curious or interesting, we were to take no action.'

'Did he, by God? I don't believe it.'

'Why, does East Africa mean something to you?'

'Never mind that. How did you answer him?'

'I said it was extremely unlikely that we should be in receipt of strange news from East Africa. I pointed out that we were not an intelligence-gathering unit, but a reactive one, and that so far as gathering intelligence in Africa was concerned, Britain had an MI6 presence in every embassy on the African continent.'

'To which he responded?'

'What he actually said was, "Oh, well, Major Fawcett, you know what Seddall's like, he has ears everywhere. Sometimes I think that if an ant farts in Arabia Deserta there will be a whole herd of Smith's gazelles on the phone to him before the day's out, or if a house catches fire in Kandahar a snow leopard will be flashing its heliograph in no time."'

'Who on earth does the fool think I am, Mowgli?' But Seddall was not irritated. A smile that held both gratification and cunning had begun to grow on his face.

Fawcett ended his wanderings and sat himself down again.

'Quite. I told him we had no wild animals on the strength. He was a bit miffed at that. I was being facetious at his expense, and he knew it. I think he'd been rather showing off his geographical knowledge, such as it is. What he ended with was this: regardless of whatever information might come our way, it must be completely understood that until further notice the East African littoral was, for us, forbidden territory.'

Fawcett had caught Seddall's expression; it was one he recognized. 'Why are you grinning like that?'

Seddall picked up his Gauloises again and they each took one. 'Grinning, am I? I'll tell you why.' He told Fawcett about the note they had found in Hillyard's study giving the name of an island in the Indian Ocean, and how it was marked in the atlas. 'It's a long way off shore,' he concluded, 'but if you wanted to get there, East Africa's where you'd make for.'

Fawcett's face was grim with thought. 'It is the closest thing to impossible not to conclude that there is a plot thickening out there in the Indian Ocean.'

'Ain't it just?' Seddall said. 'That is three warnings-off within a week. One to this office, delivered to you, and two to me as a private person. It gives one to think. We've got very little to go on. All the same . . .'

The silence ran on.

A change had come over Seddall. He still lay back in his chair, but his chin was down, his face turned towards a corner of the room, and it was as if he was aware of nothing in the office. Whatever vision he saw was far beyond the confines of these walls. His expression was as hard as any Fawcett had seen, and his eyes had a yellowish gleam to them, a wild and menacing stare, like the eyes of a beast of prey long sated of its last kill that from its lair catches on the wind the scent that draws it to the hunt.

Fawcett broke the silence. 'You said "all the same", and then you stopped.'

'Did I?' Seddall spoke like a man emerging from a trance. He became aware of the cigarette burning his fingers, and dropped it, still burning, into the ashtray. 'Then I must have been going to say a thing. Yes, I was. Perhaps I felt it was too, well, personal, even rather an extravagant thing to say.'

Seddall stood up and gave himself a kind of shake, let a shiver pass through him.

'I tell you what it is,' he said. 'I feel myself to be in the presence of dark forces. And I am not really a superstitious man.'

'No,' Fawcett said. 'You're not superstitious, Harry, but if ever a man had an instinct for dirty weather lurking over the horizon, you're that man.'

Seddall gave one of his self-deprecating ironic smiles. 'The Ancient Mariner, forsooth. Do you know, what with one thing and another, I begin to feel I'm moving in enemy territory.'

'Well, what are we going to do?'

'Officially, you're going to sit at this desk and keep on moving paper. Anything I do is going to be on the private army basis. Underground, so to speak, like the French resistance during the war. I almost feel an idiot telling you this, but I've got a man on his way out there already.'

'Anyone I know?'

'Don't believe so. He's a poet, Mick. A friend of Jane's. No connection with this office, do you see, and he's got a brain and he seems to be able to handle himself. He knew Hillyard, and he's keen to do his bit in the vengeance line. He's got no training of course, but he's going to wander out there and just scout around, and see what he comes up with.'

'No harm in that,' Fawcett said. 'Mind you, it would be good to have a professional or two to call on, and Sorrel and Mark Sedgwick are off riding horses in Colorado.'

'Well then, let's see if we can find Tony Carver, and tell him we might have a little war on our hands, if he wants to play.'

'He'll want to play all right. I saw him a few days ago. He's in Paris and he asked me if I knew of a decent hotel, not too pricey, so I can give you its number.'

'*Merveilleux, alors!*' Seddall put his hat on. 'You know, Mick, I could enjoy this, except that it looks like buggering up the Martinique expedition, and what's more, I'd found a good book to take with me.'

'A book? What is it?'

'Ah, well.' Seddall stood up. 'I think it might be a bit over your head, old chap.'

'Dear God,' Fawcett said. 'I don't know why I stay in this department.'

'You know damn well why. It beats work, any day of the week.'

They exchanged farewells, and Seddall went on his way.

Chapter Six

Harry Seddall was sitting in the sun outside a café on the boulevard St Michel with Tony Carver, having just flown in to Orly on an excessively early flight from Heathrow. On the table were the remains of croissants and brioches, for they had ordered more than they could eat, and two freshly filled cups of espresso.

Carver was lighting a cigar and Seddall was smoking one of his Gauloises. Carver was a long thin man, over six feet in height, black-haired and with a narrow black moustache. There was an old-fashioned feel to him, as if he were an actor in a wartime film.

An alsatian dog came out of nowhere and sat at his knee, with an air of confident expectation. Carver roughed up its head with both hands, by way of introduction, and then swept all the uneaten goodies on to one plate and put it down on the pavement. The dog wolfed the food down and then repeated its hopeful pantomime, but Carver bashed it on the shoulder and said, 'No more,' and the dog settled under his chair.

'Well, Harry,' he said. 'That was quite a story. What do you want me to do?'

'Don't know yet, because right now I'm wandering around in the dark. When are you planning to come back to London?'

'It's all one to me. I'll fly back tomorrow – I've got a date tonight with a lad I met at a party. I can always come back to Paris when the show's over.' Carver drew on his cigar and let a cloud of smoke issue slowly from his mouth, and watched it disintegrate, distributing its fragrance into the summer air. 'How's Jane taking all this?'

'Sad but bearing up. She's staying on at Dovestone. He left the house to her, so she's got a lot of things to sort out.'

Carver moved carelessly and his foot hit the dog, which growled. 'You don't seriously think it was any of our people who bumped off Hillyard?'

'No, I don't.' Seddall gave a yawn and stretched himself, legs and all, so that a young woman in a very short skirt and red go-go boots tripped over him. Carver's arm flashed out to save her from falling.

She thanked him and as she noticed how handsome he was and the aura of life and activity about him, her eyes lingered and went deep. But Carver only bowed his head a little, as if to say goodbye, and returned his cigar to his mouth. She tossed her hair back and went on her vivacious way.

'I like pretty women,' Carver turned to watch her retreating form, 'but the trouble is they can't always tell that I'm gay at first glance.'

Harry laughed and said, 'This town suits you. I'm sorry to drag you away.'

'Life is long,' Carver replied expansively. 'Like I said, there'll be other visits. To come back to this business, do you want to know what I think?'

'Of course I do.'

'I think we should get ourselves down to this speck in the Indian Ocean and see what's cooking there. I'm quite sure in my own mind that security-wise it doesn't matter a damn whether you go to the Caribbean according to schedule or not. Like it or not, Harry, people know how you're going to react in this kind of set-up. And you'd have a lot better time getting wired into it where it's all happening than coping with the big power monkeys in London.'

Seddall scratched his thinning hair and the lines on his face, which was much marked by life, deepened. 'You may be right. You think they'll start preaching to me again?'

'Sure of it. A chap like you is a one hundred per cent certified pain in the ass to these bozos. Tell me, do you think you're going to get sacked, if you go all the way with this?'

'It's quite likely.' His yellowish eyes were speculative. He was beginning to like what Carver was saying.

'And you don't give a damn, do you? You've plenty of other things you'd like to be doing with your life. Well, Harry, if you hang around London now, these Whitehall panjandrums are just going to irritate the shit out of you.'

Carver took out his lighter. The cigar, feeling neglected, had gone out. 'Where do they get these things? Cigars ain't what they used to be.'

Seddall hoisted an arm and asked for two more double espressos, and while he waited for them to arrive he turned Carver's thesis over in his mind. When the coffee came he put in the sugar, stirred it, and swallowed. 'All right, we'll do it. Of course we'll be flying, to Nairobi or Mombasa, so we can't take any weapons with us. We'll have to arm up when we get there.'

'In East Africa? That won't be a problem.'

'You an old East Africa hand?'

'No, but I was out there last year to spend some time with John Hynd. He's made himself a good living place out of some rondavels that were guest cottages on an old sisal plantation. The main house is derelict so he's got his own little corner of Africa all to himself. You know John, he likes his solitude.'

Seddall's head lifted. 'Hynd, by God. I've wondered now and then where he was. What's he doing?'

'Far as I know, nothing in particular. Perhaps we could rope him in.'

'Um. Don't know about that. He's first-class of course, but kind of quick on the trigger. We've got you and me and Steve Tschiffely, if he's still alive when we get there, that ought to be adequate.'

'Tschiffely's good?'

'I think probably yes. I don't know what he's like under fire, but he's a quick thinker and he's good in a punch-up, or rather a kick-up.' He broke into a smile as he remembered how Tschiffely had put down the enemy at Dovestone.

They talked about old times for a few minutes, then Seddall said,

'Time I was getting out to Orly. You'll be over tomorrow evening? Call me when you get in.'

'Will do.'

He left Carver to his enjoyment of Paris street life, and went to find his hire car, and drove out to the airport. He was followed out, as he had been followed in, by a red three-series BMW. Whether it was an open tail or just incompetent, he didn't know and didn't much care. He had a good feeling now, that with Carver and Tschiffely on the team he was going to get to the bottom of the affair that had led to Peter Hillyard's being killed, and that was all he cared about.

Back home the next morning, not such a bright summery morning as they had been having lately, he had just put down breakfast for the black cat Sacha, and was about to go out and get his own, when the phone rang. He picked it up.

'Seddall.'

'Good morning, Colonel Seddall,' a smart young voice said. 'My name is Marsden. I'm calling from Defence, to ask you at what time today it would be convenient for you to see the Permanent Secretary, Sir William Jones-Palmer.'

Yes, here it came: Tony Carver had got it right. 'It won't be convenient at all. I'm on leave.'

'Sir William is aware of that, and regrets to disturb you, but he would wish to see you for only half an hour. Could you manage eleven thirty?'

'Oh, all right. If it's only half an hour.'

'Very good, Colonel. Eleven thirty then. Goodbye.'

Seddall put the phone down without answering and looked at his clothes. He was wearing an old pair of flannels, a Swiss cotton shirt, grey with some rather engaging vertical threads of red and green embroidered on to it, and a lightweight grey tweed jacket, not so much old as antique, whose collar had utterly lost its shape. No tie.

He decided this would do perfectly well for a meeting with a Jones-Palmer kind of person, and wished Sacha good hunting and went out the door.

He breakfasted in the Hotel Rembrandt, sat about trying to do the *Times* crossword although it was one of those bad days when the man who set it clearly had a neurosis of some kind, went out and got into a cab and set off for the Ministry of Defence.

Sir William Jones-Palmer must have been knocking sixty, but he was wearing one of those trendy pin-stripe suits with a crude angular cut and the stripes set too close together, and an equally modish chromatically deranged tie. There was a lot of madness about this morning. He wondered if Sir William was a crossword man for *The Times* on the side, moonlighting, as it were, among the anagrams.

'Ah, good morning, Colonel Seddall. I am so sorry to have to interrupt your leave, however briefly. Do sit down.'

Seddall, who had sat down without waiting to be asked, said, 'What with murders and burglaries, which I daresay you know about, my leave's been pretty well interrupted already. A visit to you is the least of it. Right, what's up?'

Sir William, who despite his contemporary rig-out wore the face of one who has heard that there is a lighter side to life but hopes to remain unsullied by it, put his elbows on the desk and rubbed his hands together. They made a disagreeable papery sound but this was, after all, the Civil Service.

'Well now. As you will know, the Secretary of State has been fighting his corner with every Budget round these past years to seek to maintain the necessary level of expenditure to keep the Services – what shall I say? – up to snuff.'

'Has he now? I don't read politics, it bores me sideways. It seems to me though that, judging from the present state of Her Majesty's armed forces, he must have been fighting from outside the ring.'

This won him from the bright sparrow-like eyes a gimletty look that came and went in a flash. He could see he wasn't going to get a rise out of Jones-Palmer.

'I very much regret, Colonel Seddall, that after a great deal of anxious consultation about the Intelligence services in general, both military and otherwise, the Secretary of State has been forced to conclude that among the savings he must make is that of standing-down your own particular unit. As to your own personal position in the—'

Seddall broke in on the flow of speech. 'I take it I'll get this from you on paper?'

'Most certainly. I thought it only decent, however, to tell you in person.'

Sir William could find no clue to the other man's reaction from the expression on his face. Seddall's eyes were half shut, the lips slightly parted, the brow frowning not with vexation but with mental activity, as if he were working his way through a number of ideas; and he was at this moment so contained in himself and at the same time so distant, that Sir William found it hard to believe that the mental activity was not about some other matter altogether.

'When?' At the sudden question from the trancelike figure opposite the bureaucrat recoiled. It was as if the Sphinx had spoken after ruminating for a thousand years.

'When what, Colonel?'

'When does my unit cease to function?'

'Thirty days from now.'

'I follow. That means that I return from leave more or less the day my office closes.'

'So it would seem, Colonel. Of course, other employment for an officer of your proven abilities will unquestionably be found.'

There was nothing trancelike now about the face across from him. The mouth curled in a contemptuous sneer, the head was back and the eyes were leering at him with a mocking arrogance that Sir William Jones-Palmer had never experienced in his life from man or woman.

'Other employment? We'll see. I'm a hard man to please. Good day to you.'

To the bewildered Marsden, who showed him out, Seddall said, 'Well, it transpires that I was properly dressed after all. Fortunate chance, what?'

Marsden, who was clad in similar chic to that of his master, looked at Seddall and gave him an earnest amount of smile.

Outside, the sun was emerging from among the clouds, and
Seddall took his jacket off and swung it in his hand as he walked
along. Suddenly he stopped and looked at the hand holding the nape
of the jacket, looked at the increasingly blue sky, and then looked
around him at the street and the people walking along it.

'Good God,' he said aloud, 'I'm behaving like a schoolboy.' He
knew what he was doing: he was celebrating his freedom. The
responsibility of office, such as it was, had been whisked away from
him, and he felt good about it. After all, he hadn't quit, he'd been
told to go.

He decided that this called for a drink and caught a passing taxi.
'Take me to the Safari Club, please,' he told the driver, and gave the
address.

'But that's just round the corner.'

Seddall gave him a fiver. 'It's a whim,' he said. 'You can keep
the change.'

The club was a haunt of Intelligence people, and as Seddall was
settling down at the bar with a large Scotch, a man he knew called
Cousland, who was making a slow thing of it trying to climb the
totem pole in MI6, accosted him with, 'What are you looking so
ruddy cheerful about?'

'Just got the chop. I'm celebrating. What are you drinking?'

'I don't believe it. What on earth for? Oh, thanks, I'll have
Scotch too please. So, what do you mean, got the chop?'

'Not just me. My office is being closed down altogether.'

'Reason?'

'Saving money, don't you know. The Army's come down to two
regiments and a rusty tank, half the fleet's not fit to go to sea, and
the RAF's flying obsolete aircraft. Got to save money somehow, and
I'm it.'

Cousland laughed. 'You're exaggerating a tiny bit about the
Services. But Harry, what your outfit costs is chickenfeed, for God's
sake. That can't be the real reason.'

'No, it's not.'

'Course it's not. You've got up somebody's nose again. Who was
it this time?'

'I do believe I may have irritated the Prime Minister.'

'My word. I didn't know he had it in him. My shout. Scotch?'

'Yes, please.'

'So what did you irritate him about?'

'Something to do with East Africa, and a man called Peter Hillyard, lately deceased.'

Seddall, from a face deceptively full of bonhomie, was in fact watching him like a hawk, and saw a wayward movement in his eye.

'Hillyard? He was murdered, wasn't he?'

Seddall waited, took out a cigarette and lit it, drank some whisky, studied the minuscule shift in Tim Cousland's normally schooled countenance as the man realized he had made a bloomer, and put out a claw with the lazy grace of a cat playing with a trapped mouse.

'Slip of the tongue, old boy,' Seddall drawled. 'As far as the papers know, Hillyard died in a shooting accident.'

Cousland's face cleared. 'Ah, so you're in on it too. Well, since it was none of us killed Hillyard, I don't see why the PM's got shirty with you. And Hillyard's connected in some way with East Africa, you say? That's not my beat. The Baltic republics are my racket just now. The man who'd know about East Africa is de Salis, way above me. Know him?'

'No, not really.'

'Though it comes to my mind that a man called Derek Wood has just gone out there on some special mission. Why him I don't know. It's not his beat either and he's a good bit senior even to de Salis.'

Seddall was warming to Cousland, although he recognized that he was doing it in a regrettably patronizing way: the poor man was so fixed on making his career, and so conscious of ranks and seniorities.

'Anyway,' Cousland said, 'this can't be of much interest to you now that you've been fucked over.'

'The thing is, Tim, that's just it. I have been fucked over, and when that happens a man wants to know why.'

Coulsand frowned into his empty glass, and Seddall lifted a hand to the man serving behind the bar. 'Yes, I can see that,' Cousland said. 'Must be bloody irritating.'

Seddall weighed up how far he might go with this lad before he sensed that he was being milked, and concluded that he had a little time yet before Cousland rumbled him. After all, the man was embarking on his third double Scotch on top of whatever he had drunk before Seddall came on the scene.

He raised his glass to Cousland and said, 'I suppose that who killed Peter Hillyard is no secret to either of us.'

'Well, not specifically who, no names, I mean. Unless you happen to know that, do you?' Seddall shook his head. 'Quite. What's your thinking, why they did it?'

Seddall shrugged, he hoped boozily, and tried to appear glassy-eyed instead of crafty. 'Well, they get out of hand, don't they. We've run across that before with them.'

'I know, the cousins can be so naive. They still have the frontier mentality, some of them. Oh, lord, there's the boss, and I'm supposed to be having lunch, not getting pissed. Bad thing to get pissed in this lark. I'll go and find some nosh. Oh, I forgot, look here, best of luck with everything.'

The good-hearted Cousland wandered off, and was instantly replaced by the man he had referred to as his boss.

'I hear you've been put on the shelf,' he said, flying no signals of distress at this news.

'The country's loss, my gain, Benson. Where did you hear of it? It's only an hour since I was told myself.'

Benson was an immaculately groomed man, so vain about his appearance (which in its essence was commonplace) that he had even been seen to have his nails manicured, and awash with fastidious mannerisms.

Benson's drink, a very dry sherry, was put in front of him without him having spoken a word to the barman. He sipped it like a connoisseur, gave a pompous little nod into the glass, and allowed himself a serious, but still small, swallow.

'An hour ago? Yes. I knew long before that, Seddall. Right thing to do, if you want my view. Your office is practically free-lance, you run it as if you were a bunch of franc-tireurs. Out of date. The thing now is large organizations.'

'So you like large organizations. That accounts for it.'

'Accounts for what?'

'Where you get these extraordinary suits you wear.' Seddall peered at Benson's sleeve as if it was crawling with maggots. 'But now all is explained. You're a big-organization man. You buy your suits at Tesco's.'

'This suit, I will have you know—'

But Seddall was already on his way, for he knew an exit line when he heard it.

Back at home there was a message on his answering machine from Jane Kneller. 'I have news. I'm coming to London tonight and I'll be at your house at seven. But you ought to know this soonest, so if you get this in time to go down to that hotel where you have your idle breakfasts, I'll call and have you paged in the lounge on the hour at twelve noon, one o'clock and two o'clock.'

There was also a message from Mick Fawcett, equally brief. 'Harry, we have a thing to talk about. At the office all day.'

He telephoned Fawcett.

'Harry, I've got the most extraordinary letter here. For you, in fact. But it came in on the fax so I've read it.'

'I can guess. Is it from Jones-Palmer?'

'Yes.'

'Does it say we're being terminated?'

'Well, yes, it does. How did you know?'

'Saw him this morning and he told me. Mick, I have to rush but we must meet this evening. Can you come here – I'm calling from home – between seven and eight, and can you hold the rest of the evening free?'

'Yes, I'll be there.'

'Great. See you.'

He looked at his watch, and left the house at speed. He walked into the hotel lobby at five minutes to two and went straight to the reception desk.

'I'm expecting a phone call. Name's Seddall.' He laid his card on the desk. 'I'll be having a sandwich in there.' He pointed through to the lounge.

He went on in, got himself a drink and ordered a sandwich, and almost at once a waiter called him to the phone.

'I'll be with you tonight so I'll be brief,' Jane said. 'Also I'm in the pub and I'm surrounded, and you will be too, and you never know who's listening these days. First, I've found a file of relevant letters and I'll bring them with me. That's all I'll say about that. Second, make a mental note of this name. It's the name of a business. Are you ready?'

'Speak, wise one.'

'Idiot. Here's the name: Oceanic Enterprises. Got that?'

'Got it.'

'See if you can find an office of that company in Britain.'

'I'll do that, at least I'll put Mick Fawcett on to it. He's at the office, got all the computers and people about him who know things. And listen, Jane, finding out things about Peter Hillyard can be dangerous, so that pistol I gave you, keep it handy and keep your eyes open.'

'Yes, I'd thought of that. Don't worry, Harry.'

'And a small piece of news from my end. I've got the sack.'

'Oh,' she said, and the vowel was long. 'Then they must be really scared.'

'Yeah, the timing suggests it.'

'Well, that's great news, actually. If I give up my job, when all this is over we'll be able to have a really super holiday, we'll be able to do anything and for as long as we want. OK, I've got to get going. I'll see you tonight as planned.'

'Till then.'

He consumed his sandwich and ordered himself another. His brain was in need of fuel. There was a lot going on today. Oceanic Enterprises, hey? He wondered what that was about. Better get on the phone to Fawcett and tell him to find out things.

He got hold of the telephone and did this, then went and sat down again to put his thoughts in order, but failed to think of anything else he could usefully do before they all met in the evening.

Quite a gathering of the clans: himself, Jane up from the country, Tony Carver over from Paris, and Mick Fawcett from the office.

A self-indulgent smile grew on his face. He had rather liked being described by that creep Benson as a franc-tireur. The phrase evoked for him the free companies of the Middle Ages, the condottieri of the Renaissance, the guerrilla fighters of the Peninsular War.

A sense of anticipation grew in him. There was action ahead.

In the evening the clans gathered in Seddall's drawing-room before going out to dine. They were all wearing street scruff apart from Fawcett, who was straight from the office in his suit. Seddall was wearing what he'd worn all day, Carver was wearing chinos and a bulky designer hip-length coat, and Jane was wearing jeans and a jean jacket over a white shirt.

'You've got watchers out there,' Carver said.

'The green Saab.' Seddall handed him the pink gin he had asked for. 'Yes. I'm being followed lately. Don't know who by.'

'That's irrelevant,' Carver said. 'If they're on your tail, then they're the enemy. They'll follow us to the restaurant and we don't want that. Have you got a pistol with a silencer?'

'I have, but I don't want anybody shot tonight.'

'Not going to shoot 'em, going to stop 'em, very discreetly. And have you got an old mackintosh that you don't mind being ruined?'

'I've got one, but you won't want it in this weather.'

'Wait and see. Just get me the pistol with the silencer and the mac, and we can set off. What you'll have to do is be sure to get stopped by as many traffic lights as possible, until the deed is done.'

'What's he talking about?' Seddall asked Fawcett.

'Search me, but you might as well get them. When Tony goes for it, he goes for it. Let's repose our trust in him, and wait and see what he comes up with.'

'Where are we going?' Jane asked.

'The Romana.'

'No,' she said, and coloured slightly. 'Don't you remember that last time we went there I was half-pissed and flirted rotten with the waiters? I was feeling a bit wild and I'm just not in that mood tonight.'

Carver looked at her lovingly and smiled. 'We'll go to Agostino,' he said. 'If you don't know where it is, I'll navigate.'

They went in Jane's Renault, with Carver in the front beside her and the other two in the back. Carver was wearing Seddall's old coat and had the silenced pistol in the right-hand pocket. The green Saab followed. As they went down Knightsbridge Jane managed to get them nicely stopped at traffic lights with the Saab three cars behind.

'Won't be a minute,' Carver said as he got out.

He strode back to the Saab, took a good look at the two men in it as he passed them, so that he'd know them again, stood back from the nearside rear wheel and with the gun still in the pocket fired twice. The tyre deflated. He went round the back of the car and did the same with the offside tyre.

It had been a swift, silent and – so far as he could tell from the lack of reaction round about – unnoticed operation. He climbed back into the Renault as the lights changed. 'That horse won't ride for a while,' he said. 'Let's go eat.'

The Trattoria Agostino was an unfussy place in the Edgware Road, with red and white checked tablecloths and straw-seated chairs, and with an atmosphere of pure jollity a thousand miles removed from the complicated ways and nefarious machinations of politicians and their servants.

'This is refreshing,' Jane said, and lit the candle on the Chianti bottle on the table with her cigarette lighter. She beamed at the three men about her. 'You may order me a bottle of Valpolicella.'

The wine came and Carver poured it about.

Fawcett said to Jane, 'This find you made at Dovestone.'

'Yes,' Seddall said to Jane, 'pray spill the beans.'

She opened her leather shoulder bag and extracted a small packet of papers. 'Six letters,' she said, 'from a man called Provensal to Peter Hillyard.'

Seddall took them and laid them on the table in front of him. 'What do they tell us?'

Jane moved her head as if to clear the hair off her face but in fact to be sure she could not be overheard.

When she spoke it was with her head bent over the table, and in an undertone. To hear her, the men also bent their heads, so that the four of them looked as if they were at prayer.

'They tell us,' she said, 'why Peter was killed, and they also explain the significance of that island in the Indian Ocean. But I don't think this is the place to go into it. We need a secure location. So where?'

She, and Seddall, and Fawcett thought furiously.

Carver was puzzled by this. 'I'm not in the picture yet. Is there some reason why we can't use Harry's house, for example?'

'We think,' Seddall told him, 'that there's a lot of bugging going on. So we can't use my place, can't use Jane's and we'd probably be wise not to use Mick's.'

'Hot damn,' Carver said, 'this is keen stuff. But I have the solution. When I'm in London I stay with a chum who's got a flat near Euston. He works in theatre, stage management, so he won't be home till about midnight. Why don't we go there?'

'Sounds perfect,' Seddall said. 'That settles it. We have a quick dinner and then head for Tony's Euston caravanserai. All hands to the menu.'

Chapter Seven

The place where Carver took them struck Seddall as being a wonderfully bohemian setting for discussing matters of deep portent. It was a one-room studio flat, with two dilapidated armchairs, a mattress on the floor with a colourful bedspread thrown over it, an old pine table with three assorted kitchen chairs round it, on two walls a mixture of theatre posters and sketches of stage sets, and another lined with books almost to the ceiling.

At one end were a kitchen sink and an electric cooker and a cupboard for crockery and pots and pans, and between the sink and the cooker was a door leading through to the bathroom. The simplicity of it all won Seddall immediately.

'Good room,' he said. 'I like his style.'

'Me too. It's a bit like my little cottage in Suffolk,' Carver said. 'It's a converted mini-barn. Just one room and the fixings.'

'Yes, yes,' Jane said, and quoted dismissively, '*A Room of One's Own.*' She established herself on one of the chairs at the table. 'All very nice, but we've some talking and thinking to do and we've only got this room for a couple of hours till Clive comes back. Let's get down to it.'

The men sat down, as if chastened by the voice of authority. 'We're all ears,' Seddall said.

Jane produced a sheaf of papers from her bag. 'This is about the nuclear industry,' she said. 'The aspect we are dealing with here is the problem of disposing of nuclear waste. The agency charged with responsibility for this disposal is called Nirex, and its favoured solution is to store it deep below the ground.

'There are difficulties with this, however. Nuclear waste containing plutonium will be radioactive for at least ten thousand years, and however blithely Nirex or the government may assure people that the storage method will be perfectly safe, nobody wants it to be buried near where they live.

'The safety record of the nuclear industry is not perfect – there have been several successful prosecutions – so assurances cut no ice with local communities. There was a particularly bad example at Dounreay on the north coast of Scotland, where in the nineteen-fifties a shaft two hundred feet deep was sunk into rocks near the seafront at a place called Reay. Low-level waste contained in open-topped drums, cardboard boxes and plastic bags was dropped to the bottom of the shaft and the shaft was capped with concrete.

'Twenty years later, seawater having seeped into the shaft, the water mixed with sodium and potassium which had been used as the coolant and a huge explosion blew the cap off the shaft.'

She looked around her, saw that her audience was agog, and continued. 'Highly radioactive particles were thrown on to local beaches and "hot" material went on leaking out of Dounreay. An assurance *was* issued that there was no danger, and it was more than ten years before the beaches were actually closed to the public.'

'Why haven't I heard of this?' Mick Fawcett demanded.

'Well, for one thing it was all kept as quiet as possible. It was concealed from government experts investigating an outbreak of leukaemia among local children that the beaches were contaminated. And whatever you might have read about it would not have held your attention long. That's why nuclear installations are mainly built on remote sites with low density of population. Dounreay is seven hundred miles or so from London. It's quite possible that you read about it in a newspaper, but what meaning would it have for you, living here in the south-east?'

'It strikes a chord, but I don't recall details,' Fawcett said.

'We don't. It wouldn't have been even a nine days' wonder in the London press, and bad news has a geographical relativity. To read of two hundred people killed in a railway disaster in the Far

East has much less effect on us than reading of two people killed in a rail accident in this country. Let me go on, there is worse to come.'

'Christ.' This was Tony Carver, and he had spoken with more feeling than Seddall would have expected from a man who was, in the ordinary way, so cool and laid back.

'At Dounreay,' Jane said, 'they shovelled the debris back into the shaft and began continuous pumping at the shaft to keep it dry. But that's not going to do it. The Department of Health's Committee on the Medical Aspects of Radiation in the Environment completed a study of nuclear waste recently, and it reported, inter alia, that the cliffs at Reay are eroding and that within the next century the shaft and the waste in it will collapse into the sea, further polluting beaches and ocean.'

'Then they'll have to empty the shaft,' Seddall said.

'Yes. Not easy.' She glanced at her notes. 'The Radioactive Waste Management Advisory Committee says just that, but the waste is now such a mess, the drums corroded and the boxes and bags disintegrated, that it's going to be both difficult and dangerous. Engineers have recommended encasing the top of the shaft in concrete and using robots to extract the waste and put it into sealed containers.'

She looked round her again. 'This would take up to twenty years. Cost estimates vary. Dounreay management say between £100 million and £200 million. Others say half a billion – on top of the £2.5 billion already spent on decommissioning the plant. But that's enough of Dounreay. It was a very early atomic plant, and now we have plenty of others producing nuclear waste, and there have been enough cases – a few, but enough – of negligence over safety to make people wary. Give me one of your cigarettes, Mick, will you please? Harry's are too strong.'

'I didn't know you smoked,' Fawcett said as he lit it for her.

'Hardly ever, but for some reason I find this strenuous.'

'I'm not the least bit surprised,' Tony Carver said. 'Back when I was a lad in Cumberland, there was a fire at Windscale which threw radioactivity over most of the county. I always thought that was why they changed the official name to Sellafield – to let the fire and its consequences fade from our minds. Which it did, on the whole, but not if Cumberland was where you came from. People were scared into fits at the time. It wasn't just fear of radioactivity and its effects, like leukaemia and God knows what else. It was a superstitious fear. As if nuclear fission had been stolen from the gods, or from the devil, and wasn't a creature to be tamed by human beings. I still believe that myself, and how far it's a superstitious fear with me, and how far it's only metaphorical, I couldn't tell you.'

So, Seddall said to himself, this was the reason why Carver was focusing so intently on what Jane was telling them.

Jane said, 'Yes, Tony, I have that feeling too. That's it really, except that to round it off, in 1979 there was Three Mile Island in the United States, and in 1986 of course there was Chernobyl.'

Seddall's mind was fixed on what she was saying, but his eyes were fixed on her as she said it. He thought he knew why this was getting to her. It was the effect, on the one hand, of being in the presence of what would be called, in quaint old-fashioned language, wickedness; and on the other hand of dealing with a daemon of nature that had been let loose upon the world.

Jane caught his eye and read it. She gave him a short and appreciative nod, and took up the tale and went on to her conclusion.

'So, this nuclear waste, nobody wants it near them. Whatever assurances they are given, they will not trust them. Sellafield in Cumbria is the site chosen by Nirex to bury Britain's nuclear waste, and there is strong local opposition to this proposal. The publication of two reports which were prepared for HM Inspectorate of Pollution, on whether such waste disposal at Sellafield would put local residents at risk, was in the first instance blocked by Nirex on the grounds of commercial confidentiality.'

She put out the cigarette. 'I could go on for ages, but we don't have time and there's no need. All I have wished to do here is to illustrate the fact that civil and military uses of nuclear power leave a dangerous residue that has to be dumped somewhere; that there is in general local hostility to its being dumped in Britain; and that . . .' She hesitated.

Carver came to her rescue. 'And that government and others are willing to be less than frank, even secretive, about this problem.'

'Yes,' she said. She sat back, and waited.

'Matetendoro,' Seddall said.

'Yes,' she said again.

Fawcett spoke slowly and abstractedly, as if he was feeling his way. 'You can't mean they're going to dump the stuff on Matetendoro? That would be a perfectly demented scheme.'

Carver said with a thread of contempt in his voice, 'You're talking about government, old boy. They have a different level of sanity from the rest of us these days.'

'Demented or not,' Jane said crisply, 'that's the plan. A corporation has been formed with the name of Oceanic Enterprises. It owns four ships adapted to carry nuclear waste. There is of course, on the face of it, absolutely no connection with either the US or British governments, but that is because the façade of an independent corporation has been carefully constructed. In fact each government has a representative on the board. And it has been done quite independently of Nirex, to which no role has been allotted in the working of Oceanic.'

'How did Peter Hillyard get to hear of it?'

'From this man Provensal. Has anyone here heard of a man called Provensal? He appears to be rather well off.'

Carver laughed. 'Rather well off? Provensal is the Count of Monte Cristo of the twentieth century. He's as rich as Croesus but keeps a very low profile. Black American who made good.'

They stared at him. It was Seddall who spoke. 'How is it that you know about him and we don't?'

'I'm gay, Harry, and I travel a lot.'

'We know you're gay, what's that got to do with it?'

'When I travel I move among my kind of people. Provensal I heard of at a party in Santa Monica. There was a woman leaving. I had only a brief sight of her as she left the house and got into a gigantic limousine. She was a woman with a strange kind of beauty, and I thought she was extraordinary, and said so to a chum there. He told me about her. He said she was bisexual, and the man she lived with was this fellow Provensal, who makes no objection when she wants to make love with a woman.'

'The mind boggles,' said Fawcett.

Carver came back at him. 'Don't be so bourgeois, Mick.'

Seddall made that short jerky backhand sweep of the hand that expresses impatience. 'You can debate different moralities some other time. Tony, what did you learn about Provensal from this chum of yours?'

'Not much more than I've told you already. The lad in Santa Monica said no one seemed to know where Provensal came from. Just that there he was, reputed to be as rich as anyone else you can think of, with a string of amazingly diverse businesses all over the world.'

'And he's invisible?' Seddall asked sceptically.

'To ordinary people like us, yes. He owns everything through nominees or holding companies registered in unlikely places like Valparaíso. You know the sort of thing better than I do, I'm sure. I'm no financial expert.'

'End of briefing?' Harry said to Jane.

'End of briefing, except for one thing.'

'What's that?'

'I've got a hunch that Provensal's going to try to stop it.'

'Stop what?'

Jane tilted the wooden chair back, getting ready to relax. 'This dumping of the developed world's nuclear waste on a Third World island. That's how he sees it. He's very angry about it in his last letter to Peter Hillyard.'

'Provensal's right. It's the only way to see it. It's not at all a respectable way to go about things,' and with this, for him, unusually pompous piece of understatement Seddall got up and began to walk about.

He went to the window and looked down. There was a boy on a

bicycle making circles on the road and being yelled at by his mother from a balcony in a row of council houses opposite. An old black man with a bushy grey beard sat on a wall and watched the show. Up at the corner they were sitting at picnic tables outside the pub, making the most of the summer evening. Taxis dodging the traffic with local cunning passed down the street to take Euston Station by surprise.

He turned from the window and faced them. 'We're not going to find out a damn thing about who killed Hillyard by sniffing around in London, at least, not in a hurry. Also, I'm beginning to worry about Tschiffely. Now that I know the size of this business I think he may be in some danger. I feel responsible for him. So, I'm going out there. Who wants to come with me? Not you, Jane, if you don't mind. I think there might be rough stuff.'

Her chin came up and her eyes challenged him. 'You're saying I'm a delicate little flower?'

A laugh broke from him. 'A delicate little flower? No, that hardly fits you. You're as tough as any of us, but there's a good chance that when we get to this benighted island we'll find there's some real fighting to be done, and you've not, so far as I know, had any training in that line.'

Now her eyes were amused. 'Training, no, I haven't. I must say, Harry, how surprised I am to hear you phrase it so neatly within the parameters of political correctness.'

'Well, my love, you've taught me a thing or two. Now, who's coming with me to Matetendoro?'

'Try and stop me,' Carver said.

'God, I'd love to come, but what about the office?'

'What about the office? They're closing us down. They don't want us any more. We're surplus to requirements. They can't afford us. We're redundant. We're going to need you, Mick, so stick a notice on the door saying 'Gone Fishing,' and pack your bags.'

'What's the plan?' Carver said.

'Fly out to Mombasa, buy some hardware as if we're going on safari, charter a sea-going cruiser, or buy it if we have to, hoist the flag and put to sea. That's as far as I've got.'

'You've forgotten something,' Jane said, casting him an arch and witty look out of the side of her eye.

'Oh, I have, have I?' Harry said belligerently. 'And what have I forgotten?'

'Charts,' she said. 'There are no signposts on the sea.'

He picked up one of Clive's bright and colourful cushions and threw it at her head.

Chapter Eight

Eight days out of Kismaayo on the coast of Somalia, the dhow brought him to Matetendoro. With a fair wind they would have made the passage in half that time, but the winds had been fickle in strength and wayward in direction, and the skipper of the dhow, a man called Tepilit, was chary of using his ancient engine in case it fell apart.

So they had gone with the wind this way, and tacked that way, in a seemingly aimless voyage over the turquoise sea that put Tschiffely in mind of the Flying Dutchman, and suited his temperament perfectly, for he was not a linear man. So long as he was travelling, he did not care when or where he ended up.

But all good things come to an end and at last, on the morning of the eighth day, they raised Matetendoro with a fair wind on the quarter, and it was at a good ten knots that Tepilit ran for the entrance of the harbour of Saint-Hilaire.

'Allah be with you,' the captain said, using ten per cent of his English at a stroke as Tschiffely stood on the quayside making his farewell to the small and dilapidated craft that had brought him here.

'And with you,' Tschiffely responded, hoping this was the thing to say, and hefting his rucksack he strode up the quay towards a stone hut where three men in uniform lackadaisically awaited his arrival.

On his right, beyond the fishing boats in the harbour, he had a glimpse of a long white beach. Before him, beyond the little town, mountains of granite rose, their lower slopes thick with vegetation, and on either side of the town palm trees grew in abundance, for a part of the island's wealth, such as it was, came from copra.

When he reached the customs (or army, or police) post, one of the men, an officer, came forward and confronted him with an expression of puzzled interest that had a measure of hostility in it. His hand rested on a submachine-gun hanging from a shoulder sling. The other two stayed where they were, one sitting on the ground with his back to the wall of the hut, the other on his feet, but leaning against the wall as if it would take an earthquake to move him.

Tschiffely decided they were soldiers, doing the duty of customs and immigration staff. He dropped his rucksack and presented his passport. The officer took it without looking at it, and said something in a tongue the poet had never heard.

'*Vous parlez français?*' Tschiffely said, because he had done a little homework, and knew that the French had been here and that some of their influence had survived.

'*Oui, je parle français. Qui êtes-vous?*'

'*Je m'appelle Stephen Tschiffely. Je suis anglais. Je suis poète.*'

The face changed altogether and white teeth gleamed as the man smiled and then broke into a laugh that seemed to be at once friendly and welcoming.

'*Vous êtes poète!*'

'*Oui.*'

Tschiffely produced a pack of cigarettes and took one and offered the pack to the other, who extracted one for himself and put the pack in the pocket of his camouflage trousers.

The soldier, warmed apparently by the stranger declaring himself as a poet and by the cigarettes, spoke in English.

'Man, why have you come here? There is nothing here on this little island.'

'That's why I came,' Tschiffely said. 'To get away from the big, bad world and be on a quiet island surrounded by the ocean as far as you can see.'

'That what a poet wants?'

'Yeah, and travelling, moving from one place to a new place, that's what a poet wants.'

The officer made a circling motion with his wrist and pointed to the rucksack, and the man leaning against the wall came and squatted beside it, undid the straps, and began laying out its contents on the ground.

'You have enough money?' the officer said. 'I can't let you in if you can't afford to live.'

'I have American dollars, travellers' cheques, and a credit card.'

'Show me.'

Tschiffely extracted all these things from the pockets of his safari jacket and passed them over. The officer counted up the dollars and the value of the cheques, and glanced at the credit card, retained a fifty dollar bill, and gave the rest back.

Among the clothes and toothpaste and what-all lying at their feet were two copies of Tschiffely's collected poems. The officer picked one of them up.

'Come and sit on the pier and read to me,' he said, with a large grin. 'We are going to be friends. My name is Ombeli. Commandant Jules Ombeli.'

'You think poets are funny?' Tschiffely said to him, as they sat with their feet dangling over the water of the harbour.

'No, I think they are different. It makes me happy, meeting a poet. No poets in Saint-Hilaire. Now read from your book.'

Tschiffely, thus instructed, and feeling as if he was paying another part of the price for admission to the island, read:

> 'That door is barred,
> The other open and seductive
> And showing long corridors,
> Quietly carpeted and cool
> With light at the end.
>
> 'You have been there,
> It always tries to remind you
> Not truly, but murmuring
> Craftily deceitful of days
> You once did not live.

'The road to Hell,
I can assure you, does not begin
Within us but terminates.
Navigate superbly, you still
May not miss the path.'

As he finished he heard a movement in the water and sensed an appalling presence. He looked down into the eye of a shark. The creature hung there in the water like an uninvited audience waiting for more. Despite the heat that fell on him from the sun he felt chill: the poem which he had just read was mordant enough, but the sense – although this was plainly no more than superstitious fantasy – that a shark wandering from the ocean into the harbour had recognized enough in his poem to make it stop and listen, had strangely disturbed him.

'Shark likes it,' Ombeli said, 'but your poem sounds not happy to me, it sounds like dark night with no stars. I have not understood it. Read it again. Read it slow.'

After the second reading he said, 'Give me the book.'

The shark swam downward in a circle and came back and rose partly from the water with its mouth agape, showing Tschiffely its teeth and the path he would take down its throat and into its belly if he suddenly went out of his mind and dived into the harbour.

'This is mad. It is mad.' Ombeli was shaking his head as he spoke. 'You have to be mad to write a poem?'

The shark's intolerable eye sent its parting message to Tschiffely and the great, meaningless, soulless, primeval killer shot off at a speed that both amazed and horrified him to return to the open sea.

'Mad? It depends on where you are with yourself, and what poem you're writing. Sometimes there are moments when you feel you're mad,' Tschiffely said. 'But you have to be able to become sane again as well. You need your brain as well as your soul to write a poem.'

He watched the shark's fin vanish into the waves of the ocean and turned back to find Ombeli staring at him with his brow lined in concentration. It occurred to him that if the commandant seriously thought he was mad he might well, on that account, exclude him from the island.

He sought, therefore, to change the subject, and made his first serious inquiry as an amateur espionage agent.

'What's that over there? That quay that no one's using. And the old crane that seems to have come off its rails, what was that for?'

'That was long ago. Not used in my time.' Tschiffely put the man's age at about twenty-five. 'A mining company,' Ombeli went on. 'They took some unusual mineral from deep in the ground, over there,' and he pointed his arm, 'past the town, oh, about twenty kilometres. What was it? Bauxite? Cobalt? No – kyanite, that's what it was. They left a desert back there. Full of deep holes and caves. There are old fences, falling down now, saying to stay away, it is dangerous. A French company. They took all the money, all the profit. It was not long after they had gone that Matetendoro became a free nation, an independent republic, poor but free.'

He took out the packet of cigarettes he had snaffled from Tschiffely and gave himself one. 'That pier over there, it was poor work they did, and now the concrete is all broken up. That is dangerous too, so the pier is closed. There's a gate across to keep people out.'

His voice had gone low and there was a bitter look in his eyes. 'The French did us no good. It was all for them.'

'Hell,' Tschiffely said, 'that's what colonialism is all about, robbing the poor to feed the rich.'

'And it still goes on,' Ombeli said. 'That's all they want out of what they call the Third World. To invest in it and get profit back.'

'What is there to invest in here? What's the island's economy based on?'

'Nothing to invest in.' Ombeli's tone was sombre. 'For our economy, we have almost nothing but copra and the fishing. But I'll tell you an odd thing.' He was leaning down, his eyes on the water, and now he turned his head and looked up as if to search into Tschiffely. 'No. I won't tell you. You are not a serious man.'

'Not serious? What about that poem I read you?'

'Do not be angry. Yes, the poem is serious. But you are not a man who is serious about things like the economy of a poor place like this. But, my friend,' and his expression was open and cheerful again, 'that does not make you a bad man. Each of us has his own way of living. If you are not serious in the ways of the world, then you must be looked after. One thing the French did do, they did make a good hotel. We must find you a room there, or you will have nowhere to sleep. Come.'

He got to his feet and went over to the man who had been rummaging in the rucksack, to the extent that it was now quite empty and its contents spread before him. He exchanged a few words with him.

To Tschiffely, who had now joined him after a last look into those harbour waters which had given the poet such a startling fit of the metaphors, he said, 'Salah has found no contraband, no drugs or weapons. Wait. Now I will stamp your passport.'

He vanished into the stone hut and Salah returned to sit in its shade against the wall. Tschiffely packed his small amount of belongings back into the rucksack.

Ombeli came out of the hut and beckoned. Tschiffely went to him and received his passport, and they went round the corner of the hut to where a jeep was waiting, and set off.

The first part of the road into Saint-Hilaire was unmade, a track of dust and pebbles. On this they drove through a shanty-town where children played and hens pecked and pigs and goats wandered, all of them as if there was no purpose in life and no need for one: perhaps they were right. Tschiffely thought to himself that a man could be seduced by this, to live slowly in the great heat, to take each day as it came and offer it nothing, but simply see what it had to give to you.

They came to tarmac road and concrete houses, the walls unpainted and the concrete stained as if it was rotting in places. Further in, they came to larger houses, most of them painted white and with verandahs round them, built doubtless by the French when they ruled the roost here.

After that Ombeli drove into the old town through a warren of shabby streets, the narrow lanes populated but not thronged, and where street vendors and merchants sat or stood beside their wares which were laid out on the ground.

At last the road widened, the street vendors and the crowds diminished, and Ombeli drew into the side and parked. They had reached the hotel.

The commandant hauled the rucksack out of the back of the jeep, swung it into its owner's grasp, and marched into the hotel. It was a typical middle-market hotel-chain building, built by some French group when the colonial writ still ran here, but the dilapidation of the façade and the paintwork round the entrance made it plain that whoever now owned the place, it was clearly not a company with billions of francs behind it to spend on the maintenance of its property.

By the time that Tschiffely, who had hung back in the street while he made this judgement, had caught up with him at the reception desk, Ombeli had already secured him a room.

'Give him a hundred dollars,' he said, pointing a finger at the man behind the desk. 'Deposit.'

The hundred dollars was passed over, and Ombeli said, 'You want to see the room?'

'No hurry,' said Tschiffely, who had noticed there was a bar and restaurant combined towards the back of the hotel past the reception area. 'Why don't we go and have a drink?'

Ombeli produced his enormous cheerful smile and said, 'Good,' and heaved the rucksack over the reception desk so that it thumped to the floor beside the clerk, whose attitude to the commandant Tschiffely had marked as so much more than respectful as to be actually obsequious. 'Watch that for my friend,' Ombeli said.

In the bar there were a dozen or so men who Tschiffely took to be islanders, making a convivial noise, and off against the wall three white men in tropical suits, who had created an appearance of keeping themselves very much to themselves.

'Whisky?' Tschiffely said, as the two of them settled on to stools at the bar itself, and got a nod. Two large whiskies came.

'Who are these guys?' Tschiffely asked.

'Americans,' Ombeli said. 'Businessmen. We don't get many tourists here. Only mad writers.' He laughed boisterously and punched Tschiffely on the arm. 'Let's sit at a table, stretch our legs out.'

Tschiffely asked the barman for more whisky, and they took it to a table and sat themselves down on either side, so that both of them were facing the three white men. Tschiffely gave his companion a wry smile. 'Now,' he said, 'these three do look like serious men.'

Ombeli laughed again. 'That hurt you, hey? But yes, they are serious men. I don't know what they're here for but they're businessmen. They've been looking around that wasteland where the old mines were, and I know they have arranged a meeting with the President. So I think they want to do something with that wasteland.'

'You mean buy it? Whatever for? Who owns it now, still the French mining company you were telling me about?'

'Yes, I suppose they still own it. Nothing's happened there since they left. It's dead ground, a honeycomb of old mine shafts. Who would want it?' He lifted his replenished glass and gazed into it. 'Who would want to buy a wasteland? What use is that?'

'Seems odd, all right. Tell me though, how do you know all these things, like their going to meet the President?'

Ombeli laughed again. 'My friend, I am a man who gets to know things. I am in a position to know things.'

'You are? Why?'

'That is my secret. But let us think about you, not about me. I want you to have a happy time here, and then you will go away and write poems about Matetendoro, and tourists will hear of us, and start to visit here. So we must find you a good place to live. Or do you like to go on staying in this hotel?'

'I don't know. I'll give it time, see how I like it. Perhaps if I could get a room in a house, or a cottage, or a shack to myself, I might prefer that. But I'll wait, and see how I get on here. In fact, it's time I went to settle into my room.'

The commandant stood up. 'If you decide you want to live in a house and not in the hotel, you come to me. I'll fix it for you.'

The bedroom was of a fair size and had its own bathroom, and for all the worn state of the furnishings and the absence of clinical cleanliness, Tschiffely thought it would be comfortable enough.

He took his boots off and stretched himself out on the bed. It grew dark early here, but he put no lights on and basked in the peace of being on his own and of having reached, at last, his destination: the peace, too, to make a first estimate of his situation.

At first it had seemed to him that he had fallen on his feet in a way he had hardly expected, being taken under the umbrella of so useful a man as Commandant Ombeli. But after the reading of the poem the incongruousness of that scene, where the officer in command at the point of entry to the country almost at once offered help and even friendship to an unimportant visitor, had taken hold of him.

He had begun to doubt, and that doubt, once planted, had begun to flourish. He did not quite believe, now, in this open and amiable Commandant Ombeli, who had gone so far as to drive him here and book a room for him and to offer to find him more private quarters if the hotel failed to suit him.

Ombeli's rank was the equivalent of major, and this was a tiny country with a population of no more than a quarter of a million, so its army would be small in proportion; and a man of Ombeli's rank, therefore, a man of some importance.

Why should such a man go so far out of his way to make a visitor of Tschiffely's unimpressive appearance – a fellow who travelled with no luggage but a rucksack and little more than the clothes he stood up in – so warmly welcome, and even to establish a friendship with him?

Why? Now that he had looked for it, the answer was obvious: for no other reason than to have a pretext for keeping an eye on him.

If his scepticism about the motive for Ombeli's warmth and friendliness was well founded, and if his interpretation of the motive was accurate, then it was logical to conclude that here on Mateten-doro they were watchful of unexpected visitors.

Which might well mean that this island republic did indeed hold the explanation to whatever mystery of government had led to Peter Hillyard's murder.

He felt invigorated by reaching this hopeful conclusion. Refreshed by a warm shower, and wearing a clean shirt and cotton trousers in place of his travel-worn shorts, he went down to dinner.

The restaurant was not busy: two tables occupied by people he took to be islanders, some African and some Asian, and one table at which sat the three white businessmen he had seen earlier in the bar.

He asked for beer, and for clams stewed in wine followed by blackened redfish, and sat enjoying his beer and a cigarette with his head pleasantly empty while he waited for the clams. The food was a long time coming, so he ordered another beer, and sat sideways to the table, contentedly tracing the contours and patches on the stained wall in front of him.

One of the white businessmen came across the room and as he came Tschiffely gave him half an eye, which registered a heavy build, a big square head, and a flattened expressionless face. The man carried himself in a way which conveyed belligerence and a conviction of power, and he pulled out a chair on the other side of the table and sat down without so much as a by-your-leave. Tschiffely did not think much of this, so he looked at him briefly and then went back to mapping the patterns on the wall.

'Just who are you?' the American voice said.

Tschiffely thought of playing the game of sarcastic badinage but considered that with a hard case like this one it would fall like water off a duck's back, and decided not to bother. Besides, he was here to find things out, not to make a point of keeping the uncouth in line.

'Tschiffely, Stephen,' he said.

'And what are you?'

'A poet.'

'And what else?'

Tschiffely sat up and turned to meet the frozen eyes in the rock face. 'An Englishman on his travels – apart from that, nothing else.'

'That didn't sound like an English name to me.'

Tschiffely succumbed. 'Well, maybe not, but what would you know about it?'

'Are you getting fresh with me, mister?'

Tschiffely felt an exhilarating surge of antagonism rise in him and sat up straight and loosened his shoulders to enjoy it. He smiled a huge smile and leaned forward with an appearance of great friendliness.

'I don't like your manner, comrade, that's what it is. You talk as if I had to account to you. And if that's what you think, then what you think is bullshit. So if we're to get along together, you'll have to change your tack.' Tschiffely drained his glass. 'Want a beer? And what's *your* name, if it comes to that?'

The big man sat back. There was no change in his expression. 'Yes, I'll have a beer. You tell it like it is, don't you, mister? I guess I did come on a bit strong. My name's Arthur J. Foxberry. My friends call me Art. If you call me Arthur I'll spit in your eye.'

'Call me Steve.'

'Well, Steve. You've got a hard edge when you want to use it, don't you? And look at you now, all peaceful and friendly as if there had been no harsh words between us at all.'

Since there appeared to be a prospect of the two of them being on amiable terms (however sincerely or insincerely meant on either side), Tschiffely went for it.

'Artie, if you think those were harsh words, stick around.'

A smile and a slight barking sound, which was his laugh, came from Art. Tschiffely liked neither the laugh nor the smile. It was true that the man had backed off a bit, but his overbearing character was not displaced for a moment by these superficial signs of amity.

'So what are you doing here, Steve? Nobody else comes here unless they have business to do. It's no place for holidays. This is the only hotel and it's crap.'

Tschiffely gave a great sigh, like a man with trouble in him. He was beginning to admire his acting ability.

'Have you heard of writer's block?'

Foxberry became contemptuous, which suited him well. 'Yeah, I've heard of writer's block. It makes no sense to me. If a man has work to do, he gets down to it and does it. Where I come from, if it's time to plough and sow your wheat, you get out there and plough and sow wheat. And when it's time to get the wheat in, then that's what you do. Anything else is plain bone idle.'

'Writing's different from farming. Writer's block's like an illness,' said Tschiffely, who for the life of him didn't know whether he believed what he was saying or not, but it was his cover, so that was the tale he told.

'You talking about yourself here? Sounds wimp to me.'

'Of course it does,' Tschiffely said, 'to a thickhead like you. You asked me why I'm here, and that's why I'm here. I was getting stale, stuck in the same place too long, so I decided to travel, and go to the places the tour operators haven't reached yet.'

A waiter arrived with the clams. The American said, 'I'll leave you to eat your meal, but why don't you join me and my friends for a drink afterwards?'

'So that we can insult each other some more? All right.'

'We'll be in the bar.'

As he ate his dinner, which turned out to have been well worth waiting for, Tschiffely considered Art Foxberry. It had been clear to both of them that they had nothing in common. Foxberry had been rude to him and he'd been rude to Foxberry. So why did the American want to meet him again? To suss him out a bit more, of course.

He had felt the American's suspicion all the time they were talking together: it was clear that to Foxberry and his buddies Tschiffely's arrival here was not welcome. Tschiffely was in the way: it must be, then, that they saw him as a threat to whatever it was they wanted to achieve on the island.

When he considered his situation it was not good. First he had attracted the interest of Major Ombeli, of which he had come to take a cannily negative view; and now here were these three heavies waiting to inspect him in the bar. No, his situation was not good. He was isolated, he was weaponless, he did not know his way around.

'Yes, indeed,' he told himself as he walked to the bar. 'You are in deep shit, Steve Tschiffely, so damn deep that you're far out of your depth. And you've only been here for half a day.'

When he went into the bar the three were sitting where they had been earlier in the day, remote from the few other late drinkers. Closest to them was a man on a stool at the bar in a red cotton shirt and a hat like a collapsed straw sombrero sitting slumped, either asleep or drunk or both, with his head resting on the counter.

As he approached Foxberry and his colleagues the three of them, with a courtesy he had hardly expected, stood up.

'Steve,' Foxberry made the introductions, 'meet Will Pearce and Nathan Skolnikoff.' Tschiffely shook hands with the two men. 'We've got ourselves a house on the edge of this township, and we're going to take you out there and give you some decent liquor. I told the boys you were the worst-tempered son of a bitch I ever hope to meet, and they took to you right off.'

While his prospective hosts made jolly laughing sounds at this jest, Tschiffely thought that going off with them might be a very bad idea indeed, but then again it might not. Foxberry had the look of a hard man and his manner was as tough as you could wish, but that need not mean he was given to physical violence. Businessmen, so far as the poet's understanding went, were not generally assassins.

On the other hand, he was here because somebody had killed Peter Hillyard in the English countryside. How very much easier it would be to kill a man here and drop him in the sea for the sharks to dispose of. But it was because of Hillyard he had come, and if these were the men he had come here to get next to, there was no point in chickening out at the first prospect of getting next to them.

He quoted to himself the debonair remark of the mad earl as he launched the charge of the Light Brigade at Balaclava, 'Here goes the last of the Brudenells,' and made appropriate social sounds and went out of the hotel with his new friends.

He stood on the steps and lifted his face to the night sky, overwhelmed by the brightness of the stars. He wanted to lie on his back and have them shining there, far above him, all night long. What a waste of himself this was, risk or no risk, to spend the evening in false bonhomie with these spiritless louts.

Then he realized that he was seeing things the wrong way round. This was the sky, and these were the stars, that shone down on lands where people still lived in the tribe: and he had come here because of the atavistic call that had woken in his blood at the murder of Peter Hillyard, he was a man who had come here seeking vengeance, and to that end was going unarmed into the camp of his enemies, and he was going under the right sky.

He went down the steps and into the car, and they set off.

They had travelled no more than a furlong when he was surprised to see a red shirt and a straw sombrero scooting past them on a motorbike.

Chapter Nine

The house was on the south side of Saint-Hilaire, and when Tschiffely left the car he saw the mountains which rose in the middle of the island outlined against that starry sky.

It was a large colonial-style bungalow with a verandah round it. There were steel shutters on the windows. The grounds were composed of an inner area of about an acre with a wire fence round it, and beyond that a larger expanse of several acres floodlit by lights that rose on posts from the wire fence. From beyond the wire three large dogs shouted at them as they emerged from the car, so presumably there was another fence round the outer perimeter, and in that enclosure the dogs roamed free.

The ground on both sides of the wire was bare of flowers, bushes or trees. You would have to be as small as an ant to crawl up to the house unseen. Either the homes of Matetendoro's wealthy were as much exposed to violent break-ins as he had heard they were in, for example, Nairobi, or the firm of Foxberry, Pearce and Skolnikoff put a high premium on security.

They went inside, a black servant holding open the door for them, into a big living-room floored in hardwood with rugs on it, and a sitting area defined by three long sofas. Another servant stood by a table against the wall with drinks on it.

'What'll it be?' Foxberry said.

'Scotch,' Tschiffely said.

It was not just a bare but a barren room. There were no books or paintings in it, no art objects of any kind, and not even any flowers. The walls were painted pale blue, the colour restful in a dim light from floor lamps in the corners.

They sat on the couches, Foxberry and himself on one, with a clear yard of space between them, and the other two on the couch opposite. The air conditioning functioned perfectly. For the first time in a fortnight he was comfortable and cool. He drank some whisky and waited for all hell to break loose.

It was Skolnikoff, a man with a rough-skinned clerk's face and dark hair and dark eyes behind over-sized tortoiseshell glasses, who opened.

'Art told us why you're here, Steve. First time I ever met a poet. I'm impressed. But how'd you get here, with no airfield and all?'

'You guys got here. How did you manage it?'

Skolnikoff gave a seedy and unconvincing laugh. 'Art said you were like that. A lot of aggression, and none of the social niceties. We came by helicopter. Long-range whirlybird. She's standing out there in the yard behind the house. But poets don't have that kind of corporate facility, so how did you make it?'

There was nothing wrong with the truth, so he gave it. 'I biked through France, got a passage on a ship from Sète to Alexandria, another from Alexandria to Port Said, and another through the canal to Suez and on to Somalia. And there I got myself on to an Arab dhow that was sailing to the Seychelles.'

Will Pearce came in now, a long thin man with the classic Yankee face, deep-set eyes and a pipe between his long yellowed teeth.

'I like the sound of that; enterprising, for this day and age. I guess it makes you a kind of seaborne hippy. Must have cost a bit, though. And from what you told Art you've only just started on your travels. Did you save enough money for all this journeying just from writing poems?'

For some perverse reason Tschiffely was beginning to feel good, light and full of laughter. He drained his glass and put it on the floor and sat forward and slapped his hands on to his knees. 'Did I Hell,' he said. 'I inherited a nice little bit of money from my father.'

Money: that roused Pearce's interest. 'What was his line, your father?'

'He was a barrister, very successful, and ended up as a High Court judge.' Tschiffely narrowed his eyes and stared at the distant lamp in the corner of the room. 'What is it with you lot? I seem to do nothing but answer questions about myself.'

Foxberry lifted a hand and with no word spoken the servant took and refilled first Tschiffely's glass, and then the others.

While this took place Foxberry said, 'It makes sense to me now, you being a poet. I suppose it's about as far removed from the line your father was in as you could get.'

'Maybe,' Tschiffely said, sitting back now and rolling the replenished glass between his hands.

'And I can see why, when the poetry turned sour on you, you set out on this footloose, unplanned kind of travelling. You want adventure.'

'You might get a book out of it,' Skolnikoff said.

Before Tschiffely could respond to that, Foxberry said, after a quick look at Skolnikoff, 'I hadn't thought of that.' He went thoughtful. 'Are you going to write a book about what you see, who you meet?'

'No, I had no thought of doing that at all. I don't write prose. I don't even review other poets. The only writing I've done, the only books I've had published, are books of poetry.'

He had never seen the kind of activity in anyone's eyes that he saw now in Foxberry's. They were pouring energy at him as if lightning and thunder could be expected to follow. 'What about newspapers? Are you going to write for the papers about what you come across in your travels? Are you going to write about this island, about your impressions of life here?'

'You don't listen,' Tschiffely said coldly. 'I do not *plan* to write anything at all. When I find I'm ready, I'll write poems again.'

He came to his feet and all three of them sat up, tensed and alert. What did they think he was, a man-eating tiger?

'You know,' he said, 'ever since I met you people, you've done nothing but ask questions about me, and I find it not only extremely

98

odd but very unpleasant. You behave as if you're the police and I'm a suspect. I don't like it. So I'll wish you good night and take my leave.'

Foxberry was up and made a sign to the servant, who left the room and closed the door behind him. Skolnikoff shifted himself to stand at the back of the couch between Tschiffely and the door, and Pearce stayed where he was, drawing on his pipe, a quizzical look in his deep-set eyes.

'Not so fast, son,' Foxberry said. 'You're not leaving yet.'

'I am leaving,' Tschiffely said, 'this very minute.'

Foxberry produced a pistol from inside his jacket and took a step forward. 'No,' he said. 'I have some doubts about you and I want them settled. If you kick up a fuss I'll kill you.'

Tschiffely took out a cigarette and lit it as if he had accepted the situation, and kicked the gun out of Foxberry's hand, turned on his toes and kicked him in the balls, and as he bent over in pain, chopped him on the back of the neck.

He had stooped to gather up the pistol when Skolnikoff said, 'Drop it, or you're dead.'

Tschiffely dropped it.

Behind Skolnikoff, the door opened and a man with a black hood over his head, wearing a red shirt and with a pistol in his hand, came in and shot Skolnikoff in the right shoulder. The force of the shot hurled him forward and he lay draped over the couch where he had been standing, his eyes wide with shock or pain or both. That made two pistols on the floor.

Foxberry was moaning quietly and appeared to be still hors de combat. Pearce had gone as pale as lint, his pipe fallen to his lap.

Redshirt man pointed to the weapons on the floor and then moved swiftly till he was behind Pearce, felt inside the man's jacket and extracted an automatic. Then he swung his own pistol down and struck Pearce a violent blow on the head so that he fell sideways on to the cushions.

Tschiffely had picked up the two weapons from the floor by now and Redshirt was moving to the door, beckoning with his whole arm to Tschiffely who, as he walked past Foxberry, kicked him hard behind the ear, partly out of malice, and partly to make sure he stayed out of commission while he and Redshirt effected their strategic withdrawal.

They went to the back of the house and out through the kitchen, where the two black servants stood smiling, apparently with deep pleasure, as they went by. One of them held the back door open, and by the light from the kitchen – for the floodlights were out – Tschiffely saw a motorbike.

'Give me those,' Redshirt said, speaking for the first time, and he stowed the captured armoury in the panniers on the back of the bike. 'Get on, quick.'

He swung his leg over the saddle and Tschiffely sat on the pillion and they were away, round the house, down the drive, through the gates and on to the open road. They did not head for town, but followed the road through groves of palm trees in the direction of the hills.

His rescuer tore the hood off and thrust it into one of the panniers and turned his head for a moment and Tschiffely could see he was laughing.

'Ombeli!' he said.

'Yes, Ombeli,' the commandant bellowed into the wind of their passage, and laughed again. 'Now, hold on tightly.'

Tschiffely tightened his arms round Ombeli's waist and he found himself laughing too as the bike accelerated. It was not only that he had been saved from, quite possibly, an early grave (or being thrown to the sharks), but that this was the kind of man to be with, a man who knew how to live, unlike the ponderous, granite-faced, anally retentive yahoos they had left scattered round the living-room of that expensive house.

He wondered briefly what kind of businessmen these were who carried pistols under their suits. Then he gave a mental shrug, postponed all idea of practical thinking, and surrendered himself to the pleasures of the hectic joyride as the motorbike sped across the flat country and climbed into the foothills.

There was no traffic – he had not seen many cars in Saint-Hilaire – and they had the road to themselves. They were not running on a made surface but on a track, rutted and potholed and not made for speeding, and Ombeli kept the speed up and rode his machine like a moto-cross expert. Lush foliage rushed past them as he sped along until, after they had been going for what Tschiffely reckoned was an hour, he came down through the gears and turned off into a wilderness of trees and bushes.

This really was rough-riding, careening over bumps, roots and stones, bouncing into hollows, and at one point skidding and splashing through a stream running down the hillside.

They came to a clearing in the bush, and on the far side of it there was a house. It was a long wooden cottage, built on piles that raised it several feet above ground level, with a verandah along the front and a long stair up to it. There were two windows on each side of the door, and light shone in the two to the right of the door.

Ombeli switched off the engine. 'Here we are,' he said.

Tschiffely got off the pillion and stamped his legs to be sure they were still working. 'Boy,' he said. 'You can ride that thing, can't you.'

'Yes, I can ride that thing,' Ombeli said.

'Commandant,' Tschiffely said, 'you saved my life.' He threw his hands in the air. 'How can a man show his gratitude for that? All I can do just now is say thank-you, thank-you, ten thousand thank-yous, Commandant.'

'You can do two things,' Ombeli said, and his teeth flashed in the light from the house. 'You can put me in a poem, and you can call me Jules.'

'Honoured to call you Jules, but I can't put you in a poem. You're too ugly.'

Ombeli looked at the ground and shook his head and then punched Tschiffely in the stomach. 'You bastard,' he said, 'I knew I was going to like you. I forget your name. What am I going to call you?'

'Steve.'

'All right, Steve. Come and meet my cousin. See, there she is.'

A woman stood framed in the doorway.

She called out, 'Jules. *C'est toi?*'

101

'*Oui, c'est moi*. But we speak English tonight. I have a foreigner here.'

They climbed the wooden steps and she went back into the house. They entered a friendly and cheerful room, lit by the warm glow of paraffin lamps, the house being, presumably, too far out to tap into the electricity supply. Paintings, which looked to be all by the same hand, hung on the walls, vibrant with colour. Low and comfortable-looking chairs with cushioned seats and backs and wooden arms were placed around all anyhow. The rugs were bright and vigorously patterned in the Afro-Indian style. This was a good house to be in.

Ombeli lifted the woman's hand and put it in Tschiffely's. 'This is my friend Steve, and this is my cousin Ikwezi.'

'Hello,' she said, with a trace of South African English in her voice, 'and where did you spring from?'

'From England, France, Egypt and Somalia and over the sea,' he said, 'in that order. I arrived today – my very first day, and already this foolish man has saved my life for me.'

She had a strong intelligent face and calm brown eyes. Her black hair was cut very short, as close as a crew cut, and drew back from a widow's peak on her forehead. She wore blue jeans and a plaid cotton shirt. In the way she stood and the way she moved there was a marked sense of sureness and competence.

Ombeli threw an arm round her shoulders. 'You are going to hide Steve here, Ikwezi, and keep him safe. He and I have just left some very wicked and angry men behind us, and they will be looking for him to kill him.'

'Sit down, Steve,' she said, and sat down herself. 'Jules will pour us a drink. Jules, do you remember that my friend Shouanete is coming to visit me soon?'

He had just put his hand to the whisky bottle, but now he spun round and threw his head back in exasperation. 'No, I had forgotten. But wait, there is no harm in that. She would be on our side in this. But she must be sure, and you too must be sure, Ikwezi, to say nothing to anyone about Steve being here.'

'Of course,' she said. 'Tell me now, who are these bad men who want to kill Steve?'

'The three Americans who want to buy the old mining land.'

'Do they want to kill you too?'

Ombeli handed them each a glass of whisky and laughed. 'No, they don't want to kill me. They don't know it was me who went to their house and took Steve away from them. I wore a mask over my head.'

She looked at Tschiffely. 'Why do they want to kill you, Steve? Do you work for a competitor, a rival? Are you after the same piece of land?'

'No. I write poetry. I don't know what the hell they were on about. They took me out to their house for a drink and began to question me like the police interrogating a suspect. So I said I didn't like it and was leaving, and one of them drew a gun on me and told me I was not leaving.'

'What happened then?' Ombeli asked. 'That was the moment before I came in. I was listening at the door, and it seemed to me you did something to Mr Foxberry.'

'Well, it wasn't what he expected of a poet.' Tschiffely smiled at the recollection. 'I kicked the gun out of his hand, kicked him in the balls, and chopped him on the back of the neck. I was just about to pick up his gun when Skolnikoff drew on me. Then you came in and shot Skolnikoff in the arm.'

'In the shoulder,' Ombeli said. 'It makes a much nastier wound.'

Ikwezi was watching Tschiffely with a lot of interest. 'So you're a man of your hands as well as a poet.'

'And you're a woman of your hands as well as a damn good painter,' he said.

'How do you know that?' she said.

'Because these are your paintings.' He gestured at the walls. 'And you have a rifle there in the corner, and a shotgun in that corner, and a knife on your belt.'

She laid her head back and gave a slow smile. 'And a thirty-eight

103

revolver beside my bed. A girl has to be ready to protect herself, living alone out here.'

'Ah,' Ombeli said, 'and we have some pistols to add to your collection. I'll get them.' He went to the door and they heard his feet run down the stairs outside.

'How did you know they were my paintings?' she asked him.

'I looked at them and I looked at you, and you and they told me they were yours.'

She smiled again, and it was friendly and appreciative and in some way mocking. 'What you are doing is letting me know that you are intuitive and empathetic, because you think that to women these are attractive qualities. And you are doing it because you find me attractive.'

'Am I so transparent?'

'To some women, all men are transparent.'

He stood up and went to look more closely at one of her paintings. 'Of course I find you attractive.'

'Then, Steve, we must be friends. I think I like you quite well, and will perhaps like you very well. But, my friend, I do not sleep with men.'

He turned to see her. It was the same composed, intelligent and, it now appeared to him, wise countenance. 'You mean you do not make love with men?'

'Exactly. I make love only with women. I am lesbian.'

'Ikwezi,' he said. 'The more I know you, the more I like you, and I am very into friendship. Friendships last.'

She left her chair and kissed him on the cheek. 'Then we must drink a toast to our friendship. Give me your glass.'

Their glasses were empty, and she refilled them and they biffed the glasses together and drank the toast.

They had just sat down again when Ombeli came in and laid the Americans' pistols down on a clutter of magazines that covered a coffee table beside Ikwezi, and sat down himself.

'So, cousin,' he said, 'now you have three automatics to add to your arsenal. Three identical Colt forty-fives as used by the United States armed forces. It makes you think, that.'

'What does it make you think?' Ikwezi said.

'It makes me think our American businessmen might possibly have a connection with a branch of the US Administration, as I believe they call their government.'

Ikwezi reached out to pick up one of the Colts. 'A forty-five's a big bastard. It's heavy enough, but I could use this all right.' She turned to Ombeli. 'In the States anyone can buy a Colt like this. Why do these,' and she hefted the gun in her hand, 'make you connect these men with their government?'

'I said they might possibly have a government connection,' Ombeli said, 'only possibly; but I find it useful to hold such possibilities in my head. I find that once they are there, my mind works on them without me knowing it. And whatever these Americans are, they are certainly very unusual businessmen. They need to be explained. All three of them were armed, and they were going to hold Steve by force, and to kill him if he resisted them.'

She put the pistol back with the others. 'Why should they do that? There is nothing important about Steve, any more than there is about me. I am a painter. He is a poet. What do people like us have to do with business, or politics?'

Ombeli stretched out his legs and contemplated the toes of his boots. 'You forget your history, my cousin, which is a pity, since the only thing the French gave us, when they were our colonial masters, was an education. Poets and painters have been revolutionaries. To be a poet does not mean one has to be shut off from the world. There is more to our friend Steve than meets the eye.'

Ombeli fixed his eyes on Tschiffely, and Ikwezi looked from one man to the other with a puzzled expression. 'What does he mean?' she demanded.

'Search me,' Tschiffely said, and hoped he had said it with more coolness than he felt. 'But it does seem to me that there is more going on in this island of yours than meets the eye.'

'If there is,' Ombeli said, 'it is not your concern. But if there is more to your visit here than the satisfactions of travelling, that is my concern. It was certainly the concern of Mr Foxberry and his friends.'

Tschiffely thought about this. He concluded now that Ombeli had been doubtful about him since he arrived. He considered the fact that Ombeli had anticipated the risk he ran in accepting the invitation to the house of the three Americans, and had gone to the trouble of rescuing him, and that he had shot one of them without compunction. He reflected his feeling that Ombeli was, in principle, well disposed towards him.

He thought about all these things, and decided it was time to clear the air. 'Jules,' he said, 'if I tell you why I'm here and you don't like it, but if you see at the same time there is nothing criminal about it, what official action will you take against me?'

'If I think it is bad for the State of Matetendoro,' Ombeli said, 'but think also that you have no criminal purpose in being here, I shall expel you. *If* that is what I think, that is the worst I would do. Otherwise, who knows? Have you flogged or put in jail.'

He got up and fetched the whisky bottle and poured some into each of their three glasses.

'I would not want to do these things, Steve, and I don't believe in my heart you are here to perform some wickedness. It is even possible that your purpose in being here might turn out to be in agreement with my own view of affairs on Matetendoro. So, why not be frank with me, and we shall see.'

Tschiffely, needing some Dutch courage, drank his whisky in two gulps and told Ombeli and Ikwezi about the events that had led to his coming here: the murder of Peter Hillyard, the background to that so far as he had picked it up from Jane Kneller and Harry Seddall, and what had happened after.

When he embarked on the story he was unsure now much he would actually reveal, but as the narrative went along he was encouraged by the amount of interest his hearers showed and also by a sense that he was getting a positive response from Ombeli, so in the end he held nothing back.

As he came to the end Ombeli was sitting with his elbows on his knees and his head on his hands, staring at the floor. When the story finished he lifted his head and gave Tschiffely a long look.

'Now then,' Tschiffely said, 'do I get flogged, jailed or deported?'

Ombeli brushed this away with a gesture. 'No, no,' he said irritably, like the chairman of a meeting with a serious agenda dealing with a facetious remark. 'I don't know what is going on here, but I smell a bad smell. I think it has to do with your American friends and with those disused mines. And now I hear from you that your country is involved in it. This man, this officer, Colonel Seddall, he is in your country's Military Intelligence, and yet he is going against what his government wants? What will happen to him in the end, if he is found out?'

'I don't know. I suppose they'll get rid of him.'

'You mean, have him shot?'

'God, no.' Tschiffely was shocked. 'They'll dismiss him.'

Ombeli gave an ironic smile. 'He would not get away with it like that here. Ikwezi, can I trust this man?'

'Why do you want to?'

'That's a wise question. Because I think he and I can be useful to each other. And because I seem to like him. He's a good man, don't you think so? Think carefully. Remember that if I go down, they will come for you too; you are my family.'

Ikwezi frowned at this. 'If it is going to be too dangerous for us here, we can leave.'

'No!' Ombeli reacted so strongly at this that he leapt up. 'My place is here, in my country, and I am a soldier. We are still recovering from the colonial rule of the French, and now – do you not smell it on the air? – a new kind of colonialism is upon us. I shall fight it. So tell me, can I trust him?'

'You can trust me,' Tschiffely said. 'You saved my life.'

'Yes, you can trust him, but Steve's purpose is different from yours,' Ikwezi said. 'He wants only to avenge the death of his friend. So why do you think he will want to help you? You talk about a bad smell – yes, I can smell it too, and I know that President Sefuthi is part of it. You agree, I know you do.'

Ombeli nodded.

'All right then. You are talking about fighting the new colonialism, and you believe that President Sefuthi is in the process of making a deal with the new species of colonialists. So what are you thinking? Are you thinking of fighting Sefuthi as well?'

Ombeli broke into a laugh. 'I am not thinking at all. I am angry with these Americans and now, since I've heard Steve's story, I am angry with the British Government too, all of them with designs on our country. And I am going to throw my anger at them. How I shall do it, I do not know. Wait, Ikwezi, and see.'

She sat there in that state of intelligent composure as if she were the wise woman of the island. 'Jules, my cousin, you talk as if there is no risk in what you are going to do, when in fact it will be full of risk. Do you think it is fair to ask Steve to be your ally, and to share that risk?'

He strode away from her, the length of the room, and came back down again and stood confronting Tschiffely with his hands on his hips. He was as full of energy in need of an outlet as she was full of repose.

'Steve,' he said, 'I do not ask you to do anything. I say only that you have come here to find out who killed your friend Peter . . . What was his name?'

'Hillyard.'

'Thank-you.' He squatted down before Tschiffely in his chair so that their eyes were at a level. 'You have come to find out who killed your friend Hillyard and why they wanted him killed. And I believe that he was killed by people who mean evil to my country. I do not ask you to share the risk Ikwezi talks about; but I say to you that I think we can work well together in a common cause, and that it will serve your purpose and mine. I do not ask you, I wait to see if this is what you want to do.'

'Ikwezi,' Tschiffely said, 'should I be frightened? Is this risk which Jules means to take so great?'

'Yes,' she said. 'It is great. You should be frightened.'

At this Ombeli shook his head in vexation and muttered under his breath and went and threw himself into a chair, whose old wooden frame creaked under the impact.

At that moment Tschiffely realized how tired he was. He had

been on this island for less than a day, after that tiring voyage on the ancient Arab dhow and all his travels through France and across the Mediterranean. He was overcome with fatigue. He could think no more that night.

'Listen, you two,' he said to them. 'I'm wiped out. I only reached here today, and already I've been kidnapped, held at gunpoint, then rescued. You, Jules, you tell me we have a common cause and should work together, and you, Ikwezi, tell me I should be frightened of that proposal. At the moment I don't know if it frightens me or not because suddenly I'm exhausted. What I need to do right now is get some sleep, and then work all this out in my head. And after that I'll tell you where I stand.'

'How can I trust you,' Ombeli said, 'if you are not with me?'

'Because I'm not against you. But think about this: until we know what is going on between these Americans and your President, and where these disused mines figure in it, we can't do anything. There's an old saying, "Know your enemy," and that means know what he's up to as well.'

'He is right,' Ikwezi said. 'Unless you know what the evil is, how can you rally the people against it, and how can you justify what you plan to do?'

Ombeli stood there, remote and withdrawn, while he weighed up what the two of them had said, and then he came back with that wide smile. 'I shall think too. Perhaps you are right, both of you.'

He lit a cigarette and drew on it, and a look came on to his face. 'Ikwezi, your friend Shouanete, when will she arrive?'

'In two or three days, by boat from Mombasa. She was not certain when she would be starting out.'

'Is that man, Provensal, coming with her?'

'Yes, she said he had business here.'

'Good. I would like to talk with him. Now: we three shall meet here tomorrow. Ikwezi, show Steve where he will sleep.'

He tore off his red shirt. 'And, Ikwezi, burn this. I was wearing it in the hotel and they may have noticed it, and again when I passed them on the motorbike. It is true there are plenty of red shirts around, but it could help these Americans to identify me, so I think it must disappear. And these pistols, put them out of sight. Goodnight to you both. Sleep well. I'll go now. Till tomorrow then.'

He went out of the door and they heard him run down the wooden stair.

Ikwezi showed Tschiffely to his room. As he fell on to the bed he heard the roar of the motorbike, and then sleep swept over him like the drowning sea.

Chapter Ten

The man on President Sefuthi's right was tall and thin with a long pale face, short black hair and a neat beard, and brown eyes that were intelligent, quiet, aware and untroubled by life. The face was in a state of repose, and was that of a man who thought.

Opposite him on the President's left was a hefty man with a red face and an almost hairless head. He sat with his shoulders hunched permanently forward. He had a tough look to him and his eyes were curtained by remoteness, but if you watched them continuously for a while you noticed a recurring flicker of insecurity.

The name of the first man was Glyn Weston, and that of the second Joshua Tilden. They were respectively chairman of the board and chief executive of a corporation with the title of Oceanic Enterprises. Beside Weston sat Arthur J. Foxberry, and beside Tilden, but with an empty chair between them, sat a man called Derek Wood (the only Englishman present), both of whom had been introduced to President Sefuthi as board members of the corporation.

At the far end of the table were two of Sefuthi's personal aides, one a civilian and the other wearing the uniform of a captain in the army, as well as the Finance Minister and the Minister of the Interior, each of them accompanied by a member of his staff. The six of them sat watchful and not speaking. It was as if they had been placed there by President Sefuthi not as participants but observers of the meeting, to obviate the psychological disadvantage of his being but one man negotiating with four.

There was also a curious power in the unanimity of their silence, for it meant that the distrust and scepticism which emanated from these six men of the Third World was united into a single force; and this lay on the four men from the developed world like the weight of the weather before a thunderstorm.

'It appears then that we are in general agreement,' Weston was saying. 'Your Excellency will have no objection to Oceanic Enterprises buying the mines. Oceanic will restore the quay and lay new railtrack from the harbour to the mines all at its own expense and will employ local labour to effect these projects. Oceanic will also dredge the harbour to accept our ships.'

'It appears to be as you describe.' The President spoke in a relaxed, even enervated voice. You might have thought they were discussing a thing of no more moment than the addition of a balcony to his palace. The island dialect of Swahili was his first language and French his second, but he spoke English as if he had been educated at Oxford, which he had.

He sat low in his chair with his legs stretched out and his hands clasped loosely on his stomach. He was a man well into his sixties, with a lined face wearing a shade of melancholy about the mouth. There was nothing in his posture or his way of conducting the meeting calculated to impress the other men, but they could feel the innate strength of him: a strength which came not from the office he held, but from the nature of the man himself.

'However,' he went on, 'you have still to buy the mines, am I correct?'

'We have now traced the owner, Mr President,' Weston said. 'It is a company called La Société Anonyme des Mines des Iles, registered at Paris, France. It still functions at various sites – not all of them islands – across the world. We have authorized a written offer to be made to them and it will be presented to them by our attorneys in Paris tomorrow. It is not an offer their directors are likely to refuse since the mines here are, to their minds, worthless.'

'So far so good,' Sefuthi said. 'And we are agreed that as a quid pro quo for, and as a condition of, my government agreeing to your making use of the mines, your governments, those of the United States and of Great Britain, will use their influence to ensure that we receive the loan from the World Bank, and that your governments will service the loan, both as to interest and as to the repayment instalments.'

'That is agreed,' Weston said. 'Derek?'

The Englishman was taciturn. 'Yes. Agreed.'

'Then we shall hear tomorrow,' Sefuthi said, 'what response your lawyers in Paris receive from the company which at the moment owns the mines.'

He was obviously about to adjourn the meeting until the next day, when the uncouth Foxberry came in on the act.

'Mr Sefuthi,' he said, using none of those courtesies of locution adopted by Weston when addressing the President, 'on our side we have a problem. The administration in Washington is concerned to ensure the stability of your regime.'

This was met with a sarcastic smile. 'I should have thought, Mr Foxberry, that the stability of your own regime was what you should be worrying about, when you consider the opinion polls in your country in the run-up to a now imminent election.'

Foxberry was offended by the idea that the United States of America should figure in any sort of comparison with a one-horse republic like this one he was sitting in, and he sent a malevolent look at Sefuthi.

Glyn Weston, observing this, intervened. 'It is not quite the same case, Mr President. We have democratic elections coming up. Here in the Indian Ocean there have been God knows how many military coups and attempted coups in the last few years. Look at the Seychelles and the Comoros, where foreign mercenaries came in from outside. The chance, even the mere chance, of such an event happening here presents us with a serious reservation about the security of our investment in the Oceanic Enterprises project.'

'We have an army, Mr Weston.'

'Sir, believe me when I say that I mean no disrespect to you or to your country when I point out that you have one battalion, and that the handfuls of mercenaries – handfuls only, Mr President – who engineered the coups that Foxberry spoke of acted with a speed and ruthlessness which, if they were exercised here, would mean that you would be dead, the radio station silenced, the airport closed, and a successor government installed in the space of a few hours, a very few hours. When it was over there would be little reason for your army, unless it had a political alternative of its own, to do anything but accept the fait accompli.'

There was nothing to be read on President Sefuthi's face. 'You would not have raised this, Mr Weston, unless you had a proposal to make to me to counter the possibility of such a misfortune.'

'Yes, Mr President, we do have such a proposal. We would like to bring in sixty men picked from crack US units, Special Forces, Marines and Rangers.'

'No. I will not have foreign uniforms parading around here.'

'Of course not, Mr President. We would ask you to take these men into your national army and have them wear its uniform: so long as it is understood that they act independently in order to forestall any possibility of an armed coup. We would suggest that they be stationed, some here at the palace to protect your person, some at the airstrip, some at the radio station, some at the port, and some at our installations at the mines.'

President Sefuthi, still lying back in his chair, tilted his head up and looked along his nose at Weston. 'My dear man,' he said, 'this may sound racist, but I cannot have white troops, whatever uniform they may be wearing, allotted to protect the strategic sites you have nominated. It would look to the world outside as if I had hired mercenaries. And why should I do such a thing? I was democratically elected by my people. I am not a military despot.'

'We have thought of that,' said Glyn Weston. 'The selected men are all of African descent.'

'I see. What it would not be too witty to call a cosmetic coloration. Let me think.' Sefuthi stood up and said, 'Come with me, if you please, Captain.'

The two of them left the room, and were back again in a quarter of an hour. The captain rejoined his colleagues at the foot of the table, and the President resumed his place at its head.

'Gentlemen,' Sefuthi said, 'what you propose would be acceptable with the following emendations. Mr Weston, you have suggested that your sixty special troops should be divided into five groups, therefore each of twelve men, to be stationed at five locations. I wish each of these groups to be accompanied by twelve men of our army. Further, it will be stated to the army, as a pretext for allowing foreign troops on to our soil, that they are here as instructors to train our soldiers in the latest techniques of special warfare in order to ensure that Matetendoro can maintain its independence in the modern world.'

Weston, for some reason, looked at Foxberry who caught his look and frowned, and then, still frowning, gazed at the wall opposite him for a full minute. When he had finished communing with himself, still staring at the wall and without looking at Weston, he gave an almost imperceptible nod.

On perceiving this the chairman of Oceanic remained in a state of reflection for some moments and then turned towards President Sefuthi.

'Mr President,' he said, 'I see no possible objection to the conditions you impose. Indeed, if I may say so, there is much political wisdom in them.'

Sefuthi blinked and threw him a sardonic glance. 'I find that last sentence of yours a bit unctuous, Mr Weston. Both of us know we're engaged in a dirty business, and both of us know that you want something from me, and I want something from you. There is no need for either of us to pretend to a respect for the other which we do not in fact feel.'

Tilden gave a laugh like the growling bark of a wild boar, and spoke for the first time. 'I like that kind of talk. What you're telling Weston is, not to talk to you as if he's trying to cheat a chief of the Lakota Sioux out of their sacred burial ground so that the white man can start a gold rush and get to digging in them thar hills. Is that right?'

'That's it in a nutshell,' Sefuthi said, with some surprise, 'except that your metaphor is inverted. The white man won't be extracting gold that has been lying in the earth for thousands of years, but burying an evil that stays alive and dangerous for thousands of years to come.'

'An evil?' asked Weston, in a low and displeased voice, for he had not liked to hear his conduct being criticized by this unlikely alliance between Tilden and Sefuthi. 'It is only nuclear waste, and we shall make absolutely certain that it remains safe.'

'Yes, an evil. You could hardly call it a gift. It is we who make the gift, providing you with a place to bury it, because it has become politically difficult for you to bury it at home: you have a phrase for it in Britain, I believe, Mr Wood, which has been current in newspapers and the mouths of politicians?'

'Yes,' said the reticent Mr Wood. 'Not in my backyard is what they say. The media have made an acronym of it: Nimby.'

'Nimby. Good. And that,' Sefuthi went on, 'is why you're willing to pay so much in return, and to back the loan for us from the World Bank. It is an evil and dangerous substance, and when you in your developed capitalist world have had the use of it, your people don't want the detritus to be buried in their own backyard.'

Weston and Foxberry were each about to come back at him, when to their surprise the Englishman did it for them.

'It's all very well, Mr President,' he said, with a mildness of voice and manner which did not conceal the hard-edged thrust of his message, 'to bawl out the capitalist world for its part in the agreement between us, but is it not a trifle inept when you are a willing party to the bargain, and when you and your people stand to benefit?'

Sefuthi went silent. It was not only that he did not speak, but that his whole being had left them and gone off into a region of its own. He did not look a whit disconcerted by the reproach, it was simply that he had retreated into his mind.

The silence became one of those vacuums which weaker spirits need to break, and it was Foxberry who broke it.

'Yeah,' he said, 'Derek's hit the nail on the head. And if you're chickening out, don't think we won't know exactly what to do . . .'

Weston kicked him hard and he grimaced and clutched at his ankle. Sefuthi's head moved and his eyes searched into Foxberry's.

'Mr President,' Weston said, 'my colleague Mr Foxberry's way of addressing himself to you is inappropriate and I apologize for it.'

President Sefuthi raised a hand. 'It was rather more than inappropriate, Mr Weston. It was offensive. I wish to reflect. I beg you to be silent while I do so.'

He let the time pass, lying back in his chair and keeping up the search into Foxberry even though that roughneck had turned his face away from him, so that some of the others at the table were struck by ridiculous notions, such as that the President could make a reading of what was going on in the man's head through the very bones of his skull.

When he spoke, Sefuthi's voice was soft and inflectionless. 'I believe that Mr Foxberry has it in his head that this affair would go better if I were not here. I ask myself who he would like to see in my place.'

When the words were out, he made a quick survey of the four white men and was well rewarded. Weston threw his head back and clasped the back of his neck as if he had been stung. Under his breath Tilden said, 'Oh, shit.' Wood turned a face filled with contempt on Foxberry. Foxberry's face and neck, already red in colour, became scarlet.

'Quite so,' Sefuthi said, and then spoke down the table. 'Captain, where was Dudunzi, the last you heard of him?'

'Still in Madagascar, Mr President.'

'What company does he keep?'

The captain shrugged. 'Women, as usual. But recently he is closely followed, everywhere he goes, by two men of European extraction. It is almost as if they were protecting him.'

'My goodness, I wonder who these two men could possibly be, and what they could be possibly be seeking to protect him from. Thank-you, Captain.'

The President came to his feet and leaned forward with both hands on the table. 'Distrust, gentlemen, is a great impediment both to dealings between men and to dealings between nations. I find it will not be possible for me to allow your sixty men to be stationed on the island. When you are able to tell me that you have bought the disused mines from their French owners, I shall agree to your having twelve men down there. They will carry sidearms only, and that does not include machine pistols, and they will be accompanied by twenty men of our own army.'

He disencumbered himself of a histrionic sigh. 'You must see my position. I now perceive, thanks to Mr Foxberry, and thanks also to your reactions to my interpretation of what he was saying when he was checked by Mr Weston, more cards on the table than I saw at the beginning of our dealings together. Foreign troops here at the palace, at the radio station, at the airstrip and so forth, could as well constitute a preliminary to a coup d'état as a precaution against it.'

He came erect and folded his arms. 'The project that we have concerted between us to bury your nuclear waste in our disused mines amounts to a Faustian bargain in which I engage only because my country is poor and needs the money that will accrue. I'm not in love with it. You have heard my conditions; you must take them or leave them. Meanwhile, until you know whether you have succeeded in buying the old mines, further discussion is pointless. When you do know, you may approach me again. Good day, gentlemen.'

The Americans and the Englishman stood up. Weston embarked on a courteous farewell, which was wrapped up in diplomatic palliatives as an attempt to dissipate some of the bad feeling in which the meeting had ended. Sefuthi let him run on for a while and then smiled tolerantly and shook his head.

'Enough, Mr Weston. What has been said cannot be unsaid. When you have heard from the French, call my office. Then we will see what we will see.'

Weston inclined his head, Wood bowed, Foxberry continued to scowl, and the irrepressible and presumably insufficiently committed Tilden, who went out last, grinned at the President as if to say, 'Yeah, man, we put our foot in it again.'

When they were gone Sefuthi went over to the wall and rang a bell, then he went and sat at the other end of the table among his people. A woman came in answer to his ring.

'We would like beer,' he said and looked about him and the others nodded vigorously, 'and then more beer. We may even get drunk.'

The woman widened her eyes. 'If you're all going to get drunk, bwana, I'll send Takuli with the beer. It won't be safe for a girl in here.'

They shouted their laughter at her, grateful for release from the tension created by the fraught meeting, and she went out with a seductive swaying walk.

'Well, Captain Lobi,' Sefuthi asked, 'do you suppose they are planning to overthrow our government?'

'It's possible, Mr President, but it's hard to be sure. Of course, Foxberry is CIA – although in name he is on the board of that corporation of theirs – and as we well know, the Central Intelligence Agency will do anything. But they can have no reason to doubt our intention to go through with this project, so why should they want to displace you?'

Sefuthi laughed. 'I don't know. Why should they? I'm popular enough among our people. I'm not a tyrant or a marxist. Domuli, you're the subtle one. What do you say to all this?'

'Mr President,' said Interior Minister Domuli, 'today is the first time that you or any of us have made the slightest kind of objection to any of their proposals, apart from the usual haggling over the financial details, which won't have surprised them. But it is in my head that we may have been, as it were, outmanoeuvred. It is possible that from the first their intention was to set up the agreement between us; to buy the disused mines; for Oceanic to repair the quay and dredge the harbour: to have everything settled and Oceanic firmly in place here, and then to contrive the overthrow of your government, which is us, and to bring in a docile puppet.'

Boteleni, the Finance Minister, frowned with perplexity as he tried to master this concept. 'Why should they do that?'

'It is in their nature,' Domuli said, 'to want to be one up. It will make them feel they have been devious and put one over on us. It will make them feel they have been successfully ingenious – and appropriately ingenious, since we are merely a tiny patch of the Third World in the middle of the sea – to carry through such cunning little schemes. It helps them to feel that we, though we do not know it, are dancing to their tune.'

'That's nothing but manipulation, power by manipulation. Is

119

that an American habit?' Boteleni asked this, because he had never been to the United States, but he knew Domuli had been to Trent University in Ontario, and had spent some of his vacation time south of the forty-ninth parallel.

'Yes, it's an American habit.' Domuli laughed and shook his head in a baffled way. 'It's funny, because the Americans are very into manliness, what they call being macho, but to gain power over someone else by manipulation is a womanish thing. Yet they are proud of it, when they do it in business.'

Sefuthi made a scoffing sound. 'Running a business is a womanish thing. It is no more than housekeeping. Tell me, Domuli, what was your sense of Wood the Englishman when the fool Foxberry shot his mouth off? Do you think he is a part of this scheme?'

'Since he is on the board of Oceanic, he must be. Why, are Englishmen not into this kind of manipulation? You know more about them than I do.'

'Oh, they are. But this kind of scheme would not leave them enough scope to feel self-righteous, and when the English are engineering something to make them feel one up, they like to be able to feel self-righteous about it as well. Still, we are generalizing, which can lead to inaccuracy. Where were we when we went off on this little diversion?'

'Dudunzi,' the Captain said.

'Ah, yes. Interesting, is it not?' the President said. 'So, we conjecture that they seek Sefuthi out, and Dudunzi in.'

'Yes,' Domuli said. 'Because Dudunzi is a weakling and a fool, and would be clay in their hands.'

'For a moment, though, he was dangerous.' Sefuthi sat and remembered Dudunzi, who had stood against him five years ago, in the first free elections for the presidency. The man had gone around the island with his gang of hirelings, bullying and threatening, to secure promises to vote for him. Some of his victims were injured, and some had their houses burned down. In the end, though, Sefuthi had won by a triumphant majority, and Dudunzi had been exiled.

'Mr President.' This was Captain Lobi. 'Dudunzi lives well in

Madagascar, and yet he does no work. I ask myself, where does his money come from?'

'I can find that out,' Domuli said. 'But since Mr Foxberry of the CIA let the cat out of the bag, I am ready to bet that Dudunzi is being funded by the CIA.'

'Then we must decide what to do about it,' Sefuthi said, and waited.

Boteleni went into thought. Domuli glanced at Sefuthi and said, 'If Dudunzi disappeared, there's no one else the CIA could use instead of him.'

'Why should he disappear,' Sefuthi said innocently, 'just because it would be convenient for us? Life is not like that.' Having said it, however, he then looked long at Domuli and raised an eyebrow.

'He might have an accident,' Domuli said. 'He might have a convincing accident, so that the Americans would not know, or at least could not be sure, that we had arranged it. And we must ask ourselves how it would be possible for Dudunzi to be presented as your successor unless you yourself had been put out of the way by a convincing accident.'

'Captain Lobi,' Sefuthi said. 'Name a competent man who could arrange such an accident.' He went on, with a note of levity, 'I mean an accident not to me, you understand, but to Dudunzi.'

'I do not even need to think, Mr President. Our most able man is Major Ombeli. But . . .'

Lobi hesitated and Sufethi said coldly, 'But what, Captain?'

'The major is not what you would call an unscrupulous man.'

Sefuthi allowed a movement of exasperation to cross his face. 'He need have no conscience about this, Captain. We are talking about a traitor to this country, willing to see its government overthrown by force or trickery or both, and to sit here pretending to serve as its President while all the time he would in fact be in the service of another country. Find Ombeli and tell him I want to see him within the hour. Brief him in advance about the task I shall instruct him to undertake, so that he can prepare his mind. But do it quickly. I want him here in an hour. Go now, if you please.'

The captain departed.

Sufethi ran his eye over the men before him. 'Before I speak to Major Ombeli, I must be sure I act with the agreement of my ministers. Dombuli, it was you who first raised the possibility of Dudunzi suffering an accident. Are you in favour of having Major Ombeli arrange such an accident?'

'A fatal accident.' Dombuli was not one to mince his words. 'Yes. I am in favour.'

'Boteleni, what is your view?'

'It is the only thing to do. Yes, I am in favour.'

Sufethi nodded, and then looked round him at the three junior men, his own private secretary and the functionaries who had accompanied the two ministers. 'Does any of you three have different advice to offer?'

'No, sir,' his secretary said. 'Death to Dudunzi.' The others echoed him, 'Death to Dudunzi.'

'A little dramatic for modern times, but good. So be it. It is hardly necessary to say that nothing that has been said here today must be shared with anyone outside this room.'

Dombuli gave him a look and Sefuthi said, 'What is it?'

'It is the question of Major Ombeli.'

'What about Ombeli?'

'Captain Lobi is right when he says he is the most able man to arrange a fatal accident for Dudunzi. But he is also right when he says that Ombeli might be too scrupulous to do it. If you order him to do it, and he refuses, then he too will know we plan to do away with Dudunzi. How can we be sure he will be silent?'

'Ombeli is not disloyal,' the President said. It came out more pompously than he would have wished.

'A man's first loyalty is to himself,' Dombuli said. 'It may be that Ombeli's spirit will inspire him to act in a way that is not helpful to us.'

'I shall speak to Ombeli, and he will do what I tell him.'

'But if he does not? If he declines?'

'Since you are so pressing, Dombuli, what is your idea of what I should do in such an eventuality?'

'He should instantly be put into solitary detention, without visitors, and held there until we have created an accident and eliminated Dudunzi.'

The President grimly consulted the other men at the table. 'Any dissenters from Dombuli's proposal, speak now.'

None of them, apparently, disagreed with Dombuli.

'Very well, that is what I shall do.'

Sefuthi stood up and the others followed suit. 'I will see you tomorrow, gentlemen. Now I shall await Major Ombeli.'

They left the conference room and went about their business. The President returned to his office and told his secretary he wished to be alone until Ombeli arrived.

He slumped down on a window seat that looked over the town, over the harbour and over the sea. He did not like himself today. It was not so much the Faustian bargain he had referred to at the meeting that irked him, but this other element that had been made manifest at the meeting: the character of those who were the other parties to the bargain.

To be threatened in his own palace by that lout Foxberry was bad enough. But the speed with which Weston had cut Foxberry off showed something else: that Weston, and consequently the management of Oceanic Enterprises (which was patently a corporate vehicle for carrying out a joint British–US policy), made it crystal clear to Sefuthi that the threat enunciated, or begun to be enunciated, by Foxberry represented an underlying hostile intention on the part of Oceanic which had been part of their purpose from the beginning.

A wry twist crossed his mouth. A saying of the English had come to his mind: 'He who sups with the devil needs a long spoon.' He would have done well to think of that earlier. It should have occurred to him that the capitalist world, with its gift for practising enlightened self-interest, would think nothing of sweeping away the black President of a small country in the middle of nowhere, in order, as it were, to protect its own investment.

So many clichés in the span of one thought. Next time you find yourself in dealings with such people, he told himself, write down all the relevant clichés and proverbs you can think of before you act. When you are engaged with the European races, there is wisdom to be found in banality.

He went to his desk and looked up at the clock on the wall, and wondered how quickly Lobi would come back with Ombeli.

He was not kept waiting. Half an hour after he looked at the clock his secretary came in to tell him that Major Ombeli had arrived and, at the President's nod, ushered the major into the room and slipped out closing the door behind him.

Ombeli looked at Sefuthi and kept his thoughts from showing on his face. Sefuthi looked at Ombeli and read nothing there. He waited, making play with his technique of silence.

It had no effect on Ombeli, who walked over to the window and looked out as if to admire the view.

'Major,' Sefuthi said, 'I take it that Captain Lobi has given you an idea of why I asked you to come here?'

'Oh, yes, Mr President,' Ombeli said. 'You want me to go to Madagascar and murder that pig Dudunzi.'

Sefuthi was encouraged by the epithet. 'That pig Dudunzi, yes. In such a way that it looks like an accident. Have you thought of one?'

'Not yet. I have not had enough time. In any case it would depend on what I find in Madagascar. On how he spends his days. On how he passes his time.'

'But you are confident you will think of a way?'

'I am confident I could think of a way, if I were going to do it. But I will not do it. I am not a political assassin.'

Sefuthi went into a brown study. Dombuli had been right. Lobi had been right. He had made a fool of himself. Well, he would have to see if Dombuli's agents could handle it.

He met Ombeli's implacable gaze, and knew there was no point in shouting at him or trying to coax him into it. There was nothing for it but to order Ombeli to be held in detention until the thing was done by Dombuli's men.

'Wait here a moment,' he said, and left the room, shutting the door behind him so that he could give the necessary orders through his secretary without Ombeli overhearing.

But Ombeli was ahead of him. He had deduced easily enough that if he refused to murder Dudunzi he would be in possession of what amounted to a state secret, and that the very act of refusal would make him untrustworthy. He had not been admiring the view when he went to the window. He had been reconnoitring an escape route. Outside the window was a four-metre drop on to a stone terrace: hanging at full stretch from the windowsill and letting go, that would be no problem.

The thing was to do it now, before the word was out.

He went through the window, dropped and landed lightly, and walked briskly the length of the terrace. He turned the corner, marched along the front of the palace to the portico where he had parked his jeep, saluted the guards outside the door, and got in and drove off.

When he was out of sight of the palace he put his foot down and drove as fast as he could for the western edge of the town. He parked two streets away from the house where he lived, cast a weather eye all around, walked fast to his house, went in, put an old linen jacket over his uniform shirt, stuffed some clothes in a bag which he slung over his shoulder, grabbed his crash helmet and went out the back way.

His motorcycle stood there in the lane. He got aboard with a cheerful smile for three infants playing in the dirt, though as far as he could see none of them had noticed him, and went by narrow lanes to the north end of town where he rode like the wind for Ikwezi's house.

He saw no sign of pursuit on the whole ride out to the house, but as soon as he had turned off the road into the bush he turned the engine off and sat and listened, and looked back to those glimpses he could catch through the foliage of the winding road behind and below him, to see if perhaps anyone was following at a careful distance. He decided after two minutes that he had got there clean, and went on towards the house.

Ikwezi's car was not there, so she was away. That could be a nuisance. He leapt off the motorbike and ran into the house. Tschiffely had heard the bike's engine revving its way over the rough terrain, and he came to the door as Ombeli reached it.

At sight of Ombeli's face he said, 'What's up?'

'Where's Ikwezi?'

'She's gone to meet her friend Shouanete.'

'Shouanete? Here already?'

'Yes. Why, what's wrong?'

'What's wrong?' There was a confusing mixture of tenseness and satisfaction on Ombeli's face. 'What's wrong is that I'm on the run from Sefuthi and the whole damned army and police and government, and I'm not going to be able to tell Ikwezi where we've gone. You and I, Steve, are going to have to hide in the hills and we have to move fast. Get your stuff together now.'

'I've got no stuff to get together, don't you remember? I came out here with no more than what I stand up in.'

Ombeli smacked himself on the forehead. 'Of course. Where has Ikwezi gone to meet Shouanete?'

'To a place called Tamba Bay, is that right?'

'Temba Bay.'

'Yes, that's it. The man, Shouanete's companion or friend, I can't quite make out what the relationship is – anyway, they are on his yacht, which is moored in Temba Bay. Shouanete made a phone call, ship-to-shore, about an hour ago.'

'We must go. Ikwezi won't know where we've gone, but we must go. I dare not leave a message. Not many people know she is my cousin and that we are friends, but you never know, they might find that out somehow and come here looking for a sign of me.'

Tschiffely thought fast. 'She'll be anxious, finding me gone, and she'll hear about you, won't she? Shall I leave a message?'

'What would it say? Your note will have to be carefully written. Can you think how to say it?'

'How about this? "You and Shouanete will want to have some time alone together. Gone on a hike to see how much poetic inspiration I can find in your beautiful island. Plan to be back in two days." What do you think? I think it's innocuous, and when she hears you're hiding from the Feds, so to speak, she'll put two and two together.'

Ombeli's teeth flashed. 'Man, you think fast. Yes, do it, and I'll get out of this army gear, and then let's go.'

Tschiffely scrawled the note. Ombeli changed and stowed his uniform clothes in the shoulder bag. They placed the note on the middle of the table and went out.

'Back on the bike, Steve,' Ombeli said. 'I'm going to have a look at the road and if it's clear we'll ride up into the hills, take the bike off the road and conceal it, and find ourselves a place to hide.'

When they reached the road Ombeli did as he had done on the way in: switched off the engine and looked and listened. There was still no sign of hostile pursuit, and he set off, on up the winding hill road.

After a while it straightened and they reached a summit and began to run downhill, but almost at once Ombeli took the bike off the road and again demonstrated his skill at rough-riding, running along the side of a slope through the lush hill forest until the ground levelled, the trees thinned away, and he stopped in a flat clear stony space from where they looked far down over the treetops to the sea.

'We'll camp here,' Ombeli said.

They dismounted. Ombeli propped his motorbike against a rock, and Tschiffely walked about, getting the feel of the miniature plateau.

'Some camp,' Tschiffely said. 'No tent, no nothing.'

'If you'd rather get yourself shot by your American friends, or put in a military prison for aiding and abetting a deserter from the army, I can arrange it,' Ombeli said cheerfully.

'Why are you in such a good mood?' Tschiffely asked him.

'Because the chips are down, my friend. Battle lines are drawn. It's the waiting that's the worst part, haven't you at least read that? You must have read some books about war.'

'I fancy I have. It's a beautiful place to hole up, I'll give you that. I mean, what a view. That white ship in the bay down there . . . oh, don't tell me. That's Temba Bay?'

'Yes, that's Temba Bay.'

'And that's Provensal's yacht?'

'Yes, that's Provensal's yacht.'

Tschiffely looked at the sun, sitting on the rim of the ocean and about to vanish suddenly below the horizon, and he thought how agreeable it would be to be sitting on the deck of the yacht, watching the sun go down over one's pre-dinner drinks. And then to have dinner.

'We've got no food, have we?'

'No food. Not tonight.'

'So what are we going to do tomorrow? Go shopping?'

'No, Steve. Tomorrow we are going down there to visit the yacht. I'm not sure of this, but I think we may have things in common with Mr Provensal. Tonight we shall sleep fasting under the stars, and tomorrow, I am confident, Mr Provensal will be a generous host. So tighten your belt, my friend, and lie down on the ground, and go to sleep.'

'It's hellish early.'

'Not for me.' Ombeli shook his head and grinned. 'I have had what you might call a demanding day.'

So that night Tschiffely lay out under the stars, which shone with such brilliance and seemed so close over his head that, with his spirit laughing within him, he reached up his hand to touch the heavens.

As he waited for sleep to come, he wondered how it was going with Harry Seddall, back there at the centre of things.

Chapter Eleven

'Everest,' the Prime Minister, Philip Wade by name, exhorted his departing secretary, who stopped in mid-flight, 'an atlas.' Everett said, 'Yes, sir,' and oiled out of the room.

The Prime Minister, a tall man with black hair over a frank countenance, sat behind his desk; the candour of his look was misleading, for it hid a character of deep reserve. He regarded the Foreign Secretary and the director-general of the Secret Intelligence Service, affectionately known as MI6.

'I have no objection to your having a cigarette,' the Prime Minister said to the MI6 man, knowing that he liked to smoke.

Francis Caswell lit a Marlboro. Caswell was a man with grey hair smoothly brushed, and an air of quiet self-confidence.

'Sir David tells me you have bad news,' Wade said to him.

Caswell emitted smoke and watched it dance in the sunlight from the window. 'This Indian Ocean lark is turning sour on us, very sour. Derek Wood, our man on the board of Oceanic, the Anglo-American corporation that was set up to carry the nuclear waste to Matetendoro, that being the island in question . . .'

Caswell tailed off in mid-sentence, as if recoiling at the last minute from being the messenger who brings the bad tidings.

'Please go on.'

'Wood has reported to me that the Americans are determined to engineer a change of government on Matetendoro. The CIA are of an aggressive mind in this, though at what level the scheme for a coup originated he does not know.'

'A coup! A coup d'état? Good God!'

'Precisely so. A coup by force of arms. We cannot afford to be associated with such an adventure.'

'I should think not. We must end our connection now.'

The Foreign Secretary smoothed back the wings of hair above his ears. 'It is not quite that straightforward, since it is we who floated the idea in the first place. How else are we going to dispose of our nuclear waste?'

There was a tap at the door and Everett sidled in, his hands full of *The Times Atlas of the World*.

'You've taken your sweet time,' Wade said.

'I had to send out for it, sir. There was no atlas in the building.'

He laid it on the desk and made to go. The Prime Minister stopped him. 'Wait, Everett. Harington, it was you and Keith Moorman who hatched this hare-brained project, correct?'

Harington first bridled at being addressed by his surname, which was not customary between them, and then flinched as he saw the writing on the wall: the Prime Minister was preparing to sell him down the river.

'Yes,' he said coldly.

'Everest.' Wade spoke with the curtness of a general issuing orders on a changing battlefield. 'I want the Environment Secretary here *quam primum*.'

'*Quam . . .?*'

'Jesus Christ,' Wade said. 'It's Latin. It means as soon as possible. By which I mean now. I don't care what he's doing, he is to come here at once and as fast as possible.'

'Sir.' Everett shot out of the room.

The Prime Minister swung the atlas round and flicked through it until he found the map he wanted. 'It's pathetic,' he said. 'A spot on the Indian Ocean, and look at the trouble we've got ourselves into. Caswell, what do we know about the Americans' strategy for taking over this island?'

'They've got a puppet, Prime Minister, man who lost the presidential election against the present incumbent, who is of course President Sefuthi.'

'Of course.' This was spoken with irony, as if it was not his job to know the name of every head of state of every penny-ante republic on the globe. 'Who's the proposed puppet?'

'A man called Dudunzi. He's in exile in Madagascar. He went in for bribery and violence and threats of violence during the election, so that it became perfectly reasonable for Sefuthi to send him into exile.'

'What's Washington's objection to Sefuthi?'

'We don't know yet. We're working on it. We'll find out.'

'I know you will.' Wade was warming to Caswell, a man who wasted no words. 'We'll have a break till Moorman gets here.'

He pressed a button on his desk and a woman's voice replied. 'Mary,' he said, 'I'd like sandwiches for three – no, for four, please. And coffee likewise. As soon as you can. Yes, the usual, corned beef. With raw onion. It cuts the cholesterol.'

Harington's mouth turned down. Wade had had a fondness for corned beef since his schooldays, and had never let go of it. The man was utterly indifferent to what was proper: to offer them corned beef and onion sandwiches – a ploughboy's meal – when there was certainly smoked salmon, not to mention rare roast beef, to be had down there in the kitchen.

The dreaded corned beef and onion sandwiches had no sooner been served than Keith Moorman arrived. The Environment Secretary was a man gone to fat, with a double chin, a shiny bald head, a pouting mouth and startled blue eyes.

'Caswell,' the Prime Minister said, 'will you please fill Moorman in on what you've told us so far.'

The MI6 man did this. By the time his résumé was complete, Moorman was scowling ferociously.

'Thank-you, Caswell,' Wade said. 'Now, you had begun on the Americans' strategy for overthrowing the government of the island, and had got as far as this puppet they propose to install in place of the President. I did not collect their names.'

'President in place, name of Sefuthi. Their proposed puppet, a man called Dudunzi, currently exiled and in Madagascar. From what Derek Wood has told me, their actual tactics will not be that subtle. They have a hundred or so Special Forces men in a cruiser lying off over the eastern horizon. At first they had got President Sefuthi to agree to take sixty or so of them on to the island, on the mixed rationale that they would serve both to act as instructors to bring the Matetendoro army up to snuff in modern terms, and also to guard the old mine workings and the harbour, as well as the palace, the radio station and the airstrip.'

'Sefuthi agreed to that?' the Prime Minister said. 'Pretty naive, surely. The last of these are the classic places to take when you're mounting a coup.'

'Indeed. But as I have said, Sefuthi agreed – at first. One of the Americans seems to have been irritated by Sefuthi's manner and to have made an insufficiently veiled threat, and from this the President deciphered that it would be unwise of him to have so many American troops on Matetendoro, so he said he'd only let them have a dozen, down at the old mines.'

'What happened then?' This was Moorman.

Caswell smiled. 'I must say there are qualities to admire in Sefuthi. He adjourned the meeting, saying that when the board of Oceanic Enterprises had heard if their offer to the French company which once worked, and still owns, the mines had been accepted, they would meet again.'

'And that's where it lies?' the Prime Minister said.

'I can't say that's where it lies now. But two days after that, Derek Wood got himself on to a boat for Mombasa, and then flew home. Events may have moved on.'

'What's your view, Caswell? Did the Americans come in with us on this nuclear waste project as genuine partners, in which case their wish to have this man Dudunzi as a puppet president is to protect their commercial interest; or are they using the waste project, and the contingent ownership of the mines and the ground they're on, as a camouflage for their plan to depose Sefuthi and set up Dudunzi?'

A sarcastic little laugh issued from Harington.

'What's the joke?' Wade asked him.

'I did not know you had such a Machiavellian imagination,' Harington said.

'You are thinking of *The Prince*,' Wade said. 'You should read the *Discorsi*,' and he gave the other a flattening look.

The man from MI6 heard and observed this exchange with an impassive gravity. Now he said, 'The answer to your question, Prime Minister, is that I have formed no view on the Americans' motives. I don't have enough to go on. Except to say, as I did say at the outset, that I can see no reason for them to come into this enterprise with us, since they do not have the same problem that we do with the disposal of nuclear waste.'

Moorman, who had recovered sufficiently from the shock of what he had heard to be able to express his vexation at this, said angrily, 'They came into it in order to oblige us since we wanted to create the company, or corporation as it turned out to be, outside the UK, and the CIA – as you yourself, and Sir David, advised me – is experienced in the practice of setting up independent companies to act as secret vehicles for certain of its activities. There was nothing in that to suggest that they might have an ulterior motive, or any motive beyond giving assistance to an ally.'

'Ally.' The Prime Minister looked with a jaded and darkling eye into the space in front of him, as if he was watching the word he had just spoken being torn to pieces.

Then he turned his look on the three of them. 'Spilt milk. No use crying over it. First thing is to clean it off the carpet. The company, no, corporation – what's its name?'

'Oceanic Enterprises,' Caswell said.

'Thanks. It must be put into liquidation. I take it that you, Moorman, and you, Harington, can effect that between you. I think we should know why the Americans want their own man in the President's chair on that tiny island. Caswell, discover.'

Harington huffed. 'It was our idea in the first place. It's going to be most embarrassing to tell the Americans we want to wind up the corporation.'

The Prime Minister rolled his head and made a strangled sound. 'Don't be such a ninny, Harington . . .'

Harington rose. 'I won't be spoken to like that.'

'Then resign. I wouldn't be spoken to like that either. But before you resign you and Moorman will get that damned Oceanic whatever-it-is eliminated and all record of it destroyed. And since you're on your feet, you and Moorman may as well go now. Caswell, if I may detain you a little longer.'

The two ministers went on their way, Moorman squaring his shoulders with the air of a businessman about to put the boot into the competition; Harington as if he had mistakenly accepted an invitation to a dinner where nobody was anybody.

Chapter Twelve

Wade went to a break-front cabinet and took out a decanter of whisky and two glasses and brought them back to the desk. He poured generous measures, and gave one to Caswell and took a swallow, still standing, from his own. Then he sat down, and began to open his mind.

'I've still got to get my head round all this, Caswell. But I have to say I don't like the idea of the Yanks playing around down there between Africa and India. The Caribbean and Central America is one thing, but the Indian Ocean is another; it's not their stamping-ground.'

Alone with this man, Caswell allowed himself more freedom than in the company of others, and now he laughed out loud.

'You sound, Prime Minister, as if we still had the Empire.'

'We still have the Commonwealth, for what that's worth. You know as well as I do – you probably know better than I do in some respects – that the Americans and their confounded CIA have a history of undercover intrusions into the politics of smaller countries. We don't want them messing about too close to our friends.'

'You're talking of spheres of influence.'

'I suppose I am.' The Prime Minister drained his glass and refilled it and pushed the decanter within Caswell's reach. 'We can't talk in public nowadays about spheres of influence, but they exist, as you and I know. Colonialism throws a long shadow and British governments can't pretend that they don't hope to find it useful. We live in a time of change. We are seeing the beginning of the end – no, let's be accurate – we are in fact seeing the ending, of the dominance of the European and neo-European civilizations. We need whatever friendships we can keep or make to take us through the new world order, or more likely disorder. We don't want the Americans moving in on our patch and fucking it up for us.'

He was silent for a space, and then he looked at Caswell out of the side of his eye, curiously like a woman much given to flirtation.

'Do you know what I'd really like, Caswell?'

Caswell leaned forward. 'Yes, actually, I believe I do.'

'Then tell me.'

'You would like to intervene to prevent this planned coup.'

Wade smiled at him. 'Yes, that's exactly what I'd like to do. But we can't, can we?'

'No, we can't. Short of giving arms, advice and direction to a guerrilla movement in the mountains, there is nothing we can do that would not be visible, indeed blatant. And we can't afford that. Also, of course, there is no guerrilla movement in the mountains.'

'Guerrilla,' Wade said, and said the word again. 'Guerrilla movement. Guerrilla.'

Mentally, Caswell gathered his forces, fell back, prepared his defences, and sent out patrols to see on which part of the walls the attack was going to come. Something was gestating over there in Mr Prime Minister Wade, and God knew what that might lead to.

His efforts were useless: the Prime Minister simply opened the gates and walked in. 'Caswell, I want to do my level best to have this coup stopped. But it must be done in such a way that we don't, as it were, appear; that nothing is published anywhere to reveal the fact of our intervention.'

Caswell had seen it coming. 'Why, Prime Minister? I see no point in that at all.'

'For God's sake, man! The point is that if the coup succeeds we will be connected with it sooner or later, because we were the instigators of this thrice-damned project to dump nuclear waste on that island. As soon as it's known that the Yanks took a hand in changing the government of that bloody island we'll have the British media and the US media piling out there in their hundreds, and they'll unpick the threads of whatever tapestry we weave to cover up our part – even if our American partners are kind enough not to blow that story in the first place. And why shouldn't they? And what's to stop them? So, Caswell, I want this attempt at a coup d'état derailed.'

'How? We've already agreed that we can take no open and visible action, like sending in troops of our own to oppose the Americans, which in any case would be out of the question. I mean, we're supposed to be allies. And there's nothing that my people can do to stop such a venture. So how, Prime Minister, can we possibly derail this coup?'

And Caswell, in the not unreasonable hope that the Prime Minister, having let off steam, would be stopped short by this unanswerable question, sat back and thought about his garden.

Wade came to his feet and made a turn of the room and then stood behind his chair with his hands on the back of it. 'There are no guerrillas on the island, but what we need there is the guerrilla style of warfare. You said so yourself.'

No more roses. Caswell came back to the fray.

'No. I said no such thing. What I said was that if there had been guerrillas there we could have made use of them and hidden our own involvement.'

'Very well, but that was never likely to work.' The Prime Minister moved away from the chair and clapped his hands together and rubbed them like a man coming in out of the cold to the welcome of a good fire.

'We shall create our own guerrillas, Caswell.'

Caswell had observed with an increasing sense of distance the ebullience that had grown in Wade since Harrington and Moorman had left. At this latest pronouncement he saw that his master had the bit between his teeth, and there was no hope of reining him in. Go with the flow, Francis, he told himself.

'I perceive that you have a plan, Prime Minister.'

The reticence of his manner was honoured with a kind smile from Philip Wade. 'You won't like it, Caswell, and you'll wish me to the devil. But we're being driven on to a lee shore in this business, and any port will do in a storm.'

'I can't see my way through your metaphors, sir.'

'Damn you, stop talking like a stage butler humouring his employer.' Wade said this with perfect amiability as he heaved his chair round and sat down and put his feet up on the desk. 'Pour yourself another shot of Scotch.'

He pulled open a drawer and took from it a pipe and a tin of Dunhill's London Mixture, and began a slow process of putting tobacco into the bowl and tamping it down.

'There is one of your fraternity,' he said while he did this, 'who has a habit of gathering round him in an ad hoc way, for whatever operation he's conducting, a little band of what we can reasonably call irregulars.'

He put a match to the tobacco and got the pipe drawing well, and puffed at it and waited. He watched, with a sardonic stare, while Caswell put down some whisky and lit a cigarette.

'Angels and ministers of grace defend us,' Caswell said. 'You mean Harry Seddall. He and his unit have been stood down.'

'Yes,' the Prime Minister said, and quoted from a different play. 'Nevertheless, I can call spirits from the vasty deep.'

'So can I, and so can any man,' Caswell responded in kind. 'But will they come? You know Seddall. Obdurate, self-willed.'

Wade's pipe was drawing well, and he felt the pleasure of one who has made an inspired decision, and who has chosen to stake all on one risky throw, since no good outcome was to be expected of any of the more sensible and measured decisions that might be made.

'I think this one will come,' he said. 'The fact about our friend Seddall is that he holds politicians in such low esteem that he would not stoop to feel insulted by anything we might do to him. I shall see him myself. And since you, Caswell, are quite accustomed to hiring people from outside your service for one-off tasks, and since Seddall is so to speak unemployed at the moment, his expenses, purely for formal purposes, will come out of your budget.'

The Prime Minister drew contentedly on his pipe, and there was such an aura of self-satisfaction about him that Caswell found it intolerable.

'He would not, Caswell, being the man he is, agree to work for you or under you, so I shan't even propose it. He will be working for me. Technically, he will of course be working for the government, but I think I shall not confide this little matter to the Cabinet. Only you and I will know about it. I do not want knowledge of this to go beyond you and me.'

Another puff of the pipe.

'If he agrees to undertake this, the operation will have to be funded, and the Secret Intelligence Service will fund it. Whatever money he needs, be it twenty or fifty thousand pounds, you will pay to him in cash. There must be no trail leading from SIS to him, or from me to him. You will draw the money and have it ready to be delivered to him – delivered to him by you – tomorrow.'

'You're very confident that he'll agree,' Caswell said, 'and that he'll be able to bring it off.'

'No. I moderately expect it. That's the most I'd say. Let's face it, Caswell. If we had another shot in the locker we'd use it, but neither of us can think of one.'

'I hope it doesn't backfire, that's all.' Caswell rose and drained his glass. 'I'll have the money drawn first thing. Fifty thousand, though I doubt he'll need that much. Best to have an excess though.'

'I will notify you personally when we know whether Seddall agrees to go ahead. I don't want any of my circus to get the least wind of this. I appreciate your willingness to let your organization be used like this. I do see that it's close to abuse, rather than use, and I know it goes against the grain.'

'I don't like to be unctuous, Prime Minister, but you've been right before. And I've been wrong before.'

'Good heavens, Caswell, what an indiscreet confession. Your predecessor would never have admitted such a thing.'

'Well, after all, we're not gods, only mortals.'

'Useful to remember, that. Still, now and then we have our little triumphs. We must hope this will be one, even if it's no more than a damage limitation exercise.'

Caswell was hovering at the door, and wanted out. 'I'll arrange for Seddall to call you. I have reason to think his telephone may not be secure, so I'll ask him to phone you from elsewhere. Until tomorrow, then, sir.'

'Until tomorrow.'

With the morning's mail, in a blank envelope hand-delivered, Seddall found a note from Francis Caswell, head of the Secret Intelligence Service, saying only, 'Call me, Regards, Caswell.'

He picked up the telephone and called Caswell.

'Ah, Seddall. Good. The PM wants to talk to you. Utmost secrecy. Will you leave your house and find a safe phone and call him at No. 10. This is the number to call.' He gave the number. 'Got it in your head? Give your name to no one but Wade himself. That's vital. Got all that? Right. See you around.'

Seddall found a cab and went to a café he knew in the King's Road, where there was a public phone well placed for privacy.

'Colonel Seddall, this is Philip Wade, the Prime Minister. I would like to see you today. It must be somewhere discreet, and I have no experience at arranging this sort of thing. What can you recommend?'

'To what degree discreet?'

'Neither my driver nor my police escort must know we are meeting. In fact no one at all must know.'

'Right,' Seddall said, 'then my house is no good, it's being watched, I think by the CIA, and I'm being followed. I can shake them and meet you somewhere. A public place would hardly do. Can you come up with anywhere private?'

'This is very cloak and dagger. I hate to think what the tabloids would make of it.' The phone went silent while the Prime Minister thought. 'Seddall, I have it. My daughter has a house in South Kensington with a back gate that opens on to a mews. I could arrive there, at the front of course, leave car and driver and ever-present police guardians in the street, and you could come to the house by the back way in the mews. There is only this, that it depends on her being at home. I don't have a key.'

'I don't see how that could be bettered. Will you find out when she can be there, and I'll call you back in ten minutes.'

'I'll do that.'

Seddall got himself a cup of coffee and waited out the ten minutes. He wondered what on earth the man wanted of him, but there was no point in speculating. He sat and smiled inwardly at the strangeness of it.

His view of the Prime Minister had gone up during their talk on the phone. He would never have suspected him (or any of his kind) of being capable of breaking out in this remarkable way from the mode of conduct held to be appropriate for ministers of Her Majesty's Government.

When time was up, he called the number again.

'Maggie will be at her house at half-past twelve,' Wade said. You'll want the address.' He gave it and asked, 'Do you know where that is?'

'Yes, I do.'

'Maggie's house is halfway down the street, so the door is halfway down the mews. It's painted blue, and the others are brown or green or red or whatever, so you can't miss it.'

'Got it.'

'Can you be there at one o'clock?'

'Yes. I'll be at the blue door in the lane at one o'clock.'

'Very well.'

Seddall decided to go down to Victoria and get a hire car, since it would give him that much more chance of anonymity than using his own car or a taxi.

He went out into the King's Road, spotted the trailing car parked with two men in it, and wondered how to lose it today. He might as well do it now and be done with it. He did not have with him the silencer that Carver had used last night, and in any case he did not feel up to shooting the tyres out in broad daylight.

Then, as he looked about him for inspiration, he saw that next to the café was a shop selling music systems and radios. He went in and scouted around, and came away with the biggest (and heaviest) ghetto-blaster the shop had in stock.

He walked up to the car, a BMW this morning, beamed with great cordiality at the two men sitting in it, and heaved the ghetto-blaster through the windscreen. It made a hell of a crash. He saw no more than arms lifted to ward off the missile and the flying glass, before he was off and running.

He dodged precariously through the traffic to the other side of the road, hailed a fortuitously timed taxi, climbed aboard and directed it to Victoria. From the rear window, as his cab took a right turn, he saw that a small crowd had gathered round the afflicted and still stationary car, and knew he was free and clear.

The hire car was a black Nissan, and he drove it without haste northabout to Kensington, and had not been standing for as much as five minutes in the mews when a disreputable figure in faded blue jeans and a washed-out sweatshirt, wearing dark glasses and carrying a rusty garden rake, opened the blue door in the wall and leered at him.

The Right Honourable Philip Wade, Prime Minister and First Lord of the Treasury, clearly mighty pleased with himself, said, 'Wotcher.'

Seddall said, 'Never seen anything like it. Are you sure it's you?'

Wade laughed and said in his ordinary voice, 'I don't know. I have a powerful urge to go down the East End and play darts and get pissed, and bugger the fate of the nation.'

'You could bloody do it, too. No one would recognize you in that gear.'

'All belongs to Maggie's boyfriend.'

'What story did you give to your escort?'

'Having lunch with Maggie, and not to be interrupted on any account, meaning, whatever comes over radios or mobile phones. Maggie, in fact, has been and gone. Came to let me in and went out this way a few minutes ago. Talking of lunch, I could do with a bite. What about you?'

'Likewise. We could send out for something – a pizza, or a curry, or a Chinese meal, whatever we can come up with. We can look in the Yellow Pages and see what's on offer.'

'Carried, *nemine contradicente*. Chinese would suit me. How about you?' Wade was full of himself, all smug mischief like a boy playing truant from school.

'Yes, I'd like Chinese, but let's get in off the street, in case one of your police lads is over-motivated and comes round the back to look for assassins.'

A Chinese meal was available, and promised within the half hour. Seddall put down the phone and took the feel of the living-room, which appeared to be drawing-room and dining-room made into one. He thought he might like Maggie Wade. Her taste in furniture and paintings was eclectic; it was obvious that if she liked something she went for it, regardless of whether it might be thought to fit in with whatever else was in the room.

There was a classically designed tallboy, a Regency-looking sideboard, a chaise longue which might have been graced by a beauty of the Second Empire, and a large gilt mirror that spoke of the Adam brothers.

In among these were distributed pieces of country furniture: a plain oak meal chest, a waxed but unpolished dining-table of beechwood, a small roughly made table of what wood he could not tell, and round the beech table were set what would have been ordinary kitchen chairs but for the elegant U-shaped stretchers – an absolute find, these, he wanted them for himself.

The paintings ran from abstract to figurative, and to landscapes of this and the previous century. If there were things she liked and could not own because they were in art galleries, she had photo-graphed them or had them photographed, among them four pictures of a Gaudier-Brzeska sculpture called 'The Imp', a small primitivistic work in which the creature itself could be thought to have chosen to be stunted and unfinished, as if this best and most blatantly revealed its character of evil, and its unrestricted gift for malice and mischief.

Seddall was seized by this work, and studied the imp from the four angles presented to him like a man transfixed.

'Pound said it was grotesque,' Wade said.

'Who? What?' Seddall turned to face him like a man released from hypnosis.

'Ezra Pound. He said that the sculpture was grotesque.'

'So it is. So it should be.'

Wade raided his daughter's supplies and found a bottle of fine dry Amontillado, from which he poured into two capacious sherry glasses. By common consent they forebore to talk of the matter in hand until they had food in front of them. This came sooner than advertised, and Wade went to the front door to collect it.

'Let me fill you in.' The Prime Minister sprinkled salt over his roast duck in ginger and orange sauce. 'There's an island in the Indian Ocean – I can never remember its name.'

'Matetendoro.'

'How do you come to know that?'

'I'll tell you later, maybe. Meanwhile, we're here for you to tell me things.'

Wade laid it all out. Some of it Seddall knew already, but when he heard the report of the Americans' intention to put a new president in place by way of a coup d'état, backing it with their own military muscle, his interest sharpened acutely.

Wade went right through it, repeating the arguments he had rehearsed with Caswell, and then came to a stop and sat back, as if he was waiting for questions.

Seddall had only one. 'What's this got to do with me? What do you want of me?'

Wade told him.

Seddall's eyes wandered round the room while he digested the extraordinary proposition, pausing at the Corot-like landscapes by a Scots painter called Fraser, at the linear and spatial dynamics of the geometric abstracts and, of course, at that confusingly seductive imp.

He turned to Wade. 'You people are beyond anything. Because I had shown an interest in the murder of Peter Hillyard, you kick me out of my job and close my unit down, and then you ask me to pull your chestnuts out of the fire.'

'Yes,' Wade said, 'it's insufferable cheek, isn't it.'

'You can say that again, mister.'

A really large smile lit up Wade's face, on which Seddall reflected, that a man might smile and smile and be a villain. 'I can't tell you how much I'm enjoying this,' Wade enthused. 'It's so refreshing. No one talks like this to my face – oh, behind my back they'll call me all sorts of names I'm sure of it, but not to my face. Let me get you some wine.'

He went back to Maggie's drinks cupboard, and returned with a bottle of Rhone wine which he opened and poured.

'God,' he said. 'It's so good to be off-stage for a bit.'

'Glad you're happy,' Seddall said sarcastically.

'You were a friend of Peter Hillyard, I know. What is your precise interest in his death?' Wade asked him.

'I want to find the people who killed him.'

'And bring them to justice? I see.'

'No. Bring justice to them.'

'You mean . . .?'

'Yes, that's what I mean,' and Seddall drew his finger across his throat.

'Ah,' and Wade leaned forward, imitating a show of sincere interest and even creating a simulacrum of comradeship.

'Then you must recognize that in this mission I propose to you, our interests run in parallel. You could achieve what I want, and what you want, as part of the same exercise.'

Philip Wade was a successful politician, which meant that he was as hard-nosed as they came, but at the incongruous mixture of hostility, contempt and amusement this nimble little speech called up on to Seddall's face he experienced an indefinable sense of loss, as if a part of him had been diminished.

There was, too, a force of brutality, of an animal nature that had left civilization behind, in the set of Seddall's head on those solid shoulders, in the jut of his jaw and in the feral yellowish gleam in his eyes, that made Wade doubt, suddenly, if he really knew what toughness was about.

When Seddall spoke, it was with an intolerably patronizing drawl. 'The difference in our situations, Wade, is that you need me, but I don't need you.'

Wade explored himself for resources but found he had nothing to fall back on except his power as Prime Minister – nothing of his own self, only his status.

'So far all we've done, Seddall, is close down your unit at the Ministry of Defence. But if you don't play ball with me, I can extinguish your military career altogether.'

Seddall shook his head in a mockery of admiration. 'You're so full of bullshit, Wade. It wouldn't occur to you that a man of my age might just be a little tired of my military career? No, it wouldn't, because you boys in politics think power and career are all that there is to life.'

'Damn your insolence. I serve my country.'

'So does my postman, so does any private in the Army or rating in the Royal Navy. But they don't get as puffed up over it as you fellows do.'

Wade drank some beer, and watched him.

'If I agreed to do this, who in the government and among the bureaucrats would know about it?'

'Only me and Francis Caswell. No one else at all, even in my office. And I have been absolutely specific to Caswell that only he and I must know.' Again he leaned towards Seddall, with a great intensity in his eyes. 'Do you think you could bring it off?'

'It would depend what I found when got out there. There's always a possibility. Can't say more than that.'

'Let me top up your glass.'

Seddall's glass was still half full. 'No, thanks. This is all I shall want. I'm driving.'

Seddall lit a cigarette and cut off from Wade, and went over it all in his mind. This conversation had been useful to him: he and the lads were going out there anyway, and to know that the Americans were planning to land a hundred Special Forces on the island was useful information. It seemed unlikely that they would be able to see off that many well-armed and highly trained men, but they might find some friends out there, and with a bit of cunning they might do some successful little bits of out-manoeuvring.

His silence went on too long for Wade. 'You'll want money,' he said. 'Caswell will see to that.'

Seddall put the cigarette out and lit another one. It was time to put an end to this. 'I won't do it,' he said. 'I've had enough of you. And as for money from Caswell's secret fund, you can put that where the monkey put the nuts.'

Wade stared at him, not believing what he had heard.

'By God, Seddall, you're the most insolent shit I've had to do with since I became Prime Minister.'

'Insolence,' Seddall said, 'is a word that relies on the concept of one man being superior to the other. Whether it ever means anything, I very much doubt, but it certainly does not apply to you and me.'

He drained his glass at a swallow, and set it down and put his eyes on Wade. 'However, as to my being a shit, I'm glad I got through to you.' He smiled, with appalling, because false, geniality, and went on. 'The trouble with you politicos is that you're not democrats these days, you're no more than demagogues, so you have no interest in or understanding of real people. Ask yourself how that serves your country. There's a question for you, Mr Philip Wade. And here's another: where's the receipt for this meal?'

The Prime Minister, stiff with rage, flourished fingers vaguely at the sideboard.

Seddall went over and picked it up, and counted money on to the table in front of Wade.

'What's that for?'

'You do not qualify for the privilege of buying me lunch. That's what it's for. Good day to you.'

Seddall looked out of the window at the Jaguar and the police car behind it, and for a reason even he could not fathom, grinned at them like a fox sighting a hen run.

He went out down Maggie's good garden, through the blue door in the wall, and got into the Nissan. He did not drive off at once, but mulled over what Wade had told him. What he would dearly have liked to know was whether the crisis on that distant island was still impending, or had already exploded. Well, for that one he'd have to wait until he got out there.

Chapter Thirteen

From the deck of the *Sika Kuma*, Provensal's yacht, they saw the two figures standing on the white beach and waving.

'I think I know that man.' Shouanete took the binoculars from Wildgrave and said, 'Yes, it is Jules Ombeli, the cousin of Ikwezi.'

'Daniel,' Provensal said, 'tell them to send a boat to pick up these people on the shore.'

Tschiffely saw the launch come curving round the stern of the ship – for the yacht was entitled to this description, being a vessel of fifteen hundred tons deadweight – and sat down gratefully on the sand. It had taken them over three hours of hard going to make their way down from the place where they had spent the night. It was as hot as hell, the ground was uneven and over-supplied with dangerous pitfalls, and they had travelled all the way through a wilderness of forest and bush.

The launch ran lightly on to the beach and they climbed on to her, with a helping hand from a sailor in the bow. As the boat ran across the blue and limpid water, irradiated by the morning sun, Tschiffely looked into the depths and marvelled at the shining clarity of it.

Ombeli ran up the companionway and Tschiffely climbed slowly after, shook hands with the tall and vigorous Provensal, sank into a rattan chair and happily accepted a long drink with ice in it from the steward.

He swallowed a third of it at a gulp, and became a social animal again, exchanging greetings with two large black men, Daniel and Lucas, who had so much the build of nightclub bouncers that they

148

must have been Provensal's personal bodyguards, with a tall frozen-faced white man called Wildgrave, and then with a woman of such height (or rather length, for she was lying back languorously on her chair) and of such dramatic beauty, so golden-skinned in her white bikini-top and shorts, that his mind stopped.

'You are Ikwezi's friend,' he said.

She said, 'Yes,' and from the coldness in her eyes one might have thought he'd made a pass at her. When he heard his words again in his mind, and the way he had spoken them, he realized that it was, in a way, true. He had been seeking to placate the mysterious power he sensed to reside in her, by claiming a mutual friend.

He broke eye contact and found that Provensal, who had been conversing with Ombeli, was giving him a large and sympathetic smile. He came to sit beside Tschiffely.

'Shouanete is a difficult woman to know,' he said. 'I have been with her for four years, and even I can't say that I know her. She is like a secret walking the earth.'

'That's a potent description.' Tschiffely glanced at her again (safe enough, for she was talking with Ombeli now) and then returned his attention to Provensal.

'I am told you are a poet,' he said.

'Yes, that's what do. I was struck by the name of your yacht, *Sika Kuma*. It is African?'

'It is Asante. I am Asante, though my people have been American for three generations. *Sika Kuma* is the name of the Golden Axe which the Asantehene would send with his envoys on important diplomatic missions It is so old that no one knows its origin. It was yielded to the British, after threat of war, and presented to Queen Victoria. They were great looters, the imperial British. *Sika Kuma* was fetish, but they didn't give a damn about that, or about taking it from the Asante.'

'Fetish? What does that mean in this context?'

'It means that the axe had a mystical force within it.'

Provensal watched Tschiffely as his eyes closed over what he had just heard, and as he responded with, 'That is a story that enters the soul.'

The black man nodded as if the white man had passed a test. 'Why are you here, Tschiffely?'

'I am on a journey, wandering from here to there.'

Provensal said to Wildgrave, who at the barely visible movement of his employer's hand had come to join them, 'Do you believe him, Wildgrave?'

'No.' Wildgrave sat down on the deck. 'I think he'd spin a good story, but he's not used to lying straight out.'

Tschiffely experienced the confusions of being outnumbered, outfought, and outmanoeuvred.

He asked Provensal, 'Why do you think I'm here, then?'

'A little while ago,' Provensal said, 'a man called Peter Hillyard was killed near Dovestone, his house in England.'

Tschiffely put his face to the sky, as if it had just sent down a thunderbolt. 'How do you know that?'

'Hillyard was a friend of mine. Wherever I am in the world, my staff keep me in touch with whatever events I will want to know about. My office in England knows of my friendship with Peter. They told me of his death, and of the so-called shooting accident that killed him.'

Their eyes met, and said that both knew it had been murder.

'I had my people send inquiry agents to Dovestone to find out what they could. They heard of a woman called Kneller, who was a friend of Peter's and of yours – yes, they learned about you too – and a man whose name was not known who came with her to stay at Dovestone the weekend Peter Hillyard was shot. She was still at the house when the inquiry agents were in the vicinity, although the man she had come with was not. And, Tschiffely, as to you, they reported that after a few days you locked up your house and disappeared.'

Every last vestige of the tension that had been growing in Tschiffely since he came to Matetendoro had eased its way out of him by the time Provensal finished talking. To know that Provensal had been a friend of Hillyard and that, here on this yacht, he could let go of all the pretence and play-acting, was an unimaginable relief.

Provensal saw something of this and a great human warmth smiled at Tschiffely out of the deep brown eyes.

'Wildgrave,' Provensal said, 'can you tell me now, why did our friend Tschiffely lock up his house in England and set off on the journey that has brought him here?'

Wildgrave's penetrating eyes lanced at Tschiffely out of that stone face. 'Revenge,' he said. 'Vengeance against the men who killed Peter Hillyard. That's why he's here. But what he, a poet, thought to do here alone I can't fathom.'

'Yes,' Provensal said. 'Will you please make sense of that for us, Tschiffely.'

'I'm no more than a scout. I'd call myself a spy but I don't have the qualifications. How far shall I trust you?'

Provensal nodded his approval of this. 'As far as your own instinct tells you.'

'Far, I think. The man who went with Jane Kneller to stay at Dovestone is called Harry Seddall.' At this name he noticed a fractional movement of Wildgrave's head. 'He runs a special Intelligence unit at the Ministry of Defence.'

'I've heard of him,' Wildgrave said. 'He has a name for doing his own thing, and getting up the noses of the exalted.'

'That's the man I met, all right,' Tschiffely said, and went on, 'The Government warned Seddall off Hillyard, who had a thing he wanted to confide to Seddall, but he ignored that and went to visit Hillyard. He suspects dirty work in high places in the killing of Hillyard. He doesn't seem to care what consequences might fall on him for disobliging the government, but he likes playing tactical games, I think. He thought it would be useful for him to seem to be doing nothing dramatic about Hillyard, so we decided I should come here and see what I could find out.'

Wildgrave came in again. 'What lines of communication do you have? You can't trust the phone and you ain't got pigeons.'

'None.'

'So what happens? Do you go home and report, or does he come out here later?'

'I think we'll see him out here,' Tschiffely said.

'When?'

Tschiffely shrugged. 'When he decides it's time to come.'

Wildgrave froze suddenly and his binoculars came into play again. 'Boat,' he said. 'Let's get these people below, away from prying eyes.'

A motorboat had come into view from behind the northern headland. It was six furlongs off and moving down the coast towards the bay. 'Twin machine-gun mounting, crew in uniform, flying an ensign of some sort. She's a government vessel for a certainty. Come on, Tschiffely, down into the saloon.'

'Ombeli.' Provensal's was not a voice that would ever need a loud-hailer. 'Get below. Enemy in sight.'

As Tschiffely followed Wildgrave across the deck Ombeli looked up from his conversation with Shouanete, saw the boat, and rose at once to fall in behind.

'Man,' he said to the back of Tschiffely's neck, 'that's the Matetendoro Navy. I hope they haven't spotted me.'

Wildgrave heard this. 'If we have to, we'll sink them.' He threw the words over his shoulder. 'We carry twin 30mm cannon. They're hidden under that forward deckhouse. That boat's bound to have a natural curiosity about this ship being moored here. We'll lie low and see what develops.'

The saloon was large and luxurious. Provensal went to the dining-table. 'Let's sit here and talk,' he said. 'You should know what I know, and I want to know what's been going on and why Ombeli is on the run. Daniel, I think it would not be too indulgent to drink champagne. We'll be having lunch in half an hour.'

There were five of them there, Provensal, Wildgrave and Daniel, and Tschiffely and Ombeli. Shouanete and Lucas had remained on deck. Daniel pressed a bell, and when a steward came passed on Provensal's command: a bit different from life back at the cottage, Tschiffely thought, getting oneself a beer and drinking it out of the can.

'Now.' Provensal imbued the word with the incisiveness of a chairman calling the meeting to order. 'I have been interested in

Matetendoro for quite some time, ever since I learned that certain nations in the First World, or the developed world, whatever you choose to call it, had been sniffing around the disused mines to find out their suitability for dumping nuclear waste – high-level nuclear waste. The country that wants to dump it is Britain, and in order to maintain an initial secrecy about this it went into association with the United States so that a corporation could be set up in America without attention being called to it.'

Ombeli and Tschiffely took time to absorb this news. It was Ombeli who responded first. 'How did you find out about it?'

This won a smile with a touch of prideful irony in it, and, 'I have an excellent intelligence service.'

Ombeli pressed him. 'What's your interest in it? Are you involved in the nuclear industry?'

Provensal became grave, even stern. 'No, I'm not involved in the nuclear industry. My interest is, that I do not approve of the First World dumping its nuclear waste in the Third World. It is like a rich man getting rid of his garbage by dumping it in a poor man's garden. I intend to prevent it.'

'How can you do that?'

A slight and witty smile was allowed. 'I have beaten them to it. I have bought the French company which owns all the disused mines. They – the Americans – knew I was up to something, but they didn't know what. They tried to kill me on the way here. Wildgrave prevented it.'

Wildgrave remained impassive, as if that had been an event of yesterday, and his only concern was today and the days that were to come. As if to express this in action, he took his binoculars and went to kneel on the cushioned bench under the portholes on the starboard side and focused them.

'That boat,' Provensal said. 'What's it doing?'

'Lying off and taking photographs.'

'Well,' Ombeli said. 'You've bought the mines, so why have you come here? Do you have a use for them?'

Provensal still showed the glint of humour which decorated his seriousness of purpose. 'None at all. But the Americans don't like to be beaten. I need to see what they'll try next. And I need to talk with President Sefuthi. I was hoping to take advantage of Shouanete's friendship with your cousin, and ask you to arrange it for me, but you have told me you are out of favour. What's the whole story of that?'

Ombeli described his interview with the President, his refusal to go to Madagascar and murder Dudunzi in an arranged accident, his expectation of arrest, and his dash for freedom.

'And you thought that on this ship you might find safety and an ally? Well, you're right. We must all work together to see off this new breed of imperialists, and we must waste no time.'

He thought for a full minute.

'I shall call on the President this afternoon. Daniel, will you please tell the captain he is to lift the anchor now and take the ship round to the port of Saint-Hilaire, and also make ready to land the vehicle. Meanwhile we shall have lunch.'

For lunch they had shrimp and beefsteak out of the freezer, for though Provensal's heart and spirit were devoted to the land of his fathers, his stomach had been trained in America.

Tschiffely was glad of it, for he was starving. He was glad, too, to be out of the sun, and gloried in the air-conditioned comfort of the saloon.

He found himself placed on Provensal's left. Ombeli was on their host's right, with the golden Shouanete next to him. The dedicated Wildgrave had taken Daniel with him and gone on deck as soon as the engines started, doubtless to engage in a steady reconnaissance of the sea and the shore.

'I know it's not a well-bred thing to ask you,' he said to Provensal, 'but is it right to think that you are very rich?'

'Pah! Well-bred?' Provensal punched him lightly on the arm. 'Breeding is not a way of behaving, it is a question of a man's ancestors. Yes, I am exceedingly rich.'

'And it's a moral crusade with you, your determination to prevent the Third World being used as a garbage dump by the rich nations of the world?'

'No, it is not a crusade. A crusade, Tschiffely, is an idea of

Europeans. And the idea of a moral crusade is also a concept of Europeans, though they are better at preaching morality than practising it. I am doing what I am doing because it is the closest I can come to righting ancient wrongs. Now, you have come here because you seek vengeance for Peter Hillyard. That is a primitive and ancient thing, that is blood feud, and I respect it.'

'I seek justice.'

Provensal laughed. 'My dear man, you are trying to make it sound respectable to yourself. You have not yet killed a man? Correct me if I'm wrong.'

'No, I have not. Have you?'

Provensal put down his knife and fork and splayed out his fingers and looked at them. 'Yes, I have. I did not come by all my wealth with what, at civilized London dinner tables, they would call clean hands. Let me tell you that, when you have killed your first man in this pursuit of what you call justice, you will realize that, in truth, the killing was done in feud.'

'It will have blood, they say; blood will have blood.' The words were out before Tschiffely knew he was going to say them.

'You see. Your Shakespeare knew the ways of man. That was Macbeth, was it not? A Scottish man. Blood feud was a natural part of life in the Scottish Highlands, because they were a society of tribes. That's why the English, with their gift for the civilized art of hypocrisy, will never understand their Scottish neighbours, or us Africans, or any of the native peoples of the southern hemisphere.'

He swallowed some of the not magnificent, but sufficient, Rhone wine that accompanied the steak.

'And times, my friend, times they are a-changing.' His eyes became sombre. 'The pax Britannica is not wanted any more. The emerging world will not take to government by men in well-cut suits, based on a system that was created in the cities of what is to them a land remote in time and place called Greece. The West, as half of the northern hemisphere is accustomed to be known, does not grasp the extent of the change that is taking place. It dare not.'

'And you, you have a foot in both camps?'

Provensal laughed loudly, a positive shout of laughter. 'You know your Shakespeare. You could be more complimentary, my dear Tschiffely, to your host, and say rather that I bestride the world like a Colossus.'

The wandering poet looked at him to see if he was serious, and was met with an eye dancing with merriment.

'A joke, brother,' Provensal said. 'No. I have made my way in the capitalist world, but I have not changed my skin or my blood. I have not turned my coat. I do not have a foot in both camps. It is true I am a billionaire in the advanced – the so-called advanced and developed and highly civilized – West, but I am a seditious presence, because I am who I am, a black man whose people came from Africa. I am loyal to no country, to no flag. I am loyal to my people.'

Tschiffely regarded him with an expression of great liking. It seemed to him that this was just the sort of man the modern world needed, and one whose motives the political leaders of the Western world would never fathom, since they had so long laid their souls up in pawn to power.

He said so to Provensal. 'You are just what humanity needs today. In this affair of Matetendoro you are what the civilized West, which you so much abuse, is accustomed to call a deus ex machina. Though I don't think they would honour you with that description. You are an interloper, Provensal, that's what it comes down to.'

Provensal filled each of their glasses. 'Trust a poet to find the word. I drink to you, Tschiffely. But you know my gift for being self-satisfied. I am not an interloper, my friend, I am *the* interloper. Let us toast one another.'

He put his glass down. 'Still, the race is not yet run. I never count my chickens before I see them out of the egg and running around, and there is much to do yet. Come, Tschiffely, Let us go on deck and see how close we are to this harbour of Saint-Hilaire.'

After the coolness of the saloon, the heat smote Tschiffely like a blow. The ship was slowly approaching the harbour. There were about two dozen sailors on deck, all of them black, and all of them, to his surprise, armed, as if this were a ship of war, with pistols holstered on their belts.

The vessel did not make her way through the harbour mouth,

but was skilfully manoeuvred until her starboard side was laid against the end of the quay. A gangway was swung ashore and cables were carried round the two capstans on the pierhead, and since these were necessarily run from midships, and not fore and aft, the ship was held there with the assistance of an occasional pulse of the engines.

What happened next was to Tschiffely a wonderful piece of theatre. From an open hatch immediately astern of the deckhouse which, Wildgrave had told him, concealed a pair of 30mm cannon, a black limousine was hoisted by a crane.

He had no wish to be a millionaire, but he was exhilarated by each token of Provensal's enormous wealth. The unreality of it held him in thrall, as if he were in fact in a theatre and captivated by the stage.

The limo was swung carefully out of the hatch and over the ship's side until it hung above the quay, and then it was let down on to the stones with such perfect control by the craneman that it bounced on its springs hardly at all.

Provensal, accompanied by only one of his two bodyguards, Lucas, and by his chief of security, Wildgrave, went ashore, gave a wave to Shouanete, Ombeli, Daniel and Tschiffely, all standing in a group at the rail, and got into the back of the car followed by Wildgrave, while Lucas got into the driver's seat.

The limo drove off up the pier. As soon as it was out of sight the captain issued the order to cast off. The cables and the gangway were brought inboard, the hatch cover was replaced, and the ship eased away from the pierhead.

Ombeli took Tschiffely aside, and said to him, 'There were no men staffing the post at the head of the pier where you and I first met. That is unusual.'

'What do you make of it?'

'I don't know what to make of it. It unsettles me, though. Well, all we can do is await developments.'

'Why have we cast off?'

'Ah. That's Wildgrave's doing. He appears to be an extremely cautious man. His argument was that they had no idea what they would be getting into in Saint-Hilaire, and that a ship at sea is a useful weapon, whereas a ship tied to the shore is at risk of attack from the land.'

'Attack by whom?'

Ombeli shrugged. 'I don't know, and he didn't say, but I have a sense that Wildgrave may know more than the rest of us about what's going on, or what may be going on.'

At this point the ship hove to, about a quarter of a mile from the harbour, and the captain let down an anchor.

Tschiffely found Shouanete beside him and said, 'Are you worried about Provensal, going off into the unknown like that?'

She favoured him this time with a slight smile, although it was a smile with no warmth in it. He doubted if warmth was part of her nature, and wondered if there were people like that.

'I never worry about Provensal,' she said. 'Everything he does is successful. It would be an insult to worry about him.'

He watched her walk away, a moving image of possibly the most desirable woman on the planet, and perceived that his inner comment on her had been sexist. He knew perfectly well that there were men with no human warmth in them: he had been resisting the proposition that there might be women like that.

Your naivety is terrible, Steve Tschiffely, he told himself. You have no right to call yourself a poet.

He looked up at the presidential palace on the hill, which shone with a brilliant whiteness in the fierce glare of the afternoon sun, and wondered how that great man, Provensal, whom he had come to admire and also like so much, was faring.

Chapter Fourteen

As the Cadillac drove through the streets of the town, its occupants became aware that there were few people abroad. Here and there were groups of three or four black soldiers.

'What uniform is that?' Provensal asked.

'The uniform of the Matetendoro Army, but I have a doubt,' Wildgrave said. 'It's not a doubt for which I can offer you a reasoned explanation. It is an instinctive doubt.'

'Your instinct is part of your armoury, Wildgrave. I have never had occasion to mistrust it.'

'What will you do?' Wildgrave ignored the compliment, or his nature ignored it for him, and went straight to the point.

'I shall continue to the palace. It is essential for me to talk with President Sefuthi. And what will you do?'

'The wisest thing would be for me to get out of the car when we are close to the palace but not close enough for it to be seen that I've got out. Then I will be able to observe events from the perimeter, and act accordingly.'

'You're right, as usual.' Provensal gave one of his large laughs. 'Perhaps I am walking into a trap, but if so, who will have set it? Not Sefuthi.'

'You have only one enemy in this: the CIA.'

'Well, Wildgrave, you can handle anything the CIA can come up with. My faith in you is absolute.'

Wildgrave turned on him that impassive face and the bright stare in his eyes. 'It should not be absolute. As your security adviser, I should tell you not to go ahead with this.'

Again the laugh. 'But you know I'm set on going. If I get into trouble I'll count on you to get me out of it.'

Wildgrave very nearly made a joke. 'You've something going for you there. If I don't get you out of it, I don't get paid, and I'll have to look for a new job.'

'I like your kind of loyalty, man. It's practical.'

The car drove on, and when it was running through an avenue of trees, Wildgrave said, 'About here, I think.' To Lucas he said, 'Stop the car.'

He opened the door, looked back at Provensal and said, 'Good luck with it. I'll be out there.' He got out, slammed the door shut, and strolled on up the road, a casual figure walking to nowhere in particular with nothing on his mind, a 9mm Browning automatic concealed under his old safari jacket, and a knife in his boot, its hilt covered by the leg of his chinos.

Lucas drove on up to the palace gates, which were closed, and guarded by four soldiers. Provensal held his card out of the window to the officer who approached the car, and said, 'Appointment with the President.'

The officer scanned the card and nodded. He said nothing, but made a gesture to his men and the gates were swung open. They went on up to the palace and Lucas rolled the car on to the parking area, which was also policed by the soldiery, was waved to a stop, and got out to open the door for Provensal.

A sergeant came up and Provensal gave his name and repeated that he had an appointment. The sergeant looked at a clipboard and said, in a curiously artificial accent, that Mr Provensal was expected and he himself would accompany him to the palace.

'You,' he said to Lucas in that curious voice, 'this car cannot stay here; security reasons. Mr Provensal will be driven back in an official car.'

Lucas exchanged glances with Provensal, each saying the same thing – that this dismissal of the car sounded alarm signals. All the same, Provensal gave him an almost imperceptible nod. Lucas turned the limousine round, and departed.

The sergeant took Provensal round the corner of the palace,

along the grandeur of its frontage, in through the impressively high doors which stood open but were, of course, guarded by two more soldiers, and up the wide staircase with its thick red carpet.

He was led across the anteroom into the President's office. The man behind the desk, however, was not President Sefuthi. He was a white man, a square-headed, solidly built man. Provensal identified him at once as a foolish, belligerent second-rater who was into power.

There was a chair in front of the desk, so Provensal sat in it, and waited for words to be spoken, and studied first the fingernails on his left hand, and then those on his right. He frowned. They were too long. He must cut them soon and file them smooth, so that they did not inconvenience the act of love between him and Shouanete, the next time she wanted him.

There was a barking sound. It was the square-head speaking. 'Do you know who I am?'

'How could I?'

'I am Arthur J. Foxberry, Central Intelligence Agency.'

'Intelligence,' Provensal said without inflection. 'I see.'

'You don't seem surprised.'

'That you should be in the CIA? No, I'm not. I know the agency's reputation.'

'Don't get smart with me, mister.'

'My dear Foxberry, I have not the least thought of getting smart with you. It would be a waste of mental energy.'

Foxberry stood up as if he was going to come round the desk and clock him one, but instead he said, 'You're supposed to be lying dead in the African jungle in the wreckage of a burnt-out plane. What happened?'

'You don't know?'

'No, goddammit, I don't know. If I did, why would I be asking?'

Provensal gazed at the blue sea outside the window. 'All I can tell you,' he said, 'is that your ground-to-air missiles were stamped to pieces by elephants, and as to your men, I fear they must have fallen prey to the predators of the bush.'

Foxberry sat and glowered at him. 'You're too damn cool for my liking. Just what do you think's going on here?'

Provensal looked intelligent. 'I've been considering that question. I would hazard that your agency is staging a coup d'état on this island, and that you are even now waiting for the arrival of a man called Dudunzi whom you intend to install as President.'

Anger flushed up into Foxberry's face. 'How the hell do you know about Dudunzi? Who've you been talking to?'

A negligent wave of the hand. 'I have my own intelligence department. Surely you must know that?'

'What I know is that you're a pain in the ass, and should have been dealt with long ago. Sergeant, take this son of a bitch down to the cellar and lock him away. Get him out of my sight now!'

Provensal stood up to his considerable height and purely as a matter of form said the expected things. 'What is the meaning of this? You have no right to detain me here, on the territory of a foreign power.'

Foxberry produced a laugh. 'Foreign, maybe. But power, no. Take him down, Sergeant. I've got more important things to do than waste my time with this uppity nigger.'

There was a silence from behind Provensal, then the sergeant said in a tranquil but dangerous voice, 'Well now, Mr Arthur Foxberry, will you please kindly tell me, am I an uppity nigger too, me with this here crackerjack automatic rifle, and a full clip in it all set and just raring to go?'

Foxberry glared at him. 'Are you threatening me?'

'Bet your fuckin' ass, honky. I mean, look who we got here, just you and me and this black gentleman, and a hundred other black guys from my own outfit, and only a couple of white shitheel buddies of yours from the CIA who are off somewhere about those secret things you CIA people get into. No one's going to cry tears over you around here, Sunshine. So, you want to clean up your act; and give us two men your apology for calling us niggers, or do you want to be a mess on that fancy carpet you're standing on?'

Behind Foxberry's shoulder Provensal saw the *Sika Kuma* lying at anchor on the sun-glare of the sea, and was confident that one way or the other he was going to come out of this in one piece. He wondered when Wildgrave would make his move, and how he planned to even out the odds.

Then he saw Foxberry drop to his chair, a man filled with a choler which appeared capable of taking him off in a fit of apoplexy at any moment.

Out of lips so nearly incapable of speech that the words were barely audible, the CIA man said, 'You have my apology.'

'You can do better than that,' the sergeant said. 'Why don't you try saying, "You have my sincere apology, gentlemen."' His weapon made a mechanical sound, as if he was making ready to fire.

Foxberry was the very spectacle of infuriated impotence. The words came out in a rush, as if he was swallowing medicine with a foul taste and getting it over with as fast as he could. 'You have my sincere apology, gentlemen.'

'Shall we go?' the sergeant's voice asked Provensal, who turned from the humiliated Foxberry and saw that the sergeant had moved off to the side, so that he could cover their rear as they left the room in case Foxberry's temper should get the better of him, and send his hand to his gun.

Even when they were out of the room and the sergeant had closed the door he kept a weather eye out behind him. He maintained this wariness until they were on the ground floor.

He took Provensal to the back of the house, to a door with a man posted there on watch. The man unlocked the door and the sergeant gestured to Provensal to precede him down the stairs.

They went along a passage of whitewashed stone to another door, another soldier, this one sitting on a chair and dozing.

'Wake up, Sam, got another one for you.'

Sam yawned and stretched, and came to his feet. 'After this I'll be able to find me a job in some state penitentiary,' he said cheerfully. 'It sure beats playing soldiers.' He looked at the new prisoner and said, 'How ya doin'?'

'Good,' Provensal said, 'on the whole. Today's just an off-day, I guess.'

Sam turned the key and ushered him into his new quarters. 'You want anything, cup of coffee or cigarettes, just sing out. If you can pay for it, we've got it.'

'Appreciate it,' Provensal said, hanging in the doorway. 'You take US dollars?'

'All I do take. Enjoy. You'll need something to sleep on. We'll get you a mattress in a little while.' He slammed the door and locked it.

In the windowless chamber there were an old wooden table, two cane chairs, a mattress on the floor, and a man sitting at the table, who stood up as the newcomer came into the room.

'President Sefuthi,' Provensal said. 'My name is Provensal.'

'How do you do?' Sefuthi said, 'The yacht in the bay is yours, I believe. You are the millionaire. You have been to Matetendoro before, but we have not met.'

'A woman, Shouanete, who honours me with her companionship, has a friend here. We have been here a few times so that they can meet.'

They sat down, one on either side of the table. They studied one another, each recognizing in the other a man of stature, a man worth meeting.

'Why are you here?' Provensal asked.

'The Americans betrayed me. They came in helicopters, from a warship which has retired discreetly over the horizon. We were taken by surprise. I had suspicions but I was not careful enough. It is my own fault.'

'But you have an army of your own.'

Sefuthi smiled wryly. 'An army? Five hundred men, and they are not all stationed on this side of the island. I know that some of my government and some of the soldiers who were here at Saint-Hilaire are up in the hills, but I suppose it is not easy with such limited forces, to make a plan, to set me free and turn out the Americans.'

Provensal saw that Sefuthi expected the Americans to kill him, but there was no sign of fear on his face or in his eyes.

'I am hopeful,' he told the President, 'that we may find we are released from here quite soon.'

'Are you merely an idle optimist, or do you have good reason to be so hopeful?'

'Good reason, but I won't go into it at the moment. I want to make a proposal to you.'

Even here, imprisoned in the cellars of his palace, Sefuthi noticed himself responding to this by assuming, though he knew there was no visible manifestation of this event, the inner bearing, reserve and authority of the President.

'Then, my dear Provensal, make this proposal.'

Provensal stared into his eyes. 'First I have to tell you that Oceanic Enterprises can never buy the French company which owns the disused mines, because one of my own companies has bought it.'

Humour kindled in Sefuthi's face. 'I knew that Oceanic, Mr Arthur Foxberry and his friends, had failed to buy it. Now that they have turned to direct action, it does not matter so much to them, perhaps. But when Foxberry learned that they had been beaten to the punch by a . . .'

'By an interloper?' Provensal helpfully provided the word that eluded Sefuthi.

'Yes. Excellent. By an interloper. When he learned this, Mr Foxberry was painfully affected. Then, when he heard that the man on whom he had pinned his hopes as my successor, a man called Dudunzi, had passed away, he blew his top, as I believe they say in America, absolutely. It is almost insulting that they should have chosen such a childish creature to administer my downfall.'

'It is about your downfall that I wish to make a proposal.'

Sefuthi, sitting back with his hands clasped under his chin, bowed his head, acknowledging this as an introductory remark and indicating that he was waiting to hear what was to follow it.

Provensal adopted his grave man-of-business style, which was, he admitted to himself, a trifle pompous. 'I can't believe that you were happy with yourself over the agreement to accept nuclear waste here.' He paused to give Sefuthi room to comment on this, but the man remained still and silent. 'So may I ask you why you did agree to it?'

Sefuthi gave himself time to decide whether Provensal was being judgmental, and came to the conclusion that he wasn't. His answer was curt. 'Matetendoro is poor. I agreed to it for a very ancient reason. Money. World Bank loan, guaranteed by the United States and by Britain.'

'For how much, this loan?'

'Twenty million pounds sterling.'

Provensal meditated a while. 'My proposal will free you from accepting the nuclear waste of these great modern states. It is, that I shall lend Matetendoro twenty million pounds, a loan with no term date, and with no interest to be paid.'

Sefuthi could not believe this, and made no pretence of it. 'I know you are wealthy beyond my understanding, Provensal, but even to you that is a noticeable amount of money. Why should you do this for Matetendoro? A loan without term, and with no interest to pay: that amounts to making us a gift of twenty million.'

Provensal laughed. 'It is not for Matetendoro that I do this but for all of us who are not of the European races. With me it is a grudge fight.'

With a flowing athletic move he left the chair and alighted on the table to lean over Sefuthi. 'I do everything I can to sabotage the modern colonialism. It is not just what they do, Sefuthi, it is not only their actions that affront me. It is who they are when they treat the Third World with that contempt of theirs, it is their state of being and their state of mind that affront me.'

He shook his head and gestured wildly with his hands. 'Do you realize – a man like you, Sefuthi, I'm sure you do realize this – that they don't even know, they are not even aware, that they regard the Third World with contempt?'

He slid off the table and began walking up and down, as if there was too much activity at work in him not to be expressed in movement of his own.

He faced Sefuthi and harangued him as if he were a giant audience instead of one man.

'Oh, I do not for a moment acquit them of self-interest, but they

166

are living in the same paradox they were living in when they made their empires. They came to our countries and killed our people and despoiled us all in order to increase their own trade, but most of all to let them feel themselves to be powerful.

'And they told themselves that they did this to bring us the benefits of civilization – their civilization – and to bring us the blessings of Christianity, their religion. And now once more they are living in this paradox, this hypocrisy.

'They have developed a technological civilization that will destroy the atmosphere of the earth. They have invented ways to destroy the earth itself. And still, still, still,' he was shouting now, 'they regard themselves as the progenitors of the progress of human-kind. They give aid, in miserly amounts, to the Third World, but only because, if the Third World prospers, then world trade will grow.'

He fell on to his chair and brooded. When he spoke again he was so quiet that Sefuthi strained to catch the words.

'They have no soul, Sefuthi. They have no spirit. They are the living dead. We will not bow to them. I will not bow to them. That is why it is my wish to lend you of Matetendoro this twenty million pounds, and to prevent them making use of this island for their own degraded purposes.'

He was slumped in the chair with his eyes shut, and his face twisted as if he was racked with pain. A zealot, Sefuthi told himself. Who would have thought it? The man's a zealot.

Aloud, he said, and was surprised how gentle his voice was, 'All this is academic while we are locked in here. And even if we get out somehow, there will still be the American invaders to deal with.'

Provensal surfaced, and a smile sprang up on him, as if he relished dealing with the difficulties of turning the tables on their captors. 'Yes,' he said, 'and it will call for our guile against their force to remove them from the island.'

'Guile won't get us out of here, and that's the first item on the agenda.' Sefuthi looked at the other man sideways. 'In that regard, I think you have something up your sleeve.'

'Not up my sleeve. Up another man's sleeve.'
'So we wait. For how long?'
'Not long.'

Wildgrave saw the limousine come out of the palace gates and as it drew level he emerged on to the road. He caught Lucas's eye, and with a slow movement of the head towards the corner down the road, indicated that they would meet up when the car had rounded the corner and was out of sight of the palace.

Lucas drove on and the car went out of sight, and Wildgrave followed, in no hurry, using the careless gait of a man with no purpose in mind. He went round the corner and got into the car. He asked what had happened and Lucas told him he had been refused permission to wait and that the officer at the palace had said they would provide an official car for Provensal after his meeting with the President.

'Get the yacht on the blower,' Wildgrave said. 'Tell them I want to speak to Daniel.'

Lucas called the yacht and passed him the handset.

'Daniel. Listen close. They've kidnapped the boss. We're going to get him out. Take the launch into the bay west of the harbour, I'll meet you on the beach. Yourself and Shouanete, and Ombeli, and the Englishman too if Ombeli thinks he's any good. And Daniel, these guys have got carbines, so we need the H & Ks. Do it fast. Within the hour. Is that all clear? Good.'

They took the Cadillac to about quarter of a mile from the beach, and after that the trees and the bush were too thick for it, so they walked the rest.

The launch was already close inshore by the time they left the forest and stepped on to the white sand, so they ran down to the edge of the sea and helped to pull her bow up on the beach.

Wildgrave said to his little army, 'Council of war, up there in the trees,' and to the two armed sailors manning the launch, 'You guys wait here. Give us three hours, after that you'd best go back to the ship. If that happens don't give up on us, it just means we've been forced inland, away from the shore.'

The rescue party went up into the trees.

'Ombeli,' Wildgrave said, 'if they have seized Provensal, do you consider that means they have also taken the President?'

'Yes, either that or shot him.'

'For the purposes of this operation we'll assume they are both alive. You know the palace – how would you go about this rescue, with the Americans guarding points of entry?'

'Not the ground floor. The floor above has a balcony. I'd try for that. In fact I'd be bold and try for the President's office, which is presumably empty.'

'Where do you think they'll be holding them, either or both? Where do we make for, once we're in?'

Ombeli shrugged his shoulders. 'How can I tell? The palace has a warren of cellars, which would certainly be more secure in a superficial sense.'

Wildgrave, lightly, smiled. 'I like superficial. I think the cellars, it's what I'd do. But we have a difficulty, do we not? How do we climb the wall to the balcony?'

Tschiffely broke in. 'I'm a climber. If it's climbable, I'll go up first. We might need a rope, though, to bring up those of us not used to climbing.'

Wildgrave looked at him as if seeing him for the first time. Which, in a sense, he was, for Wildgrave had no great opinion of poets as men of action.

'There's rope in the launch,' Daniel said. 'Painters bow and stern. And who knows what they might have in a locker? I'll go and find out.'

'Do it,' Wildgrave said.

Daniel set off down the beach.

'We should approach the palace from the west side,' Ombeli said. 'There is no door there, and also, by luck, it is where the forest comes closest to it, so we will have more cover for our approach. Here, where we are now, we are of course north of the palace, so we want to go that way.' He pointed into the trees. 'Also, the sun will be down in an hour, a little over an hour, so we shall be able to go in with the darkness.'

'Surely it will be well lit?' Wildgrave said.

'Not unless the Americans have rigged up lights. Until now, the President has had no cause to worry about security.'

Wildgrave, the security man par excellence, commented on this fairytale approach to life with the sardonic lift of an eyebrow, but nodded, nevertheless, in acceptance of an alien way of doing things.

'Then we may hope for at least a degree of darkness, though we must take lighted windows into account.'

Tschiffely had a question. 'If we do succeed in rescuing the President and Provensal and in making it back to the yacht, we still have to do our best for the people of Matetendoro. I take it that we plan to find a way of getting rid of the Americans?'

Shafts of the declining sun came through the foliage and illumined the wicked cast of Wildgrave's face. 'My dear poet, there are plenty of people who'd like to knock the CIA out of the ring, but there's no one ahead of me in that queue. Our first task is to liberate Provensal and Sefuthi, and when we have done that, I promise you, we will put our minds to seeing this nice little CIA operation fall on its face.'

'Well,' Ombeli said, 'I don't know how you're going to find the answer to that one. They've got that big cruiser over the edge of the sea out there and they can pull in reinforcements any time they need to. This is the United States of America, a superpower, that you're talking about, and they could blow our little island clear out of the ocean.'

'Yes, they could.' Wildgrave looked out to sea where the cruiser was lurking out of sight. 'But they don't want to, do they? They have a reason for what they're doing here. There's something about this island that suits their book. They have a plan to make use of Matetendoro, for what, God knows – though I think the boss does too. I've a hunch that they need the island as a going concern, which means that they put in their own choice of president, probably with properly constituted elections helped by a little discreet ballot-rigging, and then go to work.'

'All right,' Ombeli said, 'but how does that help us to see a way to kick them out of here?'

'We can't kick them out. We'll have to come up with an ingenious scheme to do them down. Meanwhile, let's see what we can do about breaking into that palace. If we're lucky we might gather up one of these CIA lads and find out from him what they're after here. Knowing that might give us a line on how to bring them down.'

'Oh, come now,' Tschiffely said. 'They're not going to tell us, are they?'

Wildgrave, impassive, moved to face him. 'From what Ombeli tells me, I don't think these boys are made of very hard stuff. Even the roughneck, Foxberry, sounds like just a lot of noise. So, sure, sooner or later, they'll tell me. Oh yes, in the end, they'll give it all up to me.'

'Good God, are you talking about . . .?'

'Leave it, Steve,' Ombeli interrupted him. 'These are not good men, and they do not wish my country well. So far as I am concerned, Wildgrave can do anything he likes to them if it helps my country.'

'Well said, Ombeli,' and Wildgrave descended to irony. 'You see, Mr Tschiffely, we are the good guys, so whatever we do in the pursuit of our objective is good. So, let's go and do it.'

At this point Shouanete, at the very moment they set off, caught them literally on the wrong foot.

'I shall leave you to your boys' games. I am going across the island to see my friend Ikwezi.'

She detached first the stock and then the ammunition clip from her Heckler and Koch machine-pistol and stowed them in her yellow and white striped beach bag, and without another word began to move off.

'It will be dark soon,' Ombeli called after her. 'How will you find your way?'

'I live in darkness,' Shouanete replied. 'It is my element.' Then

171

she had a thought, and went back to them. 'But perhaps you are right. Lucas, give me the car keys, and where is it?'

Wildgrave was a man who liked to have control, and Shouanete was depriving him of it, but after a few moments he said, 'We won't need the car.'

Lucas told her, 'It's that way, half a mile towards town,' and gave her the keys of the limousine.

'Why don't you come too, poet?' she said to Tschiffely. 'We could make a sandwich.'

'A sandwich?'

Her objective and enigmatic eyes gazed into his. 'In bed. You and me and Ikwezi.'

He was astonished to find himself so overcome that he had trouble finding his voice. 'Oh, God, yes,' he said, with no bid for self-concealment or sophistication, 'but they need me to climb the wall.'

'Poor boy,' she said. 'There are better ways of climbing walls,' and without a smile or any colour of human contact, she turned and wandered off among the trees.

Tschiffely watched till she was lost among the shadows and the leaves, and felt the awe and loss of a man who has met the goddess of the place, and seen her vanish, back into her own unreachable world.

Chapter Fifteen

Shouanete followed her shadow through the trees and bushes over the red and dusty ground, wondering again why men strove so hard to do, or be, or become, other than they were.

They gave it names, all this emulative effort, all this need to be up and doing (she smiled to herself at the unintended sexual pun), names like duty and fulfilment, and even, if they were trendy and intellectually inclined, psycho-babble names like development and personal growth. And, oh, sister, had they got it wrong!

As she reached the limo the sun went down and she stood with her arms leaning on the car's roof to let her spirit intoxicate itself on the afterglow. She wondered what the poet Tschiffely was like; not the poems, only the man.

She lifted her face to the wild riot of the darkling sky and shivered in an ecstasy of being. She opened the car door, took the three pieces of the machine-pistol out of the beach bag, reassembled it, and put it on the passenger seat with the bag on top. She sat behind the wheel and reached for the gun, and then brought the weapon an inch or two closer until it was just right, until it was a fast grab with her finger touching the trigger, all one movement.

She switched on the engine and eased the big car along, came to a track and went faster, then to the road itself and faster still. It was night now, evening by the watch on her wrist, but night according to the sky. In the lights at the edge of town she saw a group of soldiers, who waved her down.

She lowered the window. 'What's up?'

'Where are you going?' The soldier was deadpan, like a cop.

'I'm the weekly cocaine run into town, babe,' she said.

'Don't fuck with me, lady.' Yup, never joke with the man, he doesn't like it.

'I wouldn't fuck with you, lover, if you were the last man living on this earth.'

A mean look. Copface. 'Quit it. Where are you going?'

'Going to see a friend, other side of the island.'

'Who?'

'Ikwezi.'

'Who's Ikwezi?'

Her hand was itching for that weapon on the seat, but there were three more men spread out round the car, it wouldn't work out for her.

'She's an artist, a painter.'

'Oh, it's a woman's name. OK, drive on through.'

'Yes,' Shouanete said, 'only a woman,' and drove on.

She went through Saint-Hilaire which was as quiet as if it were under curfew, and a hundred yards out of the south side of town was waved down again. This time there were only two of them.

Another of those hard-faced men who thought he was King of the Street, Emperor of the Universe, you name it.

These two were not so good at it as the four at the first checkpoint: the second man stood behind his companion, about four feet off.

'Who are you? Where you going?'

'I'm Shouanete. Going to visit a friend.'

'What friend?'

'A witchdoctor woman, going to ask her to melt all you soldierboys into dribbles of spit.'

'Don't you talk to me like that. Get out of the car.'

'A poor little girl like me, on this lonely road with you two mad rapists standing there? No chance, mister.'

'Get out, bitch, or I'll drag you out by the hair.'

'Eat shit, sweetheart.'

He yanked the door open and she had the gun and put a burst in his chest which threw him down. The other one was bringing his weapon to bear when the bullets from the Heckler and Koch tore into his head.

She sang as she went on up the road:

> '*Oh, the yellow rose of Texas*
> *Has bigger feet than me,*
> *But when it comes to kicking ass,*
> *Can't beat Shouanete.*'

Looking through the windscreen at the stars as the road began to climb, she shook her head at herself and said, 'Baby, you're a childish woman.'

When she turned off the road for Ikwezi's house she drove a few hundred yards along the forested hillside and stopped. That was as far as she could take the big limousine on to that rough terrain. She put a fresh clip of ammunition from her beach bag into the pistol, slung the bag and the gun over her shoulder, and began the walk to the house.

She went at an easy pace, feeling herself a creature of the night among the other creatures of the night. She stopped from time to time to listen to a movement in the dried-up grass, a rustle in the bushes; to a bird chattering at her from the leaves above and around her. She took a tree trunk between her hands and stood there, feeling herself one with the earth under her feet, and her soul one with the brilliant stars that hung so low overhead.

Once she sat down, with a picture of the English poet on her mind's eye. He was different from those other men she had been among tonight, from the soldiers on the road (living and dead: she grinned at the memory), and Ombeli and Wildgrave, and Provensal's bodyguards. He had gone with them because he was needed for the rescue of Provensal, not because of the rules of conduct that men made for themselves.

He was his own man, that Tschiffely, a being in his own world and walking his own path, not anxious to belong, to be a part of perpetuating the accepted order, any accepted order.

She heard a snake and then saw it, and sat still and said 'Hi,' and the two of them were quiet together for a while, and exchanged some essence of being. Then it went on its way leaving the depth of its eye on her memory long after it had gone.

She got up again and resumed her wandering, down through the scattered trees, Shouanete joyful in the night, until she saw the lights in the windows of Ikwezi's house.

The knock brought Ikwezi to the door.

'Hi, black pussy,' Shouanete said.

'Come on in, white trash,' Ikwezi said. 'Hey, baby, you didn't need a gun. We'll eat, and then we'll go to bed.'

'I guess we have to eat to keep our strength up, but look at your nipples, you're making me wet already.'

The door closed, and the earth went on turning, and after a while cries and groans of agonized rapture, and sometimes the sounds of laughter, went out into the forest, and into the ears of the other creatures of the night.

The sun came up in a florescence of colour so exclamatory that it might have been proclaiming the dawn of the world, but it was high in the sky before there was any movement in the house.

The women breakfasted, late and languorous, on bread and jam and coffee, and then sat looking out over the ocean.

'I wonder how the boys got on at the palace,' Ikwezi said.

'That bunch of diehards?' Shouanete tossed her head as if she had no interest in the outcome. 'I don't have any doubts about them. My Provensal and your President will be free as air by now. I can guarantee it.'

'You really mean that? You're not just saying it because you know I'm worried about Ombeli?'

Shouanete put a hand on her knee. 'I really mean it, Ikwezi, they're tough boys and they've got all these different kinds of brains going for them too. And if a girl like me can ace two of these American assholes with no trouble at all, it's a pushover for our boys.'

'A girl like you?' Ikwezi stared at Shouanete with the scorn of disbelief. 'You're a warrior woman, and you know it.'

She went on staring, running her eyes over the long golden body naked in the sun. 'I think I'll do a painting of you before you go.'

'Me as warrior woman? Sure, honey, but right now I need to stretch my muscles. Let's climb down there and have a swim.'

Ikwezi gave her an up-from-under look. 'What makes you so goddam energetic, Shouana? I could just lie down and sleep again until night time.'

'Come on, girl, it will do you good.'

They put on shorts and tee-shirts and descended the hill, not the long hike that Tschiffely and Ombeli had made to the bay where the *Sika Kuma* had anchored, but the straight mile from the house down to a small beach.

They stripped and ran into the water, and Shouanete swam out with an efficient crawl stroke as if she was bound for Africa. Ikwezi, however, who swam for pleasure and had nothing in her that heard a call to athleticism, swam up and down parallel to the shore, and dived and swam underwater, revelling in the play of light and colour, and after a while lay floating on the surface, to bask in the heat that fell from the sky and feel the heave of the sea beneath her.

She heard a shout, and there was Shouana speeding in towards her, and after that she heard the beat of an engine, and saw a large motor-cruiser come into sight, giving a wide berth to the spine of rock that ran into the sea at the southern end of the little beach.

She swam until she was in her depth, and stood with the sea washing over her knees, watching and admiring Shouanete for the speed with which that accomplished crawl brought her inshore; and watching the boat which came after her slowly, not as if it was chasing her, but as if she was guiding it in.

Shouanete found her footing and came and stood beside her, panting from the exertion. 'Of course I left the damned pistol at the house,' she said between gasps. 'So let's wait and see if these are good guys or bad guys, and if they're the bad guys we can run. We'll be out of sight in the trees in no time and once we get to the house we've got enough weapons and ammo to hold off an army. They might be OK, they didn't try to run me down or shoot me.'

As they were to discover, the men on the boat were, at least from the point of view of the two women, the good guys.

Mick Fawcett was at the wheel, and Tony Carver and Harry Seddall stood at the bow, gazing with pleasure at the two naked women who waited for them in the shallows.

The boat was an ocean-going cruiser, so they could not take her all the way in. Seddall kept an eye on the shelving sand beneath her keel and about twenty yards from the shore held up the back of his hand to Fawcett, said, 'Drop the anchor, Tony,' and jumped in, shorts and shirt and all, and swam to the women.

'Afternoon,' he said. 'My name is Harry Seddall.'

The smaller, darker woman said, 'My name is ... but wait a minute, did you say Harry Seddall?'

'Yes,' he said.

She studied him carefully. 'Are you a friend of a certain poet, who came here from England?'

'That I am. A poet called Steve Tschiffely. I've come – we have come – to find him.'

Her smile was radiant. 'He has stayed with me in my house. Up there on the hill. My name is Ikwezi. This is my friend, my lover when she is here, Shouanete.'

Seddall's smile matched hers. 'But this is marvellous. We did not think it wise, you see, to go directly into Saint-Hilaire, so we came down the coast until we saw you swimming.'

He bowed to Shouanete.

She smiled too, they were all smiles, but hers was pleasant with irony. 'So you saw me swimming, a woman swimming, and thought she's only a woman, she'll be harmless.'

'That is probably what went through my mind,' he agreed with candour. 'But now that I see you clearly, and hear you speak, I think I am looking at a pretty tough human being.'

She had already liked the look of him, experience, strength and keen intelligence in that face; friendliness in the eyes, a friendliness not yet wholly committed, which was how it should be, and at his words she liked him more.

'Pretty tough,' she said. 'Shake, Harry,' and held out her hand, and found their grips were about even.

'We must all go up to the house,' Ikwezi said. 'It seems to me we must have a good deal to talk about.'

'Is it just the three of you?' Shouanete asked him.

'Three of us, yes.'

'You have weapons on that boat?'

His eyes now were speculative. 'Hunting rifles and pistols.'

'Bring them with you. Things are happening here. I had to shoot two men myself last night.'

His eyebrows shot up. 'Did you indeed? What kind of men?'

'US Special Forces.'

'US Special Forces? Just like that, as if it was easy?'

'Shit, man, it was easy. They were a pair of dumb bunnies.'

He turned round and shouted to Carver. 'Come on shore, both of you. Bring the arms and ammunition. You'll need the dinghy.'

'We'll go and get dressed,' Ikwezi said.

'In this weather?' Seddall said.

Shouanete took a step towards him and pinched his cheek hard so that it was really painful, and kept hold while she spoke.

'I like you, mister, but watch your ass round here.'

She released him and grinned, and slapped him vigorously across the face, forehand and backhand, then she and Ikwezi went up the beach and put their clothes on.

Seddall joined them.

'You're a rough woman,' he said to Shouanete.

'The roughest,' she said cheerfully. 'Do you feel insulted?'

'If I did I wouldn't tell you,' he said, 'because I'd have to fight you, and I don't feel strong enough. No, I don't feel insulted. I feel instructed, and enlightened.'

Ikwezi said, 'I'll go up to the house and get some good cold drinks ready. Shouanete can show you the way. You two seem to understand each other.'

She set off into the rich greenery of the hillside, and the two on the shore waited for the dinghy. When it reached them, he saw

Fawcett look at her as if she was Aphrodite risen from the sea, but Carver esteemed her with a more measured eye, an eye that searched for what she was, not simply skimming the beautiful surface.

They belted on the revolvers and slung the rifles. Carver hefted one of the two game bags full of ammunition and hung it on his other shoulder. Shouanete picked up the other one.

'You can't carry that,' Fawcett protested. 'Weighs a ton.'

'Fuck you, little boy,' she said. 'We all set? Let's go.'

She set a pace up the hill that would have done credit to the Paras training on the Black Mountains, and when they came to the house at last the three men were running with sweat and heaving for breath.

'There's a war on,' Shouanete said, 'we'll talk inside.'

Ikwezi had quantities of iced lemonade, freshly squeezed, ready for them, and they fell into chairs and emptied two glasses each in short order, and lay there with their stomachs gurgling.

'Think they're able to talk now, Shouana?' Ikwezi asked with an amused irony in her voice at this scene. 'Council of war?'

Shouanete assented. 'Council of war. Harry, you tell us what you know and why you're here, and then it will be our turn.'

Carver rose and began a slow circuit of the paintings on the walls. 'My word, but these are good,' he said. 'You carry on, Harry. I know it all already, but I'll keep my ears open.'

Seddall told it all: from General Simon Ainley's approach to him at the reception, through Peter Hillyard's murder, to that bizarre encounter with the Prime Minister.

It took him quite a while, and in the middle of it Ikwezi made and offered him an outsize gin and tonic which he accepted with enthusiasm.

During the telling Ikwezi responded with exclamations, wide astonished eyes and shakings of the head, but Shouanete showed nothing at all of what she thought or felt about his story. Her face was hard and closed. He might have been making a report to a commanding general.

When he had finished Ikwezi rested her face on her hands and stared at the floor. Shouanete kept her eyes fixed on him while she weighed what he had said and formed her view of it.

'It appears,' she said, still holding his eyes, 'that even though you are English, we are on the same side, that we must agree to be allies.'

Carver, who had left off inspecting the paintings a while ago, and was sitting on the floor with his back to the wall, got his word in as Seddall was about to speak. 'Oh, I don't know about that. We haven't heard your side of things yet, and that was the deal.'

This fetched him a sideways glance of appreciation. 'You're Carver, right?' she said.

'Right. Tony Carver.'

'My side of things. Yes. I'll tell you my side of things.' She told it quickly and fluently, to the point where she left the five men about to make their bid to rescue Provensal and Sefuthi from the palace, and ending with her journey out to Ikwezi's house, and her shooting of the two American Special Forces men.

'The car,' Fawcett said. 'What did you do with the car?'

'It's up there. I drove it in a little way, so it would be out of sight from the road.'

'Has it not occurred to you,' Seddall asked her, 'that they will find these two men of theirs dead? That they will connect the car that passed the first checkpoint with their being killed, and start looking around?'

'I don't think about things like that. I was coming to see Ikwezi, other things were not important to me.'

Carver got up from the floor. 'In God's name, woman, what is important to you?'

'Living my life.'

Carver looked at Seddall. 'We need someone up there to keep an eye out. I'll go.'

'Thanks, Tony.' And to Shouanete, 'Go with him to show him the way, will you please?'

She jerked her head round at him, a stubborn petulance on the down-turned mouth. 'That sounded like an order.'

He met her cold and angry eyes with no trouble at all. 'Oh, do you think so? Just do it, will you, and when you've done it come back here.'

Ikwezi said, 'I'll do it.'

'No,' Carver said. 'Harry won't want that. He'll want you to tell him things about Sefuthi and your cousin Ombeli and the island. We're out of our depth here. We don't know the island.'

Shouanete left her chair and confronted him, glorious in her strange beauty and full of her power. 'You two should not talk to us like that, you should not talk to women like that.'

'Shouanete,' Carver said, 'we're all in this together. I can see that doesn't suit your idea of yourself. You're a woman who likes to withhold yourself from participating in the business of life and do only what will meet your needs and impulses and desires. But you broke away from that by shooting those two men on the road. That, lady, was participation. So for now, if we are going to be allies, I suggest you put your own personal idea of yourself on hold, and be useful.'

She stared at his tall, handsome, old-fashioned military figure. 'Where do you get this stuff? You look like the Charge of the Light Brigade and you're coming on at me as if you were my therapist.' She was ready to throw herself at him in her fury. 'And my own personal idea of myself – what is that?'

'So far as can tell on this short acquaintance, you perceive yourself as an isolated creature of more value than anyone else around, who gives nothing of herself to anyone else, and who feels no responsibility towards anyone else.'

Mick Fawcett, a perplexed and attentive listener, thought he had gone too far. 'Steady on, Carver. This is no way to speak to someone. I mean, damn it, we've only just arrived here. This is not our place. We are guests here.'

Carver was unperturbed. 'There are things she doesn't understand, Mick. She has to be made to understand them.'

Shouanete leaned at Carver as tense as a strung bow, and stared at him as if her eyes would turn him to dust. 'These things, giving to others and responsibility for others, are weaknesses.'

'Sweetheart,' Carver said, 'you're a great-looking kid but you're not the best thing God ever made. Why don't you climb down from your tower and join in the game till this lark is over, and then climb back up again.'

Her fist went for his face and he stopped it and held it in his hand, forcing it back. 'Baby,' he said, 'if you want to go ten rounds with the gloves on, we'll do it when this war is over. For the time being, why don't you just join in with the rest of us and be a human being? Get your gun and let's go.'

She took her hand back and stood there, running over what he had said to her. 'Ikwezi,' she said. 'Tell him he's wrong. I'm not like he says I am.'

'The honest truth is,' Ikwezi said, 'that you are.'

'Well, damn you, I thought you were my friend.'

'I am your friend, Shouana. I didn't say I don't like you for it. There are things about it that I admire. But right now we have to work together, and if we're going to have to fight these Americans who have invaded Matetendoro, we have to have a chief, and obey the chief, and it seems to me that since Harry is the chief of these men, then he is our chief too.'

'No man is my chief.'

'No woman is your chief, either, and no man or woman is my chief, but war needs generals and soldiers, not a collection of self-willed, self-indulgent heroines and heroes each going their own way. Think about it.'

Seddall had been watching the two of them with a lot of interest, but he was growing impatient. 'Tony, this has gone far enough. We need someone up there on lookout right now, or the next thing we know they'll be throwing mortar shells in on us, which will make a real mess of Ikwezi's house, apart from anything else. Shouanete, if you don't want to be one of us, then don't. But if you do want to throw in with us, I'd really be awfully obliged if you'd guide Tony to the car, and show him where the road is.'

'First,' she said, 'he must promise not to talk to me like that again.'

Seddall looked up at Carver. 'I don't see why not.'

Carver showed no sign of contrition. 'I can promise that,' he said. 'I think the message got across, or some of it.'

Shouanete closed her eyes and her brow creased in thought. The rest of them waited, as if by common consent it was agreed that she must not be distracted from what she was dealing with.

In the end she gave a sigh and opened them, and said to Carver, 'All right, soldier, let's go. And I'll stay and watch with you. If these American boys do come you might want to send back a runner.'

'Good thinking,' Carver said.

She checked the Heckler and Koch, picked up the beach bag with the ammunition in it, and went on out, jerking her head at Carver to follow. He followed.

It seemed that they were hardly gone before they were back, supporting between them a dazed-looking Tschiffely, bare to the waist and with a bloody bandage round his chest.

'Seddall,' he said, as they put him into a chair, 'good to see you. Hi, Ikwezi. I ran the motorbike into a tree. Give me a drink, somebody, that's what I need most. This,' he touched the edge of the bandage, 'is not as bad as it looks.'

Ikwezi poured him half a tumbler of whisky and he took a quick gulp, and another, and lay back in the chair. 'Give me a minute to gather my wits,' he said, 'then I'll fill you in.'

Carver said, 'We'd better get on up there. OK, Shouanete?'

'Yeah,' she said, 'and I'll come back to hear the news in case you need to know it, and I can bring it to you. Let's go.'

Seddall waved a hand to then as they left, and said, 'Take all the time you need, Steve. We can wait till you're ready.'

Tschiffely said, 'Ready now,' and took another swallow of whisky. 'It's just that it's a little complicated.'

'Tell it as it comes, we'll sort it out '

'I'll start at the end, in that case. The last I saw of Provensal, he was high-tailing it for the beach on his own. Don't know if he made it to the boat or not. The last I saw of Ombeli and Sefuthi, they were getting themselves lost in Saint-Hilaire. It's their town, so I think they'll make out. Lucas got shot and I think he's dead. Daniel and Wildgrave I don't know. They were trying to make off with that guy Foxberry as their prisoner, and that will slow them down.'

'You got Provensal and Sefuthi out? Not bad going.'

'I think not bad. Wildgrave has a kind of cold and practical determination which makes you believe that whatever he puts his hand to is going to work. And it did work, but it didn't come out quite as he had planned it. There was a place where so much happened so fast that it's clouded in my head, so now I'll go back to the beginning.'

'Wait.' Ikwezi had been listening to this with anxiety on her face. 'What are my cousin and the President going to do?'

'My dear Ikwezi.' Tschiffely's expression was one of kindly affection. 'They will be all right, I'm sure of it. They will lie low until they know what it is best for them to do next.'

'All of this sounds good,' Seddall said. 'But now, tell us what happened at the palace. Here, have one of these.'

He gave him a cigarette and lit it, and Tschiffely drew on it and put down the last of the whisky in the glass.

'I've done a bit of rock-climbing,' he said, 'and Wildgrave wanted to enter the palace by the first floor, so I scrambled up the wall at the west end of the palace and let down a rope. Wildgrave came up first, and then the other three. It was dark, you see, and that end of the palace had no sentries posted.

'We crept along the balcony, front of the palace, till we came to the window of the President's office, and there was Mr Arthur Foxberry sitting with his back to the window all by himself. Wildgrave went straight in and put a gun to his head, and we had him.'

'Can I ask you something?' This was Mick Fawcett.

'Sure.'

'You said that Wildgrave took Foxberry prisoner – I mean he didn't just tie him up and put a gag in his mouth and stuff him in a cupboard, but took Foxberry away with him. What was the point of that?'

'Yes. Well.' Tschiffely made a face. 'Wildgrave is not exactly a sweetheart. He wants to make Foxberry tell him why the CIA – with the help of these US Special Forces – are so interested in having their way on Matetendoro.'

'That would be worth knowing,' Seddall said.

Fawcett had picked up something else. 'You say make Foxberry tell him. What does that mean?'

'I think it means he'll torture him if he has to. I don't see Wildgrave as a man with any scruples about anything. Mind you, neither is Foxberry, so they're well matched.'

'Except,' Fawcett said drily, 'that when you last saw them Foxberry was Wildgrave's prisoner, so if anyone's torturing anyone, it's Wildgrave who's torturing Foxberry.'

The cast of Tschiffely's gipsy-looking face changed until he might have been a don at a university. 'Will you explain to me exactly who you are and what contribution you think you're making by filling the air with echoes of the Geneva Convention? Is that too much to ask?'

'It's simply that Foxberry is CIA, and—'

Seddall stopped him short. 'As far as I'm concerned, from the way he's been going on Foxberry might as well be a hired assassin. You're not sitting in an office now, Mick, fielding calls from an indignant Foreign Office, you're out at the sharp edge dealing with utterly ruthless and immoral men, and if one of them has run up against another ruthless and immoral man, I must say I feel no distress about that at all.'

'So who is this?' Tschiffely said.

'Mick Fawcett, my Number Two,' Seddall said.

'I think I want to get this over with,' Tschiffely said. 'So I'll get on. There was no one else on the first floor of the palace. We left Wildgrave holding Foxberry and the rest of us, four of us, went through every room on that floor. So then we went down to the floor below. There were two men in what I'll call the lobby. Ombeli knifed one, Lucas shot the other with a silenced pistol. No one on that floor either.'

'Can you cut it short?' Seddall said.

'I have,' Tschiffely said, 'and I'm nearly done, but I'll use shorthand. Found Sefuthi and Provensal in a cellar. One soldier-boy asleep outside the door so somebody hit him on the head, took his key, got them out, put him in instead. We went back upstairs, joined Wildgrave, got out down the rope, ran across the grass in the dark back into the trees, and went for the beach and the launch. And then it went wrong.'

He turned his head towards Ikwezi. His eyes were blank, as if he was back in the trees and the dark, recalling that moment.

'They had a patrol out. We hadn't expected it. Wildgrave said the reason the palace was empty was that they were short of manpower. They had men at the palace, at checkpoints, around town, at the radio station. Spread thin, he said.

'So we were careless and ran into this patrol. They heard us coming and opened up on us. I got this bullet burn across my chest. Lucas was killed, others injured. We returned fire but they were too many. We scattered, and I ended up with Sefuthi and Ombeli running for the town. As we went we saw Provensal in the starlight running down the beach. Wildgrave and Daniel, I don't know, but they vanished westward, opposite way from us, taking Foxberry with them.'

He looked round and gave a rueful smile. 'That was it, the great rescue mission. We got into town and ran through some streets and lanes and holed up with a friend of Ombeli. Then today Ombeli gave me his motorbike, and sent me out here to tell Ikwezi what had happened. And here are all you guys.'

He glanced down at his bandaged chest and smiled again. 'The President himself tore up my shirt and made a pad and a bandage out of it. Quite an honour.'

Seddall got up and planted himself in front of the empty fireplace. His face looked as tough as old boots, that mulish jaw clamped tight and his eyes quick and hard.

'Steve, you've done bloody well. They would make you Poet Laureate for this if I had my way, but I expect they have different considerations for that than I do. How do you feel? Are you out of it, or do you want to go back in there? Because we have things to do and we'll have to do them.'

'This is only a scratch. I'd like a serious dressing on it though, and then I'm with you.'

'Let me do that,' Mick Fawcett said. 'I've got medical gear with me, and wounds in the Tropics must be properly cared for. Also,' and he made an apologetic grimace, 'it will help to make up for me being so snotty back there. I hadn't adjusted quickly enough to what's going on here. Sorry about that, Tschiffely.'

'Forget it, just get me ready for the next outing.'

Seddall was chewing his lip. 'The next outing, but that's the question. What is the next outing? What do we do now?'

Feet came running up the steps outside and Shouanete came in the door. 'Carver sent me. The bad guys, six or seven of them, up there. They were following the car tracks in off the road. They'll have reached it by now. If they're thinking straight, they might be on their way down the hill already.'

'And Tony – Carver to you – what's he doing? Is he going to engage them or just keep an eye on them?'

'Carver's going to hang back and watch them. Too many for one man to handle, he said.'

'Clear thinking. Anything else?'

'Yes. He'll stay in their rear, so that if you meet them on the hill and there's a firefight, he can attack from behind.'

'Arm up, everybody. I'll go first, with Shouanete as guide, if that seems good to you, Shouanete?'

'Makes sense to me, boss,' and she threw him a grin, as if to say that she had changed her view of things, and was willing to take orders.

'Ikwezi,' Seddall said, 'what about you? Do you want to come with us, because if not, you might be wise to hide out in the bush, in case these guys get the better of us and find the house.'

'I have guns,' she said, 'and I can use them. I'll come.'

'Everybody,' Seddall said, 'please take this in. Nobody fires either till I do, or till I give the word, except in case of extreme exigency.'

Tschiffely, his wound properly dressed and wearing a top of many colours put on him by Ikwezi in place of his ruined shirt, said, 'This is the next outing. We didn't even have to think.'

'How it often happens,' Seddall said tersely. 'Shouanete, how much daylight do we have left?'

'About two hours. See, the sun is coming down the sky.'

It was indeed, a mad and blinding orb that shocked the eye.

'Come,' Shouanete said. 'We must glide as silently as the snake, and move with the stealth of the panther.'

Following her, Seddall could not find that she had anything to learn from either of these creatures.

Chapter Sixteen

They were almost at the car when they heard the voices of the Americans. Shouanete peered through the leaves. 'Three of them,' she said. 'Coming straight for us.'

She slid off to the right, as silently as the snake she so much admired, and Seddall went after, having first waved for those behind them to take the same course.

Shouanete produced a knife and looked at Seddall with the question in her eyes. He shook his head and whispered in her ear. 'Let them pass on by, if that's what they look like doing.' They lurked in the undergrowth and watched to see what line the Americans would take as they came near.

The three men came on, talking freely, blundering through the low bushes and sweeping tree branches aside, making as much noise as if they were going to a cook-out down on the beach. They went by at a distance of thirty feet and when the noise of their passage had faded Seddall rose and signalled to his followers, and he and Shouanete moved on out.

He saw first the black shape of the car, and then the four soldiers sitting in it with the engine running, making the most of the air-conditioning while they waited for their fellows who had gone down the hill to come back and report. There was no sign of Carver, woo was presumably hiding in the foliage on the far side of the limousine.

'Quite a vehicle, that. It would carry all of us.' Fawcett and the others had caught up, and they stood in a group, taking in the scene before them.

'First we have to get hold of it,' Seddall said.

'They seem to have their guard down,' Fawcett said.

'Yes, but I don't want casualties if we can avoid it, and we don't want to wreck the car.'

Ikwezi and Shouanete looked at each other, and perceived that they were two minds with a single thought.

'Perhaps we could employ our feminine charms to bring their guard down a little more,' Ikwezi said.

Their feminine charms were clear to see. They were wearing only the shorts and tee-shirts they had donned on the seashore, and there was so much sweat on their bodies from the exertions of the climb that they might have been taking part in a wet tee-shirt contest. Yes, they would lower a man's guard, all right.

'I don't think you could fail,' he said. 'But, Ikwezi, these men will very likely have been given a description of Shouanete from the men who stopped her at the first checkpoint. So you would have to do it on your own. How does that strike you? You would have to be an island girl who just happened to see the boys and felt like a bit of fun. Can you do that, on your own?'

'Watch me,' she said.

She slipped off into the trees towards the main road, and vanished from sight. Soon they saw her coming down the track behind the car, singing and switching idly at the grass with a leafy twig.

She noticed the car and stopped, and cocked her head as if to see if there was anyone in it, and then came on slowly. One of the men lounging in the front saw her in the wing mirror and sat up, and said something. The others came to life, looking round to see her out of the back window, but they had only a few seconds for that before she reached the car.

Four windows went down as one.

Ikwezi rolled her body along the side of the car, making one complete turn that brought her level with the men in the front. She leaned in the window to look at them all.

'My,' she said. 'Who are you men? Four hunks all to myself in one evening, and arrived by magic in this lovely car. Who wants to party with Ikwezi?'

To her friends, not ten paces away, it seemed, from the noise that came from the car, as if all four soldiers were keen to party with her. The man at the window where she was standing grabbed her head in both hands and said, 'I wanna party with you, babe,' and started kissing her hard.

There was a chorus of complaint from the others, and Ikwezi pulled herself away from him and said, 'Not all together, guys. How about two of you at a time? And that will be ten dollars each. That's not a lot to you but it's good money here.'

The two men on the near side, the man who had kissed her and the one behind him, got out of the car and went into their pockets and produced the money.

'This way, boys,' she said, 'there's some nice soft grass in here behind the trees. What are your names?' Their names were Joe and Eddie.

As they stepped into the ambush Shouanete put an armlock on Joe's neck and stabbed him through the heart, and Fawcett hit Eddie on the back of the head with his 9mm pistol, and then hit him again to make sure.

By the time that was done Tony Carver had emerged from the greenery on the other side of the car and got the drop on the two remaining soldiers.

'Get them out, Mick,' he said to Fawcett. 'One at a time, man in the back first. Take his knife and pistol and go over him for hidden weapons. Good. You stay there, mister, hands on the roof. Now, you in front, out.'

The two men stood disarmed with their hands on the roof and Carver's rifle covering them.

'What now, Harry?' Carver said.

'Tie their hands behind their back, and tie their ankles together, and gag them. Do the same with the one Mick knocked out, make him one of them. Arrange them round the truck of a good-sized tree, and tie them one to the other. That should hold them. Deep in the greenwood, of course. Out of sight, out of mind. The lions and tigers and panthers will do the rest.'

'Jesus Christ, mister,' one of the captives expostulated. 'You can't do that.'

'You lost the war, that's all,' Carver said, 'so don't make a fuss. It'll get you nowhere. He does this sort of thing all the time. Shouanete, will you hold a gun on these guys while I gather up the afflicted one?'

Shouanete and Fawcett and Carver went off with the prisoners and Seddall said to Tschiffely and Ikwezi, 'We might as well get in the car and be comfortable. Ikwezi, you did a wonderful job. What an actress you'd make.'

She looked at him blandly and revolved her hips. 'What makes you so sure I was acting?'

'Well, you're gay, aren't you?'

'I'm gay, but I might not always be gay. It didn't all feel like acting to me.'

'I see. I don't know as much as I might about these things,' Seddall admitted.

'I know you don't, Mister Colonel. You're so straight it's just not true.'

Tschiffely, who had been enjoying the show, said, 'So are lots of men, really interesting men, men like me, for instance. Get in the car, Ikwezi, and stop teasing the poor man.'

They sat in the car, revelling in the cooled air, and waited for the others to return.

When they did come back, the first thing Carver said was, 'Ikwezi, there are no lions and tigers and panthers on this island, are there?'

'No.'

'God, Seddall,' Carver said, 'you are a bastard, these guys are hysterical. It made them difficult to handle, and when I told them you'd made it up they wouldn't believe me. Not that it matters too much. As it is they'll just lie there and starve to death, unless we arrange for them to be got out of there.'

'Well, who's to drive this thing?' Seddall said.

'I'll do it,' Fawcett said. 'Never driven a car this size. Unless anyone else wants to. Where are we going?'

'To tell you the truth I don't have an idea in my head. I can't think of anything to do but play it as it comes. Go down into Saint-

Hilaire and see what turns up. Does anyone else have a better plan?'

Ikwezi said, 'I think we should go to Ombeli's house. He may have got something moving by now. Who knows?'

'No harm in that,' Seddall said. 'Why don't you sit beside Mick and show him the way.'

'And unless you need him,' Shouanete said, 'I'd like to take this man Tschiffely here and see if we can get out to the yacht and see what Provensal's doing and thinking – if he made it to the yacht, that is.'

'That makes sense too. Mr Tschiffely, consider yourself on detached duty until further notice.'

'It's not a duty. It's a pleasure,' Tschiffely said.

'Be cool, honey.' Shouanete stroked his thigh. 'You might not like me when you get to know me.'

'I don't need to get to know you.' Tschiffely was learning her language. 'I can like you without that.'

They drove on. Here in the tunnel of trees the light was leaving the air, and off to the left another Expressionist sunscape was in the making.

Fawcett, in his role as chauffeur, had a relevant question. 'What are our tactics going to be if we come to one of their checkpoints?'

'We shoot first,' Seddall said, 'and let them ask questions afterwards, otherwise we'll be giving it all away and they'll have us on toast.'

Carver grinned. 'Sounds like General George Patton, Harry.'

'Honey,' Shouanete said, 'General Harry knows just what he's doing. These guys are as cold-blooded as all hell. Give them an inch, and we'll be dead meat.'

Carver laughed at this. 'No Catholic like a convert, is that right, Shouanete? A couple of hours ago you were fit to spit in his eye, and now it sounds as if you'd ride into the mouth of hell if he ordered it.'

'It's not quite like that,' she said. 'Normally I've got no time for this macho shit, but if that's what we're doing, then that's what we're doing, and he's good at it.'

They came to the edge of town and, under Ikwezi's direction,

Fawcett drove slowly into a warren of sidestreets, avoiding the main thoroughfares that radiated from the centre.

'Stop here,' she said, at the opening of an alley whose far end, about a quarter of a mile off, framed the gleam of the sea. 'Shouana, if you and Tschiffely want to steal a boat to go out to the yacht, you'll find them down there, lying on the beach.'

Shouanete said, 'Come on, lover,' and she and Tschiffely got out of the car and set off down the street. She had her hand on the machine-pistol in her beach bag, which also held the flick-knife she had used once already today, and spare ammunition. In the small of his back, under his belt and covered by his shirt, Tschiffely carried a small 7.65mm Beretta that Carver had given him.

They had a clear run down the alley between the dilapidated houses, some wooden, some built of mud brick. They encountered few people as they went. Those they did meet darted into doorways or, if no such escape route offered, passed them by hastily and with averted eyes.

'God,' Shouanete said. 'It makes you feel like the Gestapo.'

'Yes.' Tschiffely's eyes were narrowed and his face dark. 'Not a happy town.'

When they reached the end of this dismal progress down the alley they found that it came to an end on the sand itself, that no road ran along above the shore. To the left they saw, as they blinked into the now familiar effulgence of the setting sun, the quay that formed this side of the harbour. In front of them the beach was littered with refuse, and on it were five of the small fishing-boats boats with outriggers called galawas.

To their right was an ill-kempt grove of coconut palms, the ground between them overgrown with bushes to about the height of a man.

Shouanete touched Tschiffely's arm and drew him back. 'Look there. Soldiers on the pier.'

'Yes, not good. What do you think? Shall we slink along the buildings as if we were part of the populace, and then choose our moment and go to ground among the coconut trees? Wait until dark before we make our move?'

'Seems good to me.'

'Let's do it. We should do our best to look unnerved and unaggressive. Are you up for that?'

Her eyes flashed humour at him. 'I'm up for that, so long as you understand it's only a disguise.'

'What else would I think?'

She laughed and said, 'Put your arm round my waist, stagger a bit, as if you were pissed and I'm a whore you picked up.'

As they set out in this mode, he said, 'This is not easy for me, I think of you as the Mona Lisa.'

'Oh, you do, do you?' and she pushed him so that he nearly fell, most realistically drunken. 'And why is that?'

'It's the purity of your look, and the gentle decorum of your demeanour. I am quite overcome by it.'

She kicked him on the ankle, which since she was wearing trainers did no more than bark the skin a little. 'You are such an asshole, Steve Tschiffely. If you're overcome by being with me, that's not what overcomes you.'

'What do you think it could be, then?'

He stumbled so effectively that the two of them fell down in a heap. She used the occasion to seize his hand and crush it on to her crotch. 'I think this might have something to do with it.' Then she lifted the hand and laid it on one of her breasts and said, 'And this.'

He ran his free hand up the inside of one thigh and down the other, 'And these,' he said.

'Hey.' She laughed again. 'You mean, the whole package?'

'When I get to see the whole package, I'll tell you.'

She jumped to her feet and, still holding his hand, pulled at it. He responded by getting up with the laborious movements of the drunkard. 'Not far now,' he said, 'then we can simply fall away in among the coconut palms.'

'And half an hour still with light in it. That's lucky. Lucky for you.'

He had his arm over her shoulders now, a man struggling to stay upright. 'What's lucky about it?'

She looked along her eyes at him, and her eyes were dancing.

'You'll have time to see the whole package. I'm not what you'd call a literary lady, but I'll bet you that kind of inspiration does a poet no harm.'

At this point in their journey the coconut palms grew right up to the ends of the houses and they walked in among them. The trunks of the trees threw a pattern of shadows which added, for Tschiffely, to the surreal state that being with her like this had brought him to.

'Here,' and she kicked off her trainers, 'is a good soft place.' She lifted the tee-shirt slowly up over her belly and her breasts and tugged it off her head. In that moment the surreal disappeared, as if it had been whisked away by the evening breeze, and to Tschiffely it was as if he had never felt so real in his life.

He stood there, waiting, and watched fascinated as a light smile came and went on her lips, and came and went, and the effect of this fugitive movement of her mouth was to enhance the profound solemnity of her face and eyes. He knew it was a poet's imagination at work, but what he saw in her was a spirit for whom making love was a rite of worship.

She felt this from him, and slipped out of her shorts and stood naked, a golden body gleaming in the bright wild glow of the sun, and caressed by the moving shadows of the palm leaves.

'Be slow,' she said. 'Let us do many things before you come into me, so that we know each other well.'

'Oh, yes,' he said. 'We shall discover each other slowly, you and I.'

He shed his clothes and she in her turn admired the sinewy leanness of him. Her eyes dropped and came up again. 'So soon, and so strong.'

With her eyes fixed on his she sank to the ground and he went down to her. They kissed, and then kissed each other's bodies, each in their turn, with kisses as light as the touch of falling leaves.

Until as their passion grew he went down on her, and she went down on him; until they would wait no longer and he entered her and at last, when she came, she made a strange sound he had not heard of woman, a 'Ha, ha, ha, ha, ha,' that went on and on, and he came after and shouted great unshaped shouts into the night, and the sun went down and left the sky a tumult of roiling colours, and not far off the sea fell hissing on the shore, and then they fell apart.

And after a little while again, and then again, and finally she said, 'I want you to come on my face.' So he came on her face, on her mouth and on her eyes, and then they lay side by side with the first stars blazing down on them and the slight wind cooling their bodies.

The sky darkened, and more stars came out. 'Well, Steve Tschiffely,' she said. 'Who would have thought it? Poets are the best, just the very best.'

'No, Shouana,' he said. 'You bring out the best in poets.'

They lay in silence again, and he turned to her and lay over her, his face just above hers. 'Two pagans,' he said, 'suckled in a creed outworn.'

'That sounds like a quotation. Who said it?'

'A poet.'

'That's all I need to know.'

The wind was rising off the sea, and the starlight flickered on their bodies, and they had forgotten everything and would have stayed there for ever. He looked as far as he could into her eyes, which was not far, because the cool impersonal woman was back in the saddle. So far as he was concerned, that was all right with him; if that was how she needed to be, then that was how she was.

He traced her upper lip with his finger, and said, 'I feel as if I've just written the best poem of my life.'

Amusement glanced from the eyes and touched her mouth. 'The best poem of your life, and you wrote it on me. Sounds as if you tattooed it on to me, but it feels like you tattooed it into me.' She moved under him, not seductively, but stretching her limbs to ease her body as if she was resting from a thirty-mile hike. 'I will say, lover, you sure know how to beat a tattoo on a girl. You've done me up and bruised me bad. Which,' and she put up a hand and ran a nail down his cheek, 'is how I like it, but it'll be a few days before we do this again. Move over, Mr Steve Tschiffely, and let's just lie here for a while.'

They lay there in silence, and watched the tops of the trees blow in the wind, and the bright silence of the stars; and in a little while, out of the silence, they began to hear the faint sounds of someone moving slow and stealthy through the trees.

Shouanete, with all the grace of a leaping cat, crossed the space to her beach bag and brought out the machine-pistol. She went down and out of sight into the bushes. Tschiffely stayed where he was, and reached out for the Beretta, and lay there trying to track the night-walker by the sounds he made.

A figure appeared out of nowhere and paused, moving his head as if he was sniffing for the scent of his prey. The bush where Shouanete lurked moved slightly. Her voice, when it came, in that first moment startled Tschiffely, until he registered the name she had spoken.

'Daniel,' she said. 'Daniel, it's me, Shouanete.'

The man's hand had moved like lightning and metal flashed in the starlight. 'Show yourself,' he said.

Shouanete rose from among the leaves.

Daniel laughed. 'I never seen you bare-assed before. It sure suits you.' He came forward, and saw Tschiffely lying naked on the ground. 'You folks sure make a lot of noise when you're doing it. Heard you half a mile away. Wasn't sure what it was, so I came to see. But I'm sure now.'

Shouanete came out of the bushes. She kissed Daniel on the cheek, laid down her weapon, and began to get into her shorts and tee-shirt. Tschiffely stood up and got into his clothes.

'So you got clear,' he said to Daniel. 'And Wildgrave, did he make it? And what about Foxberry?'

Daniel shook his head. 'Wildgrave's close to dead. Foxberry is tied up like a Thanksgiving turkey. They're not far. I'd like to get back there. Will you two come?'

'Of course we will. We were waiting for dark, before trying to find out if Provensal managed to get away to the yacht.'

'And filling in time,' Daniel said, deadpan.

Tschiffely gave him a long look. 'Oblige me. Don't make any more remarks like that.'

There was a flash of white teeth. 'You got it,' Daniel said.

Shouanete came close, dressed and with the beach bag on her shoulder. She turned her head slowly from one to the other. 'Are you two quarrelling?'

'We understand each other,' Tschiffely said.

'Then let's go.'

As Daniel led them through the grove, they filled him in on what had happened since they last saw him.

'So we've got more people on our side,' he said. 'That could help. Seems to me like the CIA and their soldier buddies must be getting edgy. Things are not going how they expected.'

'It'll make them dangerous,' Tschiffely said.

'Hell,' Shouanete said. 'We're dangerous.'

'Yeah.' Daniel's voice was low, almost subdued. 'I don't see how it's all going to end. One thing though: soon we got to see about Mr Provensal.'

They went on, held in their thoughts, until Tschiffely asked Daniel, 'So you've still got Foxberry. I take it that Wildgrave was too badly wounded, and you've been too busy, to interrogate him?'

'Christ, yes. I don't know how Wildgrave did it. He just ran and ran after he was shot back there, and we got this far and then he collapsed. That man has lost so much blood. And I had that Foxberry, gagged and with his hands tied, and I had to keep dragging the bastard along.'

'Just tell me what we need to know.' Shouanete sounded so airily confident that Tschiffely's blood chilled. 'I'll get it out of him.'

'Guess you would,' Daniel said, then, peering about him into the trees, 'It's somewhere here.' There came a faint murmur through the night, not so much a groan as a sigh. 'That's him. This is it.' And Daniel turned to the right, half-stooping as he went.

They saw a man lying on the ground and then another, sitting with his back to a tree. The first man was Wildgrave, and the other

Foxberry, whose arms had been pulled either side of the tree and his wrists lashed together.

Wildgrave was on his side with his head resting on a rolled-up jacket, Foxberry's, presumably, since that worthy was in his shirt-sleeves.

Tschiffely expected Shouanete to go to Wildgrave, since she knew him, but she didn't. She squatted down on her heels, a few feet off, as if she was a spectator, and said nothing.

He himself kneeled by the wounded man and was appalled to see how much blood had come from his abdomen. His clothes were soaked with it and it had pooled on the pebbly ground.

'Hello, poet.' Wildgrave had only a whisper left in him. 'It won't be long now. My guts are shot to hell.'

Tschiffely took the hand that lay loosely on the pebbles and felt a slight return pressure from the dying man. 'Tough luck, Wildgrave. I'm sorry.'

'It's the way I'd want to go, but Jesus, I hurt.' There was a dry croaking noise in his throat, and he said, 'I'm going. You're a poet. Give me a line, a line with no sentiment, a good strong line for a soldier.'

Tschiffely's mind flew about. He looked at the blood and he threw his head back and searched the trees and the stars.

'Quick.' Wildgrave's voice on his ear was as light as the fall of a feather on the hand.

Tschiffely leaned closer, so that they were face to face, all but touching, and spoke the line that came.

'And deep within the bloody wood, Agamemnon cried aloud,' he said, and felt the pressure, more like a tremor, from the hand that he held in his hand.

Wildgrave's mouth moved, and Tschiffely put his ear to it. 'That's good. It calls to me across a thousand years. Thanks, poet. Keep the faith.' The cold fingers drifted across the palm of his hand and a thin proud smile settled on Wildgrave's face, and he died.

Tschiffely knelt there, blind and deaf, bound to this man he hardly knew, and had not much liked, by the way of his passing.

Yes, he would keep the faith. He had no need to make a vow of it. He knew this man's dying would be with him always.

He knelt there with his head bowed, and after a while he heard the sound of the sea, and came to his feet and like a man sleepwalking went down through the trees until he felt rock under his feet, and gazed out over the rolling ocean, its surface incandescent with starlight and its depths lambent under the moon.

A hand fell on his shoulder. It was Daniel. They stood there together, two strangers, two men of alien lives, but in that hour, two brothers in the turning world.

A shooting star flew down the sky, and the beauty of it brought Tschiffely out of himself into the inmediacy of the present. 'Tell me, Daniel, is Shouanete as indifferent to the death of Wildgrave as she seemed to be?'

'Shouanete? Sure she is. She has no heart, that woman, or if she has, I've never seen her use it.'

'She is rare. I've never met anyone like her before. No heart at all?'

'No, none. I don't think she knows how to love, or even to fall in love. And I don't think she wants to know either of these things. She reckons she's doing just fine as she is.'

Pictures of the ecstasy they had shared under the coconut palms flashed on Tschiffely's mind's eye. 'I can't make out if it's a strength or a weakness.'

Daniel thought about that. 'I don't know either,' he said. 'She uses it like a strength. Mind you,' and there was a note of sardonic humour in the way he spoke, 'it could be useful to us. If we let her loose on Foxberry, he'll tell us every little thing he knows. She'll enjoy doing it, that Shouanete.'

Tschiffely turned to stare, and Daniel smiled at him.

'You've got a lot to learn about women,' he said. 'A mean woman can be as mean as a mean man, which means she can be meaner than most men know how to be. You want to think about that for a little while.'

'No,' Tschiffely said, 'I don't. I've made a mental note of it, but I don't seem to want to think about it, not tonight.'

'Time to get moving,' Daniel said. 'See what we do next.'

'See if Provensal's safely on the yacht, I suppose.'

'Yeah, lift one of those outriggers and go sailing.'

They turned their backs on the sea and the sky, and walked back to the place where Wildgrave had died, and where Shouanete and Foxberry waited.

Chapter Seventeen

President Sefuthi wiped his mouth and said, 'Well, Ombeli, a lot has happened since you left my office so precipitately. We are companions in misfortune now. We must forget that we fell into disagreement. We must put all that aside, and act together for the best interests of ourselves and our country.'

Ombeli's foot played with the loose straw on the floor. They had made a point of choosing this hovel as their hiding-place in preference to one of the more elegant homes of Sefuthi's henchmen, as less likely to be searched by the invading troops hunting for the President.

'Lately, Mr President, I have not agreed with you about what the best interests of our country were. Look what your dealings with these people have led to.'

The President acknowledged this by bowing where he sat, and his countenance showed neither resentment nor weakness, a fact which went down well with Ombeli.

'It was a bad idea in the first place, I confess it. Even if it had not transpired that the CIA had secret plans of their own, it would have been a bad idea. I did what I did, Ombeli, to get money for our impoverished country. When I was in that cellar, however, with the millionaire Provensal, he made me a proposal of such altruism that I can still hardly comprehend what the nature of such a man can be. His proposal means that if we can, somehow, get the Americans off the island, then we need look no further than Provensal for the finance that Matetendoro needs.'

Ombeli was at the door now, putting his head out, as he did every few minutes, to be sure that no search parties were on their way. He saw nothing but the usual chickens and goats on constant search for food. 'Why should Provensal do this for us, when he has nothing to do with Matetendoro?'

Sefuthi gave a wry smile, as if to comment on the difference between such a man and a politician like himself. 'It is a deep principle with him, to oppose the neo-colonialism of the former colonial powers in every way he can.'

Ombeli turned to face him. 'This being so, Mr President, can you tell me, from your heart, that you believe you and I are of one mind when we talk of the best interests of our country?'

'I believe it, and I tell you so from my heart.'

Ombeli scrutinized that strong face, touched as always with its shade of melancholy, and liked the man.

'Then tell me,' he said, 'what you want me to do.'

He thought it was remarkable that Sefuthi, sitting there on the dirt floor with his back against the mud wall, his hands clasped round his shin bones, should still present as much the appearance of the President as he had done in his own office.

'What I should like you to do is a little complicated, and perhaps even demanding. It calls for precise time-tabling. Can you please arrange for the hundred citizens who have most influence among the people of Saint-Hilaire to come here to see me, ten at a time, on the hour, over the next ten hours? Is it possible to arrange that?'

Ombeli felt his spirits rise. The President had a plan. 'You ask for the men with most influence on the people. So you do not mean the richest or most prominent, but those the people will listen to, is that right?'

'That's right.'

'Then we should draw up the list of these men together. You will know men I don't know – men of that kind – and I will know some that you don't know.'

Sefuthi's eyes, in that grave face, became witty. 'You are wasted in the army, Ombeli. Do you have any scraps of paper on you for us to write the list on? These scum emptied my pockets.'

Ombeli found in a hip pocket the form on which, before he had become fascinated by the strangeness of his encounter with the wandering poet, he had begun (in his role as the officer in charge of an immigration control post) conscientiously jotting down Tschiffely's particulars. On the back of this within an hour and a half, they had made their list.

'I have been thinking,' Sefuthi said when it was done, 'that you cannot go to see all of these men. It would take days. Let us work on the cell principle, that you see ten of them only, and ask each of them to secure nine from the list. They must, of course, come here secretly, each man on his own, so that no sign of these gatherings is given.'

'That makes sense, if speed is important.'

'It is.'

'Mr President, may I ask what you have in mind?'

Sefuthi was enigmatic. 'I intend to let the people use their power, and to wield the people as a weapon. I would like you to be here when I discuss matters with them. You will learn my specific intentions then.'

Ombeli knew he would have to be content with this. He took it to be part of his present function as a presidential aide, that he would be taken into Sefuthi's confidence only at the President's chosen time. When it was dark, he set off on his errand.

He found and spoke to four of the ten men he sought. His route to the next one on his list led him towards his own home, and at every corner on the approach to the street where he lived he paused to look for watchers in the shadows. It was not until he came to his own street that this care was rewarded. Across from his house a figure stood, motionless, almost invisible, against the wall.

He moved cautiously down the side of the street on which the watcher lurked, keeping close in to the houses, his eye on the still figure waiting there. Then there was a movement, a toss of the head to throw back the hair, which he thought familiar. He went closer, and sure enough, it was she.

'Ikwezi,' he called softly into the dark. 'It's me, Jules.'

She came round in a startled movement and saw him, but could not yet make him out. 'Jules? Is it you? Let me see you.'

He went to her and saw the relief in her face. 'I was afraid it might be one of those Americans. I have been waiting for you to come home. I was about to give you up, and join the others.'

'What others?'

She told him about Seddall and his friends.

'Good,' Ombeli said. 'Friends of Tschiffely. Then they will be our friends too. I am running an errand for Sefuthi. He and I are lying low in a hut on the east side.' He told her what his errand was. 'I don't know yet why he wants to see these men, but it is obvious that he has made a plan, which is good.'

'Shall I bring the Englishmen to see him?'

'No. He might not want that. Why don't you come with me? I have six more men to see, and then you and I can go together and see what Sefuthi wants to do about the Englishmen. Where are they just now?'

'They were going to leave the car somewhere, and then go to the Hotel Saint-Hilaire.'

'The hotel! That's reckless.'

'Maybe not. As Harry Seddall said, it would be a strange thing for the Americans to interfere with them, since they are British, and will not seem to be part of what is going on.'

'I see that, yes. And they may learn things at the hotel. No doubt some of the Americans will be there.'

They were indeed learning things at the Hotel Saint-Hilaire.

They had left the limousine in a side-street, cached their hunting rifles in a miniature wilderness which took the place of a garden and, following directions given them by Ikwezi before she went off to find her cousin, made their way to the square and walked into the hotel. Their pistols were out of sight under their cotton jackets.

Two soldiers with machine-carbines were posted just inside the door. One of them demanded, 'Where do you think you're going?'

Carver, who was in the lead, regarded him with a combination of great mildness and inflexibility of purpose, and responded. 'Think is not the operative word, laddie. I am in a state of complete certainty about where I'm going, which is, into this hotel.' He patted the man kindly on the shoulder and passed on his way.

They went into the lobby, turned towards the bar, and sat at a table. They laid the game-bags holding the ammunition, and in Carver's case the Heckler and Koch which he had received from Tschiffely in exchange for the pistol he had given him, on the floor under the table.

Fawcett went to the bar and brought back beer. There were a half-dozen officers in the room, all but one of them black. The exception was the most senior, a man who wore the insignia of a lieutenant-colonel, and who was sitting with four other white men at a table near the door.

From this vantage point he had seen them ignore the man at the hotel entrance, and now he came over to their table.

'What's your business here?'

Seddall, with an air of surprise, made a long, slow survey of the man, from head to foot and back again, and stood up. 'How do you do,' he said. 'My name is Seddall.'

The man stared at him, confused by having his assertiveness mistaken, as it appeared to him, for a sociable approach. He recovered himself, and renewed the attack. 'You mistake the position. Military law is in operation in this town, and this hotel is a military post. Civilians are excluded.'

'That's all right,' Seddall said. 'We're all army men. You have the advantage of me. We did not complete the formalities of introduction. What's your name?'

The American was a lanky individual with a long face and a lantern jaw and thinning hair, and grey eyes that showed at the moment that he was baffled by the Englishman's behaviour. He reminded Seddall of Virgil's Aeneas, or was it Homer's Achilles, 'this way and that dividing his swift mind'.

'My name is Evers,' the American said. 'You're British Army I take it, sir. What rank do you hold?'

'Rank of colonel.'

'Regiment?'

'Lancers, 17th/21st. On detachment, Colonel, to Military Intelligence at the Ministry of Defence.'

'And these men?'

'Fawcett's my Number Two, Carver came along for the ride.' He indicated which was which as he spoke.

'Very well. You understand, Colonel Seddall, that I still require to know why you are here.'

Seddall sat down and lit a cigarette from the pack on the table. 'You will understand, my dear Evers, that it would be an odd thing for an Intelligence officer to disclose his purpose to an officer of another country, when that officer is not one with whom he is on officially established relations.'

While Evers was revolving this in his head, Seddall went on. 'Tell me, who are these chaps you're sitting with? I take it they're either CIA or members of Oceanic Enterprises?'

A spasm passed over Evers's face. 'Who the hell told you about Oceanic Enterprises?'

'HMG.'

'HMG. What's that stand for?'

'Her Majesty's Government. To be exact, the Prime Minister.'

'I don't get this.' Evers glanced over, as if for help, to the four men at the table by the door. 'Are you part of this deal that's going down here? I wasn't told to expect a British military presence on this island.'

'The way your boys are carrying on, I'm not surprised to hear it.' Seddall looked thoughtful, which was in fact merely a device to keep his face straight. 'I tell you what, Evers. I'll need a bit of time to decide how much I'm going to tell you. If you rejoin your friends I shall come and talk to you when I'm quite ready.'

Evers mulled this over. 'Okay. But I must ask you not to leave the hotel until we have spoken further. You will realize, I hope, that my position here is a delicate one. Vital matters of international relations and commerce are involved here.'

'My dear sir, I do absolutely realize the delicacy of your situation.' Seddall consulted his fingertips. 'I must say that I do not envy you your present assignment. In my excessively long experience of Intelligence affairs, I have seldom found a military man drafted in to implement a CIA-led operation to come out of it successfully.'

At this, he thought he detected in Evers an instinctive wish to confide in a fellow-soldier his complaints about the nature of the operation on Matetendoro.

But the mask came down. 'We'll talk later.' And Evers went back to his table.

'God, Harry,' Carver said. 'I do believe you could talk a charging rhinoceros into doing your shopping for you. Five more minutes and you'd have had him eating out of your hand.'

'No.' Seddall shook his head. 'He's in a bad spot but he's too stiff-necked for that. A West Point ramrod, our Evers.'

He drained his glass and fixed his gaze on it in a marked way, and Fawcett went off and came back with replenishments for the three of them.

Seddall thanked him, and asked, 'You fellows got any ideas?'

'I haven't got that far yet.' Carver surveyed the room. 'So far, we must agree that in a military sense we are not doing well. We are here, and the enemy, for that's how we have to see it, has a suspicious eye on us and outnumbers us. Ikwezi has gone off to find Ombeli and the President. Tschiffely and Shouanete are seeking Provensal. Our forces, such as they are, are divided and we have no lines of communication. Where does that leave us?'

'You're right on all these points.' Seddall shifted some beer. 'But we can regard it in a more optimistic light. We're not here on a military footing. We're a group of trouble-makers with two things in mind: to screw it up for the Yanks here, and to find the men who murdered Peter Hillyard and – I hope you two have no qualms about this – kill them. Now that may well have to be done back in England, but we may get a line on them here on Matetendoro.'

'I have no qualms,' Fawcett said, and Carver gave his vote on that with a nod. 'You know, I don't feel like a soldier here at all. To me it's more as if we were in a gang war. I think what we can best do is be as tricky and ruthless as all hell, and take any chance that offers.'

'Not bad, I think I feel the same way.' Seddall turned his head towards the table by the door. 'What I'd like to do just now is have a word with the head man of these Oceanic people.'

Carver rose. 'I'll fetch him over for you.'

They watched him cross the room, a tall man with the stride of an athlete, and a commanding, soldierly air. He stood over the five men at their table and spoke a few words. Listened to a man with a close black beard speaking in reply, inclined his head graciously in agreement, and recrossed the room.

'Fellow with beard,' he said. 'Oceanic chairman. Coming to talk to you. Name's Weston.'

The fellow with the beard exchanged some words with his colleagues, got up and came over, accompanied by a man with a pipe in his mouth.

'This is Will Pearce,' he said. 'I'm Glyn Weston.' He sat at the spare chair and Pearce swung one over from an adjoining table. 'What can I do for you, Colonel Seddall? I've got the right man? Evers pointed you out.'

'You've got the right man. Are you CIA, Weston? Or National Security Agency, or Defense Intelligence, or what?'

Weston, unlike Evers, was not fazed by this impertinence. He was a man, remarkably for the circumstances, who existed in a state of quietude, but whose manner was a mixture of alertness and thought. 'None of these. I'm an academic who was called on by the Administration in Washington to take on the chairmanship of Oceanic Enterprises. I did this gladly. My field is business administration, and I liked the idea of doing it in practice.'

'But this attempt,' Seddall threw his arms out to indicate the uniformed men elsewhere in the room, 'at a clandestine military takeover can hardly be what you anticipated. It's not what you teach your MBA students, is it?'

'I'm CIA, Seddall,' Will Pearce said, 'and Professor Weston is not going to answer that question.'

Weston turned his untroubled brown eyes on Pearce. 'Be easy, Will. I can see that you must be hostile to Colonel Seddall's arrival on the scene, but the answer to his question is surely self-evident. No, this is hardly what I anticipated.'

'That's enough,' Pearce said. 'This conversation is over. The trouble with you academics, Weston, is that you don't know what goes on in the real world.'

211

Tony Carver laughed. 'The real world, Mr Pearce, according to my experience, is terra incognita to the CIA.'

Pearce took the pipe out of his mouth and pointed it at Seddall as if it were a death-dealing wand. 'What have you guys done with Art Foxberry? If you've harmed him, you're dead.'

Seddall raised an eyebrow at Fawcett. 'Name meaning anything to you? Art Foxberry?'

'Never heard of him.'

'Tony?'

'No. No Foxberries in my book.'

Seddall went back to Pearce. 'When did you lose sight of this Foxberry?'

'You know damn well when. When you guys lifted Sefuthi and Provensal out of the presidential palace last night.'

Mick Fawcett raised his eyebrows as one who despairs of the sanity of another. 'You're fantasizing, Mr Pearce, we didn't land on this island till about noon today, and we've only been in town for an hour.'

'Pray tell me,' Seddall asked the CIA man, 'who is Brother Foxberry?'

Pearce scowled at the three Englishmen as if he were Abraham Lincoln contemplating the secessionist southern states. 'If you don't know, you don't need to know.'

'Suits me.' Seddall spent some time examining and lighting a cigarette. 'This name, this Provensal. Who does that belong to?'

'Provensal is a black American traitor, and next time I see him I am personally going to blow his head off.'

Carver yawned. 'Pearce, old boy, that's a rather violent way to talk, and if I hear any more of it, I shall personally push your throat through the back of your neck.'

'Good heavens, Tony,' Fawcett said in admiration. 'Where on earth did you pick that phrase up?'

'Can't remember the name of it, Mick, but it was some mean streets crime movie.'

Pearce's chair fell over backwards as he leapt up. 'Take my advice, you three, and get out of town before it's too late.'

Weston, as if he had been off in a world of his own during the recent verbal fracas, came to his feet and said, 'Well, good to have talked with you. See you later.' He walked away, not to rejoin the table by the door, but straight past it and out of the hotel, as if he felt the need of some fresh air.

Pearce had stayed too long after his exit line to leave with the dramatic effect it was entitled to, and he went in a kind of loping gait back to his companions, whereupon they fell into a babble of talk, with many dark glances in the direction of the three intruders.

Seddall observed all this and shrugged. 'Learned something, anyway,' he said. 'Provensal got away.'

Carver got up suddenly and went to the bar, and had some speech with the barman. He was clearly pleased with the result, and came back wearing a smug and cheerful countenance.

'You're a poor corps commander, Seddall. You have forgotten that an army marches on its stomach. I asked the barman if the hotel was able to serve food despite all these goings-on and he said yes. We can eat now, in the dining-room.'

Seddall grinned up at him. 'We are infinitely obliged to you for your resourcefulness, aren't we, Mick? Let's go. Is this a late lunch, or an early dinner?'

'It'll be dark by the time we finish eating, 'Fawcett said. 'So I guess it's an early dinner. Think of it as supper before the theatre.'

'Appropriate.' Carver picked up the bag with the Heckler and Koch in it. 'I'll be extremely surprised if we don't see some theatricals before we're very much older.'

There was a stir among the Americans as they walked through into the dining-room, which they found to be empty. Seddall made straight for the far end. 'Backs to the wall is a sound tactic in hostile territory. You can see what's coming at you. Let's put these two tables together.'

'Lo and behold,' Fawcett said as they were in the act of ordering their meal. Two of the officers from the bar had come in, and were taking their places at a table in the middle of the room. 'We are under observation.'

They dined on seafood and a vegetable curry which was so hot they stared at each other speechless and with streaming eyes. They rounded off with *bananes flambées*, a good taste of burnt rum and manna to the sweetest tooth. When that was done coffee was ordered.

They sighed, replete and content. Seddall ignited one of his cigarettes and Carver one of his cigars.

A tall black man in a pale blue silk suit that Seddall had not seen, and did not expect to see, bettered, came out of the kitchen and delivered himself of a courteous greeting.

'Colonel Seddall, I believe. My name is Provensal. Imagine that I am the manager of the hotel, and ask me to join you. If these men down there know me we'll be aware of it soon enough. If not, then so much to the good.'

'Provensal? Great Scott! How do you do? Aren't you running a hell of a risk coming in here? How do you come to know my name? Ah, Tschiffely must have found you.'

'In fact, I found Tschiffely. I was coming ashore from my yacht to make a tentative reconnaissance, to see what shape matters were taking here, when I heard a man screaming and so directed the launch to where the screams were coming from.'

The coffee arrived; four cups, so it could be deduced that Provensal was on terms with the people here.

Seddall passed a cup to the new arrival. 'What was causing the screams?'

Provensal smiled. It was a smile at once wry and diabolical. 'My Shouanete was eliciting information from an American person called Foxberry. Shouanete has – how shall I put it? – a way with her. Your friend Tschiffely was not taking it too well.'

Seddall tried to picture the beautiful woman he had met on the seashore in the part of torturer, and failed. He decided he must be a trifle limited in his view of human beings. 'I would hope Foxberry wasn't taking it too well either. What did she succeed in eliciting from him?'

Carver put his oar in. 'Got to interrupt. It seems to me we ought to have a concerted plan of action as to what we do if the Americans

214

come in that door. As soon as they see Provensal they'll come gunning for him.'

'We can go out through the kitchen,' Provensal said, 'and vanish. There's a warren of backstreets out there for us to lose ourselves in.'

'Then that's what we'll do,' Seddall said.

'Still needs covering fire,' Carver said. 'I've got the Heckler and Koch, so I'll give you blokes sixty seconds, and no more, of gallant rearguard action and then I'll run for it.'

'Stout fella,' Seddall said. 'Right. If and when we break for it, we stick together, all four of us. If we scatter we'll take far too long to connect up again. Line of retreat planned and covering party detailed. We wait outside for Tony and then go. So, Provensal, what did this Foxberry tell Shouanete?'

Provensal drained his coffee cup and pushed it away. 'The answer to the puzzle,' he said. 'But from where I sit, despite the good sense of your preparations for a fast get-out from the military point of view, I think we'd be wise to go now. It would be wise for me, and what I have to tell is not just a matter of short answers. To sit here is to tempt Providence.'

'Then let's do it. Where do we go?'

'Out into the back streets behind the hotel. Get far enough in among them and we'll be tolerably secure, and if we want a place to sit and talk, I daresay we will find a café of some sort. Won't be up to much, or very clean, but what do we care about that?'

It did not surprise Seddall that this man had made a fortune or, to be accurate, several fortunes. He knew how to take and use risks, but he was also sensibly cautious; and in addition he was incisive, and had the gift of quick thinking when that was called for.

'We're moving out,' he told Carver and Fawcett. 'We go by way of the kitchen. Provensal first, then Mick and me, Tony last, just in case, since he has the most firepower.'

Provensal rose and went through the swing doors into the kitchen. His departure provoked no reaction from the pair of observers down the room, so his idea that they would assume him to be of the hotel was justified.

'Now for the tricky part,' Seddall said. 'Come on, Mick. And Tony, you come after us. We don't want shots fired if we can help it, and I don't want any heroics.'

They moved nimbly but without haste, and the element of surprise must have helped, because by the time Carver was on his way through the kitchen doors the two officers were only just getting to their feet.

The kitchen staff watched them go towards Provensal, who was waiting at the exit door, with amiable faces, so either it was understood that the departing trio were on the side of the angels, or Provensal had made them rich.

'Follow me,' Provensal said, and led them out of the hotel, and into the backstreets that lay beyond. Whatever alarm their sudden retreat had caused, they were so quickly lost in that maze of lanes and alleys that they heard no sound of pursuit.

They moved fast for about twenty minutes and then Provensal said, 'This place should do us.'

This place was a filthy establishment called the Café Babou, and they had not been sitting at one of its few tables for more than a minute when they became aware that it was inhabited by cockroaches and at least two rats.

'I bet the coffee's good, all the same,' Carver said, and he was soon proved to be right.

'Where did we leave off?' Seddall said to Provensal. 'Yes, I remember. Back at the hotel you said that Shouanete had extracted from Foxberry what you described as the answer to the puzzle. What puzzle, and what answer?'

'This puzzle: why the CIA came into this Oceanic Enterprises thing in the first place, when it's only the British who need a place to dump their nuclear waste. In the States we have all the desert we need, from the Administration's point of view. The answer: the CIA did a think-tank on East Africa and Central Africa, the usual crap, long-term visualization of the degree of political stability to be anticipated, and it came up very messy.'

'Messy?'

'Sure, messy, in their terms. They anticipate – I'm using what I suppose to be their language, I don't think Foxberry was talking quite like this by the time Shouana had finished with him – that what they regard as valuable western political institutions like parliamentary democracy, as learnt from the former colonial masters, may give way before the forces represented by the instinct of the African peoples to adopt forms of rule appropriate to their ancient heritage.'

'Which means that they anticipate what they would, I fancy, describe as chaos?'

'Quite so. And chaos, or at least visible and recognizable chaos, is not the American way. Therefore, the CIA's ambition in Matetendoro is to replace the President with a willing and subservient tool, so that they can build here on the island an airstrip from which to fly in supplies to this or that area to whichever group of combatants – they foresee this chaos, oddly enough, as adopting familiar shapes – is assessed by them as being most likely to arrange affairs in a manner that coincides with the American view of how the world should run itself.'

'Meaning, I assume, that they want to make as much of the world as possible safe for democracy and unthreatening to the American dream and to Thanksgiving and to the Fourth of July.'

Provensal leaned forward and gave Seddall a friendly punch on the shoulder. 'Man, Seddall, it sounds to me as if you and I speak the same language.'

A friendly punch from Provensal was like a friendly kick from a mule, but in the furtherance of solidarity Seddall bore it in the spirit in which it was intended.

'Yes,' he said. 'I think we have at least that in common. But, by God, that's a useful thing to know. There are countries in Europe that would not be too keen on Washington adopting an attitude like that to Africa.'

'Yeah,' and Provensal tapped his forehead sagaciously, 'but this ain't Washington, this is Langley, this is the CIA. It's run amok before and it will do it again.'

'But look here,' Fawcett said. 'If this is an independent and secret CIA operation, I still don't see how they can get Special Forces troops without Washington knowing.'

'Son,' Provensal was tolerant, 'the CIA can get troops out of the Pentagon for minor excursions on false pretences, and without the White House or the Senate Defense Committee getting wind of it at all. But I don't think these men are Special Forces. I think that's in-house propaganda. I think these men are quick recruits to the CIA from the military as a whole.'

'All right,' Fawcett said, 'I can accept that. But these men were flown in here from what sounds like a cruiser of the US Navy. She's said to be lying out of sight over the horizon.'

Provensal appraised Fawcett with a perplexed but kindly eye. 'For that, son, all you need is papers to the captain of the cruiser classified top secret, which follow secret instructions from the CIA via the Pentagon to his commanding admiral saying that this little local affair is in the national interest.'

The four men sat quietly for a space, each of them thinking his own thoughts. It was Seddall who spoke first.

'This may seem irrelevant to you,' he said, 'compared with these issues of international policy, but I'd be interested to hear how you and Peter Hillyard came to know each other. It's because of him that we came here, you see. I want to track down the men who killed him.'

The face opposite became grave and he saw anger come alive in the depths of the eyes. 'Peter gave me my first big chance. He was an investment banker in New York, and I needed a loan for this project, and I'd tried a dozen banks before I put the idea to him, and he financed it. We'd been friends ever since. He quit banking in his middle age when he inherited his uncle's farm.

'After he returned to live in England he became involved in Greenpeace. So when I learned about this little caper here we wrote to each other and talked about it. We shared a lot of thinking about what mattered in life.'

He sat back and looked at Seddall a little sideways. 'If you find out who murdered him, what are you doing to do about it? Hand them over to the law?'

'No. Kill them.'

Provensal appeared to relax. 'Good. When I find out who it was, I'll let you know.'

Seddall was astonished at this. Who was this man, that he had access to so much information that governments and their servants hoped to keep private? 'Do you seriously think you might?'

'I know that I will. If you get there first, tell me. And tell me when they're dead. I'll sleep better, knowing that.'

'I will. Tell me, did Shouanete get anything else out of Foxberry?'

'There was nothing else to be got, once he came out with that. He was too cut up by then, and passing out from loss of blood, so she shot him.'

A word had caught Carver's attention, and the way it had been said. 'Cut up. Did you mean that literally?'

'Yes, I did. Shouana is a woman from the mountains of the Caucasus. They know how to use knives there. She believes in cold steel. So do I, for that matter.'

The three Englishmen sat there, as Seddall had done some minutes before, comparing this idea of Shouanete with the beautiful and striking woman they had first come upon disporting herself with innocent pleasure in the sea.

Provensal contemplated them with a dark amusement, thinking of how many cultures there were in this wide world that had no bridges between them.

Chapter Eighteen

Ombeli had two more men to see of those chosen, in President Sefuthi's phrase, to be 'cell leaders' in the execution of his grand and mysterious design. He and Ikwezi had been running between one house and the next, in keeping with Sefuthi's exhortation that speed was of the essence.

Ikwezi was not so fit as Ombeli, and would have been glad of a break from all this exertion, and a glass of beer. As they passed the Café Babou she threw a wistful eye at the murky window.

'Stop!' she exclaimed.

'We can't stop,' her cousin said.

'No, wait just a moment.'

She went back to the window and peered through it. 'Jules, come here. It is Provensal and the three Englishmen I told you about. There, in the café.'

'I don't believe it.' He came to her and said, 'Provensal, true enough. And you recognize the Englishmen, Tschiffely's friends? In we go then.'

They received a warm greeting from Provensal, but the others saw a man in the uniform the Americans had adopted for their invasion and were instantly on the qui vive, pistols drawn and safety catches off.

Provensal stretched his arms out over their poised weapons. 'Put your guns away, these are friends of mine.'

'We know the woman.' Seddall was still wary. 'Who's the man? How well do you know him?'

'I've known him for years. He is Ikwezi's cousin, Jules Ombeli, commandant, or major, in the army of Matetendoro.'

Seddall rose and put his pistol away. 'I do apologize, Major Ombeli. The thing is that since the Americans have copied your uniforms, and the state of affairs here being exceptionally volatile, one can take nothing on trust.'

Ombeli briefly shook the proffered hand and threw himself into a rickety chair at the next table. 'I would have done the same. We are run off our feet tonight,' he said by way of explaining his collapse into the chair. 'Ikwezi, sit down yourself, you are more tired than I am, and introduce me to your friends. But first, some beer.'

He called out to the bead curtain at the back of the small room. 'Kamau! Beer for a man dying of thirst!'

'Beer sounds good,' Fawcett said, a thought which was echoed by all, and the ancient wreck of a man who presided over the café brought them their beers, two at a time.

'Let us bring each other up to date,' Seddall said when the introductions had been effected, and they did this.

'So, President Sefuthi has a plan,' Provensal said. 'I'd like to see him. Can you take me to him?'

'I have still two men to see. Can you wait twenty minutes? I shall come back here, and then take you to him.' Ombeli turned to Seddall. 'This is not easy for me to say, but I dare not take you and your friends to him. White men stand out here, and I cannot risk being followed to where he is hiding.'

Seddall told him that this was only common sense. 'But what shall we do in the meantime? I think it's not a good idea to stay too long in a place like this. And we will want, I take it, to communicate afterwards so that we can coordinate our actions, so that we don't get in each other's way.'

Provensal took out his wallet and extracted a card from it and scribbled something on the blank side. 'Why don't you go to the yacht? I sent Shouanete and Daniel and Tschiffely on board before I came into town. The launch is lying just offshore by the coconut grove where I found them. Ikwezi, if I describe to you where that is, are you happy to be their guide and also to go with them out to the yacht?'

'Of course I am. It will be a pleasant change from running around the streets with Jules.'

'Then take this card and show it to the officer in charge of the launch, and he will take all of you out to the yacht and return the launch to wait for me. You would be as well to go now. I shall wait here for you, Ombeli, or accompany you on the last stage of your errand, whichever seems best to you.'

'Come with me, if you don't object to running instead of walking.'

'Not in the least. Do me good.'

They left the café in a group. Provensal and Ombeli turned left and ran swiftly towards the fulfilment of the President's orders. Ikwezi led her charges down the street to the right.

Soon they heard the sounds of the sea and of the wind in the tops of the coconut palms. Overhead the night was alive with the intense brightness or the stars, but it was the moon that reigned, a huge white orb low in the sky.

Where the trees ended Ikwezi stopped them. The beach and the sea were bathed in moonlight. Fifty yards offshore the launch lay to her anchor. 'Wait here,' Ikwezi said. 'If they see you they will be alarmed. This is as it was when you saw Ombeli. No one can tell friend from enemy at first glance. I shall swim out to the boat.'

'Provensal's card,' Seddall said. 'That's our passport, so to speak. How will you keep it dry? They might not trust it if the ink was all run.'

'Here.' Carver produced a large bandana from his pocket. 'Tie it on top of your head with this.'

'That's good,' Ikwezi said. 'And I shall swim breast-stroke, with my head up.'

She tied the bandana beneath her chin and over the top of her head, and Carver tucked the card in securely.

She stepped out of her trainers and ran down the beach in her shorts and tee-shirt and straight into the ocean. They watched the shine and sparkle of her passage as she swam out to the launch. Two men helped her over the side, and in no time at all the anchor was up and the launch was heading for the shore.

Some hours later, wined and dined to his heart's content, Seddall fell into bed, and dreamed a dreamless sleep. He was awakened by the throbbing of the ship's engines, and heaved himself out of bed. Still a bit bemused by having just come out of such a deep sleep, he threw on some clothes and left his cabin – or rather, so luxurious was it, stateroom – to find out what this activity betokened.

He dropped by the saloon, where a steward brought him coffee. He swallowed a first cup at tongue-burning speed, so that he began to feel seriously awake, and carried a second up on deck with him.

The ship had way on and was making an easy starboard turn towards the northern horizon. Tschiffely and Fawcett were sitting under the awning, eating breakfast. 'What's going on?' he asked them.

'We're eating bacon and eggs and the most wonderful fresh rolls, warm from the oven,' Fawcett said. 'That's what's going on. I shall never travel with any other shipping line, they really treat you well here.'

Seddall drained the last of the coffee from the cup he was carrying and put it on the table. 'That wasn't quite what I had in mind. My question tended to the fact that all of a sudden this vessel is in motion. Therefore I ask myself why, and where are we bound?'

'It took us by surprise too.'

The words came from Fawcett, but it was Tschiffely Seddall looked at. Seddall had noticed last night that the poet's face was tight and enclosed, and it was the same this morning. This was not the Tschiffely he was used to. Seddall supposed that the man had been deeply shocked and disturbed by being present when Shouanete was working on Foxberry with the knife.

And yet, there was more to it than that. When they gathered for dinner in the saloon Tschiffely had made a point of staying as far as he could from her, and not a word had been exchanged between them. The look on his face was that of a man who had been dramatically disillusioned; of a lover, even, who found that he had misled himself in his admiration of the loved one.

Seddall shook himself out of these reflections. If he was accurate in his speculations, then his object must be to see to it that Tschiffely, in his disordered state, did nothing to hazard whatever kind of success was to be won here.

Fawcett completed his return to the urgent matters of the day with, 'Harry, are you feeling all right?'

'Fine, thanks. Just thinking about something. Is Provensal on board? We'd hardly be under way without his authority.'

The ship had, by now, come round in a full circle, and was on a heading for the harbour of Saint-Hilaire.

'Yes,' Tschiffely said in a flat tone. 'Saw him not long ago. I think he's on the bridge. No, look, here he comes now.'

Provensal came along the deck, wearing cream-coloured linen trousers and a yellow cotton shirt. 'Seddall, good day to you. I saw you from the bridge and I've ordered breakfast brought to you here. Let's sit down. I expect you are wondering why we are making for the harbour?'

'I must thank you for your generous hospitality to us.' At this moment Seddall's breakfast arrived on a tray, and was laid before him. 'And, Provensal, for your thoughtfulness. But yes, I do wonder why we are making for the harbour.'

Provensal laughed like a man well pleased with himself, and pleased to be part of a successful enterprise. He was in such a state of elation that he slapped Seddall on the knee.

'We are going to tie up at the pierhead,' he said. 'It is a part of President Sefuthi's plan, which Ombeli mentioned to us. But now it has been embroidered a little since I talked with Sefuthi. We, this ship, are going to be, not exactly the bait, but the lure.'

Seddall had embarked on the bacon and eggs, and had to wait until he had swallowed the current mouthful before he could say anything in response. Provensal, full of unexplained merriment, kept an expectant eye on him.

'The lure for what?' Seddall said.

'To bring the Americans on to the pier.'

'And then?'

'I am going to be very evil, Seddall, and not tell you. It will be such an extraordinary surprise when it happens. I can assure you, I almost wish I did not know myself – to see it happen without knowing about it in advance will be glorious.'

There was more hearty laughter.

'Provensal, I am your guest and eating your food, and this is a first-rate breakfast, but I tell you, you're a bastard.'

Provensal was beside himself with pleasure. 'Yes, Seddall, I am a bastard. I am a complete bastard. But wait, and when you have seen, you will forgive me. So eat your nice breakfast and possess your soul in patience.'

Seddall ate his nice breakfast, and watched with Fawcett and Tschiffely as the ship approached Saint-Hilaire, angling her way past the white beach with the town rising behind it, first a mess of nondescript shacks and above them, on the salubrious hillside, the large white houses in the better part of town.

The ship was piloted adroitly up to the pierhead and hung there with skilful manoeuvring of engines and rudder while the cables were got ashore and thrown round the bollards, all as smoothly as if the operation had been rehearsed; which it had, although Seddall had not been there to see it the first time.

'What happens now?' Seddall asked Provensal.

'We wait, and hope that the enemy will come to the lure. Which is not only the ship, but me myself.'

For this reason Provensal made a point of being conspicuous, alternately strolling the deck on the yacht's landward side and leaning on the rail to examine the town.

The three men at the breakfast table sat and drank their coffee, and waited on events. While they waited, Carver joined them, waved away the offer of breakfast, and asked for good strong coffee.

Soon after, Ikwezi and Shouanete appeared, Ikwezi yawning sleepily and Shouanete looking as vigorous as ever.

'I feel absolutely shagged,' Ikwezi said.

'That's good,' Shouanete said, 'otherwise I'd have been wasting my time last night.'

Seddall was unused to these public candours, but Carver grinned broadly. Tschiffely got up and walked away forward.

'What's up with him?' Carver inquired. 'Is he shy?'

'He's shy of me,' Shouanete said, 'since I did my number on Mr Foxberry of the CIA.'

'I confess that it's made me a little shy of you myself,' Carver said. 'But you got the goods, and by all accounts Foxberry was not a beautiful man.'

'He was a shit from way back,' Shouanete said, 'but that's not why I did it. We needed that information, and I thought I might be able to get it out of him, so I did my best.'

Carver let his eyes rest on her for a while. 'I've got a friend you might get on with. I'll give you his address before we part company, if you like.'

'Is he gay too?'

'No, he likes women.'

She nodded thoughtfully. 'I kind of fancy your judgment of people, Carver, since you called me down when we were back at Ikwezi's house, so yes, I'd appreciate that.'

'Hallo,' Fawcett said. 'Something's up.' He stood with his hand shading his eyes against the late morning sun, and looking up the pier. 'It looks as if the enemy is massing his forces.'

All of them except Shouanete looked up the pier, and saw, just behind the hut where Ombeli had held post as immigration and customs officer, a grouping of the Americans, more of them than they had seen in one place before.

Provensal joined them. 'It's working,' he said. 'Now we shall see.'

An advance party of the Americans, six men, began to come down the pier. They had not taken three paces when Provensal spoke into a handset. 'Do it,' he said.

The sides of the forward deckhouse fell outwards and the racket of automatic cannon fire beat on their ears. The shells struck on the surface of the pier sixty feet in front of the vanguard, who stopped short and threw themselves down.

'Holy cats!' Carver exclaimed. 'What is this? A pirate ship?'

'Twin 30mm cannon,' Provensal said, keeping his eyes on the shore. 'Every millionaire's yacht ought to have them.'

The six men on the pier, having realized that the cannon fire was the equivalent of a warning shot across their bows, scrambled up and ran back to join the main body.

'What are they doing now?' Seddall asked Fawcett, who was looking through a pair of binoculars.

'Conferring in an animated manner. Hallo, here come some more people. Looks like townsfolk out to see the fun.'

'Let me see,' and Provensal took the glasses from him. 'Aha, it is beginning to happen. Sefuthi is playing his master-stroke at last. Take a look, Seddall.'

Seddall took a look. They came from everywhere, trickling out of every street that opened from the town, and emerging from among the coconut palms, and coming to a stand fifty yards in the rear of the Americans. Behind the front rank they massed loosely, and still the town fed its people into the crowd, so that the mass became denser with every minute.

Seddall handed the glasses to Fawcett, their rightful owner, and turned to Provensal. 'What's going on? These people appear to be unarmed.'

'That,' said Provensal, 'is the point. Passive resistance but with a touch of menace. See how they have formed a half circle round the Americans. Not menace, perhaps, but challenge. Like they're saying, "So, what are you going to do now, kill us all, unarmed as we are, and say to hell with world opinion?" That is Sefuthi's great plan.'

Seddall took his time, weighing up, as well as he could, the implications, the invisible dynamic forces in the picture which was unfolding in front of him.

'It might work,' he said slowly. 'The townspeople will have more patience than the Americans for just standing there. To the Americans it will be a problem which requires resolution.'

'Good,' Provensal said approvingly. 'You've got the essence of it. It's the difference between two cultures, and that is what Sefuthi is banking on.'

'And where is he, right now?'

'Back in town. His judgment is that he'd be irrelevant. It is between the Matetendorans and the invaders.'

'So we wait, all of us. We here on the yacht, the Americans, and the people of Saint-Hilaire, and Sefuthi back in town, we wait until something gives.'

'That's it,' Provensal said. 'Unless we help the Americans to break the deadlock by making a move from here.'

'Such as?'

'We could make them a proposal.'

'Go on.'

'On these lines. That we have discovered why the CIA wanted to exercise its influence here: in short, that we know of their policy to intervene in the affairs of the African continent, and that they wanted an airstrip here, and why they wanted it.

'We would tell them, further, that Britain now has no interest in prolonging the existence of Oceanic Enterprises, so the corporation no longer exists effectively as a cover.

'We would say that for their purposes it was appropriate and necessary for their own intentions here to be secret, and that they are secret no longer, but that those of us who know the secret will keep it, if they go quietly, now. It suits none of us to publish it, neither Sefuthi, nor me, nor your government. And that they may use my wireless operator to communicate with their cruiser and call in helicopters to remove them.'

Seddall considered this proposal, and found it concise and persuasive. 'I have only one reservation. If you go down the pier to deliver this spiel there's a good chance they'll shoot you before you get a word out. They're wrought-up and tetchy, these lads, and they know you've done as much as anyone to put a spoke in their wheel.'

Provensal came up with another of his hearty laughs, but this one had a caustic note in it that put Seddall on his guard instantly. 'That is why I have had it written out, so that they may assess it briefly before accepting it. They must accept it, of course. They have no option. So what we need is someone to carry our message to them under a flag of truce.'

Seddall had seen it coming. 'Why are you looking at me like that, Provensal? Why the hell should I carry the bloody thing?'

He had never seen a face so refulgent with mischief joined with active intelligence. 'For one thing, you are fearless. For another, if you want me, when I have found out the names of the three men who killed Peter Hillyard, to pass them on to you, it is only fair that you should do me a favour.'

It was Seddall's turn to laugh. 'Provensal,' he said, 'I've never met a man more like me in my life. No wonder I called you a bastard back there. All right, I'll carry the bloody paper, but ask Shouanete to come with me. If she's in the right mood she'll scare the living daylights out of them, and they'll be too paralysed to do anything. And I'll take Carver and Fawcett as back-up.'

'Ah, you are beginning to value her for what she is. I will ask her, and I think she will agree.'

Seddall became brisk. 'We'll have a briefing before we go. I would like you and the man in charge of the cannon to be there, if you have no objection. Just one thing, though. As well as the names of the three men, I would very much like to know who, if anyone, in the British Government was associated with the purpose to murder Peter Hillyard.'

'Knowledge, or proof?'

'Proof will be impossible, I should think. But if you can give me the knowledge, I shouldn't wonder but I might be able to make good use of it.'

The gangway was let down on to the pier, and four crewmen, armed, stood on the pier to guard it. Seddall held his briefing at the top of the gangway.

'Tony, Mick, if they make a move to fire on us, Shouanete and I will go as quick as light to the ground and if you are quick enough you'll get the drop on them, and if not shoot at anyone who's making hostile motions with a weapon.'

He turned to the man in charge of the cannon. 'If a shooting war does start, fire into the Americans. It will have to be the last word in accurate shooting, because we must on no account injure a member of the island populace.'

'Count on me for that.'

'Document,' Seddall said, and Provensal, with an ironic bow, handed him a large manila envelope.

Seddall, remembering Waterloo, and hoping he was on the winning side, said, 'The Scots Greys will advance,' and set off down the gangway.

As they walked up the pier, he said to Shouanete, 'We'll talk on the way. It makes us look cool. Are you in a dangerous mood this morning?'

'Brother,' she said, 'today I could kill crocodiles with my bare hands and eat them after.'

'Hot stuff. Watch these bastards. The game's up, so far as they're concerned, but they may be too stupid to know it. I see Tschiffely's upset with you. Over Foxberry, I take it.'

'That's it. And also, we fucked, and I guess it meant more to him than it did to me. It was great fucking, you know, but that's all it was. That's all it ever is with me. So because it was great he began idealizing, and then when I cut Foxberry he lost his ideal.' She shrugged. 'Tough tit, but I guess it's not unreasonable that, even nowadays, some poets are romantic.'

She looked at Seddall with a lovely smile that transformed her tragically drooping mouth. 'It's funny. I like him for it.'

'No, I can make sense of that,' he said. 'It's bewildering, sometimes, how complicated life can be.'

'It doesn't complicate anything for me,' she said. 'Life can be simple if you make it simple, and that's what I do.'

'You have unique attitudes and a unique way of living,' he said. 'I could talk to you for hours. I really believe I would learn a lot.'

'I think you would too, but this is not the moment. We're getting there.'

She moved off to one side as they came to the hut where the leaders of the Americans were grouped. Seddall approached them and, though he was not in uniform, gave Evers a formal salute, and extended the envelope.

'A proposal, sir, for your consideration,' he said. 'If you will be kind enough to peruse it, I shall return to the ship while you and your colleagues come to a decision. We shall be happy to receive your answer on board. Good day to you, sir.'

He saluted again, turned about, and went down the pier with Shouanete once more at his side, and following, this time, Carver and Fawcett.

'Hot damn,' she said, 'you turned on the high-toned lingo there, all right.'

'Diplomacy,' he said, 'is best conducted in such forms. It serves to eliminate the interaction of personalities from the conduct of business.'

'Maybe I could learn things from you too,' she said.

'Maybe,' he said, 'but there's nothing worth learning in that area. It's a load of bullshit. Got nothing to do with life and living.'

She slipped forward to walk backwards in front of him, and her sexual appeal was so strong and palpable that he wished he had fucked her in the coconut grove last night himself. He made an effort to pull himself together, and remembered Jane, but he still wished there had been just one night among the palm trees and under the stars with Shouanete. Damn it, he was behaving like a schoolboy. What was she saying? Oh yes, a reference to his use of dispassionate multisyllabic language.

'You move in and out of it, though, just like that. Doesn't that make you a hypocrite?'

'No, it makes me an actor. Though I may well be a hypocrite into the bargain. In fact,' he said, detecting a truth recently demonstrated, 'I know I am. Do you know what, Shouanete, I'm going to miss you when I get home.'

'Well, I won't be dead,' she said. 'You can always call me. So long as there's none of this what they call falling in love. I've got no time for that. This friend of Carver's he wants me to meet, do you know who that is?'

'Friend of Tony's? No idea.'

'I'm going to go for it. Carver's a good man. If he says we'd do well together, he's likely right. And he knows what I'm like, so he won't be thinking grand passion stuff.'

Talking in this suddenly and surprisingly intimate fashion, they came to the pierhead and went up on to the ship, to be met at the head of the gangway by Provensal.

'Well, that went off without fireworks,' he said. 'What did they say to you?'

'They didn't say one word,' Shouanete said. 'This Colonel Harry Seddall bamboozled them with fancy talk, and just turned round and came away.'

'I told them we'd hear their answer on board,' Seddall said.

'We shouldn't have too long to wait,' Provensal said. 'It's a simple enough proposal.'

The sound of singing came to Seddall's ear. It came from the gathered Matetendorans. The arc they stood in had come even closer to the Americans. He could see them sway rhythmically to the music as they sang, sway with their whole bodies and their arms above their heads.

'What are they singing?' he asked Provensal.

'They are singing of freedom, and of their traditions, their ancient tribal traditions. It will get into the blood of the Americans, and weaken their resolve, if they have any left.'

Seddall cast his eyes up to the mountains in the centre of the island, brought them down to Saint-Hilaire, and then turned to the sun-smitten radiance of the ocean. He turned again to face the Americans assembled at the head of the pier, who now looked to him ridiculous; in spite of their array of automatic weapons they appeared impotent before the huge crowd of unarmed people, singing and moving to their own music.

He was sure, now, in his own mind, that it was the Americans who had killed Peter Hillyard.

'You're right,' he told Provensal. 'We won't have long to wait before we hear from them. They've run out of options.'

'Waiting's over.' Provensal pointed. Two men had started on their way towards the ship. 'They're coming now. Let's stage it a bit, as if we think it's all settled. Let's look as if we're all here on vacation. Work on their mind-set.'

Chapter Nineteen

It was Lieutenant-Colonel Evers and the rancorous CIA man, Will Pearce, who came down the pier to the ship.

They were brought to Provensal by the deckhand who had been manning the entry at the head of the gangway. Provensal and his guests were sitting under the awning, drinking cool drinks.

Pearce stopped at the sight of them: Provensal himself; the women, Ikwezi and Shouanete, in their bikinis; Seddall and his two sidekicks; and Tschiffely, whom he had met before and who did not evoke pleasant memories.

'The Unholy Alliance,' he said.

'Well,' Provensal said, 'we are not members of the Little Church Around the Corner in New York City, but neither are we the children of the Devil.'

'Speak for yourself,' Shouanete said lazily, without going to the trouble of opening her eyes.

Provensal got up and went over to the visitors. 'What is your response to our proposal?'

'I accept it,' Evers said.

'Good,' Provensal said. 'Do you want to use my wireless to contact the USS Whatever-it's-called, and call in helicopters to evacuate you?'

'I do. Our own wireless equipment is damaged.'

'Then let's go, and get it done.'

Pearce held up a hand. 'Wait one moment. I need to know what has happened to my colleague Foxberry.'

There was a slight pause, and then Shouanete, still with her eyes closed, said, 'He got dead. He stepped in front of a bullet.'

'I had supposed as much. Where is his body? I wish to have it transported back to the States for proper burial.'

'You're too late, dude,' the languid Shouanete said. 'We put his body out for the sharks, and with the blood and all, they came running. So you could say, he's been buried at sea.'

'Who shot him?' Pearce demanded.

Shouanete opened an eye and looked at him.

Seddall intervened. 'Details of that kind are not inquired of after hostilities have ceased and when a truce has been negotiated. I take that to be how you would view the state of affairs which now obtains, Colonel Evers? I speak as one professional soldier to another.'

'Yes,' Evers replied. 'That is how I see it. I wish to move ahead with this business so that my men can be flown out as soon as possible. If you are ready to proceed to the wireless shack,' he said to Provensal, 'I'm with you.'

They set off, and Pearce followed in their wake. They were done in twenty minutes, and Provensal accompanied them to the gangway and saw them off.

He came back well pleased with himself. 'That is the last time we shall have any dealings with them,' he said cheerfully. 'Now we shall have lunch, and later, after the helicopters have been and gone, I shall have a little conference with President Sefuthi, and then we shall set sail.'

'Back to Mombasa?' Shouanete asked him.

'No. I may have some business to transact in London. I plan to sail through the Suez Canal and get a plane from Cairo. You must be ready to go back to London yourself, Seddall, you and your compadres. Why don't you all come up to Port Said on the yacht, and we can fly from Cairo together?'

This felt good to Seddall. It meant he would be back with Jane Kneller a damn sight sooner than if they went back to Mombasa on the charter boat.

'I would certainly like that,' he said. 'But we've got the charter boat to return.'

'I'll take her back to Mombasa for you,' Tschiffely said. 'I'd like some time alone. To have the boat to myself would be ideal.'

He was still closed in on himself. Yes, not only would it be convenient for Seddall and the others, but it might be of some help to Tschiffely. He had a dream and a nightmare to consign to the past, and when a man needed to do that, some of it was best dealt with on his own. And it was as clear as daylight that he could not stand being near Shouanete.

Out of respect for the man's feelings, Seddall pretended to know nothing of this. 'Steve,' he said, 'I really am extremely grateful, if you're certain that would suit you.'

'No,' Tschiffely said. 'No need to thank me. It does truly appeal to me, to have that boat to myself. Since she's in the bay below your house, Ikwezi, if it fits in with your plans, we could go there together.'

'That would be fine,' Ikwezi said.

When the helicopters came in, the crowd of townspeople fell back to give them room to land, but stayed to see the intruders leave their island. The singing stopped while the embarkation took place, but when the last of the helicopters had risen and headed out across the sea, it started again.

In the evening President Sefuthi and Ombeli came to the ship, and when Sefuthi had thanked the others for their help, he and Provensal retired to discuss the financial rescue scheme they had agreed on during their incarceration.

Afterwards, Tschiffely and Ikwezi went on shore with Sefuthi and Ombeli, and the ship cast off and headed north for Suez.

At dinner that night, the sepulchral air of anticlimax that hung over them was dispelled when Carver broke into laughter.

'What's up, Tony?' Fawcett inquired.

'Those men we tied round the tree. They're still there. I'd forgotten all about them.'

'Ombeli will pack them off,' Provensal said. 'Even I forget things in times of crisis. I have left the limo on the island. Well, it will make a good enough car for the President. It can be the first instalment of our financial package.'

Seddall viewed Provensal with respect and admiration, but he had a sudden revulsion against the environment of extreme wealth. It was, so it appeared to him, too remote from real life, or real life as he understood it. He was out of place in it. He had a longing for a commonplace English pub, or a simple Italian restaurant in some out of the way street in London.

By the time the ship had journeyed up the Gulf of Suez, along the Great Bitter Lake, and made the slow passage through the canal, the excess of luxury in which he was bathed had reinforced this attitude. He castigated himself for being so, as he thought of it, priggish, but there it was, a hard fact: billionairing did not go down well with him and he sank into his seat on the Boeing at Cairo with a sigh of relief.

All of which might explain why Jane Kneller, after their enthusiastic reunion back in London, found herself whisked off in a cab to Camden Passage, without being given time to dress up, and told not to fuss, she looked terrific in her leggings and black leather jacket.

'But don't wear that shirt-tail hanging out at the back,' he said. 'I want to see your ass.'

Her eyes danced at him. 'You're getting very down to earth,' she said. 'It's the influence of all these Americans you've been dealing with. You're aware that in American the word ass, when referring to that region of my anatomy, has a choice of meanings.'

She swung her pelvis around with a fluid and obscene grace that he had not known was available to Home Office high-fliers, and in a coquettish and seductive voice said, 'The next thing I know you'll be telling me I'm a nice piece of ass.'

He kept his face straight, as far as he could manage. 'Well, babe, a nice piece of ass is all you are. Why else do you think a guy would want to be with you?'

She laughed. 'The hoodlum from the Bronx is not an accent you're ever going to be able to do.' Then she gave him a straight eye. 'All the same, Harry, you've grown a lot less stuffy even in the time I've known you. I like it. It's a hell of an improvement.'

'It must be your influence.' A raffish smile turned one end of his mouth up, the other down. 'Who'd have thought a senior civil servant would have such a liberating effect on a man?'

She put her hands on her hips and became serious. 'A senior civil servant no longer. I've sent in my resignation. I told you I was thinking of it, didn't I?'

He sat down and got his cigarettes out. 'By God, good for you. Yes, you told me, but that was quick work.' The lighter flared and he drew in, and blew out smoke. 'But quick was the best way to do it. Why hang about?'

She sat on a stool in front of him, with her elbows on her knees and her chin resting on her hands. 'It's a solemn thing to me, Harry. I don't know who killed Peter Hillyard, whether they were British agents or American, but it was done in the furtherance of a British Government policy, and even if it was not ordered at government level, the reason for his death will have become clear to at least one government minister, it will be known of at government level, and I will no longer work with that government.'

He stood up, and bowed theatrically. 'I salute you. Now let's go out and celebrate.'

'It's me we're celebrating, and I don't even get to dress up? I'll just go and denude myself of this shirt.'

She came back with a white blouse tucked into her waistband and a black belt round the join, and stood with her leather jacket hanging from one shoulder. 'How do I look?'

'You look like a piece of street scruff, and it suits you. Come on, chiquita, and I'll tell you of all the strange things which happened on that island in the Indian Ocean.'

They went out and walked to the corner, and caught a taxi.

They had a good plain Italian dinner, with two bottles of wine between them, and came home and took glasses and a bottle of Armagnac into the bedroom, and went to bed.

Three hours later she said, 'You're tired already? What were you doing down there? Wrestling with the sharks?'

'A few sharks, but mostly crocodiles.' He yawned. 'And if you want to know, they took a lot less out of me than you do.'

'Yes, but I'm prettier.'

'There is that,' he said, and his eyes kissed her all over, and Jane, since she was the one with a surplus of unexpended energy, blew the candles out, and they slept.

They were awakened at noon by the telephone.

'I don't want to talk to anyone yet,' Harry said. 'Do you?'

'No, I don't. And I've resigned, and you've been sacked, so we are beholden to none.'

An hour later, when they had showered and dressed and were drinking coffee, and Harry was smoking his first cigarette of the day, the phone rang again.

Jane raised her eyebrows and he nodded, and she picked up the phone and listened. 'I'm afraid Colonel Seddall is terribly busy,' she said, the Sloane personal assistant to the life. 'Is it frightfully important?'

Her face became all at once bright and alive. 'Yes, I'm Jane.' Pause. 'He's been talking a lot about you. Holds you in high esteem. Lunch? I'll ask him – he's a bit played out, poor fellow. Harry, it's your friend Provensal. He says do we want to join him for lunch? Yes, that sounds lovely. Where? Give us half an hour. Look forward to meeting you.'

She put the phone down. 'What a beautiful voice he's got. Up and at 'em, Seddall, you've got to make yourself respectable in five minutes flat.'

'I have no intention of making myself respectable. I'm fine as I am.'

'What about me? I wasn't planning on a luncheon party. I was going to have a day like last night, if you follow me.'

She was wearing a black leather miniskirt, black high-gloss tights, shiny black disco boots to the knee, and on top of that a bright blue silky fitted shirt. 'This, what I'm wearing – I went shopping as soon as I resigned. I felt amazingly liberated and I wanted to ride that. I haven't worn this outfit yet and I just don't know about it. You don't think it's too young?'

'You look like approximately a million dollars,' Harry said. 'I'm not going out to lunch today with anyone who doesn't look like you

238

look now. But, God, one more cup of coffee. Where are we having this lunch?'

'Quite odd, for a billionaire. Not a famous restaurant. It's in White Horse Street, between Piccadilly and Shepherd Market. Eastern food. I've been there, and it's good. I can take us straight to it. He said it was Shoo . . . Shoo . . .'

'Shouanete.'

'Yes, Shouanete. He said it was her choice.'

'I can see it. Her kind of scene, not his. A change from the high life.'

'I remember. That's his girlfriend, who you told me about last night? Gosh, the one who cut up Mr Foxberry of the CIA?'

'Absolutely. She's sort of his girlfriend, but also she's bisexual, and he's quite happy with that. Unusual couple.'

'You didn't tell me about that.' She flashed her eyes at him. 'I could be bisexual too now, now that I don't have to be the Home Office high-flier any more. What a lot of fun I've been missing.'

'You can start today, with Shouanete. You just want to make sure she's not carrying a knife.'

She looked at him sideways, threw a black, beautifully cut, long and waisted jacket over her shoulders, and led the way out of the house. Seddall followed, not quite so smart as she, in his old linen suit and cotton shirt.

'The car's going to be towed away,' he said, as she parked the Renault on a profusion of yellow lines.

'Then we go and collect it and pay the fine. Come on, lover, we're late as it is.'

He could see that unless he woke up his ideas, he was going to he left behind by the new liberated lifestyle.

He woke up his ideas. 'Yeah, fuck it,' he said.

'That's my boy.' She took his hand and walked at a sprightly pace towards lunch, swinging their arms as she went.

Provensal was tieless too, although the suit was, of course, made of silk. Shouanete was wearing scarlet velvet jeans and a yellow shirt and gold ankle boots.

'Hey,' she said to Jane as they were introduced, 'I'm glad it's you. He's a good man, he deserves a real woman. Like you.'

'I think I'd like to sit beside you,' Jane said. 'Will that upset Mr Provensal?'

'No,' he said, 'it won't. Means I can look at you. Please don't call me Mister. People mostly call me Provensal.'

'Don't you have a first name?'

'I do, but I'm not grateful for it. They called me Achilles, would you believe?'

'Yes, not easy, somehow. It works all right in French, but in English . . . Anyway, Provensal is a good name, and it feels right for you.'

'Seddall, I don't care what Shouana says, you don't deserve this woman.'

'Sour grapes, my dear Provensal, but I don't mind. Anyone who knows you both must realize that Shouanete's judgment is far superior to yours.'

'We're drinking beer. What would you like?'

They chose beer, being aware of curry and spices in the air.

They had a cheerful meeting, during which Shouanete and Jane made a date to lunch on their own the next day.

'Ladies who lunch,' Provensal said with light mockery.

'Don't patronize us, boy.' Shouanete was in there like a shot. 'And maybe not just lunch.' She made certain her point was unambiguous by running her eyes over Jane's thighs.

'Are you flirting with me?' Jane asked, feeling oddly excited and stimulated, and alarmingly skittish.

'Flirting with you? I'm coming on to you, babe. Does that make you uncomfortable?'

'Not in a way I don't like.' Jane felt the colour come up on her face. 'Damn it, I'm blushing prettily, as the books say.'

'It's pretty, all right, and it turns me on.'

Jane decided it was time for straight talk. 'Shouanete, I think you're a great woman and I want to get to know you, but though I've nothing against women having sex together, and to tell you the truth I have fantasized about it, I'm not ready for it at the moment, and also, I'm certainly not going to be unfaithful to Harry.'

'That's telling it how it is. I want to know you too, and we'll have a good time when we meet tomorrow. And don't worry on my account. If I want a woman after we've had our lunch, I have friends here in London.'

Provensal listened to this exchange with understanding and the pleasure he always got from Shouana's openness, and Harry with the interest of a man who was learning things.

When they had reached the coffee stage Provensal passed a piece of paper to Seddall under cover of the tablecloth.

'Three names,' he said. 'Three London station CIA names. I'm still working on the rest of it, but nothing there yet.'

Shouanete looked over her glass at Seddall. 'If you want any help with the three names,' she said, 'I'm in.'

Seddall crumpled up the paper and put that hand in a pocket from which he extracted a pack of cigarettes and as he did so deposited the scrap of paper in the pocket. 'How did you get these so fast? You only got here yesterday.'

'My people have been working on it since our friend was killed. It took a little time because our, ah, contact is a desk-based man in the States. The United Kingdom is not part of his assigned area, so he had to use a certain amount of guile, and find the right moment, to access London embassy material.'

Seddall gazed absently into the sunny street outside. 'So, we have the US Embassy in Grosvenor Square to thank for this. They were taking quite a chance. If the police had tracked them down there would have been hell to pay.'

'It would have been covered up,' Jane said.

'Most likely. Short of a leak to the press from the police or the Home Office. They were taking a chance.'

'The whole darned thing was taking a chance,' Provensal said, 'not just the murder of Peter Hillyard, but the whole business of trying to get rid of Sefuthi and lay down a goddam airstrip for covert operations.'

Shouanete was tilting her liqueur glass this way and that, watching the play of light in the Grand Marnier. She went on doing this, and spoke as if she was asking the most casual question in the world.

'They take a lot of chances, and they take them to keep what they're doing under wraps. Why do we seem to think they've stopped taking chances? There are four of us here, and three who were with us on that island, who know far too much about what they've been up to and what they've done.'

'What are you saying?' Seddall asked her.

'You know what I'm saying. I'm asking why we're acting as if we're all safe now, just because we're in London. As for me, I can tell you I'm carrying a gun right now and I'm keeping my eyes and ears open.'

Provensal's eyes travelled from her to Jane and rested on Seddall. 'She's right,' he said. 'Had you thought of it like that? Like we're targets now, because of what we know?'

'No.' Seddall put his mind to it. If it made sense, and if Shouanete was not just letting her imagination run away with her, why had it not occurred to him? Because he had thought, no, had let himself believe without any thinking at all, that the mission part of it, the finding out what was going on, was over and done with; and all that was left was to deal with the three names Provensal had given him.

And to learn, if that was possible, who if anyone in the government had been party to murdering Hillyard. Though what he would do about that last, he had not the remotest idea.

Yes, Shouanete was right. They might well be in peril, and that meant Jane too, damn it. 'No, I hadn't thought of it like that, but I begin to think you're right, Shouanete. I don't see what we can do about it, except go armed and keep all our wits about us.'

'We can't go on for ever like that,' Provensal said. 'Given a little time, though, we'll think of something.'

'Yes, but look here, Provensal. If Jane and Shouanete are to be lunching tomorrow I want two good men in the same dining-room.'

'They can have Daniel.'

'Daniel and Carver then. And Carver can bring Jane here and

Daniel can bring Shouanete, and take them home afterwards. Is that acceptable to you two?'

'It's all a bit sudden,' Jane said. 'But yes.'

'So long as they sit two tables away,' Shouanete said. 'We have things to talk about, when we're being ladies who lunch.'

'Good, I do think that's wise. In fact, Jane, you'd better move into my house altogether for now, and I think I'll ask Carver to move in with us.'

'So long as he has the farthest away bedroom,' Jane said without blushing at all, 'that's fine with me.'

Provensal produced a card. 'That's got my London address on it, Wimpole Street. I'll write the phone number, it's not listed.' He did so, and proffered the card to Seddall, who reciprocated with one of his own. 'We'll keep in close touch, right? Every day.'

'Best thing,' Seddall said. 'And, in any case, not at all unpleasant from my point of view. Now, we'll go straight home and I'll call Tony Carver.'

They said their farewells and collected Jane's Renault, which, mysteriously, had been neither clamped nor towed away, although there was a ticket on the windscreen. They went to her flat to collect clothes and other necessaries, and then on to Seddall's house in Sumner Place.

At the far end of the hall was the black cat Sacha, waiting with dignity to receive the honours due to her position, and on the mat was an envelope of good quality, hand-delivered, from the Ministry of Defence.

'It's from Wardlaw,' he said, and passed it to Jane. Wardlaw was the Secretary of State for Defence. 'Wants to see me at the earliest opportunity. I'll phone Tony. Oh, hell, I'd forgotten this place was bugged. We'll go down to the hotel and telephone from there. One thing, Jane, I'm not going to leave you on your own. Wardlaw can wait till he gets here. If Tony's not at home till midnight, Wardlaw can wait till tomorrow.'

Carver was at home. When Seddall asked him to come and stay with him and Jane for a while, he didn't even have to explain.

'You're thinking what I'm thinking,' Carver said. 'We know too much for our own good, and now, I fancy, Jane does too.'

'Right,' Seddall said. 'It's a bastard, isn't it, Tony?'

'Oh,' Carver said, 'we'll straighten them out, one way or the other. I'll come over right away, armed to the teeth.'

He was as good as his word. 'My,' he said to Jane, 'You're a sight for sore eyes. I like the style, down and street, unusual for a Civil Service mandarin.'

'I've quit the Civil Service,' she said.

'And Harry's got the heave-ho. What vistas of unrestricted bliss open before us. Where's he off to?' he asked, for Seddall had gone upstairs, saying he was going to change.

'Wardlaw – Defence Secretary – wants to see him.'

When Seddall came downstairs again, and into the drawing-room, he was every inch the well-dressed, well-groomed, brisk and businesslike man on the career ladder. He found it amusing that it was so easy to adopt this fraudulent disguise.

Carver leapt up making histrionic gestures of surprise. 'You can't go out dressed like that. Here, wear this, Harry.'

He picked up the wide-brimmed straw sombrero he had been wearing and put it on Seddall's head. 'Perfect fit. In these clothes and with that hat, you look like a high-class drug dealer. I'd buy from you any time.'

'Thanks,' Seddall said, 'but it doesn't consort with the way I'm going to play this meeting.' He chucked the hat on to the piano beside the black cat Sacha, who sniffed at it and then went back to meditating on the eternal verities. 'But you can give me a couple of your cheap and revolting cigars, Tony. I'd like to have just a touch of ill-breeding on show.'

Carver stuffed four of the long thin cigars in behind the handkerchief in the breast pocket of the elegant jacket, and Seddall sashayed off down the street feeling oddly exhilarated. There was something about Carver's approach to life that put even the direst difficulties into the shade.

Chapter Twenty

By Seddall's lights, which usually presented politicians as a species that would be better extinct, Wardlaw was not such a bad chap. He was about fifty, about six feet tall, and about two stone overweight. He had a big blocky face, which showed the unhealthy tone of the excessive cigarette-smoker, and though he was wearing a good suit, he was a man who gave his personality to his clothes instead of being made by them.

Also he knew how to behave. He stood up and came round the desk to shake hands when Seddall entered, and indicated not the seat placed in front of the desk for visitors, but one of two armchairs canted towards the windows.

'I owe you an apology, Seddall,' he said. 'I understand that my Permanent Secretary, or rather my department's Permanent Secretary, has arranged for your office to be closed down and your unit disestablished as part of the perpetual economies with which we seem to be afflicted. When I asked him why I was not consulted he said it was because yours was too small an operation for me to be concerned with.'

He offered Seddall a cigarette and added, 'Do you have any comment to make on this?'

Seddall was unable to make out if this was part of a game, or if the man was sincere. 'First, thanks for your apology, which was mannerly of you.' He paused to reflect, throwing his mind back to the event itself. 'I have a feeling that I was, as it were, purged, not wholly for economic reasons.'

Despite Wardlaw's experience a flicker of interest appeared in his eyes. Seddall asked himself if it was possible that the man had asked him here to get some information from him, as if perhaps the Defence Secretary had been left out of something. The balance of unlikelihood was great, but stranger things had happened.

'What do you mean?' Wardlaw asked him.

Seddall gave him a quick sketch of the happenings that had led him to Matetendoro: the Prime Minister's message, delivered by Simon Ainley, warning him off Peter Hillyard; the death of Hillyard and Tschiffely's witnessing of it – though he kept the poet's name out of it; the break-in at his own house; the Prime Minister's request to him to undertake a mission to the island of Matetendoro and his refusal.

Wardlaw's attention appeared to sharpen as he took all this in. When Seddall had finished he waited and thought, and then said, 'But you went to Matetendoro, on your own account.'

'You know that?'

Wardlaw sat back in the armchair, pensive, fingering the corner of his mouth. 'I've had the Foreign Secretary on to me,' he said. 'He had it from MI6, who had it from the CIA. He said you had been interfering, while on leave, with the execution of government policy and ought therefore to be deprived of your commission and retired.'

'I was thinking of retiring anyway,' Seddall said, 'but all the same, it is in my mind to say that it's none of his damn business to propose that Army officers should be disciplined, never mind how they should be disciplined.'

'Yes.' Wardlaw regarded him carefully. 'I myself felt it to be an intrusion on to my own bailiwick.' As if he had made his mind up about something, he said, 'Seddall, I'd very much like to know what exactly you found was going on at Matetendoro.'

Their cigarettes were long gone. Seddall produced his packet of Gauloises and offered one to Wardlaw, who took it and ran it under his nose and put it in his mouth. 'I'd smoke these too, but I smoke so much I'd have a permanently sore throat.'

They lit their cigarettes, each his own, and then Wardlaw said, 'You're playing for time while you think, aren't you?'

'This is damned difficult to say to you, Wardlaw, because so far as I know I've got nothing against you. But this has been a very nasty business, and government was behind it, though how far it knew what was actually going down on the ground I have no way to know. The thing is, I don't know why you're asking me what went on down there: whether it's to find out how much I have found out, or if it's because you yourself truly don't know, and want to know.'

Wardlaw was still serious, but he gave a dry laugh at this. 'What you're saying is, you don't know if you can trust me. I think that's perfectly fair. After all, we have little or no acquaintance with each other. However, I'm not a fool, and I can see the other man's point of view. I did foresee that you might feel like this. How does this strike you: if Simon Ainley told you I was to be relied on, would that be good enough?'

Their eyes met, two men beginning to appreciate one another. 'Yes,' Seddall said. 'That would do it.'

Wardlaw called his secretary in and asked him to say to General Ainley that it would be convenient if he were to drop into the minister's office. Ainley arrived so rapidly that it was clear he had been standing by. He put an upright Sheraton-looking chair in front of them and sat on it.

'What's the score?' he said to Wardlaw. 'I take it Seddall's not sure of you.'

'That's it.'

'Well, Harry,' Ainley said, 'I know you are sceptical of politicians, and that you two don't really know each other, but I am here to tell you that I trust Richard Wardlaw above most men I know, and I know absolutely you can trust him in this.'

'That's good enough for me,' Seddall said. He turned to the Secretary of State. 'I am embarrassed to have exposed you to what Simon calls my scepticism towards politicians, but you were kind enough to say that you understood me.'

Wardlaw waved a careless hand. 'It's done with. Do you feel able now to tell me the whole story of this Matetendoro affair?'

'Yes, I do.' He looked at Ainley. 'Are you ignorant of it too? I mean, are you going to stay and hear this report?'

'I am ignorant, and should like to hear what you know.' He cocked an eyebrow at Wardlaw.

'Yes, you should hear it,' Wardlaw said.

Seddall opened with his extraordinary meeting with the Prime Minister, and then recounted everything that had happened on the expedition to the island. The telling took him an hour and a good bit over.

They were so seized by his account that they heard him out without breaking in to ask questions. He concluded with the suggestion by Shouanete that they might still be in danger of their lives, saying that he had taken it seriously enough not to leave Jane Kneller unprotected.

He did not say that Provensal had given him a piece of paper with names on it, the names of three men due for retribution.

When he had finished, Wardlaw stood up, and said, 'Excuse me. I need time to absorb all of this. It's quite a story, and it has all kinds of implications.' He crossed the room, sat down behind his desk, put his feet up on it, and settled back with his chin resting on his clasped hands.

Ainley, on his part, gave Seddall a long, unblinking stare, and then sat with his hand to his forehead, his pose close to that of Rodin's sculpture 'The Thinker'.

Wardlaw picked up the telephone and embarked on a quiet and, so far as the other two were concerned, discreetly inaudible conversation. At this sign of activity Ainley emerged from his contemplation and sat up.

'Am I right about this?' he said to Seddall. 'The PM asked you to go to Matetendoro and pull his chestnuts out of the fire after he heard that the Americans were planning a coup d'état, and you turned him down, but went anyway on your own account?'

'That's almost right. I went on Peter Hillyard's account. I wanted to find out who killed him and I thought I'd be more likely to learn things out there than I would here at home.'

'And did you?'

Seddall furrowed his brow, or hoped he did, and adopted a

serious and regretful mien. 'Alas, I didn't.' Which was true, it was Provensal who had come up with the three names.

Ainley's look was ironic and humorous. 'In fact, a result of your going there has been that, from your efforts combined with those of this black plutocrat Provensal and a few locals, the Prime Minister's chestnuts have been pulled out of the fire?'

'And what do you think of that?'

'I think, apart from the benefit it's been to the island, that it's rather a pity, really.'

'Yes, so do I. It was a crazy scheme. I wonder how it came about in the first place.'

They had not noticed Wardlaw put down the phone, and his voice took them by surprise. 'It came about because Harington had been at Oxford with Sefuthi, the President. They were on the same staircase in their first year, and became friends.'

Ainley looked up. 'David Harington? The Foreign Secretary?'

'Yes. And it wasn't that crazy in one way, if it could have been kept under wraps. The government's got a real problem with disposing of nuclear waste, since nobody in Britain, naturally enough, wants it planted in their own backyard.'

He leaned against the wall beside the window facing them, and sighed. 'We shall have to find a solution to it, but I myself have a revulsion against the idea of dumping nuclear waste resulting from the scientific sophistication of the developed world, and which is the residue of a process of which we have had the benefit, on the innocent land of people in the impoverished undeveloped world.'

He went into his thoughts for a moment or two. 'I suppose you two will have gathered, but all the same I am saying this to you in the strictest confidence, that the matter did not come before the cabinet, although I imagine it would have been passed before us in some form if the scheme had ever got up and running.'

'Yes,' Seddall said. 'I thought it smelled like that.'

Wardlaw smiled, and said, 'Smelled. That is rather the word.'

Seddall came up on to the alert at once. It had been a smile of unintended eloquence. Wardlaw was not carrying himself with the appropriate regretful gravity of a minister of the Crown whose government has just avoided, by the skin of its teeth, the political misfortunes of a prime balls-up.

It was clear to Seddall that Wardlaw had moved on. He had seen leap into Wardlaw's eye the bright, prophetic glow of a man who sees the world open before him – it might have been the eye of Alexander of Macedon advancing upon Asia.

'I've just been talking to Loring, the Energy Secretary,' Wardlaw told them. 'He, of all people, did not know about this either. Harington had been to him with some nonsense about licensing a mining company to exploit the old mine-workings on Matetendoro. He said he didn't like the smell of it – your word again, Seddall – and told Harington so to his face.'

He lit a cigarette and blew the smoke casually out of the open window. 'I'm going to meet Eddie Loring this evening, and have a talk about all this. It could have been very bad for the government, and for the party. It was foolish of Wade and Harington to take the risk of invoking the Americans. Before you do a thing like that, dealing with another government, you simply must realize that they won't come into it unless they have an axe of their own to grind, and you have to find out what that is.'

Seddall's and Ainley's eyes met and moved blandly on: it was plain to both that Wardlaw was not really talking to them, he was rehearsing what he was going to say to Loring, and what he and Loring, running in harness, were going to be saying to a lot of other people.

Political ambition was afire in Wardlaw's blood. Seddall had a low enough opinion of Wade and Harington, Prime Minister and Foreign Secretary respectively, to wish this alliance of Loring and Wardlaw good fortune.

It was, it seemed to him, time to go.

He climbed out of the excessively comfortable armchair. 'If you have no further need of me, Wardlaw, I'll be off.'

'No, indeed, Seddall. And I'm very grateful to you, both for giving me the detail of what has happened with you in all this, and for what you have done for your country. I don't know what you would regard as appropriate recognition for such a thing, but I shall consult with Ainley, and we shall see.'

Seddall made to go.

'One thing more. I think it is on the cards that I may soon be able to lift this threat you feel yourself and your friends to be under from – ah, what shall I say – maverick elements of our American cousins.'

'That would be good. Thank-you for that, Wardlaw. Ainley, good to see you.'

He left them, and went out into the evening sunshine.

Back at Sumner Place he found Sacha sitting on a pile of luggage in the hall, and in the drawing-room, not only Jane and Tony Carver, but Shouanete and Daniel as well.

'This is very pleasant,' he said, 'but what's up?'

Jane gave him a kiss and put a pink gin into his grateful hand. 'We're all going to Suffolk,' she said.

'What the hell for?'

'We're being followed,' Carver said. 'Three men, almost certainly American by the look of them. The thinking is that they may well be the men who hit Peter Hillyard, and that if we put ourselves in an isolated place, they might make a move on us. You know I've got this little one-roomed cottage near Hadfield. So the plan is that Jane and Shouanete stay there, go in the Renault looking as if they're set for a sexy weekend, and we go separately, put up at a pub nearby and, moving silent and invisible through the night, lurk in the bushes outside the cottage. In short, we stake the women out to attract the tiger, and then turn out to be the tiger ourselves.'

Seddall downed his drink and demanded another. 'I'm not at all sure I like this. It sets Jane and Shouanete up to be the target for these CIA hitmen.'

Shouanete went up to him and ran a sharp fingernail down his face. 'I know, Harry, we're only women, poor defenceless little creatures.'

He gave her a ferocious grin and said, 'One of these fine days, Shouanete, I'm going to put you across my knee and smack the living daylights out of you.'

'There you go, good old male chauvinist unreconstructed you. Do it if you can, honey, I won't mind. But,' and she gave him an indescribable look, part evil merriment and part as deadly as the cold and basilisk eye of the cobra, 'if I don't want you to, I don't think you can.'

'No,' he said. 'Neither do I.'

'Oh, come on, Shouana,' said Jane. 'He's not that much of a chauvinist.'

'I know that, honey. I just like being bad.'

'Carver,' he said. 'What sort of site does the cottage stand on? And how isolated is it?'

'Half a mile to the nearest house. It's got a slope with thick scrubby wood behind, and it has a big garden in front of it, mostly down to grass since I'm not there all the time and it's easier to keep. A big long field in front, woodland to the right rising to a sort of plateau with another big field.'

Seddall looked round at them. Daniel smiled and gave him a lazy nod, and his whole look said he was looking forward to putting it to these people who kept getting in the way. Carver appeared to be in a personal state of military preparedness and eager to go. Shouanete wore that detached uninterested face from which she could move like lightning to stick a knife in a man, or contemplate spending the night with a girlfriend. Jane was, clearly but to him unaccountably, enthusiastic.

'Why are you so keen on this?' he asked her.

'One, I want to get free of this constant sense of menace, and I'd rather be proactive than reactive about it. Two, excitement, this kind of stuff is all new to me. Three, if these men murdered Peter I want to see them dead. Also, this is our holiday, Harry, and so far we're not having one, and this is sunny weather, and Shouana and I can sunbathe in the garden.'

He went to the piano and stroked the cat, which had taken up its familiar station there, while he weighed it all up.

'All right, yes, let's do it. We must sort out what weapons we want. So the women go in the Renault. What do we go in? If we're trying to be inconspicuous we don't want to go in my car. So do we hire, or what?'

'Aha,' Carver said. 'Surprise. I have recently acquired one of these cross-country jobs, four-wheel drive and all that jazz. It's a Mitsubishi Shogun, secondhand but only thirty thousand miles on it. It's in the underground car park at Park Lane, and if the three of us can't get there without being followed, we're poor fish indeed.'

Seddall rubbed his hand over his chin. 'Daniel, what would Provensal think of this, using Shouanete as bait? And where is he, anyway?'

It was Shouanete who answered. 'I can't get through to you, man, can I? Provensal doesn't get to have an opinion on what I choose to do. If I want to do a thing, I do it.'

Daniel grinned. 'She's right, you know. And the big boss, tonight and tomorrow he's talking business with some guys.'

Jane came in. 'I'm not a shrinking violet either, Harry. I'm not expert with that pistol you gave me, but I'm a damn good shot with a twelve-bore. So I can make my contribution. And if it comes to in-fighting, Shouana will slice them open before they know they're bleeding.'

Seddall stared at this budding Amazon.

'There's a kukri on the wall of the cottage,' Carver said. 'Sharp as a razor. That's a good weapon, Shouanete.'

Seddall became impatient, partly because he was still uneasy about the risk Jane was taking, being the bait in this trap.

'We had better get on the road,' he said. 'It will take two hours and more for the women to get to your cottage, Tony, and we have to collect your car, check into some hotel or other, and move into place round the cottage. So let's pack up and roll.'

Shouanete came up to him. 'Don't worry about Jane on the journey,' she said. 'I've still got that machine-pistol. If their car comes anywhere near us I'll blow them off the road. And once we get there, we'll be the ones with the strong hand.'

'How did you manage that? To get the H & K through the customs?'

'Certain things are easier,' Shouanete said, 'when you travel with a millionaire.'

Seddall stayed inside to pack the little he needed, while Daniel and Tony Carver put Jane's and Shouanete's luggage in the back of the Renault, and waved them off. Up at the end of the street, they saw a black Mercedes pull out to follow.

'Good,' Carver said. 'They're on the way.'

They went back into the house, where they found Seddall ready to go. 'We want a clear run,' he said. 'Unlike the women, we don't want to be tailed, so I think the form is this. We start off in my car; drop you off, Tony, at Speaker's Corner. You walk down to the underground car park and collect your vehicle. Meanwhile, I'll dump my car in Belgrave Square, and Daniel and I will wait for you to pick us up in Grosvenor Place, between Halkin Street and Chapel Street.'

'Sounds good to me,' Carver said. 'And if we do spot a tail on stage one, in that Lancia you can shake 'em off before we head for Hyde Park Corner, even if it does mean going a bit round about.'

They said goodbye to Sacha, piled into the Lancia, spotted a car that might have been following and might not. Seddall did some smart weaving and smart turns, blasted the wrong way down a one-way street, and they were free and clear.

And so, in the early evening, to the sublimities of Mahler on the Mitsubishi Shogun's tapedeck, they headed at a rate of knots for leafy Suffolk.

Chapter Twenty-one

They came to the village. Jane stopped the car and she and Shouanete looked at the map Carver had drawn for them to find the way to his cottage.

It showed their road passing between a pub one side and a hotel on the other, leaving the village, and then a by-way diving off to the right down into a dip; going along there at the foot of the dip until they passed the house with the white gate, and then up a lane to the right, climbing again, and after a mile turning up a track to the right, past a farmhouse, the track climbing all the way, a big loop to the left, then right again and the straight run in to Tony's cottage.

'I wonder what these guys behind us are going to make of all this,' Shouanete said. 'There's going to come a point where they have to stop, or else they'll be crowding after us into the cottage to put the kettle on. Well, we'll see. You ready for this?'

'I'm ready,' Jane said, 'so long as you have that machine-pistol of yours handy.'

'It's so handy,' Shouanete said, 'that my hand's on it. We got these guys outclassed already.'

'Here we go,' Jane said, and put the car in gear.

When they reached the run-off to the track, Shouanete said, 'They went on past. They'll be planning on doing their scouting on foot.'

The track was rough and falling away in places so that Jane had to take the Renault up it with great care, in first gear all the way. At last they reached the cottage, which proved to be a tiny stone barn that had been converted for habitation.

'It's like a studio flat,' Jane said when they went in. 'And my goodness, only one bed.'

She had flashed a look sideways along her eyes as she said it, and Shouanete said, 'My, are you flirting with me now?'

Jane realized that she was, and that she'd had a sudden rush of excitement when she saw that they would be sharing a bed. God, she didn't know if she wanted this or not. She felt such a strong sexual force drawing her to Shouanete. It would be like a loss for her to resist it, and once, what harm could once do, when the pleasure to be enjoyed would be so strange to her and, she knew this for certain, so wild and glorious.

'Flirting with you? It seems that I am. Come on, Shouana, let's make ourselves at home.'

They hefted their dunnage into the cottage. There was one room which had everything, bed, table, chairs and electric cooker, and beyond that a narrow bathroom running the width of the cottage.

Shouanete checked the place out: one tiny window in the bathroom, enough to air it but not big enough to admit a human body; one window in the studio room, looking over the garden, and at the far end from the bed; and the door, a solid wooden door, in the middle of that wall. The facing wall was unbroken, solid undressed stone, and beyond that, as she had seen from outside, the rising hillside covered with scrub oak.

'Honey,' she said to Jane. 'I'll just run out and look over this garden, and then have a quick look at that field over the garden wall, to see what gives there. Be about ten minutes.'

While she was gone Jane unpacked the few clothes she had brought, and put on the electric kettle to make coffee. She stood at the window to watch Shouanete, who had changed at Sumner Place into jeans and a white cotton shirt, ranging the garden in the gathering dusk, vaulting the wall into the field, running with a long athletic stride to its far side, standing there to look all round her.

The excitement in her was intense, a kind of happiness. She marvelled at herself. It was true that she had fantasized about making love with a woman, but never with a particular woman, so that it had always been, as it were, unlikely to happen. And now, here and now, was the woman, and it was going to happen.

She had said earlier to Shouana that she would not respond to her, would not be unfaithful to Harry. But now, and she did not care whether she was rationalizing or not, it seemed to be nothing to do with Harry. It was between two women, and it was nothing to do with a man, even the loved man.

Shouana was running back over the field with that athletic and graceful movement of hers. Jane put the grounds in the pot and poured the boiling water on top of them.

She sat on the table with a foot on a chair. She was still watching Shouanete, but now, she noticed, there was in her that slight touch of objective inquiry, which she would have if she was with a man who wanted to go to bed with her for the first time, and she with him. It put no restraint on her. It was the wish to have some intelligent knowledge of the other being, before the free and flowering abandon of sexual knowledge.

Shouanete, she saw, did not seek this, but had nevertheless an instinctive awareness of what Jane was doing. Shouanete – and Jane would not have expected it to be otherwise – was not fazed by this.

'All we've got with us to eat is eggs and bread and butter,' Jane said. 'I wonder who makes the best omelette.'

'I make a mean omelette,' Shouanete said. She said it with a sly and allusive smile, and either from that, or because there was more sex burning in Shouana's eyes that she had ever seen in man or woman, Jane felt, for a moment, faint.

'Then you're the chef,' Jane said. 'I'll just sit and watch. But first I'll draw the curtains. Harry and Daniel and Tony will be out there soon, playing at tigers stalking tigers, and we'll want to be private, won't we, Shouana?'

'Yeah, babe, that's what we'll want.'

She made her mean omelette, which they accompanied with a bottle of Carver's Pouilly-Fumé. When the meal was over Jane made no bones about it; she could not wait. She put out the overhead light, leaving only the bedside lamp on, and took her clothes off and stood there at the foot of the bed.

Shouanete left her own clothes in a pile beside the table, and came to her. She ran her eyes halfway down Jane's body, and breathed deep, and said, 'I want to drink you into me,' and gave Jane a gentle shove so that she fell back on to the bed with her legs wide, and Shouana, with her tongue, began to create the ecstasies of the night.

Much later, as they lay idle, they heard the fluttering call of an owl on its nocturnal hunt.

'Not the only hunter out there tonight,' Shouanete said, and let a hand slide lazily over Jane's stomach to settle on her right breast. 'We've sure got the best of it.'

'Haven't we?' Jane gave a sigh of pleasure. 'If this is what it's like being the goat staked out to bring in the tiger, I'm sorry I didn't know about it sooner.'

'That's only because you didn't meet me sooner. Who was the hunter in this one, babe, you or me?'

'It was you first, and then it was both of us.'

The owl, quartering the ground about the cottage, was displeased to find three human beings on his territory, and what was worse, spread about it on three sides of the house, and appearing to have established themselves there for the night: a most unexpected and unnatural phenomenon.

He called to his mate, who answered from a beech tree on the far side of the field, and their complaints rang musically over the heads of Seddall and Daniel and Carver, who appreciated the sound without understanding the content.

It was a hunter's moon, and the three men, Carver in the scrub oaks behind the house, Seddall in the field in front of it, and Daniel lying by the track that led to it, lay still, and waited. They had long to wait, and the moon had passed far across the sky, before their patience was rewarded.

'Fuck,' a voice said.

It was Daniel who heard it most clearly, for they came along the track, as city-bred men would, but the others heard it too.

'Cut it out,' another voice said, 'and you, Samuels, try to make less noise with your feet.'

All three of them, in short, were coming up the track in a group. Carver moved down through the trees as quiet as a lynx, feeling with his hands before him for bits of twig and branch that might break under his feet. Seddall came silently to the wall between field and garden. And Daniel, when the men had passed, moved lightly in their wake with a knife in his right hand and a pistol in his left.

When the men came to the cottage, the moonlight showed them clear, like wondering shadows frozen against the stone.

Seddall came over the wall and into the garden. He looked to his right for Daniel, and saw him as no more than a movement that came and went in the dark, by the entrance from the track. From his left came the soft call of a third owl, and this was Carver, who knew that owls do not hunt in threes, a fact which is not taught to agents of the Central Intelligence Agency.

Carver came in from the left, drifting from bush to bush in a garden that he knew like the back of his hand. Seddall moved up warily, a stranger in a strange land, and Daniel waited by the gateway, since there was no cover for him if he came past the wall.

Inside the house, Shouanete sat up suddenly, hearing the voice of instinct, put a finger to her lips, and got off the bed. She bent to the floor and as Jane sat up put a pistol in her hand. Then she went to her bag, lying against the wall, and took from it the machine-pistol. Naked, she hung this from her shoulder by the sling, and took the Nepalese kukri from its hook on the wall.

She signalled to Jane with her arm to get down behind the bed on the far side from the window. As Jane slid to the ground Shouanete went to the far corner of the room, and knelt there.

In the garden, Seddall and Carver had achieved a conjunction of forces to the extent of being no more than six feet from each other. Carver, with his left hand, pointed to the pistol in his right and lifted his head inquiringly. Seddall bowed his head deeply, for in the moonlight a nod might not have been visible.

Placed as they were, it was obvious that Carver would take the man on the left, Seddall the man on the right, and then both of them the man in the middle. Seddall lifted his left arm above his head, looked at Carver to be sure he had seen this, and brought the arm down.

Their pistols crashed on to the night air. The man on the right was flung against the wall of the cottage, the man on the left collapsed at the knees and began to issue a woeful noise. The third man, with commendable reflexive responses, sprinted for the gateway. Daniel stepped out and received him on a knife blade that was nine inches long. The man made a sound between a scream and a shout and fell his length on to the start of the track. Daniel bent over him as if to be sure, and struck again, and came up with his knife hand holding also the man's pistol. This had an unusually long barrel, which signified that it had a silencer attached to it.

'Dead?' Seddall called to Daniel.

'Dead as he'll ever be,' Daniel called back.

'What have we got here?' Seddall said to Carver, who was looking at the two against the wall before him.

'One dead, and this groaning fellow, I don't know how bad he is. Do we want to ask him questions, or settle him now?'

'Settle him. One in the back of the neck. We don't want a mess of brains to clean up.'

Carver stooped, and fired one shot. The moaning stopped. The man was silent, now, for ever. Three souls had fled, but the two owls were not appeased, and continued to proclaim their tuneful lamentation to the stars.

Carver stood at the door and shouted to those within. 'This is Tony Carver. It's all over. We've got all three of them.'

Jane stood up beside the bed and from her corner Shouanete rose, and walked demurely across to replace the kukri on its hook.

'And now, sweetheart,' she said to Jane, 'do you want to do a fast elimination of the traces? Make the bed and smooth it down, all that kind of thing?'

'No,' Jane said. 'I'm not into concealment. Let them in.'

'We're bare-ass naked, you don't mind that?'

'No, I don't mind that. I look good, and you look good.' She went to the door and opened it.

'Hi, Tony, come on in. You made a lot of noise out there.'

'You two look gorgeous,' Carver said. 'There are a couple of bathrobes through there, if you want them.'

Shouanete went into the bathroom, brought them out, put one on and handed the other to Jane, who wrapped herself in it just as Harry entered the room.

'I had a glimpse of the two of you stark naked,' he said. 'What were you going to do? Stun them with your beauty? Do we have a strong liquor situation here, Tony? I've been in a state of discomfort for hours. Well, all three of us have.' He looked round the room, bedclothes on the floor, wine glasses beside the bed. 'You two been having a good time? I knew you would.'

He said all of this in a tone of perfect good humour, and in his eye, when he went over to kiss Jane, there was a pleasant glint of friendly, even loving malice. 'But just tell me,' he said, 'am I still your fella?'

'Bloody right,' Jane said, and held him at arm's length with her hands on his shoulders, looking at him with eyes aglow. 'I have never met a better man, and will never need to.'

Carver had come up with a bottle of Scotch. 'Do all this, somebody. I'll run out to the top field and fetch the tarpaulins so that we can get these bodies out of the way.'

'Tarpaulins?' Shouanete said.

'Bought them on the way down,' Seddall said. 'Plastic sheeting, in fact. We came prepared, because we have to transport the dead elsewhere, can't leave them on Tony's doorstep.'

'How did it work out?' Jane said.

'Equitably,' Harry said, 'if that's an appropriate word to use. We got one each. Daniel caught the boss man on his knife as he was running for the tall timber. A sight to see, that.'

It seemed to Jane that this description ought to make her feel at least a little unwell, but it did nothing of the sort. Euphoria ruled the small room, and when they heard the sound of Carver's vehicle coming down off the high field, she went out with Shouanete to watch the disposal of the bodies.

Carver produced a Nikon camera with flash, and took pictures of each of the dead faces. Then they rolled each one up in its plastic sheet, and heaved them into the back of the Shogun. After that they returned to the house and toasted their success, in what felt to Jane, in the light of all that had been done that evening, a healthily pagan way.

'What are the photographs for?' Jane asked.

'So that we can show them to Tschiffely, when he gets back, and see if he recognizes any or all of them from the time when Peter Hillyard was killed,' Carver said.

'Well, that was good,' Seddall said, putting down his empty glass, 'but we still have work to do. Got to get these fellows to their destination.'

'Where are you taking them?' Shouanete asked him.

'We're going to take them to Thetford Heath, which has some good lonely places, unroll them from the plastic and dump them there, and then we'll come back here. It'll take us, I can only make a rough guess, three or four hours.

'Tomorrow, with the benefit of daylight, we'll find their car, and I'll leave it on the heath, in the vicinity of the late lamented. Tony and Daniel will follow me in the Shogun, and then I think we'll head back to London, and meet up with you there. Sumner Place, say, at about lunchtime.'

Daniel, who had no driving to do, lifted his glass. 'Best night's work I've ever been on, and the best people to do it with. I thank you, one and all.'

'We'll come and see you off,' Shouanete said. 'Let's give them a treat,' she said to Jane, and shrugged off the robe. Jane did the same, and they stood there, naked in the night, and waved the Shogun on its way.

They stood there under the moon, looking at each other bathed in its light, and then went inside. Before, at last, they fell asleep, they heard the owls rejoice in having their hunting ground to themselves again.

Chapter Twenty-two

Refreshed and energized by their rescheduled three weeks in Martinique, Jane Kneller and Harry Seddall arrived at Sumner Place about noon.

She had a quick shower and then he embarked on a long soak in a hot bath. He was still in the bath when the doorbell rang, and Jane went to answer it.

A man stood there holding a case of wine. Behind him she saw a van with the name of a first-rate wine merchant painted on the side. 'For Colonel Harry Seddall?' the man said.

'Yes,' Jane said. 'Will you bring it in, please.'

He carried it in and set it down in the hall and departed.

Jane poured herself a glass of sherry and settled in the drawing-room with Sacha and a book, until Seddall came downstairs, as red as a lobster from his bath and with a towel round his waist.

'Do you want a drink?' she asked him.

'You know what I like after a hot soak. Black coffee and some cigarettes. It's a combination that cools me down somehow. Don't move. I'll get it.'

'No,' she said, 'I'll get it. You just sit down and sweat.'

So he sat himself down and sweated, and Jane brought him a pot of good strong coffee and poured herself more sherry.

'Damn,' he said. 'I've left my cigarettes upstairs.'

He shuffled in his ancient slippers out of the drawing-room and she heard the scuffing sound they made fade away towards the stairs, after which there was silence until she heard them coming back again, but in the hall they stopped, and Seddall's voice came to her.

'What's this? When did this arrive?'

She went to the hall. He was kneeling over the case of wine, looking at a claret bottle he had taken from it. 'It came when you were in your bath, of course.'

'Was there a note, or a message? I never ordered this.'

'No. nothing. I assumed it was from your wine merchant.'

He stood up with the bottle in his hand. 'No, these people are not my wine merchants. With his foot he touched a label stuck on the side of the case. 'Mind you, they are first-rate. And this is Pichon-Longueville. It's my favourite claret, and a bloody good year, too. What a mystery.'

Later in the day, at the end of an afternoon of blue skies and balmy summer weather, they drove to Dovestone.

'How pleasant,' Seddall said, as the car was approaching the turn-off from the motorway, 'to go wherever we feel like without having those American creatures on our tail.'

'Not only pleasant,' Jane said, 'but liberating as well, don't you find?'

'That too,' he said agreeably, though he smiled privately. If the Knellers were a Highland clan, he thought, 'Liberation' would, by now, have become their slogan. But why should I laugh at that? he asked himself. I myself could do with a lot more of this liberation that seems to have reached me with Jane.

He fell quiet and set himself to relish the beauties of the countryside through which they were passing.

They came to Dovestone at the fall of dusk. The reflection of the setting sun, gleaming gold on the windows, hit so bright on the eye that almost you could not see the house. They stood on the gravel and looked out over the garden and the fields, at the rolling hillsides and the scattered bits of woodland.

'Why is it,' Jane asked, 'that I don't feel sad, or at least not as sad as I expected?'

'Perhaps,' Seddall said, 'because he wouldn't want it.'

'Yes,' she said. 'And perhaps because we – well, in fact it was you, Harry – have done what he would have wanted.'

'I think – I feel,' and he put his arm round her, 'that Peter is at peace. Tomorrow we shall take some flowers to his grave. Flowers from his own garden. He'd like that.'

She turned to him, her thoughts clear in her eyes. 'You're a good man, Harry Seddall.'

'Nobody ever told me that before.'

'Well,' she said sweetly, 'that will be because everybody else knows you better than I do.'

He took her round the neck and smacked her Wrangler-denimed bottom. 'If you think you're going to make the bad jokes round here instead of me, you've got another think coming.'

She pulled herself free and stood with one foot forward and a hand on a hip, and gave him the long cool look. 'That's not all I've got coming, lover, so, if you want to whack my ass, let's go upstairs and you can do it in bed.'

'Two things,' he said, but before he could get them out he burst out laughing. 'Oh, God, Jane Kneller, how I like you.'

She shrugged. 'That's reasonable. What were the two things?'

'First, I'm not going upstairs till I've had something to eat. Second, whatever happened to those well-bred women I used to read about?'

'You can still read about them, old chap,' she said in the manner of a twenties anyone-for-tennis girl, 'if you like that sort of thing. But you know what the song says.'

'What does the song say?'

She sang the line, ' "A good girl nowadays is hard to find." '

'You can say that again. Let's go into the house and see how well Mrs Taylor has done in preparing for your return.'

Mrs Taylor had excelled herself. There were smoked salmon and a duck. There was a salade Niçoise which she had prepared. There were Roquefort and a large chunk of mature Cheddar, and all the usual household provisions.

Seddall scanned the range of goodies on offer, and surprised himself. 'Do you know what I feel like?'

'No,' Jane said. 'What do you feel like?'

'Bacon and eggs, of all things.'

'For dinner?'

'That's just it. I don't feel like dinner. I just want to sit down at the kitchen table and tuck into bacon and eggs. And perhaps fried bread. I'll cook it myself, because I'm the only one who knows exactly how I like it.'

'After all the cooking I've done for you.' Jane pinched his ear painfully. 'But that suits me. I don't feel like roast duck and all that. I like the look of the salad, so I'll have that while you have your bacon and eggs, and in the meantime I'll have a drink while you're showing the world what a great chef you are. What would you like? Scotch?'

'Yes, please, and quite a lot of it.'

Jane got their drinks, and threw some knives and forks on the kitchen table. She sat down with her gin and tonic to watch the great man at work and turned on the radio to catch up with the news, expecting the usual menu of banal political infighting and reports of violence in the streets.

As it turned out, what she heard interested her, and the aspiring chef at the stove, a great deal. The country had a new Prime Minister, and a new Foreign Secretary.

Philip Wade and Sir David Harington had resigned, and been replaced by, respectively, Richard Wardlaw and Eddie Loring. She smiled as she listened to the desperate attempts of the political staff to speculate intelligently on the reasons that might lie behind these changes, and was intrigued by how many words could be produced when there were no hard facts to go on.

Seddall, meanwhile, had turned from the frying-pan with a face frozen in astonishment. A huge and complicated smile, at once mischievous, sardonic, delighted and childish, came on to his face.

'Well, I'll be damned,' he said. 'The good guys – or at least the relatively good – have triumphed for once, in a way. Great Scott! What a convulsion. Well, we knew Wardlaw was up to something, and that's what he was up to.'

'Yes, Harry, that's what he was up to. And it was you who helped him to it: what you and the boys did in Matetendoro, and afterwards, when you gave him the scoop on the whole thing.'

'Yes, well, I don't care about that, but I'm glad it served to get Wade and Harington out.'

As he returned to his cooking they heard the sound of the knocker on the front door. Jane went to see who it was.

'Three for supper,' she said as she came back. 'Look who's here! Mr Steve Tschiffely, back from Mombasa.'

'I saw the lights,' Tschiffely said. 'Hope I'm not de trop.'

'Not in the least,' Seddall said. 'I am so pleased to see you. We're roughing it tonight. Are you in a salade Niçoise mood or are you for bacon and eggs and fried bread?'

'I'll take the cholesterol, if it's not too much bother.'

'It's no bother,' Jane said. 'He's displaying his abilities as a short-order cook, and it's making him terribly happy. It's the only thing he does really well.'

'Steve,' Seddall said, 'get yourself a drink, and when you have imbibed enough Dutch courage, punch her on the mouth. She is making it a point to disturb my concentration.'

'Couldn't do that,' Tschiffely said. 'Might hurt my knuckles on her teeth. But thanks, I'll get myself some beer.'

Seddall was pleased to see that the man had apparently come out of the dark state he had been in when he last saw him on the island.

Soon the three of them were round the table, and exchanging news. This began with Jane asking Tschiffely if he was aware that his activities in Matetendoro had contributed to the changes in the government.

'Tell me,' he said.

So they told him what had passed since he and Seddall went their separate ways in Matetendoro, and added some appropriate comments about the splendours of Martinique in the by-going.

'What about your journey home?' Seddall asked Tschiffely. 'How did that go?'

'It was good.' He threw the black hair off his brown gipsy face. 'It was good having the boat all to myself to make the run to Mombasa: the boat and the sea and the sky, that was good for the spirit.'

He looked Seddall straight in the eye. 'I know you realized I was in a poor way about Shouanete. I was tremendously taken with her. I don't think I was falling in love exactly, but she has great sexual power and another power as well, which I can't find a name for, but it comes to me as something primitive and unsullied by civilization.'

He smiled. It was a smile with no trace of bitterness, but with a touch of self-irony. 'As it turned out, she is unsullied by civilization, but in ways I hadn't thought of. What she did to that American with her knife held me spellbound. It was as if I stopped being human. Through my head kept running the line of Eliot's I had given to Wildgrave when he was at the point of death – 'deep within the bloody wood, Agamemnon cried aloud' – and do you know, it was as if I was more possessed by the poetry of the line than by her mutilating Foxberry.'

He stopped, but it did not seem that he had finished. He took up his glass, which still had some beer in it, and put it down again without drinking from it.

'Perhaps you'd like something stronger?' Seddall asked, and stood up. 'Whisky, for example?'

'Yes, please. I would like that.'

Seddall went off to get it.

While he was out of the room Jane asked, 'Are you saying that Shouanete tortured a man by cutting him up with a knife?'

'Yes, that's what she did.' His eyes ran over her face, and studied her eyes. 'Dear Jane, have you made love to her too?'

'Yes.'

'And you're fond of her?'

'I was fond of her. Now I . . . I don't know. It's hard to get hold of, a thing like this.'

'It is. It knocked me sideways.'

Seddall came quietly into the room and put a glass of whisky at Tschiffely's hand. He sat down and listened to them.

'You're not knocked sideways now, though, are you? You've got past it somehow.'

'Not got past it.' Tschiffely took a swig of Scotch. 'Taken it with me. I wasn't that quick to work it out. I was alone on that boat, on the empty sea under the empty sky, and I let it come up in me slowly. I realized first that I was trying to run away from it – to get past it, as you put it. A couple of days later, I realized I was in fact running away, hiding, from part of myself.'

'What on earth do you mean?' Jane's face was intent on his. 'Are you saying there is a part of you that wants to torture men by cutting them up with knives?'

Tschiffely shook his head. 'Not that, no. It was too much for me, that. It was beyond anything, what she did. What I was hiding from, though, was an aspect of me that had recognized what she did, recognized who she was.'

'Recognized?'

'Best word I can think of. Recognized it as if in a previous incarnation I might have had that depth of evil in me.'

Seddall's eyes met Jane's. This was not a way of thinking they were used to. But they said nothing, and waited for him to continue.

Tschiffely's face, watching this silent exchange, was clear and calm. To Seddall it seemed, also, that the poet's countenance was complete in a way it had not been when they had first met, as if it now held a maturity that had been lacking. The man had not let himself be damaged by his experience of Shouanete. Instead, he had gained from it.

Tschiffely had gone silent, as if he had forgotten what he had been telling them, so Seddall spoke.

'If it was, by your lights, in a previous incarnation, then I don't see what there was for you to hide from.'

Tschiffely lifted his head and sat there as if he was gazing at a distant mountain. 'It threw a shadow, and the shadow is in me, in this incarnation. You see, what I have learned is that I am not only words, life is not only words, just because I am a poet. What I've learned is that life is not as pure as that, and I am not as pure as that. There is evil in me too. That is what I have learned from knowing Shouanete.'

Seddall felt himself to be out of his depth, and it was Jane who spoke now. 'There's evil in everyone.'

'Yes,' Tschiffely said. 'I knew that, but as an abstract idea only. Now I have felt it move inside me, and I am coming to terms with that, emotionally and spiritually. You can't come to terms with it if your only knowledge of it is an abstraction. If you don't come to terms with it, then there is a part of you which you cannot truly say you know, so that, in effect, you don't know who you are.'

To Seddall this was all very strange. His mind called up the glorious time with Jane on Martinique, the sun and the sea and the long nights, the extrovert style of life and the magical mixture of France and the Caribbean; his mind called up these ways of doing things, these ways of living, and they made strikingly incongruous what was coming from the poet.

He said what it came into his head to say. 'You don't sound like a modern civilized European at all. You sound like a man from the dark ages, or a tribal savage in some hidden land not yet discovered by the outside world.'

To his surprise Tschiffely's face lit up with pleasure. 'You could not say to me anything more agreeable or rewarding, and I doubt if you know why.' He gave a dry smile. 'Or want to know.'

'No, not particularly.' Seddall felt profoundly serious, but did not know what he felt profoundly serious about. He shook himself, metaphorically, as if to be sure that he still fitted into the skin of his own understanding. 'This sort of thing is quite beyond me, I confess it. All the same, Steve Tschiffely, you did a top-class job in that business from first to last, and I'm glad it brought you something that you find of value, even if I don't understand it.'

Tschiffely gave him a pleasant and friendly look. 'It was a good thing for me, that whole expedition, and I have you to thank for it.' He laughed. 'I find it amusing – and I expect you do too – that there is still the same gulf between us, in the way we see life, which has been there from the first; and yet it seems to me we have quite a lot in common as well.'

'It's often that way with people one likes,' Seddall said, and noticed, even as he spoke, that he was pontificating. 'It's the difference that makes the other chap interesting.'

Jane had been concentrating hard on Tschiffely, both on what he was saying and on the man himself. 'What do you feel about Shouanete now?' she asked him. 'Do you feel you are her friend, or is that impossible for you?'

He contemplated her with an expression of great charm. He was, by the look of him, in a state of peaceful exhilaration. 'I don't know the answer to that, not yet. But tell me, Jane, are you asking me that question, or are you asking yourself?'

'Good point,' she said. 'Yes, I was asking myself, and at the same time testing the question on you.'

'And what's your answer?'

She looked at him, and at Seddall, and back to Tschiffely again, while she thought about this.

'I think I've decided that yes, I'm still her friend. By all accounts, that man Foxberry was a horror of the first water. I know that doesn't excuse what she did to him, and I know it was horrific, but I don't seem to need an excuse for her. I like her, and that's that.'

'So do I,' Seddall said. 'I liked her from the start, and I still like her.'

Jane turned to him swiftly. 'You've been very understanding about me and Shouanete, but you haven't said that before.'

'Why should I dislike her for what happens between you and her?' He mimed a patronizing and chauvinistic smile. 'After all, she's only a woman.'

'Oaf!' she said, and took the chunk of bread which she was breaking up to eat cheese with and threw it at him: but she was laughing while she did it.

He caught it and ate it himself, and then became serious. He turned to Tschiffely and said, 'We have pictures of the men we killed at Tony Carver's cottage. Tony photographed the faces of the corpses. I'd like you to look at them to see if you're able to identify them as the men who killed Peter Hillyard. Will you do that? If so, I'll go and fetch them.'

'Of course I will. We have to be sure. That's what this was all about, to get the men who killed Peter.'

While Seddall was upstairs Jane and Tschiffely sat silent in their thoughts, now and then catching the other's eye. There was no need of speech between them. Each was inhabited by the idea of what Shouanete represented.

Until at last Jane said, 'We do live rather sheltered lives, don't we?'

'We do. And when we venture out of them, out of our Northern European bourgeois safeties, we're too easily shaken.'

They said no more, but returned to their private thoughts.

Seddall came back, with the pictures and laid them out in front of Tschiffely. He picked them up one at a time, and gave them careful scrutiny.

'Dead men's faces,' he said. 'Yes, these are the men. I can recognize each of them. Peter Hillyard has been avenged.'

There was a sound at the front of the house. 'Wonder what that was.' Seddall got up. 'Front door, do you think?'

'I think so,' Jane said. 'Maybe it's Mrs Taylor.'

Seddall went to investigate. When he returned there were three men at his back, two of them carrying automatic pistols.

'Surprise callers,' Seddall said. 'I think you know them.'

They knew them at once. It was the three men who had gone off with their tails between their legs after pretending to be Special Branch and demanding to search the house.

'How boring,' Tschiffely said. 'I thought all this sort of stuff was over and done with.'

He had already, with what Jane saw as incredible coolness and presence of mind, slid the photographs under the plate in front of him.

Seddall resumed his seat at the table.

'I suppose you have what you would regard as a reason for being here,' he said to the intruders.

The chief man, who was wearing a fairly respectable black overcoat, as against the shoddy raincoats of his pistol-packing acolytes, came further into the room.

'We are here to search for evidence of treasonable activity. I have good reason to believe that you, Henry Seddall, making use of information that was of a highly confidential nature, and which had been passed to you, in your capacity as a senior officer of HM

Forces, by a member of the government, misused that information in order to prevent the execution of official policy, to the detriment of the interest of this country.'

'You talk like a policeman,' Seddall said, 'which I know damn well you're not.'

'That's immaterial,' Black Overcoat said. 'The department to which I belong works in close co-operation with the police.'

'I find it odd,' Seddall said, 'that a magistrate would sign a warrant empowering you to search a house belonging not to me but to a friend of mine, namely Ms Jane Kneller.' He indicated her with a gesture.

'Yes,' Jane said. 'Show me your search warrant, if you will be so kind.'

'My department,' Black Overcoat said, 'does not require to have a magistrate sign a warrant when we perceive the necessity of searching premises. You will remain here, under guard, while I and my assistant search the house.'

'Coffee,' Seddall said.

'Absolutely,' Jane said, and went over to the Aga and moved the kettle on to the heat. She sat down again, saying to Black Overcoat, 'Do try not to break anything. If you cause damage, I shall go to law to obtain restitution.'

'See that they don't leave this room,' Black Overcoat said, and went off with one of the raincoats. The other raincoat shut the kitchen door and stood leaning against it with his arms folded and the pistol symbolically visible, although not aimed at his prisoners.

'Harry,' Tschiffely said, 'do these assholes remind you of another lot of assholes we met abroad not so long ago?'

'Don't be so cruel, Steve.' Seddall produced a reproachful frown. 'They don't know any better. The poor fellows haven't had your advantages.'

'Damn your eyes, both of you,' Raincoat said. 'I got a good second in history at Cambridge.'

'I don't think that's quite how he meant it,' Tschiffely said. 'I mean, I went to a comprehensive and then got sacked from Edinburgh University in my third year for being idle.'

'What did you do with your time?' Jane asked him.

'Played bridge all day in the common room at the Old Quad, as it was called – when I wasn't in the pub, that is. Went to parties, went to the theatre, walked in the hills, and in the summer went along the coast and spent the day on the beach. And wrote poetry.'

'As good an education as any,' Seddall said.

'Not what the government thinks,' Jane said.

'That's an oxymoron,' Tschiffely said.

'Remind me,' Seddall said. 'What's an oxymoron?'

'Remind you? You mean instruct you.' Tschiffely smiled kindly. 'It means that a sentence in which there is implicit the proposition that the government thinks, holds an interior fallacy. The government is incapable of thought.'

'Oh, I say.' Seddall saw an opportunity to make use of this game that they were playing with words and attitudes to follow a hunch. 'We don't know that yet about Wardlaw. He's only been Prime Minister for a few hours so far.'

He got his reward. Raincoat took a step towards them. 'What are you saying? Wardlaw is the Prime Minister? Since when?'

'Since,' Seddall consulted the watch on his wrist, 'between two and three hours ago. You didn't hear the news?'

'No. We've been sitting in the bloody car for half the day watching the house.' Seddall and Jane, who had the door within their vision, saw it begin, slowly and quietly, to open. 'Still I don't suppose it makes a blind bit of difference to us who the Prime Minister is. Governments come and governments go, but we go on for ever.'

A hand came round Raincoat's body and took the pistol by the barrel and wrenched it from his grasp.

'You're quite right, laddie,' Inspector Radley said. 'It's going to make no difference to you at all, because you'll be behind bars. Handcuffs, I think, Sergeant, don't you?'

'What the hell is this?' Raincoat, his wrists yanked behind his back so that the sergeant, whom Seddall recognized as the sergeant of the local force who had been here on the day of Hillyard's death, could handcuff him – Raincoat was in a state of shock.

'I'll need to consult myself about that,' Radley said. 'What have we got? We've got illegal entry. We have armed robbery, attempted or realized, as we'll discover when we know what your friends have been doing. We have threatening use of firearms, which is at the very least assault. I wouldn't wonder if we have conspiracy to commit murder.'

'God damn it, you'll pay for this,' Raincoat was shouting now. 'I was only following orders, you fucking idiot.'

'Abusive language to a police officer,' Radley said. 'And a threat, however obscure. Sergeant, do you want to see how the other lads are getting on? And can you spare a constable to put this buffoon in one of the cars and keep on eye on him?'

'Easy. We've got two of the lads waiting outside and six in the house. Come on, you. And don't swear at me, or I'll be very unhappy.'

Radley closed the door behind his departed colleague, and said, 'Good to see you, Seddall.'

Seddall was out of his chair and gripping him by the hand. 'You're one of the two craftiest police officers I've ever met. How on earth did you come up with this piece of timing? Jane, meet Inspector Radley. And this is Steve Tschiffely, Radley.'

'I'll make that coffee before the kettle boils dry,' Jane said, after she had welcomed Radley.

'Who's your other crafty police officer?' asked Radley, giving Seddall a careful look.

'Commander Kenna, Special Branch.'

Radley's face relaxed. 'Kenna. To be spoken of in the same breath as him is a compliment indeed.'

'Sit down, Radley, and explain how you just happened to turn up so conveniently. But first, I give you my deepest thanks for this. The leader – the one in the black overcoat – is a loose cannon if ever I saw one, so God knows what he might have done if you hadn't put a spoke in his wheel.'

There was an outbreak of noise from the front of the house, and the voice of Black Overcoat shouting, 'You can't do this, damn you,' and the quiet voice of the sergeant, followed by the slam of the front door and silence.

'Well,' Radley said, settling himself at the table, 'there they go: in the bag. Now, you want to know how I come to be here. As you know, I don't trust these people, and I thought it quite likely they hadn't finished with you. I've got a man and a woman in my lot who are criminally good at computer-hacking, and I had them play their little games with the Security Service and, just to be on the safe side, the Secret Intelligence Service.'

Jane put a mug of coffee in front of him, and he thanked her and sugared and stirred and tasted. 'Delicious coffee. I need this, I can tell you. Where was I? Yes, I was breaking the law, or rather suborning my juniors into doing it for me, which comes to the same thing. They couldn't get into everything, but they found references to you now and then: secret talks with the Prime Minister, wild doings in the Indian Ocean, talks with other eminencies who shall be nameless, and obscure matter about the deaths of three Americans in East Anglia when you happened to be there.'

He gave Seddall a bland stare and swallowed coffee. He eyed the packet of Gauloises on the table and Seddall tossed it over to him. Radley lit a cigarette and said through the smoke, 'Of course, I knew you'd have had nothing to do with the killing of three CIA men. After all, the Yanks are our glorious allies and you would never lay a finger on their representatives.'

He kept up the bland stare.

'Lay a finger,' Seddall repeated. 'No, I can't recall that I have ever actually laid a finger on a CIA man. I'm a lazy man, and I don't like to have to wash my hands more than necessary.'

'Good coffee,' Radley said, 'and good cigarettes. Amounts to bribing a police officer. Therefore I can cheerfully say, I'm glad to be assured by you that I was correct in my judgment.'

'I think your estimate of me is pretty accurate,' Seddall said, with an affectedly inflectionless voice. 'It takes one to know one. Chuck me a fag, if you can spare it.'

'Catch.' Seddall caught. 'Then my hackers,' Radley went on, 'learned that you were away on holiday to Martinique, and then they learned that you were back again. And they learned that you were to receive a visit.' He sat back with a satisfied air. 'So I thought

276

I'd crash the party. I phoned the local force, since this is out of my ground, and they were willing and ready to co-operate with me.'

He leaned over the table and tapped his forefinger on it as if to add emphasis. 'They were very willing and ready, in fact, because they had met with some surprising difficulties in pursuing their inquiries into the death of Mr Peter Hillyard. They thought it had been a shooting accident, but nevertheless, since there were no witnesses, and shooting caused the death, inquiries had to be made in the case. These were, shall I say, discouraged? Yes, discouraged.'

'By whom?' Seddall asked.

'My lips are sealed.' Radley produced what could only be described as a conniving leer. 'But if you made a guess, it would probably be the right guess.'

Tschiffely, who had kept a wonderfully impassive countenance when Radley said there had been no witnesses, asked him, 'Why do you think these men came here tonight? I mean, how far do you think they would have gone in the way of violence?'

'This lot?' Radley said. 'I doubt if they know themselves. I think that man, call him the team leader, is out-of-his-mind angry with you, Seddall, for cocking up their end of whatever wheeze they were involved in with the CIA. You know more about that than I do, and that suits me fine. I don't need or want to know about that. I've got them on illegal entry and waving guns around and whatever else I can make of it. That'll do me.'

'What will it do to your career, getting across the hawse of the powers that be?' Seddall asked him. 'You said it didn't do you a lot of good once before.'

'I don't care about that, not any more.' Radley nodded to himself. 'I work for the legal system that is a safeguard for the people of this country, not for whichever bunch of moguls occupies the chief offices of state.'

The telephone rang. Jane picked it up and spoke and listened and beckoned to him.

'Colonel Seddall? The Prime Minister wishes to have a word with you.'

Wardlaw's voice. 'Seddall, how are you? I want you to know

277

that Eddie Loring summoned the American ambassador to see him this morning, and told him in the most categorical terms that if anything injurious happened to you or any of those who have been associated with you in your recent enterprise on behalf of this country, it would play havoc with the relations between Downing Street and the White House. I think your mind can be at rest in that regard.'

'Much obliged, Wardlaw, I appreciate that.'

'Good. You've been away, Seddall, so you won't have heard that a man walking his dog a few weeks ago on Thetford Heath found three men violently done to death, and that they bore the identification of members of American Embassy staff?'

'No, indeed. What a frightful thing. Still, we do live in violent times, Prime Minister. These disasters happen, alas.'

Wardlaw laughed a little. 'I'm afraid they do. Before I go, one last thing. I hope you like Pichon-Longueville.'

'That was you, was it? Then, Wardlaw, I thank you a thousand times. I prefer it to any other claret, prefer it to any of the First Growths.'

'Happy coincidence, because that's my view, and I'm glad you share it. I like it so much, that only once in my life have I felt able to give it as a token of esteem to another. Another last thing. Do you want that post restored that you recently vacated?'

Seddall looked at Jane. 'Thanks, but I truly don't think so. I'm enjoying life so much at the moment that I feel like resting on my laurels, if I have any to rest on.'

'If my judgment is worth having, I think you have earned enough laurels to make a most comfortable couch to rest on. But do let me know if you should change your mind. Failing that, I would feel comfortable if I thought I might call on your wisdom if the need arises.'

'You're very kind.'

'I'll say *à la prochaine*, and go well, Seddall.'

When he came back to join the others at the kitchen table he saw that Radley's face was a study, and Tschiffely had a small and witty smile lurking at the edges of his mouth. As for Jane, she simply gave him a wink.

'Was that . . .?' Radley had lost his coherence. 'That was, wasn't it? That was our new Prime Minister?'

'Yes, it was.' Seddall stretched his legs under the table and tilted his chair back, acting the negligent English gentleman in a *Punch* cartoon of the 1880s. 'Rather a good sort, really, for a Prime Minister in these times.'

'Do you mean to tell me,' Radley said, 'that for once in a way I've backed the right horse? Damn it, Seddall, you're in like silk with that man.'

'That's not quite the way to put it, Radley. Wardlaw is lucky enough to be in like silk with me.'

Tschiffely laughed and stole one of his Gauloises from the table. 'You're an arrogant bastard, Seddall.'

'I'd like to think I have come across a better description of myself than that,' Seddall said languidly.

'Oh, yes? Then share it with us.'

'Very well, here it is – but first, you must understand that I just don't fit in the present age, which is why so few of these idiots in high places can make sense of me. So here is the portrait in words I came across which seems to apply to me: "A stone abandoned in a field, cut by an unknown hand, according to unknown rules." '

Tschiffely went deep for a moment, and then emerged again. 'God, I like that, and I admire the writer. Wherever did you find that?'

'It is Roberto Calasso, writing about Talleyrand, in his book *The Ruin of Kasch*. And no, I won't lend it to you. I won't lend it to anybody. Buy it yourself. You'd take to it, you know, Tschiffely. We have some things in common.'

Radley came to his feet. 'I must go and take these fellows to justice. Thank-you, Miss Kneller, for your hospitality. We must meet again, Seddall.'

'No question. When we're back in town next week, I'll see if you can make time to lunch with us. Thanks again, Radley. You did us proud tonight.'

'I'll come and see you off,' Jane said, and tucked her arm in the inspector's, and they went out.

'I'll be off too, when Jane comes back,' Tschiffely said. 'You two will want to get to bed.'

'Yes,' Seddall said. 'Bed seems the right thing.'

This judgment later proved to be unanimous. As Seddall, having locked the doors and checked the windows, made to go upstairs, from behind the angle of the wall on the landing above there appeared mysteriously an arm, wearing not even a vestige of white samite, which beckoned three times in a seductive arc and then vanished.